LOST VALENTINES

*

THE COLLECTED VAMPIRE STORIES

S.P. Somtow

ILLUSTRATED BY LOUKAS STOURMWITCH

DIPLODOCUS PRESS
LOS ANGELES · NEW YORK

DIPLODOCUS PRESS

First Edition
Hardcover ISBN: 978-1940999-76-0
Trade Paperback ISBN: 978-1940999-81-4

to David Zink

who supported one of my wildest projects
for a whole year,
freeing me to dream

LOST VALENTINES
VAMPIRE STORIES

S.P. SOMTOW

Me, My Mom, and the Count

I have often told the story about how my mother used to take me to horror movies when I was little. This is partly because, when my parents were in living in Europe during my childhood, my dad was still doing one of his many PhDs and hiring a babysitter was often out of the question. My deep love for *Psycho* stems from the fact that I saw it so many times at a precocious age. In fact, I was too young to understand the dark psychosexual underpinnings of Norman Bates's personality. I was not too young that the film made a huge impression.

In fact, there's a scene in the movie that I remember with absolute vividness. It's where the police are digging up Mrs. Bates's grave, and it is empty. This scene is not in movie. When, years later, I watched it on commercial American TV reruns, with commercials, I assumed the scene had been cut out. No way. I created it. False memory syndrome. Some people have this problem and remember hideous traumatic events, rapes, tortures, that happened to them, except they didn't. I have the syndrome too, but I remember scenes from non-existent movies ... in one case, vividly, an entire John Ford western I have been unable to find anywhere and which everyone assures me is not part of the received canon.

Thus, when it comes to vampires....

I was no older than when I saw *Psycho (way* before puberty) when I saw the 1958 Christopher Lee *Dracula.* I saw every subsequent one, ending with *The Satanic Rites of Dracula* in 1973 — with my mother. She covered her eyes during most of the key scenes, but somehow, she still knew them intimately. She would often say that Christopher Lee was not only terrifying, but *handsome.*

And this, I think, is the crux of the fascination with vampirism that really started with Bram Stoker. There were vampires before that, of course, but they weren't really sexy. Well, you've have to have pretty unusual tastes to be attracted to F.W. Murnau's *Nosferatu,* but vampires were indeed more akin to werewolves and zombies before they became eroticized. During the twentieth century, they became steadily more romantic, until they passed through the velvety feel-goodness of Anne Rice and then metastasized via the spiky coolness of the hormone-laden teen sensibility.

But vampires were always about taboos, death being the first and most daring of all, for what separates a nip on the neck from being savagely raped by a corpse? Arguably, not much, if the barrier between the two is Victorian morality.

So, arguably, it comes down to necrophilia. But necrophilia with what, who, what social status, what age? These become the next taboos. Once you've summoned up the courage to open the fridge, it's only a small step to start eating whatever's in there.

So, in these vampire stories, it seems, we will binge it all. Because it seems that, over my almost half-century in the field, I've had a stab at pretty much every taboo when it comes to vampires. Well ... not coprophillia, yet. I leave that to Pier Paolo Pasolini.

So: van Helsing was a fictional vampirologist. Today's tend to be more academic and don't actually skulk around carrying stakes and mallets. One famous one is Gordon Melton, who's written scholarly books about vampire literature. He wrote the introduction to a stunning new edition of *Vampire Junction* which sold out before it was even released.

Another is the aristocratic Lloyd Worley, who runs an order of chivalry on the side and teaches in Colorado; he once presented *Vampire Junction* with the "Devendra P. Varma" Award. I believe that Varma was a major figure in gothic lit. criticism; in Wikipedia, he's noted as having received honours from both a real university and a fake one. Dr. Worley has been a great advocate of my vampire work.

But in this essay I want to mention Dr. Leonard G. Heldreth, who wrote fascinatingly about vampire literature and who said something very illuminating to me about my work when I first met him at the International Conference on the Fantastic, decades ago, in Boca Raton. He said, "*Vampire Junction* has something in common with *Dracula* – Bram Stoker pushed against the most forbidden taboo of his time — and until *Vampire Junction,* there wasn't a taboo quite so forbidden as the one you deal with." He was referring of course to the fact that the protagonist of *Vampire Junction,* while he's actually two thousand years old, has never physically aged since the age of twelve. The "object of desire" can therefore, tactfully, be described as "barely legal" — depending on what country you live in. Timmy Valentine is also a eunuch, compounding his ambiguity. And therefore, the more sympathetic he is, the greater his charisma, the more the reader is challenged to delve into the most disturbing areas of darkness in his own unconscious.

Heldreth's thesis about my book and about why it's scary is that in Bram Stoker's novel "the sexual and social fears of the nineteenth century's *fin-de-siècle* years, identified by many critics as the major substructure in *Dracula*, are replaced in the trilogy by the sexual phobias of the last decades of the twentieth century." — That's a quote from his book.

Often critics don't know what they're talking about, but what Leonard said was quite chilling to me. I had an attack of boss-sneaks-up-on-you-watching-a-naughty-video-at-your-desk syndrome.

The problem with *Vampire Junction* wasn't only the unprecedented gore and bad sex. It was also that on top of that, it had literary pretensions, composed in a fragmentary style derived from the editing style of a brand-new genre, the MTV video. Robert Bloch compared the book to William S. Burroughs.

The book appeared almost forty years ago and in my opinion it is *less* publishable by a traditional publishing company than it was in the 1980s. Even then, it was rejected by thirty publishers, before three editors who had *almost* been able to buy the book at different companies managed to end up at the same publisher, Ace/Grosset & Dunlap. They could then gang up on their boss together. It was only then that I could get it published — and they even made me change my name. They gave me a tiny advance — less than I got for my science fiction novels. After all, with the new name, I was a new author.

But ... there came a barrage of astonishing reviews, spearheaded by the frequently visionary Ed Bryant. And Phil Nutman naming the book as one of the four ancestors of "splatterpunk." And, eventually, canonization on the Horror Writers' Association's "all time greatest forty books" in 1996.

Since Leonard Heldreth explained my novel to me, it's taken me thirty years to understand *why* the book is that way. You see, it comes down to my mother, and all those Christopher Lee movies, impacting the deepest regions of my prepubertal mind. In a sense, there is something of an Oedipal triangle going on. (The book has a triangle, too — the Jungian analyst, the Wagnerian conductor, and the curious little vampire boy.)

It's clear now that I was experiencing what science fiction people have called "the golden age" — but in horror, just as in SF. Now that I am approaching 70, I see that I was projecting *myself,* at the age of 12, onto the "obscure object of desire." The ultimate outsider, too young to have any real power in the world while often knowing so much more than the adults around him ... I know now I was a thoroughly unlikeable child. But by morphing into a vampire, I turned the tables on the world that didn't get who I was.

I have been writing vampire stories, here and there, for most of my career. This book brings together all the ones I could find from the various anthologies, including some standalone Timmy Valentine stories — some were incorporated into the *Vampire Junction* trilogy, some weren't. My first vampire story was science fiction, part of the popular *Mallworld* series, but George Scithers, my editor at Isaac Asimov's Magazine, couldn't take "a vampire named Fred." Two were created for a series of anthologies which demanded from me "something controversial that'll get us banned."

To my disappointment, genre books aren't important enough to attract the attention of book banners. So let's hear it for genre — one of the few places where a writer doesn't have to look over his shoulder all the time, wondering when the thought police are coming, and whether they will raid the house from the left door or the right.

— Bangkok, December 5, 2022

S.P. Somtow

The Vampire of Mallworld, the first story in this book, is the first vampire story I ever attempted. It was designed to appear in my *Mallworld* series, which were then popping up in *Asimov's,* but the late George Scithers just didn't like it. Ostensibly, it was a vampire named "Fred" that bothered him. I wonder what it really was, and now, alas, he's no longer talking. It took the uninhibited Jean Marie Stine, then Hank, to take the story for *Amazing,* where he made it the cover story. I *think.* I never actually understood the cover.

Lost Valentines

The Vampire of Mallworld

Clement barJulian was a quadrillionaire with eyes in the back of his head. I was a reporter for the Holothrills-National Enquirer Syndicate, stiffly snapping at my live turtle soup in the middle of a gourmet restaurant in the middle of a thirty klick-long shopping center floating in space, trying to get the man to talk about a vampire—and he wasn't talking.

"I hate to presume on our old friendship—" I was saying. Above, a holoZeiss projected a shimmering stardome. My turtle swam half-heartedly in its bowl of bluish nutriliquid, and I was only waiting for it to hold still a moment so I could jab it with my fork.

"You presume," said Clement barJulian, "too far. There *is* no vampire in Mallworld." The candlelight flared up for a moment, playing flicker-shadow with his face. It was, of course, a deliberately contrived effect; I knew that Clement liked to affect a menacing mien. "Go home, Milton. Aren't you supposed to be covering the atrocities of the seven-veiled sect or something?"

"Yes, I was. But they assigned someone else. Got some kind of notion that I'm slipping—hell, Clement, you've seen the ratings! I'm only the most popular holovee personality in the Solar System! Remember when I covered the time in Mallworld when the mini-demat-booths backfired and left six hundred shoppers minus their heads? Remember when the Selespridon governor of Sol System was molested by a hundred Girl Scouts from bible-belt? And here I am investigating filler material. Sticking me with a moderately gory carnival act when I could be covering the war in Luna or interviewing a Selespridon ... " Carefully I maneuvered myself to get some good shots of barJulian. I was incognito, of course, covered with mounds of plastiflesh; indeed, the pot belly I'd snapped over my well-muscled torso was a pouch to carry my camera in, and it was operating surreptitiously through my navel.

"Always whining, Milton Huang, always whining," said Clement barJulian as he slurped the last of his Denebian whiteworms. "I know very well that whenever you get a Mallworld story you come to me first and whine and hope I'll bail you out—not to mention that I own a not insignificant share of the network. But I've never heard of a vampire in Mallworld, and I don't even rightly know what one is—some kind of geek, no?—and if anyone would know, *I* would."

He was right: his family *owned* Mallworld. He was worth enough to buy Phobos and Deimos and use them for juggling balls. And yet—he was edgier than I'd ever seen him. He'd always been very cordial with me, though you can't really ever know what the super rich have clicking in their minds. But today he was downright hostile. Was there something goingon?

"I'll investigate, of course," I said. My career was slipping and I could hardly do otherwise.

"That," said Clement portentously, "is life."

It was a relief to step out of the Galaxy Palace restaurant. Clement barJulian owned it, of course. It was the only place in existence where you could see the stars—the way they used to look, before the Selespridar came and shunted everything inside the orbit of Saturn into a pocket universe "for your own good"—projected via the last surviving holoZeiss recording. It's a beautiful restaurant; depressing, too. I'd gotten some good establishing shots there—only 2-D unfortunately, but they could be superimposed into a holo-collage, very in and arty that year, back at the studio.

***

Once in the corridor—

Mallworld was as it always was. Crazi-gravi corridors corkscrewing precariously and mobiustripping around straight corridors lined with demat-booths, and you could look up and see level after level after level on either side of you, vanishing into infinity, above and below; signs yelling at you, garish holo-ads with sensual young men and women selling perfume, airbeds, spacecars, relics of the Cross, pet salamanders, laxatives, compact sensuosurrogates for asteroid miners, rut pills, skating gloves—and the people, streaming by like space truckers' convoys, and the robots weighed down with shopping bags, and the jabbering, the jabbering...

Setting off at random—figured I should do some more establishing shots—I found a courtyard with upside-down fountains. An orchestra of Rigellian semisentients was playing squeaky music from their synthesizing rituals.

Perhaps I've been a little too Machiavellian, going straight to barJulian, straight to the top like this, I thought. Resolutely I turned to summon a comsim. Why not try the direct approach?

The comsim landed on my shoulder, a bearded six-inch man in pink.

"Hello. I am computer simulacrum Mallguide 227719," it buzzed. "Can I help you?"

"Yes. Uh, where's the vampire?"

"Hee!" it snickered, fluttering around my head. "You must be loaded! Show me your thumb."

Satisfied by my creditworthiness, it went on, "Honored sir"— it had suddenly become very obsequious, being programmed to react favorably to well-heeled thumbprints — "I cannot talk. But for one of such a bottomless expense account—"

"What do you mean, you can't talk?"

"You will be contacted!" And it was gone. I hadn't even been able to turn quickly enough to get a good angle through the camera eye in my navel.

All there was left to do was find a hotel and wait, so I got into a booth and asked for the Gaza Plaza, and in a split second I was walking into the hotel that was a scale model of the Great Pyramid of Khufu. Or perhaps it *was* the Great Pyramid-the ads were deliberately ambiguous there.

I felt a bit strange in the pyramid-shaped room, which was kept at a half-g for comfort. There was a crazy, queasy feeling in my stomach ... but wait! It wasn't the gravity!

Ali right, you can come out now, I subvocalized. My belly ripped open at the command from my throat gizmo, and my camera flopped all over the bed, wires and tentacles and micromikes wriggling like Medusa's head.

"Well," I said. "What do you make of it all?"

"Pretty weird," it said. " I still think it's a hoax, but—what do I know?"

"Shit," I said, "It's just some guy drinking blood. Why should Clement barJulian get all defensive about it? And what about all this cloak and dagger stuff with the comsims? I don't like it—"

Suddenly all the lights went out. "What the—" I stuttered, thinking, Uh oh, not a repeat of last season's blackout!

An eerie green light flickered on, cold and faint as in a dream. Then a comsim matted in: almost a foot tall, hovering in the air, with a dark black cloak that trailed behind him and rippled ever so gently. Its eyes were closed, and its lips were thin, red, sensuous.

"Quick, Clunko, get this on tape!" I murmured.

"Whaddya think I'm doing, dummy?"

I just stared and stared at the comsim. I almost recognized it; it was like a forgotten childhood image, an old story, a racial memory even.

The eyes flashed open. They were bloodshot. I was transfixed. Terror lanced my stomach for a wild moment before I could regain control.

Then—

A horrible cackle reverberated around the room, the mouth opened, the hideous fangs glistened, death-white, the eerie light shifting, darkening. gigantic shadows twisting...

"Good evening," it said. A sinuous, cold voice. " I am a comsim reproduction of Bela Bartok, the most famous vampire of the ancient earth myths. If you will kindly follow me, we will demat into the Cellars of Doom... participation is twelve credits only, observation twelve thousand credits to ensure only the most discriminating clientele... and now, the secret Vault of Horror of The Way Out Corporation. Your credit identification, please... this way! this way! this way!"

So this was it! I resisted an impulse to clutch Clunko's tentacles, abandoned myself to a deliciously creepy shudder, and followed the comsim through a wall that had begun to shimmer and turn to mist.

***

TIRED OF LIFE? said the sign in a mellow, father-image sort of voice. WHY NOT ... KILL YOURSELF? 300 WAYS POSSIBLE AT *THE WAY OUT CORP.!* MOST REVERSIBLE! MONEY BACK GUARANTEE IF STILL ALIVE AFTER PROCESSING!

I noted with some perplexity that The Way Out Corp. was a subsidiary of the Clement barJulian Group. "The plot thickens," I subvoked to Clunko the camera. I'd discarded my pot belly and donned a cloth-of-iridium loinshield; Clunko clattered behind. I still did not dare reveal my true face, of course, since I had some pretty overpowering fans.

Our personal comsim led us inside. Abruptly, a soundscreen cut off the crowd and we were each immersed in our own little silence.

"Your seat, sir," said the comsim resonantly. A dim green light shone on an antique coffin, done up to make a padded couch.

"Yes, but what about the vam—" He had dematted. I found a piece of paper with writing on it on the couch, program notes or something: since I can't read, of course, I scrunched it up and threw it behind me. *Okay.* I subvoked. *Spread yourself out and start shooting.* Clunko subdivided into little cells—ah, the miracle of subatomic circuitry! and began to drift around the place. For holovee you need at least four or five shooting angles or you can't get a good "in-the-round" feeling.

In the dimness I could make out some breathing. When my eyes adjusted I saw others in the audience. The bored and rich, all of them. Not since Pope Joan the Fifteenth's funeral had I seen such an array of garish clothing and outlandish, extravagant soma-models: purple skins, vestigial heads and other paraphernalia, grafted-on limbs and appendages, lewd looking women wearing gilded potato sacks, and all of them heaving with a sort of vulturelike ecstasy. I even saw a Selespridon, occupying a couch by himself—tall, blue-skinned and magenta-haired and looking decidedly uncomfortable. A subtle, sickly sweet odor pervaded everything. It was so dark there wasn't any scale to it. I mean, there could have been thousands of people there...

I subvoked an amplicommand to the olfacto track: there's nothing better than a wicked, nasty smell on holovee to really drive a point home...

A voice broke the silence. It came from everywhere at once, as the darkness deepened still more.

"Humans, aliens and semisentients," it began, "we are proud to present a genuine reconstruction of the day-to-day life of an ancient mythic vampire. The vampire of Earth—whose name has come down to us in various forms as Bella Abzug, Bela Bartok and Clarabelle—was a monstrous alien who devoured... human blood.

"Today we have the Vampire of Mallworld. A psychopath of unknown origin, this vampire came to The Way Out Corp. wishing for a release from life. Today, instead, he has earned a permanent place to live out his dread fantasies... all his victims are our customers. All the death scenes are genuine, and no victim will be revivified; each has signed an irreversible contract with The Way Out. We warn you-many who have come to watch as members of the audience have eventually found their way onto the stage of death!... And we sincerely hope that the desperadoes, the depressed, the schizoid, and the merely bored among you will think of us when the time comes for *you* to seek—*The Way Out!*"

Spotlight on a single coffin on a dais, old and dirty. The audience was quite still. Slowly, agonizingly slowly, the lid creaked open. The sound system was hyperamped to give you the shivers. It creaked... creaked... and then crashed onto the floor.

Very slowly he stood up. He was tall, over two meters. A black cloak flapped from his shoulders. His face was painted white, unearthly white with a glowing tinge of green. It was a long, bleak face, the black hair merging with the black cape, the lips Mars red and seductive, the eyes empty, dead. He hardly seemed to notice the audience.

"The first victim," said the announcer. "Miss Emily Smith."

A little old granny tottered onto the stage. She was shaking all over as she crossed the stage's lines of shadow. The vampire took her into his arms, towering above her.

She seemed to see nothing but his compelling eyes.

Teeth glistened. She whimpered once before he ripped her apart, and then she fell to the ground with a crash. A robot dragged off the body.

That's all? I was thinking. I looked around: couples in the audience were intertwined, some shamelessly indulging in erotic little games. *Talk about the rich and bored!* Clunko buzzed in my ear. *Shut up,* I subvoked. *Keep filming.*

A few more victims, mostly women. And then—number ten or eleven, I forget the name, but she was shatteringly beautiful, only a girl. she wore a white gown, and her long black hair streamed behind her in the stagewind they had set up for her she just stood there, half in the shadow, deep brown eyes moist and meltingly lovely, and I was on the edge of my seat. So was the audience. A throaty murmur escaped them, was stifled.

"Come, my dear, my little one " The voice was heard for the first time, and the sound system distorted it into a terrifying, nightmare voice. She advanced as though hypnotized. The vampire caressed her face with a large, slender hand that half glowed with some luminous grease paint; they embraced chastely, then more passionately, and then she was flinging aside her gown and he was biting her all over, and pools of red were spreading all over the white, and her sighs turned into shrieks of terror—

The whole audience cried out all at once. She flopped lifeless to the floor.

A burst of thunderous applause, cheering, the vampire bowed and dematted and the lights came blindingly on—

"We hope that you have had a pleasant fright," the announcer said warmly. "And thank you so much for choosing The Way Out Corp. for your entertainment today...

Good evening."

I glanced cursorily at the audience. Many were still under the spell. Then I got up to look for the stage door.

This was stupendous! This man had turned a simple geek act into a work of art. I could imagine him wowing them all on the lunchtime news now—the ratings'd put our rivals Astroco in the sanitization club for bankruptcy. Mind you, he *was* a psychotic... but one might daydream. He had an air about him. There was no vulgarity here. This had power. This had panache. This had class.

It wasn't just a filler. This had to be a special. Pocket History of Earth's Ancient Vampires. Panel of psychologists human and robot. The works. There was a fortune here, if only I could get the right angle on it.

***

... found a little autodoor that whispered STAGEDOOR, AUTHORIZED PERSONNEL ONLY, so I muttered "Holovee, holovee" in that urgent, well-rehearsed tone of voice that I always used to get into forbidden places. It accordioned open. Then it banged shut behind me and Clunko, and I took a look.

I found the vampire alone, being helped off with his clothes by a rusty-looking robot. Everything stank of poverty and degradation in the dressing room. Cloaks and props cluttered up every centimeter of the floor. And then I looked at the vampire's face.

He was standing in front of a mirror. I saw him first in the mirror, a dazed, sad face, a trace of blood on his lips. With a shock, I realized he was only a meter-fifty tall or so. He'd been wearing leviboots.

He had an earnest young face, mousy hair, freckles, a mild, undernourished look.

"You the vampire?" I couldn't believe it.

"I'm the vampire," he said sadly. The robot had whisked the cloak away and he stood naked in front of me. His soma was emaciated, pitiful. I was still in shock as he went on. "I don't know how you got in—"

"I'm Milton Huang!"

"Who?" The man didn't even watch holovee.

"I'm a holovee personality. I want to do a special on you. You look like you could use the money," I added in a confidential sort of tone. "Listen, what do I call you? Mr. Vampire? Vampey?"

"My name is Federico barJulian," he said emotionlessly, "and my friends usually call me Fred. But then again I have no friends."

I was shaking inside, the way you always do when a terrible humdinger of a story is about to break. "You're a *barJulian?* How could the scion of one of the richest families in the universe-"

"I told you. My father owns the place. Now leave me alone."

"You're *Clement's* kid?"

"Leave me alone!" I saw his face freeze and a look of deep tragedy come over it. It would be perfect for holovee: this man was a born actor. Lucky he didn't know everything was being committed to tape.

"Can't you people leave me in peace?" he said. "You've already turned me into a ridiculous parody, a stage show, forcing me to abase myself because of my terrible hunger."

"Look, I just want to do some filming. Name your price, for god's sake! Holothrills-National Enquirer is willing to pay any amount within reason ..." I walked around him slowly, thinking, *Why does he need to do this? With his kind of credit he could buy up an azroid full of pretty people and bite them all to death.*

As if in answer to my thoughts, he said, "I've been disowned. Father wishes to hush me up, completely. I make a living the only way I know how." The pathos was just stunning. Loonies are always good material; they're so unpredictable, so *genuine.* And a quadrillionaire loonie geek was the acme of ratingsworthiness.

He stared me full in the face and said, "I just want to be normal."

"Huh?" I was taken aback. "You can't mean that. Hell, look at what you've got; they all love you out there. Your show has everything an audience could possibly want: a little bit of sex, a little bit of sadism, and a whole lot of archetypal, mythic mystery... come on," I said frustratedly, "you can't be *that* psychotic. Money's money."

"But you don't *understand,* " he said, practically in tears. Nothing could have been further from the imposing, terrifying figure he had portrayed only a moment before. "I loathe this life. I don't want to be a freak! I want to be normal! Help me! Help me!" And he had gripped my arm so tight that it was hurting. Gently I twisted loose. I took a long, stern look at everything I'd seen. Should I cut my losses... and lose the most potentially staggering holovee special I'd ever had the chance to make? There was pathos in the way this little man, childlike and torn by uncontrollable desires, was weeping his heart out in the dressing room. There was tragedy, even depth.

Then I got my brainstorm.

"Look here," I said, "we'll *get* you cured! We'll buy you

the best psychocomputer in Mallworld. We'll have experts come and root out every trauma, every complex. We'll even slip you back into society afterward; we've got the megacreds to do it, and-"

"There's a price," he said truculently. "There's always a price."

"Let us tape everything."

"Well... " I saw a little gleam in his eye now and smiled smugly. How well I knew in those days that *everything* has its price.

Taking advantage of his confusion, I went on quickly, "Why, don't you see? As a sensation show it's pretty cool. We could maybe get a thirty-five to forty on the ratings. But as *human interest*—the private anguish of your tormented soul as it finally finds peace-it's incredible! I can see the whole thing," I went on, losing all caution in my enthusiasm, "a three-hour feelietape special. We can get the sponsors. Hell, The Way Out Corp. will do it for the publicity, maybe even the Vatican! The eyes of billions, in their living rooms, in their spacecars, in their azroid hideouts, eyes, ears, tacto-olfacto electrodes all glued to the holo-screen, from Titan to Mercury 'The Vampire of Mallworld finds truth and meaning, and a new life.' It's warm it's wonderful-"

"Help me! Oh, help me!" cried the Vampire of Mallworld.

***

Time passed and the best psychocomps in Mallworld were unable to extract any but the most extraneous information from Fred. We drugged him with every drug we could think of. We had him trussed up in a booth on the fifteenth level of Auntie Annetta's Do-It-Yourself Shrink Shack, alternately pumping him with sensory dep and sensory overload. A biochemcomp stood by, flashing every molecule of his endocrine system onto a strobomanic vidscreen. Even tried some medieval therapy from an old recipe book where you electrocute the victim-patient half to death.

I toyed with the idea of getting help from the Selespridar, even...

The best shrink shack in Mallworld was by definition the best shrink shack in the Solar System, and this was all it yielded: Federico barJulian had shown a propensity for bloodletting and other violence from the earliest. He was a virgin at twenty two, twice the normal age. His obsession had crystalized when he watched some ancient two dimensional tapes of mythological vampire epics from Earth: his favorite was a character called Dracula after whom he was later to model his act most consciously. Every six hours, the hunger would come upon him and he would rush down to the suicide parlor for another session. They were certainly milking him for all he was worth, paying him peanuts, and screwing the creditful thumbs of some fairly heavyweight clients... the Selespridon, a xeno-anthropologist, for instance, being one of the regulars. The six-hour interval between each feeding session was totally reliable. You could tell time by him. In fact, I gave up checking my eyelid calendar completely.

For a person with such a peculiar social problem, he was astonishingly sane: witty, full of tragicomic one-liners, and a great holovee personality. He seemed undaunted at first by the constant failure of the therapy machines. I had a great time with his steadfastness, his courage, his obvious longing to be normal. But it was all wearing thin, and you don't make a good holovee show with failure. The audience has to have a satisfying climax and denouement, or you're stuck with three hours of pathos and gore and sex and human frailty and witty characterization and not a peg to hang the story on...

My boss called me while I was taking a respite in the hotel's automassage-sauna. It was a transmat call; must have cost a fortune, all for the convenience of not having to wait ten minutes in between remarks. The boss materialized right in the middle of my tub of water. It was only a holo-image, but nonetheless unnerving.

"Got anything yet?"

"We're working on it—"

"Now see here, Huang!" The boss began to gyrate wildly around his tripod. "I don't want to catch sight of you in a sauna again, you hear? You've run way over budget and I'm giving you a hundred hours—" Abruptly his twenty seconds were up.

It's hard working for a machine; they have no sense of human dignity.

That was the day some kind of breakthrough happened. I was too depressed after the boss called, thinking of my career going to seed and my ratings tumbling. After being poked at, prodded by machines, Fred was not feeling too hot either, so we decided to walk through Mallworld. We floated through the corridors in a holo-bubble, because I'd donned my all-too familiar true somatype and I didn't want to be mobbed by the fans.

"It's not Bela Bartok anyway," he was saying, "it's Bela someone-else. They don't give a damn about accuracy at The Way Out, all they care for is their lousy show."

We turned a corner and sailed past the Galaxy Palace restaurant. We both shuddered, knowing who owned the place. I was becoming quite fond of Fred, even outside my professional capacity. We streaked past a bevy of shopping bags, their wares fairly bursting their seams, sauntering down a slidewalk as if they owned the place. A huge animated tomato demonstrated dance steps on a whirling dais flanked by twittering comsims. Up a crazi-gravi corridor that gravi-flipflopped so we saw the whole world upside down-

"Tired of this?" I said.

"Yeah. How about some nature?" We turned into the Earthscape Safari Park.

Striding boldly out of the holographic sea, one of Mallworld's most famous landmarks, the Statue of Limitations, patroness of merchants and thieves...

As we winged down a klomet-wide pathway lined on either side with Grecian columns, with lions (actually leonoids) and tigroids and zebroids and okapoids and crocodiloids acting out the primal drama of nature, and shadows from distant dueling triceratopses blotching the wild wheat brown savannah, we did not speak much. I saw that Fred was moved by what he saw. I sensed that he felt as they did, was part of this savage world. And then, without warning—

"Mommy!" he shrieked. He crushed me in his arms and tried to bite me, then began to wail like a baby and press hard against my chest, sobbing, "Mommy, Mommy..."

"What's wrong?" I looked ahead and saw nothing but a herd of chimpanzoids, playfully cavorting inside a plastiflesh carcass of an elephant.

"Mommy—"

I was shaken. I mean, I knew he was crazy, but he'd never *acted* crazy before, except for this little quirk of sucking people's blood. I tried to calm him down, but he would not rest until we had gone way past the chimpanzee exhibit, into the aquarium hall where they showed dozens of fish being happily devoured by larger and larger fish...

This new turn of events would keep the studio happy for a day or two. But now we needed results, and fast.

I beckoned to Clunko, who was trotting along behind, and asked for its advice. Meanwhile, Fred was staring at the chains of fish eating fish, smiling happily to himself.

"Maybe he was raised by apes in the jungle—" my camera began.

"Oh, be quiet."

"And acquired carnivorous habits, and when he was adopted back into civilization—"

"Watch enough ancient twodee tapes, you'll soon be as crazy as he is," I snapped. "Besides, he only bites humans. Besides, we found out that he was born right here in Mallworld, at Storkways Inc., in fact, who have never been known to deliver a defective baby—"

"Or so they claim."

"He's never so much as stepped off this thirty-klick hunk of metal! And what place could be safer than Mallworld? Where in hell could he possibly have picked up a chimpanzee specific mothersurrogate response? I think... that it's time for a human psychiatrist, Clunko."

"A witch doctor?"

"Don't be silly. They have had human psychiatrists for centuries—"

"What are you, some kind of back-to-nature ecologizer?"

"You machines are such impossible chauvinists," I said,

thinking of my boss.

We spent the day trying to relax: watched lion eat lion, vulture eat vulture, shark eat shark, and, in a rousing climax to the park's entertainments, a passably convincing tyrannosaur eat tyrannosaur.

And then Fred shambled off to assuage his six-hourly hunger, and I went off to look up Dr. Emmanuel Varhite. He and I had gone to St. Martin Luther King's Traditional Strict and Snooty School when we were kids, so presumably he—like Clement barJulian himself-was on the Old Boy Network.

I found him running a psychiatric concession at Gimbel and Gamble's Department Store and Feeliepalace on level T67. He'd come down in the world, and had also grown inordinately portly. He accepted the case at once, insisting only on one condition: that Holothrills buy him at least one meal a day at the Galaxy Palace restaurant. That was how low he had sunk, my old schoolmate. It was his own fault for picking such a pointless career, though. As useful to have chosen alchemy or window-washing, or to have learned how to read.

A few hours later. Emmanuel Varhite was wolfing down Denebian whiteworms with great relish beneath the dome of artificial stars in Clement barJulian's restaurant. We had a table right beneath the starfield, and special wraparound seats that really felt snug. Invisible, too—they were Selespridon force-mechanisms—they made us look as though we were spacing out on Levitol. Clunko was casually disguised among the cutlery. Above, the "stars" shone—fake, but still beautiful. It was a masterstroke, I thought, to film in the Galaxy Palace: thestarsweredazzling, and every human being yearns for those outside our space and time...

Here the tables were turned, and we, the underdogs, got served by real people dressed in exotic alien costumes. Probably inaccurate.

I'd settled for the echinoderms stuffed with soft-shell malaprops; Fred, in full Bella Abzug attire, was eating a steak. Rare.

Varhite, whose face resembled a trampled rosebush, was expostulating at the camera. "We know." he said, "that the subject likes to drink blood-preferably killing the victim in the process."

"Come on, Varhite!" I stage-whispered. "Try to sound a little more witch-doctorly... our audience can be a little dumb, you know?"

"Relaxen Sie... I mean, relax, my boy," he said, warming to the image I'd created for him. "There are other clues. For instance, he reacts violently to chimpanzees, calling them 'Mommy, Mommy' in a petulant child's voice... clearly an anguished plea from the Unconscious.

"He is a product of Storkways Incorporated, the most blue-chip, influential baby factory in the Solar System, whose main showroom is, of course, in Mallworld..."

As he spoke he never stopped sucking in the whiteworms as they wriggled in their death throes, thus releasing the intoxicating hormone that was the whole secret to their appeal ... for sheer taste, give me spaghetti.

"He first, as it were, concretized his urges when accidentally exposed to an old twodee movie. Now he watches it every day, in between meals, in his little one-room apartment tucked inside the labyrinthine corridors of The Way Out Corp. And every six hours—"

"They've heard that."

"Now, from these facts, what strange, tortuous, twisted trauma can we glean? Ah—"

"Not much to go on, is there, Doctor?" I said glumly. "Frankly, Doctor—my boss is thinking of dumping this whole project."

"And not cure me?" Fred suddenly looked up from his steak with those hopeless, despairing eyes.

"Come on, kid," I said, patting his hand. "Doctor Varhite and I, we *believe* in you." At that moment, I confess to being moved. He seemed so helpless ... a baby, really. Trying to look professional, I skewered another echinoderm, watching as it deflated in a messy splat of rheum. "We *will* cure you!" I was almost choking. I'd lived with this thing for days now.

"And yet," said Doctor Varhite, "it seems to be most difficult to isolate the primal trauma. It must be very deep, very deep."

I knew the doctor was up to something, so I subvoked to my camera. Several forks and spoons levitated to surround the doctor from all sides. He pulled out something from his armpit pouch and threw it on the table. It was an inflatable hologram. He touched the stud —

A chimpanzee was sitting on the table.

"We've already done this a hundred times, you don't have to be cruel—" I began.

And the vampire screamed! He tried to clutch me, the empty hologram's throat, tried to bite it, began to sob. I was so involved, subvoking instructions to all my hardware, that it was practically happening to me. And then he sank down on the table, wracked by convulsions, as other diners on their motorized tables swung by to see what all the fuss was about. *"Ah-ha!"* Doctor Varhite cried. "Positively Pavlovian!" Abruptly the screaming stopped. Fred pulled himself together, whispered "Mommy" very softly, and gathered his cloak up around himself. He stood erect and tall in his levi-boots, menacing in his deathpale makeup.

His face seemed to shine with a pallid, luminous coldness. "Blood," he whispered harshly. "Blood, blood, blood!" Then he swept out of his seat and strode to a demat-booth in the middle of the restaurant and disappeared, leaving behind him a giggling audience of diners.

"Well," I sighed, "that's another thing we know."

"Ja," said the doctor,"regular as clockwork. In the middle of a word, in the middle of an action, when the six hours come, the urge comes. It's uncanny." With a fingertip he deflated his hologram.

"Well, let's go back to the hotel and talk more strategy, eh?" I said. But I wasn't feeling very hopeful.

"What about dessert?" I sighed; the contract was binding, of course, so we ordered. While we were waiting, a six-inch high hologram of my boss appeared on the table.

"Oh no," I gasped, "not another holo! And this time *I'm* going to get the convulsions."

"Huang!" spluttered the hologram. "Something terrible has happened! Holothrills-National Enquirer has been completely bought up by the Clement barJulian Group!"

I could feel my stomach turn. "Does this mean-"

"Yes it does! Now look, you have twenty-four hours to come back to Soaprock, or your expense account is up. Orders from on high say you're fired... whatever the cost! Someone in the new administration's after your ass,

Huang. Now this is a regular real-time call. I'm not waiting ten minutes just to see you answer, lounging about in a sauna or... dining at the Galaxy! I bet that's where you are, isn't it? Now see here—"

He vanished and was replaced by two chocolate sundaes.

I shuddered. There was my whole career, flashing before my eyes. I tried not to think at all, and applied myself greedily to the sundae, an exotic dish made entirely from the blubber of specially cloned whales.

"You see the situation I'm in," I said. "I've raised the kid's hopes sky-high and now I'm to dash them all." Maybe I should have been thinking more about my own career than about Fred the vampire. But I'd seen his show, I'd been touched by it. The kid had fallen all the way from riches to rags because of his obsession, yet... in the moment that he killed, he was a king. I'd seen it, I'd captured it on film, and I was starting to see him as a martyr symbol of the human race... or maybe just falling victim to my own skillfully worded holo-scripts. I don't know.

"We still," Doctor Varhite said kindly, "have twenty-four hours."

"What can we do? We've tried everything!"

"Except... confrontation therapy."

"Oh?"

"I have already figured it out. This will be so dramatic that you can run to the competition with it if you have to--"

"BarJulian owns the competition."

"You want to help Fred, don't you? Regardless." "Regardless." I knew this was the wrong time for altruism, but I was in too deep to quit.

***

"Confrontation therapy was a popular Dark Ages treatment," Varhite explained as Clunko whirled around the table, "invented by one Marcus Welby, whose tapes have survived the ages in truncated form. It involves confronting the patient with the locale, the flavor, the *presence* of his infancy, in order to drive the hidden trauma or *engram* to the surface. Tomorrow, then, we will film at Storkways, Inc., and the patient will come to find himself, there, at the very moment of his birth."

"It sounds very farfetched to me."

"My boy," he said, "what do you know about Storkways Inc.? Did *you* have the good fortune to be a Storkways child?"

"Of course not! I was born in the regular way, with an android host mothersurrogate, delivered by Caesarian straight into my mother's arms."

"That's the problem, then. You don't understand the peculiar loneliness, the *angst,* of a baby factory. I'm sure we can find an answer there... won't you give it a try?"

"What's in it for you, Emmanuel?"

He shrugged. "It's complicated. I guess I want to vindicate us 'witch doctors' and destroy the ascendancy of the psychocomps. I've been on a downhill trend lately and I need something. And besides, another day of the Galaxy Palace's food—"

Just then a waiter slunk up to our table. "Excuse me, sir," he said, floundering about in his half-donned fuzzy suit. "Mr. barJulian has asked me to inform you that you and the doctor are no longer welcome in this restaurant. A comsim will escort you—"

With a grand gesture Doctor Varhite slung the remainder

of his sundae in the waiter's face. He stood dazed for a moment, then toppled into a heap of arms, legs, fur and chocolate sauce.

Clunko had filmed the whole thing. "Bravo!" I said. "Let's get out of here."

"You have no idea," said Doctor Varhite, "how much it cost me to do that."

It was a sorry troupe that matted on the level Y99 an hour or so later; we had just caught the last of Fred's act at The Way Out, and he had just done away with a pair of beautiful tangerine-eyed twins. Varhite led the way through a conch twisty passageway; I followed, not even caring that, even in my normal soma, I was not attracting the attention of any rabid fans. Clunko trotted behind, and the Vampire of Mallworld lagged in the rear. I knew I wouldn't get a chance to see the act again—not at twelve kilocred a throw and no expense account—and so the killings had been tinged with an exquisite sadness. You might wonder why these people have elected, of their own free will, to die, and the exhibitions of suicide parlors are a natural consequence of man's innate commercialism ... but I found myself thrust into a state of profound longing which no competent newsman should have felt. I began to wonder about myself. Did I really belong in the holothrill trade?

Too soon we reached the lobby of Storkways Inc., a gigantic stylized uterus, painted pink, with transparent walk-levels jutting from the sides, which you approached from below by means of a diagonal slidewalk through a tubular passageway. The symbolism lent a grave dignity to the proceedings. Storkways was the oldest of the baby production firms, and was known to be incorruptible. No one had ever purchased a faulty baby from Storkways ... or so they claimed.

Theprimeval womb would make an excellent final scene, I decided, my spirits lifting a little. I could almost hear the script: *Here, in the very womb of humanity...*

I had to stop and remind myself that I was just doing the day's filming as an empty gesture, an attempt to wring every last microcred from the coffers of the company.

Soon we were greeted by a buxom human attendant in an oversize diaper and nothing else. She was wearing Storkways' Radiant Motherhood Smile.

''Ah,'' she said, not at all perturbed by the strange sight of a vampire in full regalia, a fat little psychoanalyst, a talking camera, and me. ''A charming menage you have here, I see! What kind of baby were you interested in, and at what price range?"

I looked a bit indecisive, I suppose, so she quickly went on, ''Aquatics are in this season, as are little fuzzies and of course our ever-popular *normal* model, and—''

She looked at us expectantly. The smile hadn't changed at bit: I knew that it had been soldered on surgically.

"Why don't you nice fellows just browse through our catalogue?" she said. Instantly the air was full of holographic toddlers, solemnly filing past our faces. "Just point to the one you want... oh!... you're ... *Milton Huang!"* she shrieked suddenly.

It was the only good thing to have happened all day. "I'm sure you'll be wanting a custom-made, then," she said thoughtfully. ''Are these your husbands?"

"Miss—"

"Could I have your thumbprint, please? Just a formality, credit check, you know, and—well, actually I wanted it for my collection, I watch your show almost every fourday—"

"We'd like to do some filming here. If you'll just thumb this release—" I fiddled around with spools of minitape from my loinshield.

"O-o-oh!" She just stared at me, hardly taking in a word, while I explained the situation. "I'll get the manager. Oh, we'd be proud. Very proud indeed." She hopped into a demat-booth.

"What do you think?" I whispered to Emmanuel.

"Let's be patient," he said. Then, "Oh, look at all the darling babies!"

A seductive voice was saying, in warm, motherly tones. "Number 17 of our 'exotic' line is green-skinned, adapted for Deimos gravity, with a power-steering option for those difficult visits to high-gravity worlds. Choice of three hair colors and two basic personality indexes—'passionate and profound' or 'excitable and extrovert.' Actual personality will depend, of course, on environmental factors and your own parental proclivities."

The baby spun around and toddled off in midair. "Number 18. The two heads are perfectly adapted for —"

"Can't we turn this thing off?" I shouted impatiently.

Doctor Varhite nudged me gently, and I saw that our friend Fred was gazing, spellbound, at the tot parade.

"Normal... normal ... " he was murmuring, as a charming little number with vestigial wings, four arms, and belly-gills drifted by. Poor Fred. I made sure I got a shot of his wistful face. I was in my element now, capturing the very essence of the man for the audience that was never to be. More and more the situation was getting urgent—anyone who'd envy an 'exotic' baby for being normal. they're usually intended for Babylon 5, and if you call anything to do with *that* colony normal, you really have flipped your chips.

Miss Perfect Mother came flouncing in with another matriarchal figure, this time in a golden diaper that radiated higher authority. This was Mabel Murray-Pentecost, regional manager of Storkways Inc. She too sported the infamous patent smile.

"Welcome!" she boomed. "I am most honored to be able to conduct you through our venerable halls myself, though I am *sure* that whatever is troubling that poor, poor young man will not be found here. And let me say for the benefit of the audience"—she certainly was making the best of her airtime, not knowing that she'd never make it on to the holovee screen— "that Storkways is *dedicated* to the infinite recomplexification of our human gene pool. Why be the same when you can be different? I know it's conservative and old fashioned of us, but let me say that I *believe* in those values. Here at Storkways Inc. we always say: 'A clone no more!'"

Having said her piece, she beckoned us into a booth. "Fred has been tranquilized," Varhite was explaining, "so that only the most primal memories will precipitate his convulsions." Nevertheless, I noticed that Miss Murray-Pentecost was keeping her distance and even seemed a little leery of Clunko as he clambered after us.

***

" ... and this is the viewing room," she was saying, "where the little dears all rest and where they can be examined by prospective parents through a sophisticated audio-video-tacto-olfacto projection device in the privacy of their own holoview cubicles." We were standing in a tremendously long hall lined with floatcribs, five in a row, with narrow lanes between each row, and little comfort-robots whizzing back and forth between the rows. The din was really heady; with some reluctance I resisted the cheap trick of switching up the audio track. I was damn well going to be artistic even if no one was going to experience this show.

"My god!" I exclaimed for the camera. "How many babies do you have here at any one time?"

"Three, four thousand," she said. "We change them every sleep shift."

"But... don't they ever get misplaced?" said Doctor Varhite slyly.

"What, sir? Incompetence here at Storkways Inc.? You ask the impossible. Are we not *dedicated* to the preservation of human life? Are we not a byword for ethical behavior throughout the Solar System?"

"All right, already!" I said. "Varhite—any luck on the patient?"

Fred was stalking up and down the aisles. He seemed a little restless, with his cloak flying behind him and his hands trembling a bit, but benign enough for now. Every now and then he stopped to croon over one of the babies.

"He won't... you know, *eat* one?" asked Mabel Murray Pentecost anxiously.

"Oh, no. His 'attacks' come every six hours exactly, and he's just been fed," said Doctor Varhite.

"Curious," said the matriarch. "We've just had our feeding too—we run the feeding system every six hours, and it's all computer controlled, obviously—"

Doctor Varhite and I exchanged a quick look. "It's probably fortuitous," I said. "It seems a pretty unlikely connection to me..."

I subvoked Clunko and told him to heel. We had a lot more to squeeze into my last day and I was getting impatient. We weren't going to find a solution anyway. Clunko had been having a grand time snapping all the babies-his 'human interest' programming was very deeply ingrained. I had to squeeze to negotiate the aisles, and the manageress's fixed smile had become extremely wearying to look at. The hall was *not* designed for people, but for robots; and the nearest demat-booth was a good five hundred meters of squashing and squeezing away.

The next hall was a very murky one. It was two meters across but seemed to stretch forever. The walls were high —about twenty-five meters—and lined with shelves. On each shelf squatted a row of bored-looking chimpanzees, each with a baby in its arms.

"Ah-ha!" said Emmanuel. I saw his point. Now I was sure there was a connection, but what was it? I glanced at Fred, who was shaken but still in one piece-thanks to the massive dose of tranquilizers.

"This," said the guide, "is our feeding room, where our little ones are breast-fed by genetically altered chimpanzees, as you can see. It's ever so hygienic, and you know it's much better psychologically for the child to be able to relate to a living creature."

Now I knew that all the pieces belonged to the same puzzle. But I still couldn't see the answer. Nothing fell into place. What could possibly be traumatic about being breast-fed by a chimpanzee? The idea certainly didn't worry me, and I had been a regular baby.

But they gave me a creepy feeling, those rows and rows of apes, each clutching a baby in its arms, each with a dead, glazed look which betrayed ... what? Genetic tampering?

"What now?" I asked Doctor Varhite.

"Is there anything else?" He turned to Miss Murray-Pentecost.

"I don't think so-this represents all the stages that a baby would go through— "

"And yet the patient has exhibited no unusual anxieties yet." Fred had retreated into his cloak but was still calm. "You've never discovered"— the doctor began to hem and haw, choosing his words with great care— "any instances of traumatization from these breast feedings?"

"Heavens no, Doctor," she said with some revulsion. "Our research department—not to mention our discriminating clientele—would never have let us get away with such a thing!"

"And the babies are placed with chimpanzee mother-surrogates immediately after parturition?" said Doctor Varhite.

"Well, yes, of course."

"And if no chimpanzees are available?" I said.

"Well, it sometimes happens, and then we take some of the older babies off the chimpanzees temporarily to make room... we have excellent temporary facilities, of course, for the temporarily displaced little ones."

"Show me," Varhite said grimly.

"You don't ask for much, do you?" she said through her implacable smile. "Come with me." Her golden diaper gleamed in the half-light.

" I do apologize for our lack of demat-booths," she said," but we usually only have robots here." A little passageway opened up at our feet, and she motioned us to descend. "We don't usually want any unnecessary infection, you know, and one can't very well put a prospective parent into an autoclave... " She chuckled heartily at her own joke.

The steep passageway was cramped: we had to go single file. Fred and the doctor lagged; I think Fred was reluctant and had to be coaxed. A strange unease hung in the air. The manageress and I were the first ones to enter the little room. There were perhaps ten circular tables, stacked with hardware. "On peak seasons," she was saying, "we do sometimesuse these."

She indicated one of the round machines on a table, from which half a dozen padded cribs jutted, in some of which babies lay, some gurgling, some asleep. A plastiflesh pacifier extended over the mouth of each infant, and was connected to a vat of milk under the table. Most of the berthlets were empty.

"Seems efficient enough," I said.

She beamed maternally. "It's usually only for a day or so, until a new shipment of fastclone chimps can be transmatted from the farms on Earth."

"What's this here?" I pointed to one of the unoccupied cribs, where a pacifier looked a little odd.

"Why," she said, "I've no idea."

The plastiflesh had broken off, rotted away somehow, revealing the pointed steel of the milk-injector underneath, sharp and ugly. A baby could...

"Are you telling me-" I began.

"Oh, no, our equipment is inspected *daily*. That must be why the crib is unoccupied, you see." I thought I could detect a slight wilting of the permanent smile, even though I knew it was anatomically impossible.

"But isn't it just possible that, if you had a defective pacifier, that a baby could accidentally get assigned to it ***before*** the daily inspection, and-"

Just then the others came down and crowded around the

table. I was just pointing out the faulty pacifier when—

Fred gave a hysterical cry and began to pummel the machine with his fists. Doctor Varhite and I stepped back in shock. He was banging, now his fists were sore and bloody, he was yelling over and over, "Mommy, Mommy, Mommy, you betrayed me you hurt me you made me drink blood you gave me blood Mommy Mommy Mommy —"

My blood was racing with excitement. I sent the camera flying every which way. Fred was beautiful. The way he clawed at the metal, the way he moaned and shrieked-

"Inspected daily?" I turned to the matriarch grimly.

"I assure you, sir," she said without losing her smile for a moment, "your accusations are impossible! We'll sue! We'll sue!"

"Mommy Mommy Mommy—"

How big a story could you get? Incompetence—in *Storkways!* Corruption within the very bastions of everything we held good in society! I'd shot the show that would undermine the very foundations of our beliefs! No matter that no one would see it—

"I'll sue, you can't go exposing us like this, I can explain!" screamed the matriarch, smiling beatifically and grotesquely the whole time.

Above the tumult I turned to Emmanuel Varhite. "And now let's talk to the expert himself," I said in *my* suavest holovee voice. "Now that the pieces have come together, what are your conclusions?"

"Dark are the ways of the Unconscious," he began dramatically. (The screaming in the background never stopped. It set the babies off, and *they* were all hollering their lungs out.) "The essence of Confrontation Therapy is truth, sheer truth. Here we have seen an unfortunate trauma: the patient was made to substitute pain and blood for a mother's love and milk. No wonder he felt hostility toward the chimpanzee mother surrogate who came too late to aid him from his terrible torment! No wonder he could not forgive! Yes! It was in this very womb that the seeds of schizophrenia were sown..."

"Mommy Mommy Mommy—"

"I'll sue—"

"Waaaaaaagh—"

Seizing the moment, I gathered up *my* most melodramatic phrases and stood in a heroic pose, full face in front of Clunko. *Go, Clunko,* go, I subvoked, and then began rhetorically: "What have we seen here, friends? We have traced this unfortunate, tragic man's career back to its very roots. We have shown him the source of his terrible inner conflict; and now we have freed him to emerge, a fully *human* being, from the living hell that was his domain. Yes! What we have witnessed today — is Death and Rebirth ! Total Catharsis! In a monumental, heartwarming victory for the human spirit!"

I spread out my arms in the famous "crucified" pose that has since made me a household word, held for ten seconds, and turned around to see if I could stop all the screaming.

***

"—so you see," Clement barJulian was saying to me, "I had to see the finished product. Federico was—is—my son." He downed another glass of angels' tears. "I should havebelieved that a cure was possible, and yet-and yet—"

"I know." He had wept four times when they showed him

the rough edit of the special. He'd rehired me. He'd re-adopted his son. I didn't want to go into all that again—I was trying to ferret out some scandal about his sister-in-law. After a whole year in which I'd become rich, in which Storkways had paid damages through the nose-and hush-up money, too, when a dozen other cases of criminal negligence came to light, and vampire imitators popped up all over Sol System, and glamorous Fred being chased everywhere by an army of amorous groupies begging for a gentle nip on the neck in memory of the old days—

Yes. Things certainly turned out right for him. And yet—

"Clement," I said, "I don't like what I do anymore."

He hardly looked up from his main course, a succulent crablike purple thing with splotchy tentacles swimming in a bowl of strawberry Jell-O. I looked away, watching the stars wheel. "Eh?"

"I'm a phony, you know," I said. After a whole year I had to blurt out my heart to someone. "All holovee personalities are. We're really drab. And yet, when I think of when I first watched Fred's show, and saw love and death and beauty and mystery all mingled together, and I knew that this was *Art*—nothing *I* do will ever be as beautiful, or as terrifying, or as *real* as Fred the vampire's lunacy. Will it?"

"He was crazy!" Clement said. "You cured him, and earned a few creds yourself from the whole thing. You should be happy."

"But I'm scared. I'm scared. I feel like I've destroyed something very personal, something like a soul, I suppose. I almost regret it—"

"Come on!" Clement roared. "Here, take your mind off it, let me tell you some juicy gossip--"

I could not bring myself to confess to Clement barJulian that, for a few moments, when his son the vampire squeezed the life out of a particularly beautiful woman in a passion beyond ecstasy and terror, I would have given anything to feel what he felt... for a few seconds that will haunt me forever, I had envied the Vampire of Mallworld.

***

This next story first appeared in an anthology for the *World of Darkness* series. The editor was the controversial Ed Kramer, but in those days we didn't know how controversial he really was. He said to me, "I want a biblical story that will get people so angry they'll ban the book."

In my innocence, I thought that depicting Jesus as a gay vampire would do the trick. I was wrong; no one complained at all. Thirty years later, maybe they will. Times have changed.

Beloved Disciple

First off, I never fucked him.

I know, I know, Your Holiness, Your Eminences, Monsignor, distinguished fathers of the Roman and other churches; some of you are going to be disappointed. I've heard that there's even a church named in my honor, the Church of the Beloved Disciple, with the implication that I'm the patron saint of homosexuals, which is all very flattering, especially knowing how many of you reverend fathers suffer from certain ... proclivities which you hypocritically practice even though they are forbidden in your religion.

Not that it never occurred to me. For in any other country in the Empire or beyond, it would have been perfectly natural. But this was Judaea, and Joshua barJoseph, Jesus to his Greek friends, was very, very Jewish: no pork, no graven images, and no buggery.

He was so pure that I don't think he ever even masturbated. But he had a passionate hankering for all those things that make a man immortal: philosophies, ideas, poetry. And a hankering for me, too, since I was what, at the time, he was not: I was, so to speak, the real thing.

I am immortal. I am a vampire.

He was a dreamy boy — no more than a boy when I first met him, though old enough to turn a few heads in Cornwall — for the Celts, when it comes to boys, were more Greek than the Greeks, as you would know if you read Caesar's *Gallic War* unexpurgated.

Cornwall, you protest! Jesus was never in Cornwall. Oh, but you surely know William Blake's poem:

And did those feet in ancient time
Walk upon England's mountains green?

As late as the nineteenth century there still lingered some memory of the truth: that Joseph of Arimathea, one of the most influential men in Judaea, owned shares in a Cornish tin-mine, and had become rich from the manufacture of bronze; that he once had occasion to bring young Joshua to distant Britannia, the most barbaric outpost of the Empire.

Joshua's father was another Joseph, a rabbi of the Essene sect, so learned and so diligent that they nicknamed him The Carpenter. His mother, Miriam, doted on his little brother James, and ignored him. They were, in modern parlance, dysfunctional.

I learned all these things when I was in Cornwall for the winter solstice.

The solstice was a marvelous thing. You cannot imagine what you have lost by turning your backs on the paganism you so shamelessly plundered for the trappings of your own religion. You still burn the yule log. But the Celts burned living things: virgins, children of particular purity and beauty, lambs, chickens, cattle, all imprisoned within monstrous wicker statues, so tall they dwarfed the trees, the houses, even the menhirs or votive monoliths that the Celts loved to erect in honor of Bridget, their great goddess.

This was, you understand, before the rampant Romanization of the area. I visited it less than a century later and found a health spa, a marble shopping mall and slave market, next to a temple to the God Vespasian. The Old Religion had become unfashionable. I see you're smiling, Your Holiness; the same thing seems to have happened to your own Old Religion.

But not to digress, the solstice was a wonderful time for hunting humans, and on the night of the great sacrifices I was mingling with them, sniffing the night air, redolent with the fragrance of excited blood. Bloodlust was blowing in the wind. Druids strode among the populace, and so did I, in the same white robes, a wolf in wolf's clothing.

The feet of the wicker men were already aflame. They held the lowlier life forms; the humans, lashed together inside the statue's chest and head, would have ample time to reflect on their mortality. Most seemed resigned, though a few screamed and tried to free themselves, much to the merriment of all. I moved through the throng. There was snow on the ground, but the heat from the wicker men was turning it to mush. Boars were roasting on spits, and tourists were being fleeced by cunning vendors into buying any number of sacred stones, elixirs, mistletoe love charms, and the like. Among those tourists was a small group of Judaeans; and one, apart from the others, was gazing intently at the holocaust, almost as though he were feeling the victims' suffering with them. This was the boy called Joshua barJoseph.

I could single out the peculiar scent of his blood, even in this chaos. It was a sweet blood. In today's all-too-scientific parlance, you might say that I detected a complete absence of adrenaline; his was a terrifying kind of inner calm, almost as though he were already one of us. It was this calm I found most beautiful about him. I wanted to make him kindred to me. I did not want to feed on him, and then abandon him to the worms and fishes.

I do not breathe, and so it was I was able to stand behind him, quite close to him, without his noticing. I wanted to hold off the moment of attack, to savor the fragrance of his blood, as a mortal lover longs to delay his climax till he can bear no longer.

At last I could no longer rein myself in. The sacrificial victims were on fire. Smoke billowed through the crowd. Blood, I thought to myself; blood, blood. I coiled, prepared to pounce.

"Don't," the boy said.

It suddenly occurred to me that he had known I was there all along; perhaps he had even been toying with me.

"I have a sense about these things," he said, and turned to me. Looked me over with his soulful, serious eyes. "Joshua," he said. "And you... I suppose you have many names. I'll call you John."

"All right."

"You're not a druid at all, are you?"

"What am I?"

"I'm not sure, really. I think you're sort of an angel."

"Hardly. I'm what you might call a fisher of men. You often talk to angels?"

"My whole family does. They're always at the house. An angel told my mother she was going to get pregnant with me, you know. Other people laughed when she said it was an angel; they said it was a Roman centurion named Pantera. Another angel told my father he should marry my mother anyway, but he still doesn't like me."

"You're here without them."

"Yes, I made a scene at my own bar mitzvah, got into a big argument with some learned men, so they sent me away with Uncle Joseph to cool off. Wasn't a scene, really. All I said was that the whole of the Torah could be boiled down to a single sentence — 'Do unto others what you would have them do unto you.' Rabbi Hillel says that all the time. I was just quoting him. They don't call *him* a dangerous radical."

"I'm assuming this Rabbi Hillel is a learned, venerable scholar rather than an insolent pipsqueak like yourself."

"I keep trying to go about my father's business, but I never seem to get it right."

"So they don't think you should be a rabbi."

"That's right. They want me to get into bronze, like Uncle Joseph." The Roman occupation had made Joseph of Arimathea a very rich man.

We did not talk for a while. The wicker men were fast being consumed, and the Celts were rolling around drunk and indulging in the usual debaucheries. The druids were droning an interminable paean to the sexual forces in nature, and I needed to slake my thirst. A suitable prospect ambled by at just that moment. I entranced her with a look, sipped a little from the nape of her neck even as she stared into empty space, seduced by my eyes, which seem to mortals like an yawning void. Joshua watched me, alarmed and fascinated. "You're a strange kind of angel," he said at last, as I let the woman go and she stumbled into the crowd. "You're beautiful, and that in itself is dangerous. The way your skin sucks in the moonlight. It's probably really cold, as cold as the moon."

"Yes." If only he knew how cold. I have stood in the country of the midnight sun. But what I am is a thing more desolate still. "Tell me about that sense of yours," I said. "Most people are completely clueless about what's lurking in their very midst."

"Well," Joshua said, "I just make myself go very still, and then it's like I'm outside myself."

"Samadhi," I said.

He started. "What language is that?" Almost as if he had heard it before.

"A language of India. It's something ascetics know how to do... leaving their own bodies, turning themselves into creatures of pure spirit, floating above the world. Only they have to meditate for years first."

"Oh!" he said. "You've been to India!"

"Occasionally," I said. I did not tell him how long ago.

"So have I," said the boy. And he told me all about it. I'm not sure how much there was to it. It was all so mythic: the massacre of the innocents, a flight by camel across a great desert, then forests, palaces, sages, teeming cities; and him so young through all of it, he could not possibly have remembered so much. I think he was told some of it, surmised some, imagined most of it. He had the gift that all great leaders have; he could take the wildest fancies and make them palpable.

Before long, I was telling him some of my own adventures in India. Encounters with hermits in the jungle. How I once sipped the blood of a maharani as she rode to a tryst with a secret lover on the back of an elephant. How I had sat at the feet of the Buddha and heard him tell me that the world is only a dream. He came alive as we talked. I was almost convinced he had been there.

"You see," he said, "we do have something in common."

"More that something." For he had seen the void, and he had not been afraid.

From that moment on, I wanted to make him my beloved disciple, to teach him the ways of love and death, to be his guide through the labyrinth of night. But he had other ideas. "One day," he said, "they'll hold this festival in my name. But I think I'll get rid of the human sacrificing." Even then, Your Holiness, he was suffering from what has come to be known as a messiah complex.

A bearded man, richly attired in the Hellenistic fashion, his head covering the only indication of his Judaean origins, called out to Joshua: "Let's go back now, Joshua. This place reeks of pork."

Joshua surprised me by putting his arms around me, and his lips to my lips, also in the Hellenistic fashion; I held him a little longer than was seemly, but only because I wanted to savor the pure still fragrance of his blood; perhaps, though, he mistook my meaning, for he then said, "I'd love to, but you see, I'm Jewish; we're not allowed to."

He stepped away from me, a slender, shadowy figure that soon blended into the crowd. A hint of that strange fragrance hung in the air, for the fires had died down and the celebrants mostly passed out from too much partying. I wandered among them for a while, feeding here and there. But their lust-drenched blood was too rich, too ripe.

He's only a minnow, I told myself. I've tossed him back in the river. But I couldn't shake the suspicion that it was I who had been let go. Who was fishing whom? It depressed me so much, I went to a cave in the Himalayas and slept for thirteen years.

***

When next I saw him, he was in his thirties. I, of course, had not aged.

"John," he said. I hate the name John. You will note that I have contrived to omit it from that gospel. But Joshua had changed. Getting dunked in the Jordan by his cousin the mad guru had caused him to undergo what you might call a religious experience. The messiah complex was in full swing, and he'd caught a bit of the infallibility bug, too, Your Holiness. Yet he was no fool. He knew me at once. Even though night was falling, and thousands of people had gathered to hear him preach.

I had braved the twilight to come and see him, cowled and caped like Mr. Death to protect myself from the dying sun. He had been preaching all day, mostly, it seems, a rehashed rendition of Rabbi Hillel's doctrines; but there was a healthy dose of Buddhism in it too, the whole non-violent "blessed are the meek" angle, half-remembered from the stories I had told him about India.

Like a guru in Benares, he was surrounded by disciples, fetching him wine, bread and fish, sitting at his feet so that not a pearl could escape.

They stared at me, with my pallid mien, my unblinking gaze, the fact that I do not breathe except occasionally, for a touch of verisimilitude. One of them, tall and bearded and reeking of fish, was about to shoo me away, but Joshua barJoseph silenced him with a barely perceptible flick of the wrist. I smelled the strange tranquility of his blood. I knew at once that this was the memory that had drawn me back from the sleep of the dead.

"Now I'm old," he said, laughing, "and you're the callow boy. You'll have to be my beloved disciple this time round." We both laughed, but the companions didn't. I made them uncomfortable. "Peter," he said to the tall one, "don't you know an angel when you see one?"

Warily, the disciples looked me over. One of them — I could tell from the family resemblance that this must be James, the favored younger brother — said, "Is he Jewish?" They were eating, you see. It wasn't as rude as you might think; dining with goyim violates one of their innumerable *mitzvot*.

"Don't be such a brat, James," Joshua said. "Haven't you been listening? I've changed the rules."

"You're such a fucking egotist," said James. "No one minds your being the messiah — everyone and his mother's the *kwisatz haderach* these days. But you start saying 'I've changed the rules' and people are going to think you're crazy." He wouldn't eat another bite, but the others were less fastidious.

"I'm not crazy," he said slowly. "There's got to be five thousand people camped out here tonight. They need something. I'm giving it to them. There are miracles. The blind can see. Today" — he looked straight into my eyes — "you've seen the dead walk." Peter poured me a krater of wine. "He never drinks wine," Joshua said, and made me laugh again, and baffled the others even further; grumbling, they turned away from us and began debating some arcane aspect of the Torah.

"We've got to talk," said Joshua to me. He got up suddenly from the rug they'd laid out for him. He gripped my hand. The coldness of my flesh didn't make flinch. I didn't feel his blood quicken. Only the preternatural calm. He led me a little further uphill. It was sheep country here, crags protruding out of sparse vegetation; the moon was rising now, and you could see all the followers, bundled up, dotting the slopes and on down into the valley; the sheep analogy felt particularly poignant. "I've been... well... waiting for you to come back," he said.

"What for?" I said.

"You're still the same. The childlike eyes. You don't need to breathe the air. You are an angel. I know I wasn't wrong when I was a boy, in Cornwall, at that awful sacrifice."

"Maybe a dark angel."

"You have to help me, John. I'm the captain of the ship, but I don't know which way to go, and I don't recognize any of the stars."

"Rabbinical teachings are hardly my thing. You haven't tried asking your father?"

"Which one?"

"Touché," I said. Inside the head of this brilliant, radical rabbi there was still the angry little boy, uncertain of his parentage, whose mother saw angels where others saw centurions.

"I've been suckered into this whole messiah scheme," he said, "but I'm all wrong for the role. I don't understand politics. I've never led an army. I don't even believe in an independent Jewish state. Have you heard of this guy Herod Agrippa? Now he'd make a fine messiah. He's had military training... and he went to school with everyone who's anyone in Rome, so he knows the enemy... speaks Greek like a native... plus he's got royal blood. The messiah's supposed to have royal blood."

"Genealogies can always be faked."

"Yes, but —"

"So why don't you just endorse him?"

"Yes, but... well, I know it's hopeless. The Romans are the greatest nation on earth... well, the only nation on earth. No messiah has ever succeeded before... it's essentially a losing proposition. Unless.."

He had no intention of asking my advice at all. He was bouncing ideas off me. Well; we cast no reflection, you see. That's because we are your reflection. We hold up the mirror to your dark souls. Chew on that one, Your Holiness. I stood beside him, on the hilltop, overlooking the sea of sheep, showing him his true self in my vacant eyes.

"Unless," he went on, "the redemption of Israel is really a metaphor for something much bigger, something cosmic. Unless the kingdom is not even of this world. Do you follow me? Like the world you come from, the world of shadows. That's it, you see. If I build my church on reality, then I'm building it in the sand, and Rome is the infinite sea."

"What are you saying?"

"Nothing really. Except ."

"Except?"

"Can't you stay, this time? I know I can't turn back the clock to that time in Cornwall, and of course I'm just as Jewish as I was then, so I don't do abominations, but... you're the only one who understands. There's more to life than... you know, life."

Had I been human my heart would have raced, my hormones would have started to hum, because Joshua was on the verge of admitting that he loved me, even though he couldn't quite bring himself to suck my dick. He still didn't quite get it, Reverend Fathers. I was going to have to use the direct approach. You never have much time, with humans. You blink and they're dead.

"I'll stay, but you're going to have to give me something," I said.

He sighed.

"No, no, you fool," I said. "I only want a little blood."

"Wouldn't be kosher," he said. "But I guess you wouldn't care about that. Well... why not? The whole world's going to be drinking my blood soon enough."

He pulled back his right sleeve and offered me his wrist. I knelt down, worried a little scab with a fingernail, then sipped it, one drop at a time. It was something to savor. That otherworldly calm seeped into me. A memory of my mortality surfaced for a moment. My mother's milk. I had not thought of mortality in a thousand years. For a moment I almost thought my heart was beating. As I drank, he stared out over the sleeping congregation. His eyes shone in the moonlight. Some humans become aroused when I feed on them, and cry out as in orgasm; he only made himself go far away.

Finally, faintly, I heard him say, half to himself, "They crucify you through the wrist; did you know that? A lot of people think it's through the palms, but that would just rip right through."

And that, Your Holiness, Your Eminences, Reverend Fathers of the Church, was the extent of the Beloved Disciples's carnal knowledge of the Son of Man.

***

It took some time for Joshua's followers to get used to the idea that I was there to stay. Judaea was a pretty tense place, a messiah under every rock, political activists railing in every street corner, and the Romans sitting around crucifying people almost at random. I wasn't a spy, and I wasn't one of the peasants, and I was surely no theologian. But it was necessary, for various numerological and historical reasons, to have twelve apostles, and Joshua always got his own way.

I was there for it all: the miracles, such as they were, though you people have become a lot slicker at these things; the triumphal entry into Jerusalem, carefully stage managed so as to function as an elegant midrash on selected passages of the Tanakh; I was there for the passover shabbat, wherein Joshua made no mention of his body and blood, such pagan concepts being quite distasteful to him; and I was there for the awful climax and its bathetic denouement.

After they dragged him away, the apostles called an emergency meeting at Joseph of Arimathea's house. Joshua's parents were conspicuously absent, as usual; but there was another Miriam, an ex-prostitute, who was Joshua's first and most devoted groupie and could not be kept away. Joseph — a liberal — didn't mind having harlots in the house, though he did draw the line at publicans.

"It can't end this way," James said. It was as if, having been the family's darling all his life, he couldn't stand the thought of being permanently one-upped by Joshua's martyrdom.

"So what do you suggest?" said Peter. "We can't very

well storm the dungeons; we'll all end up getting strung up." He stared shiftily about; on his way to the meeting he had denied knowing Joshua three times. The foetor of his fear permeated the chamber. They were all stinking drunk, except for me.

I sat in the shadows, thinking of other things. Between mortals and immortals, love always ends in an unending longing. I wished we could have gone to India together. Or even to the world on the other side of the ocean, which I had heard about from a sage whose skin was the color of wine. I relived our first meeting again and again. Their lives rush by so fast, I thought. Larva to chrysalis to butterfly to putrefaction.

It was Joseph of Arimathea who said, "But it's so simple. Let John bring him back from the dead."

They all looked at me, looked away, drank deeply; I said, "It's a gift that can't be taken back. And he has never asked me to make him immortal."

"We need him," Peter said. "You can see that. We're like a chicken with its head cut off. If he comes back, everyone will see that the God of Abraham, Isaac and Jacob is more powerful than idols of stone and brass."

"When's the execution?" I said.

"Friday," said Joseph of Arimathea, who, being a man of influence, had a tendency to know these things. "The Romans'll give him a fair trial, but there's really no way they can let off someone who's being openly called King of the Jews."

"But his kingdom's not of this world!" said Thomas, who never believed anything he was told.

"The Romans," I said, "are completely literal-minded. That's why they own everything."

"It's politics as usual," said Joseph, "and Pilate has to protect his own ass back home. Can't blame him, really." But he was on the verge of tears. I've often wondered whether it was not he, rather than the legendary Pantera, who stuck it to the rabbi's fiancée; for he loved Joshua far more than the other Joseph ever did.

It was Joseph who convinced me, not the squabbling, self-righteous rabble who called themselves his apostles. No, I take that back, Your Holiness. It was I myself who convinced me. Perhaps it was selfishness. But you, Reverend Fathers, have never faced eternity. You just wouldn't understand.

Oh, but you preach eternity from your pulpits. Eternal bliss, eternal damnation. Fleecy clouds and fiery brimstone. You don't know what the fuck you're talking about. After the first few hundred years, every color becomes gray. Every song is a single note. Every mortal is another scurrying piece of vermin, and all that is left is the ache that can never be slaked, and the loss than festers forever. You are fools to say forever so lightly. A long long time, my friends, is not forever.

"I'll do it," I said softly. "But somehow, we have to get him to drink my blood."

"Is that kosher?" said James. No one so much as looked at him for the rest of the evening.

***

Humans can never get used to crucifixions, but for me an almost clinical detachment was possible. In their own way, the Romans bent over backward to accomodate the practices of their wayward subjects. Usually it takes days for the victim to die, but the Judaeans had a religious taboo against leaving corpses hanging after sunset (or was it only on Saturdays?) so they had compromised by using novel techniques for speeding up death: the flogging and the nails were, grotesquely enough, designed to shorten the agony. That was Roman knowhow for you.

The "display" crosses you see in religious paintings were not a common feature of these operations. Actually, criminals were strung up only slightly above eye level; you could look right into their faces, even spit in their eye; and people did. Public executions bring out the worst in mortals. You all know that Joshua barJoseph was crucified between two thieves, but actually the whole hillside was crammed with crosses; under Roman law, virtually everything was a capital offense.

It was afternoon, and so I almost didn't make it there. But about three or four o'clock it became preternaturally dark; a nightingale began to sing outside the room at Joseph of Arimathea's mansion where I was lying. I came to suddenly, bewildered because my sleep seemed so short. There was no one in the house. I made my way to the crucifixion hill.

In the tribal north, there had been at least a sense of elation and celebration about the wicker men. Here there was nothing of the kind. Here only beggars and lepers lurked about, and a few idle curious; the Roman soldiers, jaded, went about their business, nailing them down and stringing them up. Unrecycled crossbeams lay on the dirt; the smell of stale blood clung to them, mingled with the scent of fresh-gushing blood which permeated the hot, dry air.

I made my way through the forest of the dying, and at length spied Miriam — the whore, not the mother — standing almost at the summit of the hill, where three recent crosses formed a sort of triptych of suffering. The smell of Joshua's blood was faint, but it still held that eerie calm. I went up to Miriam, told her we had to go through with the plan.

She said, "Wait. His mother's here."

Then it was I saw another woman, one who had remained conspicuously absent throughout Joshua's ministry. She looked up at her son now, and I do not think she wept.

And I too looked, and did not weep, but for another reason; I cannot.

It was going to have to be done soon. And still I was unsure, because, Reverend Sirs, it takes more than an invitation for a man to enter my eternal kingdom — not a sprinkle of water over a baby — not a few murmured phrases. To borrow a cliché of your modern pop psychology, Joshua had to want to change. I was almost sure I had seen that longing in him, at our very first meeting... but might it have been something else?

I watched for a sign. His agony beggared description, but then all agony does, in the end, doesn't it? They had crowned him with thorns. Blood caked his forehead. There were flies. Vultures, too. The causa poenae, tacked to the cross, read "Rex Iudaeorum." He gazed back at me, his eyes already beginning to dull. In his mother's eyes I saw... disappointment, perhaps. She looked at Miriam the prostitute and for a moment I thought she was going to claw her eyes out. Then she saw me.

I do not look Jewish. I am clean-shaven as I was in life, which the Judaeans considered a sign of Hellenistic effeminacy. I have a certain clarity of complexion, a glow; all vampires do. That is why the ugliest of mortals becomes beautiful once he has heeded the call of night. I could tell that she did not admire my otherworldly looks; rather, she instantly assumed the worst — that I must be the masculine counterpart of Miriam the whore. She looked at me, and her dying son, and I could just imagine her thinking maybe I was the reason her Joshua could never settle down and have kids.

Then Joshua gasped, "Mother, he's your son now. John, kiss your new mother."

She gaped at the outrageous insinuation. I wanted to tell her it wasn't what she thought it was, but I daresay it would have made even less sense to her. Just like human beings, to stoop to a bit of domestic bickering at a moment like this.

I was surprised that he could still speak. The process of crucifixion is actually one of asphyxiation, of the body slowly sagging and collapsing the lungs. The power of speech soon goes.

"I'm thirsty," he said.

A small detail was marching uphill, pausing in front of each cross to smash the criminal's legs. Without the anchor of nailed-down bone, the body caves in on itself and squeezes the life right out of itself. Another practical Roman solution to the Jewish taboo about corpses being strung up past nightfall. No time to lose. I found a sentry, nodding off against a boulder. I shook him. "Let me give him something to drink," I said. I dropped a silver denarius in his helmet. He grunted, let me borrow his javelin for a moment; I pierced my left wrist with a fingernail and squeezed out enough blood to wet a sponge, held it up to his lips; blood trickled onto his tongue, which was already beginning to protrude.

When he tasted blood, something about him changed. Was it the touch of the first breath of eternity? Softly, he said, "It's done." But what was done? Surely not his crazed masterplan for establishing the perfect Jewish society, god's kingdom on earth? Or was it an acceptance of his vampiric destiny? Only the night would tell.

He closed his eyes. The darkness gathered. But I left swiftly, for these unnatural darknesses have a way of lifting, and I did not want to be stranded in sunlight even on the short distance from the execution site to the tomb that Joseph of Arimathea had prepared — a luxurious tomb, for he had intended it for himself.

***

Once inside the tomb, I waited awhile; in time, my circadian rhythms, interrupted by the unnatural darkness of the afternoon, forced me back into slumber. I slept more than twenty-four hours; when I go out by day, even in darkness, my body needs a little longer to repair itself.

When I awoke, he was hunched on the lid of the stone sarcophagus, tearing the bloody linen off himself. "I'll get that," I said. I ripped away more pieces of his shroud. His wrists were regenerating nicely, but there was a deep puncture in each one, wide enough to stick a finger through.

"What did you do to me?" he said. "What have you made me?"

I said, "They begged me, your apostles. And I've seen it in your face. You want this. You've looked eternity in the eye before, Joshua, and it didn't scare you."

He didn't answer. He was staring at his hands. They were white as the limestone sepulcher itself. Yes, I knew he was no longer mortal. There was no source of light in the tomb, and yet he saw with the eyes of night; and for those who see as we see he himself was light, cold, phosphorescent, pale.

"This isn't what I had in mind, John," he said.

"Don't call me John anymore," I said, and instead cried out my own true name in the language of night, which only the dead can speak. In that instant he knew his true name, too, which cannot be spoken here.

I sensed his confusion, sensed also the incipient pangs of the great hunger; and slitting my wrist once more with my fingernail I gave him sustenance, becoming mother to him as well as midwife. He did not complain that the blood violated his dietary taboos; he knew already that to cross into our world is also to abandon the very concept of god. "I was hoping to be resurrected," he said. "But at the last minute I despaired; I tried to pray but all I could hear were the words of the psalmist about having been forsaken by god; that's true, isn't it? Instead of god, you came."

"And once you called me an angel."

"You still are. Angelos: messenger. But who sent you? That's what I can't figure out. Is this how we're going to defeat the Romans... by turning Judaea into a kingdom of the undead?"

"Just the sort of harebrained grand scheme you'd come up with. Get the long view, Joshua. You already have defeated the Romans. Do you know how old I am? I was old when the citadel of the Hittites was plundered and razed. Where are the Hittites now? A few scratches of cuneiform in other people's history books. Where are the Trojans now? The Minoans, the people of Thera, the Carthaginians? I've already defeated them, because I'm still here, remembering the taste of their blood, and they are dust. If you ask me a question, and I pause till the fall of Rome before I answer you, it is only a blink. The mortals cannot see the grand spectacle of their own lives; they cannot be as passionate as we, nor as pitiless. Don't you feel the thrill of it?"

"If you say so," he said.

But perhaps he didn't. I recalled the odor of his blood. The tranquillity that had so intoxicated me... it had survived the transformation. Why had I been lecturing him about the sweep of history? He had felt all of that without even having experienced it, even as a mere mortal. It occurred to me that perhaps it was not my blood that had brought him back from the dead. Maybe he was some kind of natural vampire, self-creating, self-sufficient. I had never encountered anything like that, but if you think about it, there's got to have been at least one vampire to start the whole cycle off..

This was a disturbing line of thought. So I said, "Well, Joshua, if not for the sweep of history, then at least knowledge. We've spoken of India, but there are other lands too... Cathay... there are some of us who have found a whole new continent to the west... there are more worlds to conquer than your Roman Empire."

"And we shall conquer them, my friend," he said. He had freed himself from his winding-sheet now. He embraced me, and said, "We'll find new worlds and fresh philosophies." "You mean it?" I said.

"You know that I can't lie," he said. Such is the loneliness of eternity that I welcomed what he said without considering its ambiguity.

***

Your Holiness and others... I see that you are becoming

heartily troubled by my narration. But it gets worse.

You all know the story of the empty tomb. We met up with the rest of the apostles at Joseph's, and a couple of other times. They all thanked me — somewhat perfunctorily, to be sure — for bringing Joshua back from the dead. Miriam and Joseph (the rabbi, not the tin tradesman) and the rest of that mixed-up brood went through a transformation of their own. Having shat on their wayward eldest all his life, they resolved to put him on a pedestal; the fat, spoiled little brother led the campaign to make Joshua's proto-Marxist precepts into the biggest new sect of Judaism.

A book of those down-home little parables and precepts was circulated underground — much like Chairman Mao's little red book — it's the "lost" book that biblical scholars — which many of you, reverend fathers, are not — call "Q". I know, it was a cheap trick, using xeroxed pages of my personal copy of "Q" to cause this, ah, ecumenical support group to be convened, and, yes, I will present you all with the entire manuscript after I've had my say — but how else was I going to get your reverend asses all in one room and to believe in the authenticity of my tale?

In any case, you'll find that the scholars were quite correct: virtually all of "Q" is quoted at length in the four canonical gospels. You won't find anything new in it. The scoop, Reverend Fathers (oh, I do apologize, Sister, I didn't notice you amongst all the male chauvinists) is in what I'm telling you. I know you're all spazzing already, but please hold your sphincters for just five more minutes.

Something really, really weird happened next: Christianity.

Joshua and I were gone for, oh, twenty years or so. It was wild and glorious... the vampiric equivalent of a honeymoon. Yes, we went to India. We fed on pilgrims as they stripped to bathe in the Ganges. I did most of the hunting. Joshua saw the necessity of it, but was still queasy; he was still adjusting. We rode through jungles, were received by maharajahs, drank the blood of virgins, were venerated as gods in some cities, reviled as demons in others. Yes, we did set sail to what you now call America, so you Mormon elders may consider Mr. Joseph Smith's febrile imaginings, at least in part, vindicated. Joshua did not preach. Instead, he listened. He was like an empty vessel into which men poured what was best and worst in themselves. And I admired him for that, because in transcending mortality he had not lost compassion, which is usually the first thing to go. He grew in compassion, in fact. I had not known that was possible.

In time, we came back to the Levant, and it was in Ephesos, a town most famed for its huge gold statue of the Great Mother, that we first encountered Jesus Christ.

It was, in fact, in front of the famous statue (in Ephesos they call the mother-goddess Diana) that we first heard the name being bandied about. It was night and they were sacrificing — strange how that motif crops up again — and we were hunting. The place was a spectacle, all towering columns and clouds of incense and everything gold and ivory and the statue itself tall as a ten-story building. No babies being sacrificed here, though; we were well inside the civilizing boundaries of Rome. In the shadow of a fluted column, voices were whispering about Nazareth.

Joshua pricked up his ears. "They haven't forgotten

me," he said, and smiled.

Good news. Baptism. The Kingdom of Heaven... the redemption of mankind... the resurrection... it sounded hauntingly familiar. There was a meeting later that night, we overheard. In a back room of a local synagogue.

The crowd was an odd one. I had never seen so many goyim in a synagogue, and they didn't cover their heads. There were women, too, sitting right alongside the men. A lot of riff-raff — slaves, the homeless, prostitutes — Joshua liked that. He had always gone down well with the proles, with that stuff about the first shall be last and blessed are the poor and camels going through needles' eyes and all that. One or two rich people, too. We blended right in; no one so much as stared at us.

The thing was as brilliantly stage-managed as a contemporary revival meeting. There were warm-up speakers, who gave testimonials about the efficacy of using the ineffable name of Jesus as a kind of mantra; Joshua chuckled a little at this, but as the meeting went on he became more and more solemn.

The keynote speaker was a man named Paul. Bit of a flamer, a Liberace type... a real-live Roman citizen, as he never tired of pointing out. The tale he told was an amazing one, a sort of throw-it-in-the-blender mélange of every popular cult in the Roman Empire. Jesus was the son of God (like Hercules) and that bitter yenta of a mother was transformed into an eternal virgin, much like the Great Mother herself who was worshipped at the Temple of Diana down the street. Like Adonis, Jesus had died at the beginning of the spring fertility rites and been resurrected on the third day. Like Odin, he had been strung up on a great tree. Adam's dismissal from Eden was no longer what everyone had always thought it was, a profound, poetic metaphor for the human condition, but a temporary inconvenience to which Jesus would soon put an end, especially since he was coming back any moment now to snatch up the faithful and punish the sinful. The whole of the Tanakh was just Part One. All this was gospel truth because Paul, formerly Saul, had once persecuted Christians... and Jesus had come to him in a vision and set him straight.

Mixed in with all this fantasmagorical mythology were many of the homely parables and radical sociological viewpoints that Joshua had actually preached. It was very inspirational, very feverish, very much like a rock concert. Women were weeping and fainting and having orgasms; men were having attacks of glossolalia; cripples were tottering around and blind men claiming they could see while banging their heads on pillars.

As Paul's rhetoric climaxed with an appeal not to resist persecution — to welcome martyrdom as it would mean instant acceptance into the bosom of Jesus. Crucifixion, flaying, burning, being devoured by lions, all were but painful preludes to paradise.

It got better. Next came a magic ritual — a pagan parody of that sad last passover meal we had all had together, the night they came to take him away. They broke bread, and after a few incantations pronounced that it was Joshua's body; a flagon of wine became his blood. Such irony! It made me relive once more the moment I had first savored that blood, so innocent of inner turmoil. Eating the sacred body of the god-king was a custom as old as the Stone Age, but Paul had managed to trivialize even that most ancient and potent of metaphors. Fucking

Roman citizen indeed. He certainly had their literal-mindedness.

"I can't take much more of this," I said, and we fought our way through the throng as someone bore down on us with a collection plate.

But suddenly Joshua stopped me. "We have to talk to him," he said. "This is insanity. We have to stop it."

"They're only humans," I said. "This will all blow over."

"But it's my name they're using," he said. "It's my name they're dying for."

"Your human name," I said scornfully.

"Yes," he said.

You know, we don't change all that much when we cross over to the darkness. Alive, Joshua had attracted me because he grasped eternity so completely; now that he was dead, I saw that his comprehension of mortality far surpassed my own. He had not been comfortable in their world, and now he had still not found his home.

I had to humor him. It was not in my power to douse this spark of difference in him; it was what I loved most about him.

Easy enough for us to blend into the shadows, to drift along the dusty columns until we found a back room, where a young man stood flexing in front of a polished shield. We stood behind this youth, too absorbed in his narcissistic endeavors to look over his shoulder — we cast no reflection in the shield, of course — and waited.

Presently we could hear a hymn being sung, fervently and discordantly, by the crowd outside, and Paul came storming into the room. We stepped back into gloom. Paul and the young man kissed passionately. "A strong showing tonight, Timothy," Paul said. "I think we've collected enough to hit the big time."

"You think we'll actually get to play Rome?" said the boy. The adoring gaze he had for the old man turned sour when Paul looked away, and I recognized the sullen mien of the street hustler. Definitely rough trade.

"Rome? Honey, we're going to own Rome!" said Paul.

Many theologians and sociologists have argued that St. Paul was a closet homosexual who imposed his misogyny on the misguided Christian masses; but let me tell you, Your Holiness — in spite of your recent encyclical — that civilized people in the first century were far too sophisticated to be hung up on such minutiae as sexual preference. Later. of course, when St. Augustine decided that sex was dirty..

We interrupted before the scene could become x-rated, materializing out of the shadows. "Paul!" Joshua said. "Do you know who I am?"

"No," he said, mystified. Timothy shrugged and went back to flexing.

Joshua held up his pierced wrists. You could see the smoky flicker of the wall torch through the holes.

"You're not," said Paul.

"I am," said Joshua barJoseph.

I stayed out of it. It was Joshua's fight. I lurked in the background. Outside, the hymn singing crescendoed to a cacophonous climax.

"Why are you doing this to me?" Joshua said softly.

"James and the others... they said you'd risen from the dead, said they'd seen it with my own eyes... thought it was the greatest new gimmick... but it's true, then. Dear me, who would have thought it?"

Joshua said, "I'm not Dionysus. God didn't come down from heaven to screw my mother. I'm not Osiris, come back from the dead to guide mortals beyond the grave. I'm not the Corn God, ripped in pieces to fertilize the earth and then reborn as king. I'm just a rabbi who hung out with hookers. I wanted my friends to become better Jews, to understand what the Torah's really trying to say instead of hiding behind their petty regulations."

"What good are the Jews? They crucified you."

"No, they didn't. The Romans did."

"They made them do it."

"You don't make the Romans do things. I broke a Roman law. I would not render unto Caesar something which belonged to Caesar — sovreignty. I wasn't talking about political sovreignty, but you know how literal-minded the Romans are. Why would the Jews have had me killed? For claiming to be the messiah? There's a new messiah every week, and they don't get crucified."

I had to speak up. "He has to blame it on the Jews," I said. "He's preaching to the Romans. Roman complicity in your death would be a real no-no. What do the goyim know about the workings of the Sanhedrin? As far as they're concerned, a bunch of swarthy, middle-eastern religious fanatics is capable of any depravity... even Deicide. Have to bend the truth a bit here and there, don't you, Paul?"

"The truth! And what, as Pontius Pilate said to you, Jesus, on the morning of your crucifixion, is truth?"

"He didn't say that," said Joshua. "He didn't even talk to me. He had a dozen other death warrants to sign that morning, and he didn't want to miss lunch."

Paul was fuming. "You're just like your brother

James," he said. "I've built this majestic structure of powerful, rich images that trigger the imagination, that make men's spirits soar. I'm giving hope to the downtrodden and picking up a few denarii along the way. So what if it's a house of cards? So what if it didn't really happen that way? I've found the core of mythic truth in your tawdry little bio, and I'm going to make you the biggest thing since the invention of the wheel, you ungrateful insect. This new religion is going to take over the world. It's got everything. Tragedy and pathos, terror of judgment, the catharsis of forgiveness. It's the grandest religion yet invented."

"But I don't want a new religion," said Joshua barJoseph. "I'm Jewish."

***

After a while, Paul seemed to calm down a little. "I'll need to regroup a little," he said. "Maybe I can still salvage some of this."

While he guzzled wine, we told him some of our own adventures. We got drunk together... he and Timothy on a couple of kegs of Samian wine, Joshua and I from a pint of Timothy's blood which he obligingly let me draw... after I told him I could do it painlessly.

Paul became so drunk he even stopped speaking Greek. In tearful Aramaic, he told us searing childhood tales about his father whipping him for sucking off the stablehands. No wonder he preferred being Roman to being Jewish! No wonder he wanted to bring the gospel to the goyim!

That was what it all boiled down to after all. He wanted to be accepted, to be loved for what he was, this poor little sissy boy who had the misfortune to be born into the one culture where they stoned sissies. One could almost sympathize. After a while, indeed, one did. "Forgive me," Paul was weeping into his goblet.

"I forgive you," said Joshua.

"Thank you... thank you, abba," said Paul. I realized then that he wanted his real father to forgive him... that the source of the angst that drove him was his fear of having disappointed his earthly father... he had created in his mind a surrogate father, all-merciful, all-forgiving, to succour his own self-loathing. And Joshua understood all this... truly understood it... and felt compassion for this lonely little man... a compassion as deep as any love he felt for me.

I envied the world, because not even death had sundered Joshua from his love for it.

Paul invited us back to his home. "I want to hear more stories," he said. "I want to learn everything you can teach me. After all, you are my redeemer. You ought to have a hand in the religion, especially since it's all about you."

Very softly, Joshua said to me, "He just doesn't hear me."

But we went home with him anyway, and as dawn approached we bedded down for the day in a cosy wine-cellar.

Night fell and I rose from my dreamless sleep. I found my beloved disciple lying on the dirt floor, unmoving, in a pool of still, cold blood, with a stake through his heart.

Paul and Timothy had gone on to Rome.

And I too fled, for the inchoate feelings that raged through me were too much like my memories of pain.

***

He must have known. He had a sense about such things. He must have realized that Paul could not long abide the shattering of his great glass cathedral with the hammer of blunt reality.

He loved the world. He loved beautiful things, cities, trees, animals, and even more so, people. It must have pained him more than I can imagine, to choose to leave the world behind. Why, then? Was it that he could not face the prospect of his name being taken in vain by thousands, thousands who would become millions, billions? Did he sense that his homespun stories about shepherds and widow's mites and mustard seeds would become the official religion of the Roman empire, that that religion would plunge the western world into a Dark Age for a thousand years, that it would spawn senseless massacres, enslavements of entire peoples, wanton destructions of countless noble, ancient, beautiful cultures?

I don't know.

Your Holiness, Reverend Fathers, Your Eminence, and... yes, Reverend Sister... this is what I know.

He was good. I have never known anyone before or since who has truly deserved that adjective. He was brilliant. He loved, deeply and with complete commitment. He possessed an absolute empathy even for the dispossessed. These qualities were in his very blood.

The blood of mortals is spiced with the hormones of desire and fear, but his was not. It was to other blood as a sparkling mountain stream is to the murky effluvium of a city faucet. It was the Platonic absolute of blood. It was pure. It was the holy grail of bloods, the true taste of which all other tastes are but an echo.

We are much alike, you who have hocus-pocused a

million gallons of cheap wine and call it redemption, and I who have savored your savior's actual blood. We cannot believe he is gone forever. Love such as ours, we desperately think, can not stay unrequited for ever. The Absolute is by its very nature Eternal.

We live — you for a few heartbeats, I for all time — in the hope (the fear, too) that he will come again. He must come again.

The river of time is long. I know. Trust me. One day he will. Suddenly. Without warning.

Like a vampire in the night.

S.P. Somtow

Here's a story, *The Voice of the Hummingbird,* that exists in two versions — San Francisco and L.A. No doubt completists will want both, but the only reason both exist is that the original anthology it was commissioned for took place in San Francisco, but I longed to also have it in my book of L.A. Fairy Tales. So I changed the local color, but not the essence of the tale.

The Voice of the Hummingbird

Huitzilopotchtli.

It was the will of the god named Hummingbird that our people should cease to be a wandering people, a desert people, an impoverished and simpleminded people … that we should journey down into the rich green valley at the world's heart and claim its lakes and forests for our own, and rule over all the nations of the earth. We were a people with a grand and glorious destiny; we had been called to a special covenant with our god; and if there were things that our god commanded us to do which, to those who did not share our special relationsip with him, appeared brutal, cruel, uncompassionate, it was only that we alone could see the higher purpose; that we alone were charged with the guardianship of the knowledge of the secret workings of the universe.

It was the will of the god named Hummingbird that I should be the one to hear his voice and bear his message to my people; that I should lead them from the wasteland into the place where they would build the greatest of all cities, set in the center of the world as a turquoise in a circlet of gold. And it came to pass that I spoke, and the people obeyed, and we sealed our covenant with our own blood and the blood of the countless conquered. This was as it should be. Our people had been chosen.

Later I would come to understand that there were others, people no less proud than our people, no less confident of their moral rectitude, no less certain that the salvation of the entire universe lay in the application of secret knowledge that only their tribe possessed; there was even, across the great ocean to the east, a people whose god had called them to cross a great desert and seal a covenant and conquer and build a great temple. We Mexica were not, after all, unique; we were merely a repeating pattern in the wheel of history; and our history was not even the only wheel that was in motion at the time.

We didn't even *have* wheels then, anyway. After a dozen centuries I suppose one might be forgiven a few anachronistic metaphors. I learned about wheels a long time after the covenant was broken, in San Francisco.

I learned about the *other* chosen people from Julia Epstein.

***

There is a gap of about five hundred years in my existence. One moment, the fire was raging in the streets of Tenochtitlán, and I was watching the stars fall from the sky, and cursing the silver-clad man-beasts called Spaniards who had blundered into shattering the equilibrium of the universe. Then, in a blink's breadth, it seemed, I was lying in a glass case, an exhibit in the San Francisco Museum, being pointed at by a petulant youth.

That I might have slept for an time — a century or two even — would not have been surprising. I had done that before, though only of my own volition. I had slept all the way through the conquest of the people of Tlatztelhuatec; I knew it would be dull; they were little better than cattle. But there were no signs that I had been in suspended animation … no cognitive disjunction … no sensation of falling, falling, falling into the bottomless abyss.

The room was gloomy; it had been designed to simulated the rocky chamber in which I had been found. There was no daylight. Torches flickered, yet they did not burn; the fire in them was cold and artificial.

Even lying under the glass, unable as yet to move more than the twitch of an eyelash, fighting the inertia of the dreamless sleep, I was aware that the world had become far stranger than I could have imagined. The youth who stared down at me was a mongrel; he had the flat nose and dark skin of the Mexica, but there was also something about him that resembled the man-beasts from across the sea. He had no hair save for a crest that stood unnaturally tall and was dyed the color of quetzal feathers. His robes were of animal hide, but black and polished to an almost reflective smoothness. He was not utterly inhuman — his ears were pierced at least — but from them hung, upside-down, a pair of those silver crucifixes that symbolize the man-beasts' god, whom they call Hesuskristos, who is in reality Xipe Totec, the flayed god, as Hummingbird once revealed to me in a dream.

He called out to a companion; this one's tufted hair was the color of fresh blood, and he wore a silver thorn through his left cheek. The language, at least, I knew, though the accent was strange and there were unfamiliar words; I had taken the trouble to learn the language of the man-beasts. There are two dialects; one, spoken by the black robes, is called Español; the other is the language of their enemies, known as English. It was the second of these I heard, in a boyish voice muffled by glass.

"Dude! It says he's been dead for five hundred years."

"Pulled him out of the foundation of a fifty-story office building after that big Mexico City quake ... yeah, perfectly preserved and shit. A hollow in the rock, a natural vacuum ..."

"Yeah, I saw it on 20/20."

"Did you see that? He *moved*, dude!"

"Yeah. Right."

Five hundred years ... but that was impossible! Hummingbird himself had told me that in a few short years the world would end in an apocalypse of blood and fire. How could five hundred years have gone by? Unless, of course, the world had already ended.

That would explain the surpassing alienness of my surroundings. Even the air smelled strange. Even the blood of the two boys, which sang to me as it pumped through their arteries, exuded an unaccustomed odor, as though infused with the pulped essences of the hemp and coca plants.

The one with the crimson hair said, "No, dude, I ain't joking. Look at him, man, I swear his eyelids are like, flickering."

"You shouldn't have dropped acid at the Cure concert last night. You're still blazing, dude."

I turned my head to get a better view.

"Jesus Christ!" they screamed.

So the world had ended after all. The time of Huitzilopotchtli was over. There had been a fiery apocalypse — my memories had not deceived me — and we were now well into the World of the Fifth Sun, foretold to me by the god, and a new god was in power, the hanged god whose name those boys evoked, Hesuskristos.

I was full of despair. I did not belong here. Why had I been suffered to remain alive? Surely I should have been destroyed, along with the city of Tenochtitlán, along with the great pyramids and temples and palaces of my people. Could the gods not have been more thorough? But then that was just like them; come up with the grand concepts, leave their execution to imperfect mortals … I raged. My heart gave a little flutter, trying to bestir itself from its age-old immobility. My fury fueled me. I could feel my blood begin, sluggishly, to liquefy, to funnel upward through my veins like the magma through the twisty tunnels of Popocatapetl.

Soon I would erupt.

I lashed out. I heard shattering glass. The smells of the strange new world burst upon my senses. Then came the hunger, swooping down on me as an owl on a mouse in the dead of night. No longer muffled, the rushing of young blood roared in my ears. The odor was sour and pungent. I seized the first creature by the arm, the one with the quetzal-feathered hair; the second, screaming, ran; I transfixed the prey with my eyes and filled him with the certainty of his own death; then, drawing him down to me, I fed.

I do not know how long we lay together, locked in that predatory embrace. His blood was youthful; it spurted; it permeated my pores; I drank it and I breathed it into my lungs; for a fleeting moment it brought back to mind those nights of furtive, unfulfilled encounters in the chill desert night; the burning curve of a young girl's thigh, the aroma of her liquidescing pubes. Those were the times before the god called me, when I was mortal and barely man.

At length I realized that I had completely drained him. I let go and he thudded on the polished floor like a terracotta doll. It was then that I became aware of a noisome clanging sound, a whirling, flashing red light, and men in strange blue clothing who brandished muskets of a sleekly futuristic design as they surrounded the plinth on which I lay. The boy who had fled stood beneath an archway, babbling and shivering and pointing at me and at his friend's desiccated corpse.

Perhaps, I decided, it would be more prudent to play dead for a little while longer.

***

I awakened in another chamber. It was lined with leatherbound codices of the kind the black robes favored. The room was lit by candlelight, and I sitting on a wooden chair. I tried to move, but I had been bound with ropes — metal ropes, artfully strung, and padlocked, the way the Spaniards keep their gold. Across an immense desk, cluttered with the artifacts of my people, jeweled skulls and jade statuettes and blood-cups, sat a woman.

She was of man-beast extraction, but not unattractive. I had never seen a woman of their kind before; they had brought none with them from their country, which was perhaps why they had become so ferocious. She was sharp-nosed, and had long brown hair. When she spoke to me, it was, to my amazement, in Náhuatl, the language of the Mexica people.

"I'm Julia Epstein," she said. "I'm the curator of our Latin American collection. Would you care for a little blood?"

"I'm quite full, thank you," I said.

"In that case, you might want to start telling me what the hell is going on. It's not every day that a museum exhibit gets up and starts attacking the public. Who are you?"

"It's not proper for me to give my name to you … a man-beast."

She laughed. "Man-beast! I know … you Aztecs used to think that the Spaniards and their horses were some kind of hybrid monster… but times have changed. We drive automobiles now. I think it's safe for you to tell me your name. I'm not going to acquire any mystical power over you. Besides, you're just going to have to trust me; I'm the one who talked the cops into believing that that punk's story was just some kind of acid-trip fantasy; they have him under wraps now, the poor child, deciding whether to get him on murder one."

"Very well," I said, "I am Nezahualcóyotl."

"And I'm Santa Claus," said Julia Epstein, frowning. "So you say you're *the* Nezahualcóyotl, who claimed descent from the great gods of Teotihuacán, the greatest poet, musician and prophet of the Aztecs, their first great ruler, a man who was an ancient memory when Moctezuma was king and the Conquistadores swept over Mexico?"

"You are well informed," I said.

"Well, why not? It's no harder to believe *that* than to believe that an exceptionally well-preserved mummy, just dug up from the newly discovered catacombs in Mexico City, and my museum's prize exhibit, would get up, walk around, attack a few punks, and drink their blood ... and to think that I dug you up with my own hands."

"So it is to you that owe my continued ... existence."

"If you want to call it living."

"What else *would* you call it?"

"You're a vampire."

"I'm unfamiliar with that word."

"Oh, don't give me that bullshit, Nezzy. I know everything about you guys. I can't get anyone to believe me, but I've gathered a shitload of information. Yeah, I'm an archaeologist, sure, but vampires are kind of a hobby with me, know what I mean? And this city's *crawling* with them. I know. I've got *tons* of evidence ... clippings, photographs, police files ... tried to sell this shit to the *Inquirer*, and you know what? They rejected it. Said it wasn't, ah, convincing. *Convincing!* From the people who did the *Alien Endorses Clinton* story and the piece about the four-headed baby! Let me tell you what really happened. *They* found out about it. They're everywhere. Big cities mainly, but even the smallest town has one or two. They're running everything. Your worst nightmare about the Mafia, the CIA, the Illuminati, all rolled into one. They read my submission and they *squelched* it! Sounds pretty damn paranoid, doesn't it? Welcome to the quackpot world of academia."

"But what is a vampire?" I said. I was beginning to feel the hunger again; just a prickle in my veins. Normally the blood of a whole young male would have kept me going for days, but it had been so long ... I glanced down at myself ... saw my papery skin ... knew it would take a few more feedings to restore me to the semblance of life.

"A vampire?" said Julia. "Why, *you're* a vampire. You drink blood. You live for a long, long time. You are a child of the shadows, a creature of the night."

"True, but — are you saying that there are others?"

"Are you saying that there *aren't* others?"

"There *was* one other ..." It pained me to think of my young protégé ... the one who had betrayed King Moctezuma to the man-beasts, the one whom the black robes called *Hortator,* which signifies, in their language, the man who beats the drum to drive the galley-slaves who row in the Spaniards' men-o'-war ... because of the drum he stole from me, made from the flayed skin of the god Xipe Totec himself ... the one I thought would succeed me, but who instead had destroyed my whole world. "There was the god at first. He called me to his service. I had thought to hand on the power to another, but...."

"That's where you're wrong, my friend," said Julia. "There's a whole network of you people. You have your tentacles in everything ... you *run* this whole planet. You're in Congress. In the U.N. In the damn White House, for all I know. And all top secret. Don't worry ... I won't give you away. *They* have a certificate on file that says I'm a paranoid schizophrenic; so who'd believe me anyway?"

"Even among the white men, people such as I?" It was hard to grasp.

"The New World was a universe unto itself in 1453. Maybe you *were* the only one here. Maybe your god came over the Bering Strait, nurtured his secret alone for twenty thousand years ... perhaps he forgot, even, that there was a race of creatures like himself ... perhaps, after milennia, he became lonely; who knows? Or he needed another cowherd. He made you. You, Nezahualcóyotl, coming of age with an entire continent for your domain, completely ignorant of the customs, traditions, laws, identities of your kindred … a law unto yourself. They're not going to like you."

"I think I'll have that drink now."

Julia Epstein rose and went to a white rectangular cabinet. She opened it. A searing cold emanated from it, as though winter had been trapped within its confines. She drew out a skin of chilled blood; not a natural skin, surely, for it was clear as water. "It's my own," she said. "I have a rare blood type, so I keep some around in case something happens to me and I need a quick transfusion … yeah, more evidence of paranoia."

She tossed the skin to me. I sank my teeth into the artificial skin. The blood was sweet, a little cloying, and freezing cold; then I remembered, from my childhood, how much I had enjoyed the snow cones flavored with berry juice that the vendors used to bring down from the mountains; I savored the nostalgia. Twice today I'd had a remembrance of the distant past, before my changing. It is strange how one's childhood haunts one.

Julia herself drank coffee, which she poured from a metal pot and blended with bleached sugar. She shook back her hair. I was taken aback at the immodest way she stared at me; truly my god had no more power in this world, or she would have been trembling with awe. There was a faint odor of attraction about her; this woman desired me. And that was strange, for no Aztec woman would have dared think sexual thoughts about one who spoke directly to the gods.

"You need me," she said. "You'll be flung into a cutthroat society ... dozens of your kind, with bizarre hierarchies, internecine politics, games of control and domination. You been asleep for five hundred years, and since then there's been a mass emigration. They like it better in the New World; fewer preconceptions, the American dream and all that ... and the prey are a lot less careful than back in old Wallachia ... where everyone believes in vampires, it's hard for one to catch a decent meal."

"What? They do not give their blood willingly?" For that was the hardest new concept to grasp. Was it not the duty of humans to give freely of their flesh and blood that their gods might live? Was blood not the life-force that kept the sun and the stars in their courses?

"Willingly!" said Julia. "You *do* have a lot to learn."

"You'll help me."

She smiled. "Of course. But only if you help *me.*"

"How?"

"By telling me all about yourself."

She unchained me, and I told her about the coming of the white men, and about Hortator's betrayal. And she in turn told me of her own people, who had once been nomads, who had crossed a tremendous desert to find a land flowing with milk and honey; who had made a covenant with a great and terrible deity who spoke in the voices of wind and fire; and I came to know of the vastness of the earth, and of how my people had been but one of many; how nations had risen and fallen, how even mankind itself had not always been the pinnacle of creation; how the great globe had formed out of the cold dust of the cosmos, and would one day return to dust.

In time, I came to love her; and that in itself was a strange thing, for our kind do not feel love as mortals feel it.

***

The man who came to be called Hortator belonged to me. I had captured him in the Flower Wars, which we hold each year when there are not enough captives from normal wars to feed the altars of the gods.

This year the war was held in a plain not far from the city. Moctezuma himself had come to watch; on a knoll overlooking the battlefield, he and the enemy king, Cozcatl, picnicked on tortillas stuffed with ground iguana, braised in a sauce of pulped cocoa beans, which the man-beasts call *chocolate.* I, as the mouthpiece of the god, sat above Moctezuma on a ledge lined with jaguar skin and feathers. It was a pleasant afternoon; the courtiers were wolfing down their packed lunch while I sipped, from a sacred onyx cup, the blood of a young Mayan girl who had been sacrificed only that morning; yes, the blood had been cooled with snow from the slopes of the volcano.

"It's not going well," said the king. "Look — the jaguar team has only snared about a hundred, and the quetzal team less than half that."

Once touched by the sacred flower-wand which was the only weapon used in these artificial wars, a soldier was sent to the sacrificial pen. It was a great honor, of course, to be sacrificed, and a thing of beauty to behold those hordes of young men, oiled and gleaming, rushing across the grass to embrace their several destinies. "They seem more reluctant than usual, Your Majesty" I said.

"Yes," said the king darkly. "I wonder why."

"I think," I said, trying to put it to him delicately, "it has something to do with the man-beasts from the sea."

"You'd think they'd be all the more anxious to get sacrificed, what with the present danger to the empire."

"Yes ... but ... they've been spreading sedition, Your Majesty. I've just come from the prison; they've been interrogating that black robe they captured — a high priest of sorts. He says that our sacrifices are ignorant superstition; that the sun will rise each morning with our without them; and he's been babbling about Hesuskristos, their god, who seems to be a garbled version of Xipe Totec."

"You shouldn't say bad things about the man-beasts. Last night I dreamed that the Plumed Serpent was returning to claim his kingdom." He was speaking of Quetzalcoatl, the god-king who left our shores five hundred years before, vowing to come back.

"Quetzalcoatl will not come back, Your Majesty."

"How do you know? Am I not the king? Don't my dreams have the force of prophecy?"

"You may have dreamt of him, Your Majesty; *I,* on the other hand, was his friend." It was because he lost the land in a wager that he had been forced to cross the ocean to look for a new kingdom, though that part of the story never made it into our mythology.

"So you say, Nezahualcóyotl. You say that you're a thousand years old, and that you personally led our people out of the wilderness ... that sort of thing is all very well for the peasants, Nezahualcóyotl. But I'm a modern king, and I know that you often use the language of metaphor in order to enhance the grandeur of the gods. No, no, I'm not blaming you; I'm a mean hand at propaganda myself. It's just that, well, you shouldn't believe your own —"

It would not do to argue. I finished my blood in silence.

"Anyhow, I think we should have a bit of propaganda right now, Nezahualcóyotl. Why don't you go down there and lead the jaguar team personally? Give them a bit of that old-time religion. Stir up their juices."

"Sire, at my age —"

"Nonsense. Guard, give him one of those flower wands."

I sighed, took the wand, and went down the hill.

The war was being conducted in an orderly fashion. Seeing me, members of the jaguar team made a space for me. I gave a brief and cliché-ridden harangue about the cycles of the cosmos; then it was time to charge. Boys banged on humanskin drums; musicians began a noisy caterwauling of flutes, cymbals, and shrilling voices that sang of the coming of Huitzilopochtli to the Mexica. The armies ran toward each other, chanting their war-songs, each soldier seeking out a good quarry. I too ran; not with supernatural swiftness, but like a man, my bare feet pounding the ground. Above us, the whistle of the atl-atl and the whine of flower-tipped arrows. The armies met. I searched for a suitable captive that would honor the god. I saw a man in the farthest rank of the enemy… more child than man, his limbs perfectly formed, his eyes darting fearfully from side to side. There was someone who saw no honor in dying for the god! I elbowed aside three pairs of combatants and came upon him suddenly, looming above him as he ducked behind a tree.

"I am your death," I said. "Give yourself up; give honor to the gods."

I touched him with the flower-wand. He glanced at it,

took it, stared me defiantly in the eye.

"I won't do it," he said.

I knew then that he had been polluted by the preachings of the man-beasts. A fury erupted in me. I said, "Why have you been listening to them? Don't you know that they're only human beings? That they bleed and die like ordinary men?"

But he began to run. I was surprised by his speed. He leaped over a bush, sprinted away from the mass of warriors toward a field of maize that bordered the battleground. My first impulse was to let him go — for there was no honor in sacrificing so abject a creature to Hummingbird — but my anger grew and grew as I watched him shrinking into the distance. I could stand it no longer. I called upon the strength of the jaguar and the swiftness of the rabbit; I funneled into the very wind; soon I was upon him again. He turned, saw me running beside him, matching him pace for pace. I could smell his terror; terror was only natural; what I could not smell was the joy, equally natural, that a man should feel when he is about to embrace the source of all joy, to die that the sun might live. He was less than a man. Only an animal could feel this terror of dying without also feeling the exhilaration. I decided to kill him as he ran. I reached out. He struggled, but I drew on my inner strength; I pinned him to the ground. The corn encircled us. Only the gods heard what we said to one another.

"I won't go," he said again. "Kill me now, but I won't die to feed a god that doesn't even exist."

"Doesn't exist!" My anger rose up, naked and terrible. I startled to throttle him. The odor of his fear filled my nostrils. It was intoxicating. I wanted to feed on him right then and there. I could feel his jugular throbbing against my fingers. I knew that his blood was clean and unpolluted with alcohol or coca leaf … his blood was pure as the waters of the mountain; but I could not kill him. "How long were you among the man-beasts?"

"Three years."

I had to let him live. He knew about the foreigners … their languages, their savage ways. I could not kill him until he had divulged all he knew. With a fingernail I scratched his arm, sucked out a few droplets to assuage my hunger. I had to bind him to me. He could become a secret weapon; perhaps I could stave off the end of the world after all.

If only I had listened to the voice of Hummingbird! But I wanted to halt the wheel of time, and though I was a thousand years old I was still too young to understand that there is no stopping time.

"Who are you?" I said.

"I don't know. I don't have a name anymore; I've forgotten it … the Spanish called me Hortator. It pleased them to let me beat the drum on one of their galley ships. I've even been to Spain … that part of Spain that they call Cuba."

"Why aren't you still with them?"

"Pirates, Lord High Priest. I escaped; the others … dead, every one of them."

"And the man-beast who is called Cortéz, who the king thinks is the god Quetzalcoatl, returned to reclaim his inheritance?"

"I don't know of him. The man-beasts are many — dozens of nations and languages. And all of them are coming here. They want gold."

I laughed; what was so valuable about gold, that would make these creatures come across the ocean in their islands made of wood? Was gold then their god?

"No, my Lord. They worship Xipe Totec; their name for him is Hesuskristos."

When I escorted my prisoner back to the pen, it was getting late. Moctezuma was bored and listless; Cozcatl was annoyed at having lost the war, though it would hardly have been good manners for him to be victorious over his sovereign lord. The two kings applauded as I approached them, and bade me eat with them; they had a fresh haunch roasting. "Excellent meat," said the king. "She was good in bed, too."

"You did her great honor, Sire, to inseminate her, sacrifice her, and eat her, all with your own hands."

"It was the Queen's idea, actually; she had been getting uppity. But what have we here?" He eyed my captive with interest. "A powerful-looking fellow; I didn't know you had it in you to bring in so fine a specimen."

He cast his eye about for his obsidian knife; when the king particularly favored someone, he was apt to sacrifice him on the spot. I had to think quickly to protect my source of information. "Your Majesty," I said, "the god has told me that this man is to be the next Unblemished Youth."

"Oh," said the king, disappointed, "we'll have to wait until the big ceremony, then." To Hortator he said, "You're a very lucky young man; you'll have the best in food, drink and women, including four holy brides; until you're sacrificed, a year from now, you'll be worshipped as a god. Even *I* will have to bow to you, though you mustn't get any grand ideas."

"Yes, Sire," said Hortator. I could tell he was grateful for his reprieve. Perhaps, in time, I would be able to wash away the silly notions the man-beasts had planted in his mind. A year was time enough, surely, to persuade him to look forward to being sacrificed properly.

***

"You were planning to deprogram him!" Julia said, having by then become somewhat drunk. I myself was on my second skin of blood; my appearance was far less corpselike than it had been in the exhibit hall.

"I'd better take you home with me," she went on. "At least until you figure out what you're going to do with yourself. I mean — no credit cards, no social security number, no car — you could be in for some culture shock."

I was not sure what she was talking about, but a few hours later I was numb from confusion. I had ridden in a thing called BART, which is a cylindrical metal wagon that runs through tubes under the earth; I had been driven in a horseless chariot across a bridge that seemed to hang on wires above the ocean; I had seen buildings shaped like phalluses, strutting up into the sky; and the people! Tenochtitlán at its most crowded had not been like this. San Francisco — named, so Julia told me, after a nature god of the Spaniards — was a hundred times as crowded. There were people of many colors, and their costumes beggared description. In my feathers, leggings, and pendulous jade earrings, I must have looked a little odd; yet no one stared at me. This was a people accustomed to strangeness.

At length we reached Julia's home, an apartment within one of those tall buildings, reached by means of a little chamber on pulleys which seemed much more efficient that stairs; I could see that I was going to enjoy the many conveniences of this alien world.

Her home was an odd little place; she lived alone, without parents or children, without even any servants; and the apartment, though crammed with laborsaving devices, was little bigger than a peasant's hovel, and considerably more claustrophobic.

We had been there for only moments when she thrust herself at me. Her blood was racing, and scented with erotic secretions. She kissed me. I tasted blood on her chapped lips. I pulled away. "Be careful," I said. "I don't have the same desires as you. I don't feel lust … not like that."

"Then teach me the other kind of lust."

"I'm afraid you would not like it."

"Yes, yes, I know … the desolation … the loneliness of eternity … I don't care! Don't you understand? I've always wanted to be a vampire … I've never been able to get this close to one before … not for certain … I'm a historian. I want to get the long view. I want to see man's destiny unfold, bit by bit … I *hate* being a human being."

"It's not what you think it is." How could I tell her about those flashes from my childhood … those faded images that still haunted me with their unattainable vividness? My world is a gray world; only the infusion of blood brings to it a fleeting color, and that only a simulacrum of color, awakened by long-lost memories; now, five hundred years beyond the end of the world, I had become even more of a tragicomic figure. How could this woman ever know … unless I *made* her know? And then, poor thing, there would be no turning back.

I did not want to make her like me. I had tried that once.

It had not eased my loneliness. And my creation had betrayed me. But the woman could be useful. For now I would pretend to hold out the possibility that she might one day become immortal.

"Make love to me," she said.

She smiled a half-smile and beckoned me into an inner room. There were mirrors everywhere. With great deliberation, she began to remove her clothing. There was a pleasing firmness to her, though she was not young. An Aztec woman of her years would have been worn out, her fists hardened from pounding laundry or tortillas. It would be necessary for me to go through the motions of lovemaking. In the end I did not mind. She had been menstruating.

Afterwards, I lay on the bed and watched her sitting at the mirror, painting her face. She opened a drawer and took out a gold pendant in the shape of a crucified man. Suddenly I understood why I had not perished along with the rest of the world. I had unfinished business.

"Where did you get that amulet from?"

"You recognize it, don't you?" She stood up, clad only in the pendant and her long dark hair. "I'm afraid you're not the first vampire I've dated. Actually I wasn't entirely sure he was one ... until now. They don't make a habit of telling. But you've just confirmed it."

"I have to find the person who gave it to you."

"I'll take you to him," she said.

***

Once more we crossed the bay in the steel chariot; once more my memories came flooding back.

They had seemed insane to me, those man-beasts; there were only a handful of them, yet they scoured the land as though they were an army of thousands. In only a short while they had conquered a city but a day's journey from Tenochtitlán. But in the palace of Moctezuma there was a strange calm. I did not know why. Each day, I sacrificed the requisite numbers of victims at the appropriate hours; I did nothing that dishonored the gods.

Except, of course, for the little lie I had told my king; it had not been Huitzilopochtli who had commanded that the man Hortator be consecrated as the Unblemished Youth. I had said so to ensure that the man would survive and remain useful to me. It was not the first time I had invoked the voice of the Hummingbird to bring about some personal decision. When one has been the mouthpiece of the god for centuries at a time, there are times when one's identity becomes blurred. Besides, what harm could it do? Hortator was the perfect choice, even if the god had not made it himself.

I visited him each evening in the compound sacred to Xipe Totec, where the four sacred handmaidens dressed him, bathed him, and tended to his sexual needs, for he was no longer free to walk about the city at will. He was, indeed, unblemished, a prime specimen of Aztec manhood, lean, tall, well-proportioned, and fine-featured. The god would be pleased when the day came for him to be flayed alive so that his skin could be worn by the priest of Xipe Totec in the annual ceremony that heals and renews the wounded earth and brings forth the rains of spring. There was only one thing wrong with it all; the Unblemished Youth did not seem particularly honored by the attention. It was all most unusual, a sign of the decadence of those times.

"I don't want to do it," he told me, "because I don't

believe in it." For a nonbeliever he was certainly reaping its benefits — being massaged by one handmaiden, being fed by another, and the gods alone knew what was going on under the gold-edged table behind which he sat. "I mean that it's no use; the blood of human sacrifices isn't what makes the sun rise each morning; the god of the man-beasts is clearly more powerful than Huitzilopochtli even as Hummingbird was mightier than the gods who came before. I don't mind the pain so much as the fact that I'd be dying for no reason."

"You've been poisoning the king's mind, too, haven't you?" I said. For Moctezuma seemed to have lost all interest in the future of his empire.

"I *am* the Unblemished Youth," he pointed out. "It was your idea. And as you know, that means that my advice comes from the gods...."

"You hear no voices from the sky!" I said. "It's all pretense with you."

"And what voice from the gods told *you* that I was to be kept alive to teach you the ways of the white men?"

He knew I had lied. Only one whose mind had already been tainted by the man-beasts' ideas would even have imagined such a thing. "But I do hear voices," I said.

"Then let me hear one too."

"All right."

I told him to follow me. We took a subterranean passageway — for he could not be seen to wander the streets of the city — that angled downward, deep under the great pyramid of Huitzilopochtli. The walls were damp and had a natural coolness from the waters that seeped underground from the great lake of Tenochtitlán. Hortator stopped to admire the bas-reliefs which depicted the history of the Mexica people in their long migration toward the promised land; there were sculptures in niches in the stone, some decorated with fresh human skulls or decaying flowers, some so weathered that they could no longer be identified, being the gods of unremembered peoples who had long since been conquered and assimilated by the Mexica; many parts of the tunnel were ill-kept; our torches burned but dimly here, far from the outside air.

At length we reached a chamber so sacred that even King Moctezuma had never set foot within it. It was guarded by the god of a civilization far older than ours — Um-Tzec, the Mayan god of death, whose skull-face was etched into the stone that blocked the entrance.

I whispered a word in the long-forgotten Olmec language, and the stone slid aside to reveal the chamber. Hortator gasped as he read in the flickering torchlight the calendar symbols and the glyphs that lined the walls.

"But —" he said, "this is the lost tomb of Nezahualcóyotl, your namesake, the first great king of the Aztecs!"

I smiled. I held up my torch so he could see all that the room contained — treasures of gold from ancient cities — magical objects and amulets — and a great sarcophagus, carved from solid obsidian.

"The tomb is empty!" he gasped.

"Yes," I said, "it is, and always will be, by the sacred grace and will of Huitzilopochtli, Hummingbird of the Left."

"The black robes told me of creatures like you. I've never seen you eat; you seem to subsist on blood ... you're one of the undead ... a creature of the devil ... you sleep by day in your own coffin, and by night you prey on human blood...."

I laughed. "What strange notions these man-beasts have! Though I admit that I have sometimes taken a nap inside the sarcophagus. It's roomy, and very conducive to meditation."

I showed him the treasures. Every one of them had an ancient tale attached to it, or some mystic power ... the ring of concealment and the jewel for scrying the past ... the great drum fashioned from Xipe Totec's skin, which, when beaten, confers the power of celerity ... "Feel it, touch its tautness ... that is your skin too ... for you are Xipe Totec."

"There is only one Xipe Totec, who gave his life for the redemption of the world, who was killed and rose again on the third day...."

"I'm glad the Spaniards haven't robbed you of *that* truth!"

"On the contrary," he said, "they taught it to me. And they say that theirs is the real Xipe Totec, and yours is an illusion, the work of the powers of darkness." He pulled out an amulet from a fold of his feather robe, and showed me the image of Hesuskristos; a suffering god indeed, nailed to a tree, his torso cruelly pierced, his scalp ripped by thorns. "It is an admirable god," I said, "but I see no reason why, accepting one, you must heap scorn on the other."

"Oh, they are not so different, the new gods and the old. The black robes have sacrifices too; they burn the victims alive in a public ceremony called *auto-da-fè,* after first subjecting them to fiendish tortures —"

"Wonderful," I said, "at least they have *some* of the

rudiments of civilization."

"I did not say their god was better, Nezahualcóyotl; only that he is stronger. Now show me how your god speaks."

"I will need blood."

"Take mine," he said.

I took my favorite blood-cup, carved from a single, flawless piece of jade, and murmured a prayer over it. I did not want to scar the Unblemished Youth; I knelt before him and pricked him lightly in the groin with the fingernail of my left pinky, which I keep sharpened for that purpose; I drained a ounce or so into the bloodcup, then seared the wound shut with a dab of my saliva. The drawing of blood caused the man to close his eyes. He whimpered; I knew not if it was from pain or ecstacy. I called on Huitzilopochtli, drained the blood-cup, tossed it aside. The warmth shot through my ancient veins, pierced my unbeating heart; it was a bitter blood, a blood of destiny. I emptied out my soul. I waited for the god to speak.

And presently it came, a faint whisper in my left ear, like the fluttering of tiny wings. I could not see Huitzilopochtli — no one has ever seen him — but his still small voice lanced my very bones like the thunderous erupting of Popocatapetl itself. *The world has turned in on itself,* said the god, *and the fire of the sun has turned to ashes.*

"But — what have we done wrong? Didn't we slaughter hecatombs of warriors to your glory? Didn't we mortify our own flesh, build pyramids whose points grazed the very dwelling places of your kindred?"

The god laughed. *The cosmos dances,* he said. *We are at peace.*

In my trance state I saw Hortator standing before me, no

longer in the consecrated raiment of Xipe Totec, but naked, nailed to a tree, the skin scourged from his back, the blood streaming from his side and down his face, and I cried out, "You abomination! You travesty of the true faith!" and I rushed toward him. When I was with the god I was more powerful than any human. I could rip him in pieces with my bare hands. I had him by the throat, was throttling the life from him —

You will not kill him, said the god. All at once, the strength left my hands. *Instead, you will make him immortal.*

"He doesn't deserve—"

Obey me! He too is a prophet, of a sort. Do you not understand that he who rises to godhead, who creates a world, a people, a destiny, plants inevitably within his creation the seeds of his own destruction? All life is so — and the gods, who are the pinnacle of life, are as subject to its laws as any other creatures.

It seemed to me that I no longer understood the god as clearly as I had once, when I came down from the high mountain to bring his message to a tribe of wanderers. His words were confused now, tainted. But he was the god, and my obeyed him without thought. I knelt once more before Hortator, and I began to feed, mindless now of damaging his flesh, for I knew that he would never have to suffer the rites of Xipe Totec ... I fed and fed until there was no more blood at all, and then, slashing my lip with my razor fingernail, I moistened his lips with a few drops of my own millennial blood, blood that ran cold as the waters under the earth.

I cried out: "Do you see now the power of Huitzilopochtli? I have killed you and brought you back from the dead; I have awakened you to the world of eternal cold...."

But Hortator only laughed, and he said to me, "I heard nothing. No hummingbird whispered in my left ear. The black robes were right; your gods do not exist."

"My gods have made you immortal!"

"I am already immortal; for the black robes have sprinkled me with their water of life."

I could not understand what had happened. Why had the god commanded me to make him my kindred, then allowed him to mock me? Why could Hortator not hear the voice of the deity when it reverberated in my very bones? The very fabric of the world was unraveling. For the first time in a thousand years, I was afraid. At first I could not even recognize the emotion, it was so alien; it was almost thrilling. I reached back farther and farther through the cobwebs of memory ... I saw myself as a child ... scurrying beneath my mother's blanket ... fleeing the music of the night ... with fear came a kind of melancholy, for I knew that I would never again truly feel what it was like to be alive.

Once, it seemed, I walked with my god; daily, hourly I heard his voice echo and reecho in my heart. Then came a time when he spoke to me but rarely, and usually only in the context of the blood-ritual. And now and then, I began to speak for him, inventing his words, for the people did not hear him unless I first heard him; it was I who was his prophet. Was it those little lies that had made my god abandon me now?

I cried out, "Oh, Huitzilopochtli, Huitzilopochtli, why hast thou forsaken me?" But the god did not see fit to respond.

***

We stopped at a bazaar to buy clothes more suitable to my surroundings. Julia picked out some black leggings which could be pulled over my loincloth, shoes made from animal skins, and an overshirt of some soft white material; she paid for the items with a rectangular plaque, which the vendor slid through a metal device, after which she made some mysterious marks on a square of parchment.

Then we drove on to another part of the city, one where the buildings were more ornate, not the monolithic towers of stone and glass I had seen before. We stopped in front of a low, unpretentious-looking building; Julia bade me follow her.

Inside, the surroundings were considerably more ostentatious. There were paintings, a floor covered with some kind of red-tinted fur, the pieces joined together so invisibly that one could not tell what animal it had come from. The place was full of all manner of people, jabbering away in many accents, though I did not hear anyone speak Náhuatl; perhaps my native tongue had gone the way of the language of the Olmecs.

We stood, a little uncomfortably — for though no one questioned our being there no one made us welcome — and I began to notice a pervasive sickliness in the air — the sweetness of putrefying flesh that has been doused in cloying perfume — I knew that it was the odor of the dead — I knew that I was in the presence of others of my kind — not one or two but *dozens* of them. What had happened in the past five hundred years? Had I been reborn into a world of vampires? Again fear flecked my feelings, the same fear I had felt when I doubted my gods for the first time.

"Your friend is sometimes to be found there," Julia said.

She pointed to a door, half-hidden by shadows. "Go along. I'll stay here and have a glass of wine."

"You're not coming with me?"

"I can't," she said. "No human being has ever come out of that room alive. But if you're really what I say you are, you won't have any trouble. That room," she went on, her voice dropping to a whisper, "is the Vampire Club."

"Why are you whispering?"

"I'm not supposed to know." Her eyes sparkled. I could see that she loved to flirt with danger … that was why she was so obsessed with my kind.

I put aside my fear. I had to confront Hortator. Already I knew that he was close by. From the dozens of clamoring voices in the building, my attenuated senses were able to isolate him. I could even hear his blood as it oozed through his veins; for every creature's life force pulsates to a personal rhythm, unique as a fingerprint, if one has only the skill to pick it out.

I was becoming angry. I stalked to the door and flung it open. There came a blast of foul and icy wind. I stepped inside and slammed the door shut. There was no mistaking the odor now. I descended steep steps into a tomblike chamber where several outlandishly attired men and women sat deep in conversation, sipping delicately from snifters of blood.

"Rh negative," said one of them disgustedly, "not exactly my favorite."

"Let me have a sniff — *pe-ugh!* Touch of the AIDS virus in that one; oh, do send it back, my dear Travis."

"Whatever for? I think it lends it a certain *je ne sais quoi,*" said Travis, "that ever-tantalizing *bouquet de la mort….*"

Two other creatures looked up from a game of cards;

their faces had the pallid phosphorescence of the dead; their eyes glittered like cut glass, scintillant and emotionless.

A slightly corpulent man, sumptuosly clothed in velvet and satin, waved languidly at me. "Heavens," he said, "what a surprise! We don't get many Red Indians here."

"Get him out of here," one of the cardsharps hissed. He was attired like one of the Spanish black robes.

"Yeah, dude," said a young man, of the type Julia had described to me as *punk*. "Or card him at least." He cackled at some incomprehensible joke.

"Whatever for? He's obviously one of us … either that, or he's in desperate need of the services of an orthodontist," said the man in the velvet.

"We don't know him," said the other cardplayer, a woman, whose hair stood on end and fanned out like the tail of a peacock, and who wore a full-length cloak of some thick, black material.

"Perhaps we should ask him who he is. See here, old thing — very, *very* old, I'm afraid — I'm Sebastian Melmoth, your humble host. And you are —?"

"I am Nezahualcóyotl," I said, "the Voice of the Hummingbird. I'm looking for a certain person. He calls himself Hortator."

"Oh, I see. Well, you really mustn't get to the point quite so fast; it's not very dignified, you know. Let a century or two go by first."

"I have let *five* centuries go by."

"Perhaps you'd care for one of our sanguinary cocktails?"

"I've already supped tonight, thank you."

"And might I ask you what clan you belong to?"

"I know nothing of clans. If you won't tell me the whereabouts of Hortator, please direct me to someone who can."

"Are you an anarch?" asked the woman with the peacock hair. I could only look at her in confusion.

The other card player rose and sniffed at me. "Unusual bloodline," he said. "Not a pedigree I'm familiar with."

"Now look here," said Sebastian Melmoth, "he's obviously a vampire. But he doesn't seem to have the foggiest notion about how to behave like one. Tell me, Nezzy old chap, if you *were* in fact to find Hortator, what would you do?"

"I shall kill him."

The others began to laugh at me. I felt like some peasant on his first trip to Tenochtitlán. "Why do you mock me?" I said.

"Well!" said Sebastian Melmoth, "that's simply not done anymore. Not without the consent of the Prince. Who doesn't even know who you are, so I don't see why he would grant your request."

It was then that I heard *his* voice. "Kill me?" The voice had deepened with the centuries, but I still recognized it. There he stood, towering over Melmoth, in the full regalia of a Mexica warrior, the jaguar-skin cloak, the helmet fashioned from a jaguar's head, the quetzal plumes, the earrings of gold and jade. Behind him there hung a life-sized painting of the white men's Xipe Totec, the god nailed to a tree; a soldier was hammering a stake through his heart; a beautiful woman watched with tears in her eyes.

"Kill me?" he repeated. "Why, Nezahualcóyotl?"

"Because you tried to kill *me!*"

"That was a foolish thing. I admit it. I placed too much credence in the Spaniard's superstitions. I know now that you're not that simple to kill. In fact, you look very well for someone who hasn't had a drop of blood in half a millennium."

"You are part of the old things, the things that should have died when the world ended. I understand now why I have been preserved by the gods. It is so that I can take you with me, you impious creature who twice refused the honor of a sacrificial death. I have been sent to put an end to your anomalous existence so that no part of the Old World will taint the New."

"Did your god tell you this, old man?"

Suddenly I realized that I had heard no voices from the gods since awakening inside the glass box in the San Francisco Museum. There was no more certainty in me … there was only ambiguity and confusion. My grand revelations no longer had divine authority. Perhaps it was true that they were the hallucinations of a madman. Perhaps if I had my votive objects I could summon back the voice of the hummingbird — the sacred blood-cup, the drum, the gold-tipped thorns for piercing my own flesh….

"Huitzilopochtli!" I cried out, despairing.

"You fool," said Hortator. "No god brought you to this place. There is no divine plan. It was I who told Julia Epstein where to dig … it was *I* who chose the moment to bring you back out of the earth … it was *I,* not Huitzilopochtli, who summoned you hither!"

"Why?" I said.

"Oh, don't imagine that I want to renew some monstrous cosmic struggle between you and me. It's much simpler than that. Buried with you … in the chamber at the heart of the pyramid … there were certain artifacts, were they not? Magical artifacts that will enhance my power. Your coming back to life along with the items I need is something of an inconvenience, but I'm sure you won't last long … because you simply don't understand how things work in this new world, this age of vampires."

***

Then it was that the memory of the apocalypse returned to me, bursting all at once through the wall I had erected to shield myself from its pain. I could not bear these creatures of their future, with their petty rules and their ignorance of the great cycles of the cosmos. I turned and strode away, taking the steps two at a time until I reached the Alexandrian Club, where Julia was sitting nervously at a corner table.

"Where did I come from?" I screamed at her. "How did you come to possess my body? And where are the artifacts I was buried with?" I had to have them. I had to try to summon Huitzilopochtli. Surely I would hear his voice again if I went through the ritual of the sacred blood-cup. …

"Quiet now," she said, "you're making a scene."

"I have to know!"

"Yes. Yes. But not here … it's dangerous for me."

We drove into the darkness. San Francisco sparkled with man-made stars. A thousand strange new odors lanced the air … frenzied copulations … murderers and thieves skulking through the back streets … and the blood music, singing to me from every mortal inhabitant of the city … from within the topless towers of stone came the pounding of a million hearts, the roar of a million bloodstreams … oh, one could be a glutton in this city, if one were a creature such as I … no wonder they had congregated here.

"I told you," said Julia. "Things are different now."

"What did Hortator mean when he said that *he* had summoned me back from the dead — by telling you where to dig?"

"Oh, he was being melodramatic. But he did drop a few hints."

"Before or after he made love to you?"

"You're not jealous, are you?"

"Of course not." I was silent for a while. The woman had a way of baldly confronting me with the truth. I didn't like it. I loathed the very idea of a city crammed with vampires, living by complex rules, observing silly hierarchies. But could I do? The car raced over the bridge once more; Tenochtitlán too was a city of many bridges, a floating city … San Francisco was like a bloated, savage parody of my vanished kingdom.

Julia said, "I'll tell you, if you like. We have a series of weekly lectures at the museum … Hispanic studies, you know. Hortator came to a few of them. He would ask penetrating questions. Then he started telling *me* things. There was a big earthquake in Mexico City, you know. The Velasquez Building was leveled to the ground. He told me — convinced me — that there was a major find hidden beneath it … a secret room, he told me … next to a secret passageway. He told me he'd seen it in a dream. I laughed when he drew me a map … well, that was the thing, you see. We had been using sonar to excavate those tunnels … and the computer scan matched his drawing … to the centimeter."

"And you found me there."

"You were lying in a massive obsidian sarcophagus. You had a stake through your heart. I assumed — foolish me — that because of that, you were quite, quite dead — too many *Dracula* films, I suppose — so that it would be safe to put you on exhibit...."

***

Memories of the apocalypse....

The king in all his splendor ... this time not on the crest of a grassy hill, watching a pretended battle, but atop a pyramid of stone, looking down on the conquistadores as they swept through the city in a river of blood and fire ... man and beast conjoined now, the man-things glittering in their silvery skins, the beasts whinnying and pawing the pathways paved with the dead ... arms and legs flying in the air as the canonballs smashed through stone and adobe and human flesh....

And I beside him, I the mouthpiece of the god of the Mexica, aghast and powerless, raging. "You didn't have to play dead for them. They're just mortals. You're treated them like gods."

"They *are* gods," said Moctezuma. "There was nothing I could do."

Hortator had poisoned his mind. He had fed Moctezuma a diet of his own bad dreams ... told him that the Spaniard was indeed Quetzalcoatl.

I looked into the eyes of my king; and I saw such sadness, such desolation that I could not bear it. It must be a terrible destiny to be the one chosen to preside over the end of the universe. Was there no way to turn back the sun? No. Beside us as we sat, each one wrapped in his private melancholia, my deputy priests were grimly carrying on the day's duties, plucking out the hearts of victims who waited in an endless queue that stretched all the way down the thousand steps and into the conflagration in the market square.

"Don't tell me that you accepted the word of this man-beast as the word of a god!" I cried.

"Wasn't it?" the king said. "In truth ... I felt a certain ... wrongness about it all ..."

"Then let me call on Hummingbird to turn back the tide of time!"

"What difference does it make now?"

"Majesty," I said, "when the king himself no longer believes in the old truths, how can the earth sustain itself?"

"Perhaps I've been a little ... distracted," said the king. He was wavering.

I knew that *I* could not stand idle. I left the king's side, I entered the sacred chamber behind the altar, whose walls were caked with the blood of ten thousand human sacrifices. I paused only to suck the juices from a fresh, still palpitating heart that one of the priests handed me. The soldiers were hacking off the limbs of the still convulsing victims, casting down the arms and legs, as has always been the custom, for the poor to dine on. The sight of the city's daily routine being carried out even now, on the brink of utter annihilation, would have moved me to tears, except that I had shed none in a thousand years. The priests worked quickly and efficiently, up to their elbows in coagulating gore. I hardly looked at them; I chucked the drained heart onto a golden platter before an image of Hummingbird, then entered the secret passageway behind the altar that led downward, downward to the hidden chamber where lay my sarcophagus and the tools of my art.

In the tunnel, the sounds of death were muffled. Canon like the distant whisper of thunder in the rain forest. The screams of the dying faint, like the cries of jungle birds. The clash of metal on stone like the patter of rain on foliage. I took the steep steps two at a time. Soon I was in the heart of the pyramid.

When I reached the chamber, I found that the seal was broken. Not with the magic words, but shattered with gunpowder. Several of the man-beasts were already there, ransacking the place, gathering up the treasures into sacks ... "How dare you?" I screamed. The man-beasts rushed at me. I summoned up my inner strength. I struck out blindly with both fists, and two of the Spaniards slammed against the stone walls. One of them died on the spot; the second more slowly, a little string of brain oozing down from his helmet. The third man-beast gaped, turned tail, started to run ... then his greed got the better of him and he returned to gather up one of the sacks of gold. He glanced at me; I was draining his dead friend's blood into the sacred blood-cup so that I could call on Hummingbird.

I closed my eyes. I called on the name of my god.

Huitzilopotchtli....

I felt myself sinking into the well of unconsciousness that was the presence of my god. I heard the familiar buzzing in my left ear that presaged the coming of Huitzilopotchtli. I smiled.

My child....

Came the whisper of the Hummingbird's wings, the tiny voice from the heart of the flames. I thrilled to its dark music. I allowed it to wash over me like the currents of the sea. I relinquished my being. The presence of the divine was more fulfilling even than the taste of blood, than the memory of women.

My child....

Abruptly, the trance was broken. I was jolted into consciousness. Even now, telling the story to Julia five hundred years later, the memory will not come back as a woven fabric; it is in tatters.

Hortator stands before me, no longer in the attire of the Unblemished Youth, but wrapped in a metal skin from head to toe, like one of the conquistadores. With him are a dozen of the whiteskinned creatures. He has delivered to his masters an entire world, an entire civilization.

"I know what you are now," he cries, "creature of Satan ... they've told me everything." Several more of the Spaniards come in behind him, brandishing their swords and their flaming torches and their muskets. Seeing their dead comrades they cry out, back away; but Hortator laughs. "I know what you are now, and the Jesuits have told me what I must do to kill you."

Confused, uncomprehending, I lash out —

He dodges my blow, leaps across the sarcophagus, seizes the drum of Xipe Totec ... and begins to pound on it, a slow relentless rhythm ... I scream ... he pounds ... I lunge ... he leaps, each leap drawing more celerity from the power of the drum ... he flies along the walls, he twists, he turns, he is a whirlwind, a tempest —

Huitzilopotchtli! I cry out.

No answer. I reached into the profoundest darkness of the well within. Where was my god? Then I saw Hortator bearing down on me, brandishing a sharpened wooden stake.

As though from infinitely far away I seem to see the

stake rive my stony flesh, rip apart my ribcage, pierce my heart....

Huitzilopotchtli!

Huitzilopotchtli!

Then, and only then, the god responds. The pyramids above us start to tremble. Cracks appear in the ceiling. Rocks start to rain down.

"Flee!" cries Hortator. I hear, through the fog of pain, their footsteps, metal clanking on stone. I hear some of them cry out as the cave-in crushes them.

I clutch at the wooden stake. But it is too late. I feel its leaden weight within me, feel it still the sluggish pump that is my heart, I feel the blood slow from a spurt to an ooze. I feel my heart muscle tighten around the unyielding wood like a vagina. I feel violated. I feel powerless for the first time since my changing. Then, all at once, I am spiraling downward toward the long sleep of ultimate forgetting.

***

... and now, another underground passageway, another secret chamber ... five hundred years in the future, in a world I did not belong in ... I stood with Julia Epstein among the shelves and shelves of artifacts of my people, all labeled, boxed, marked in white paint in the strange curlicuish script of the man-beasts.

Crate after crate I ripped open. "What is it you're looking for?" said Julia. "This is valuable stuff — you can't just throw it around like it belonged to you."

"It *does* belong to me."

"Half a millennium ago. But they're priceless antiquities now. And they haven't been appraised by the insurance company yet, so —"

I saw a tattered quetzal-feather robe that had once belonged to King Moctezuma's grandfather ... I saw my sacred blood-cup, chipped now ... I lifted it from its box....

"Careful with that thing! It dates back to Olmec times."

" I know. I made it."

She was silent for a moment. "The drum!" I said. "There was a drum ... fashioned from human skin...."

"I've seen that," she said, "in Hortator's apartment."

So that was how he had made it out of the collapsing tunnels ... with the power of celerity conferred by the drum of Xipe Totec! I was furious now. He had no right to my ritual objects. I was more determined than ever to exact revenge. Perhaps *he* thought I would be a useless anachronism, but I would teach him not to usurp my magical tools. They had told me at the Vampire Club about new laws that forbade the killing of vampires without permission from some prince ... but what did I know of princes? What did I care? I was more ancient than any prince.

But even as I spoke, we heard the sound of shattering glass, and the high-pitched wail that I now knew to be an alarm that would eventually summon the museum's security. Then came a distant thumping sound, uneven, like a fibrillating heart. I knew that sound well. The hollow pounding contained in it the scream of a dying man.

"Hortator!"

"Why do you have to go on fighting him?" Julia said. "Don't you realize that the war between you two has no meaning any more?"

"Julia, I must have a little of your blood."

She closed her eyes, craned her neck, bared it to me as a

warrior bares his heart for the sacrifice. "I need the blood," I said, "so I can summon forth the voice of the Hummingbird."

"There's no voice," she whispered. "It's in your mind … the right brain speaking to the left … a hallucination of godhead. Don't you understand that people don't see visions and hear voices anymore? You come from the age of gods; we live in the age of consciousness; it's not the god who commands us anymore, it's we ourselves, our ego, our individual being … people like you, people who still hear the voices of gods … they put them insane asylums now."

What was she telling me? It made no sense. How could humans exist without prophets to transmit the commands of the gods? How lonely it must be for them in this future … to be like little islands of consciousness, not to be linked to the great cycle of the cosmos … to be not part of one great self but merely little selves, with little, meaningless lives. I could not, would not live that way. I took her in my arms; I made a tiny incision in her neck with my little fingernail; I drew a thumblefull of blood into the sacred cup; deeply I drank, and as I drank I prayed: *Huitzilopotchtli … Huitzilopotchtli … do not forsake me now.*

Hortator burst into the chamber. The alarms were screeching. "The rest of the treasures of the room have now been brought to San Francisco," he said "That's why I told Julia where you could be found. I need the other ritual objects … I need the powers they can bestow on me. As for you … you're just a historical oddity."

But I could feel the strength of Huitzilopotchti course through my flesh.

As Julia, faint from her bleeding, sat, dazed, on my old

sarcophagus, still in its wooden crate, Hortator and I battled. He threw me against the wall; I lacerated his face with my fingernails; he whirled about me, pounding his drum, *my* drum ... each of us drew on his dark powers. A mortal would not have seen us battling at all. He would have felt now a tremor, now a flash of light, now a ripple of darkness. I leaped onto the ceiling, I sped along the walls, defying the earth's pull with me speed; but Hortator was equally swift. His fangs glistened in the man-made light. We fought hand to hand on the lid of the sarcophagus where Julia still lay. We tussled on the concrete floor of the storeroom, and still the siren wailed.

"I'll really kill you this time," Hortator shouted. "The black robes told me a stake through the heart would kill you ... I know better now."

And still I had not heard the voice of the hummingbird. It was beginning to dawn on me that there was something to what Julia said; that perhaps this was no longer an age of gods. The last time the god had spoken, had he not said, *Do you not understand that he who rises to godhead, who creates a world, a people, a destiny, plants inevitably within his creation the seeds of his own destruction?* I did not understand then, but I understood it now. My existence showed to ordinary men that there was something beyond mortality; but beyond my own immortality there was also a kind of entropy. In being granted the ability to see the grand scheme of the universe, to live for centuries and know the higher purposes of mankind, I had also learned that all, even the most sublime, is vanity. I was full of despair. How could I belong to this future? How could I live amongst dozens of creatures like myself, arcane hierarchies all selfishly struggling for domination over one another? I knew that Hortator would hound me to my death. I could not live in a world where I could not hear the voice of my god.

We had battled for what seemed like days, but I knew that only seconds had passed; so quick were our movements that time itself had seemed to stand still. He had me pinned to the ground. I felt not only his weight but the weight of this whole bizarre new universe. And with a free hand he continued to drum, frenzied now, his eyes maddened, his lips frothing. I waited for him to drain me of all my blood, to desiccate me, to consign me to the well of oblivion for ever.

Then, at that moment, the siren ceased. Hortator relaxed his hold on me. A shadow had fallen over us. I smelled the presence of another kindred. I could feel the concentrated power, a puissance that matched my own.

"Prince," Hortator whispered. He stepped back from me, then fell to the floor in supplication. I could not see this Prince, so thoroughly had he cloaked himself in magical darkness. But I knew him in the shadow that suffused the air.

"Oh, Nezahualcóyotl," said the prince, whose voice was as reverberant as a god's, "what am I to do with you? You have arrived in this city, yet you do not even come to pay homage to me as is our custom; and already you've created all sorts of controversy. The vampire club talks of nothing else but you. You're an anomaly; you challenge our most basic assumptions about our people's history."

I said, "I did not mean to offend you. My quarrel with Hortator is an ancient one, and not your affair; and I see now that the things we quarrel about have become irrelevant. I have no real desire to live. Let Hortator take my ritual objects and grow in power; and let me return to the earth."

"It is true," said the prince, "that I have the authority to grant you death. But how can I? You are older than I; you are so old that even the concept of the masquerade is foreign to you; it is I who should bow to you, but I cannot. There can only be one prince. Nezahualcóyotl, you must find your own destiny in some other place. Or else there will always be some who will look to you for leaderships, anarchs who will revere your disregard of our rules of civilization and who will claim that your greater age gives you greater authority. Nezahualcóyotl … you must leave. I cannot command you. I, a prince, must ask it of you as a favor."

And now the security guards were entering the room. It was just as it was in Tenochtitlán, the enemy storming the secret chamber just as my world was disintegrating all around me. The prince did something — used his powers of hypnosis perhaps — for the guards did not seem to see me, Hortator, or the rippling darkness that was the prince of San Francisco.

"Are you all right, Ms. Epstein?" said one of them.

Julia was struggling to get up. "I — must have passed out," she said. "Something — someone — perhaps a prowler —"

"No one here now, ma'am. But they've made quite a mess."

"Are you sure you don't want me to get a doctor?" said another guard.

"I'm fine, thanks."

"Let's see if we can find him lurking around somewhere," said the first guard, and they trooped away.

Astonished, I looked up. I thought I glimpsed something — a swirl of shadow — vortices within vortices — the eyes of a ancient creature, world-weary, ruthless, yet somehow also tinged with compassion. I knew that I he was right. I could not stay in San Francisco. I knew nothing of the feuding factions of the vampire world, the warring clans, the masquerade; I belonged to a simpler time.

"I will go," I said softly.

Then Julia said, "And I will go with you."

I said, "You don't know what you're saying. You think it's some romantic thing, that there's glamour in being undead. Look at us; look at how we have relived, again and again, ancient quarrels that the world has forgotten; the vampires that rule the world are but shadows, and I am less than a shadow of their shadow."

Julia said, "Only because you have not loved."

She came toward me. In her eyes there shone the crystalline coldness of eternity. I had not wanted to transform her into one of my kind … I had sought only to use enough blood to sustain me, to let me see my visions. She had not yet become a vampire; what I saw in her eyes was the yearning. "It's a historian's dream," she said, "to pass through the ages of man like the pages of a book … to perceive the great big arc of history. It's not just that I love you. Even if I didn't, I could learn, in eternity, to love."

Hortator hissed, "Only the prince can grant the right to sire new kindred!"

But the prince said only, "Peace, peace, Hortator; will your anger never be slaked?" And then — and I could feel him fading from our presence as he spoke — he said, "Do what you wish, Nezahualcóyotl. Be glad. We will not meet again."

***

I have returned to Tenochtitlán. It is a gargantuan madhouse of twenty million souls, but it is still called by the name of my vanished tribe, the Mexica. My official title is Meso-American Studies Advisor to the San Francisco Museum Field Research Unit, Mexico City. Julia and I have a charming apartment; one side overlooks one of the few areas of greenery in the city, the other one of the worst slums.

Julia tells me that a philosopher named Jaynes has written a book called *The Origin of Consciousness in the Breakdown of the Bicameral Mind.* It is a book that explains how, in the ancient world, men did not possess consciousness of self at all, but acted blindly, in response to voices and images projected by the right side of the brain, which they perceived to be the direct commands of gods, kings, and priests.

It is a strange world indeed, where people see no visions, and where a book has to be written explaining away the gods in terms of ganglia and synapses. I do not like it. I do not like the fact that I have been cut off forever from the divine; that I am no longer a prophet, but merely one vampire among many.

Yet the city does have its charms. Its nightlife is thriving and decadent; its music colorful; its alleyways quaint and full of titillating danger. And then there are the people ... the descendants of my own people and the Spaniards who overcame them. Julia and I often make time to enjoy the inhabitants of our new home.

There are many poor people here. They pour in from the country, seeking out a better life; often they end up working as virtual slaves in huge factories that pump out cheap goods for their richer neighbors to the north. Sometimes they become gangsters or beggars. Sometimes they find a charitable person to take them in, as domestics, perhaps, or live-in prostitutes.

***

For this next tale, I was asked to contribute *another* taboo-destroying tale about religion, so I picked the Old Testament. A constant theme in the Bible, in my opinion, is that God rarely chooses ideal people to be his representative. I think Lot is a prime example of that. He does, after all, sleep with his own daughters. And more.

I also wondered ... we all know what they did in Sodom, or think we do. But what did they do in Gomorrah?

S.P. Somtow

Brimstone and Salt

And what, you ask me, did they do in Gomorrah?

It's a reasonable question. We all know what they did in Sodom. They sat around buttfucking each other until God, in his wrath, rained down fire and brimstone, and blew the place to kingdom come. Everyone knows that, right? It's all there in the bible. An angel told Lot that if he could find ten righteous and upright men in all of Sodom and Gomorrah, the twin cities would be spared; Lot couldn't, and that was that. Boom. Apocalypse. Mushroom cloud hanging over half of Mesopotamia.

Of course, Lot's own righteousness was pretty questionable; the bible tells us that he screwed his own daughters, so he was probably not the very best judge of character. One wonders what gave him the right to pick ten honest upstanding citizens out of that double den of iniquity.

As usual, alas, the good book has it all backwards; and we must, in fact, look elsewhere for the facts. Ask me anything. I know. I was there.

Don't laugh, Mr. Big-shot Shrink. You run a tight support group. Melvin the Multiple's pretty damn entertaining, and Mildred's regressions to her four-year-old closet of satanic abuse are truly Hard Copy material. Nothing to complain about there. Maybe Jack-in-the-box, who doesn't do a fucking thing except rock back and forth, isn't that much of an asset to the group, but on the rare occasions when he does talk, he goes wild. One of these days I'm going to get Entertainment Tonight in here for you, but for now, we just have each other, don't we? As if that weren't enough.

I've been watching you guys go at each other for three weeks now. You know I haven't said anything. I've sat, and I've watched, and maybe you people think that my hundred bucks an hour are wasted because I haven't had the chance to spill my guts all over the plush white carpet of your elegant art deco office. Tonight, my friends, you're going to get your money's worth. This is one child abuse survivor support group that's never going to be the same.

Melvin, you had such a hideous time when you were four years old that your mind fractured into a dozen personalities. I've had a thousand.

And not because of one cruel stepfather — because the entire world hurt me. To survive, I've become a thousand people over the years. Oh, Melvin, you have me beat on one thing — all your people are inside your brain now, fighting among one another. My personalities came one at a time. Each of them grew up, grew old, and died, yet I went on.

As for Jack, rocking back and forth — I like you. You had a narrow escape from a serial killer when you were seven years old, so you don't talk much. Look into my eyes. I'm a lot worse than the one you escaped from. I've dined on the kind of man who made your life a living hell. I'm a serial killer's serial killer.

Mildred: maybe you were a victim of that satanic abuse bullshit, and maybe not. False memory syndrome is a big thing right now, and your last analyst is being sued by half her ex-patients. I don't really believe it personally. You think you hung out with Satan? Satan was a personal friend of mine, back in the days when he was somebody.

So here I am. Just a visitor, in a sense, although I too am a survivor of what happened to all of you; I just happen to have survived a few thousand years longer than any of you have. Don't laugh, Mr. Shrink; I am not delusional. I am not suffering from any psychosis, though, after all these centuries, I probably ought to be. I'm not some rich bitch paying through the nose in order to play elaborate mindgames or live out arcane fantasies, two evenings a week.

I am a vampire.

I am Shoshana, the youngest daughter of Lot.

I am probably the oldest incest survivor in the world.

You want the support group confession to end all support group confessions? You want a night to remember, full of spectacle, bloodshed, debauchery, greed, insanity, shame, lust, angst, orgies, bellydancers? Hold on to your horses, my friends. Tonight, after five millennia or so, I finally

feel like talking. And you, my friends, are a captive audience. Not because I compel you to stay, but because we of the ancient kindred possess a seductive glamour that makes it nearly impossible for you to resist us. You fear us, but you desire us too.

Look at me, Mr. Big-shot Shrink: am I not beautiful? Is it the moonlit pallor of my complexion, the lurid carmine of my lips, the dusky splendor of my shoulder-length hair? Or is it perhaps the sensuous contralto of my voice, or my indefinably foreign accent, or the bizarre way that I lisp sometimes, as if the air had been trapped in my lungs for decades at a time, because I don't seem to need to breathe? Surely it's not the way I dress — about four centuries out of style — passing for gothic chic in today's strange, alienated youth culture? I am, you know, forever young. And I do mean forever.

Maybe you want to know, if I'm really this immortal creature of the night, why I need to be here with you at all. You're beyond all this, you tell me. You're not even human. Psychiatry is about helping human beings come to terms with their humanity, is it not? If you're really a vampire,

presumably you don't have to worry about such mundane things as night terrors, bad dreams, neuroses, obsessive-compulsive behaviors.

But you have to understand that before I changed into what I am today, I once was human, and the bad thing my father did to me started long before I even knew vampires existed....

***

It was at Ur that my father first came to me in the middle of the night. We had come for the funeral of Enkidu, the king's lover. Our people had long since been displaced from the land we called Eden, the fertile valley of the Tigris and Euphrates, by a technologically superior people, smelters of bronze, builders of cities; the desert had become our home. We lived in a manner not much different from the Bedouin tribes today; but in theory the King of Sumer had suzerainty, and now and then it was necessary to send an official mission to the court. A formality, really. Abraham, the patriarch, didn't need to come himself, so he sent Lot.

My sister and I came with him, sharing a camel. We were not important. They didn't even lodge us in the palace, but allowed us to set up our tents in walled garden that had once been part of the royal harem.

As the lowliest of the subject peoples, my father was not even granted an audience with Gilgamesh. But on the morning of the funeral, they gave us a perfunctory tour of the city. We were a convoy of litters, each one carrying a visiting party from some distant outpost of civilization, and they were doing their best to impress us with the splendor and spectacle of their superior culture. But everyone was in mourning, so there wasn't much to see. The marketplace was closed, and all the houses shuttered; from inside came the constant sound of weeping. The king had decreed that anyone caught not acting suitably doleful would be impaled.

The only action within the city walls was at the temple of Ishtar, which couldn't very well be closed down. Our palanquin moved slowly past it, and our guide, a minor functionary of the court named Turak, lectured us about sacred prostitutes. I had no idea what he was talking about. But my father covered our eyes with his fat palms.

"Abomination, abomination!" he murmured. "Don't look!"

"But father," I said, trying to pry his fingers off my face, "you're looking. In fact, you've got that look in your eye. The one that usually gets you in trouble."

My sister Rachel was a lot less defiant than me. She turned her back on the temple and squeezed her eyes tight shut. But I got in a good look. It was a spectacle! There was a ziggurat in the midst of a plaza, and it was all limestone, shimmering in the sun. On the front steps of the temple sat women of all shapes and sizes. Most were young — some as young as me, even — but a few were haggard and hideous, and there were one or two leviathans among them. They weren't wearing very much. Except for their makeup, that is: they were kohled and rouged and powdered until they looked more like statuettes than human beings.

One of the women winked at me and beckoned with a languid hand. She was, I thought, very beautiful. The thick layer of makeup made her seem quite unreal. My sister saw me gawking and poked me in the ribs. "Don't let abba catch you staring," she whispered.

"But he's staring himself," I said.

"He's a grownup," she said. "Not like you."

Turak was explaning to us bumpkins, in an self-important drone: "When a girl reaches the age of her initiation, she must come to the temple of Ishtar and wait to be deflowered by the first man who desires her...."

"What's 'deflowered', abba?" I asked my father.

He slapped my face.

My sister began giggling. "You'll soon find out," she said.

My father grew very red. "Faster," he said to the litterbearers. "Faster. We don't need any of this heathen nonsense." And he flailed at the nearest one with a little lead-tipped flagellum. The slaves marched a little faster. They narrowly avoided a six-palanquin pileup with a little fancy footwork. The streets in Sumer were narrow, the buildings leaning inward, mostly in that white adobe style you still find in places like Tunisia.

Enkidu's funeral was an obstreperous affair, with bevies of women beating their breasts, and slaves, animals, ex-wives and catamites of the deceased being drugged and buried alive along with him. We, the visiting diplomats, watched the whole thing from a specially erected pavilion. We caught a glimpse of Gilgamesh, the god-king, but he was wearing a golden mask of grief, so we couldn't be sure if it was really him or whether it was some priest, subbing for him so he could sulk in his private apartments.

As is customary at funerals, the last clod of earth shoveled over the dead (and the half-dead) was the signal for a different mood, a kind of desperate merrymaking. There was a banquet to be held in the throneroom, and yes, there were plenty of dancing girls and all sorts of food and drink. Gilgamesh didn't bother to show up.

My father drank deeply of the wine, which was cooled with snow that had been brought down by runners from mountains, they said, a thousand leagues away. He was in a foul mood. Ambassador though he was, he wasn't being well treated. And the incident at the temple of the goddess seemed to have put him into a severe depression. My sister was deep in conversation with some Akkadian prince, which didn't please my father either. I loved my father, and I hated to see him this way. So I took it upon myself to sit by him, to fetch him a fresh beaker of wine now and then, and to cool his brow with a piece of damask dipped in spring water.

Turak, our erstwhile guide, had taken a shine to my father, for some unearthly reason. Perhaps it was because he was being snubbed by everyone else at the party. In between gnawing off great mouthfuls of leg-of-lamb, he insisted on informing us who all the guests were. Not that I really had any idea what was going on.

A long time after sunset, when half the guests were already sprawled out snoring on pillows stuffed with rose leaves, there was a brief commotion. Conch-trumpets blared. My father rubbed his eyes and bestirred himself a little. Several acrobats and fire-swallowers entered the throneroom, followed by slave girls strewing flower petals.

I overheard some of the guests talking: "The impertinence! Getting here this late, how can they get away with it, not even showing up at the funeral itself," and other gossip that I didn't understand. It was at that point that the mystery guests entered the throneroom.

One was a young man dressed as a woman, his hair delicately hennaed, his eyebrows brushed with kohl. "Abomination!" my father whispered, and tried to cover my eyes again; but I was able to peep through his half-separated fingers, and I thought the man-woman was really very goodlooking. "Such a creature has no right to exist on this earth! It is an abomination; it should be stoned to death."

"Nonsense," said Turak. "You Hebrews are so provincial. That is the King of Sodom, you ignoramus. Their priest-kings take the form of the Sacred Hermaphrodite out of respect for their god, who possesses both sets of genitalia; he is said to have impregnated himself, grown himself inside his own womb, and at length given birth to himself."

"What arrant superstition," said my father.

"You think your little tribal thunder-god, whose name you don't even dare utter, is any more believable?" Turak said, laughing. My father simply fumed.

At that point, I took a good look at the other guest. She had long black hair that went all the way down to her knees, and it was artfully draped around her body. To my amazement, I realized that it was the only thing she was wearing, apart from her earrings. Her skin was as pale as the snow on the mountaintops on a moonlight night; her hair was blue-black, like a raven's feathers. Her eyes had an unearthly glow about them, and when she smiled something glistened in her mouth, shiny and pointy-sharp.

I found myself staring at her. Amazingly enough, she appeared to be staring at me too. I saw her whispering to some confidante, perhaps trying to find out who I was.

I did not have to ask; Turak was already explaning. "The Queen of Gomorrah," he said. "The less said about Gomorrah, the better."

I went on staring at her, and I thought I could hear her voice inside my head, murmuring of cool springs and fragrant gardens, telling me of a land of eternal starlight, or perpetual night.

Later in the evening, I found her seated next to me. I didn't see her move across the room. She touched my shoulder. Her hand was icy. She said, "You are beautiful, daughter of Lot. You are wasted on these ill-mannered nomads. One day you should come to my city.

Thenyou'll know what love really means." And she smiled, and I turned to see my father scowling.

That was the night my father stumbled onto my pallet, his breath sour with alcohol and vomit. That was the day he caressed me with gnarled hands, tossed aside the coarse woollen covering, and lay next to me, touching me in places where no man had ever touched me. I lay awake, but dared not open my eyes. My father started to speak in a harsh, strained whisper: "Oh, Shoshana, I'm a wicked man, I'm a man who's drawn to abomination and darkness, but you shouldn't have stared so hard at the sacred whores of the goddess you bitch cunt whore look what you're making me do you bitch oh, oh, Shoshana, I can't help myself, you're such a fucking bitch you cunt you whore...."

Oh, god, it got worse. He ripped open my sleeping robe. I felt something hard drive into my body. I felt torn up somehow. I knew I was bleeding. I couldn't help crying out. My father whispered, "Go to sleep, go to sleep, nothing's happening," and at that moment he began to shudder and — most heinous of all — began to utter the sacred Name of our tribal thunder-god — "YHWH!" he cried out. "There, I've done it, just as I do it every night with the other bitch, and you haven't struck me down, you haven't turned me to stone, you haven't seared my abominating body with a lightning bolt, YHWH YHWH YHWH," and each time he screamed out that word he thrust deeper into me and once I opened my eyes and I saw that his eyes were the eyes of a madman and I thought to myself, This is the worst worst moment of my life and I wish I could go away far far away....

It was in that moment that I saw, in my mind's eye, the

face of the Queen of Gomorrah, saw her thin-lipped smile, saw her eyes grow wide and bloodshot, and heard her voice inside my head again, speaking of endless night. And I was comforted.

In the morning, there came gifts to my father's tent from the court of Gomorrah: a pound of salt for my father, and a terracotta doll for me. My father made me smash the doll in little pieces. "It's a graven image," he told me. He divided the salt into several pouches and put it away in a cedarwood chest. "Salt, after all," he said, "is the most valuable thing in the world. It's only because of salt that the people of Sodom and Gomorrah can be so arrogant, so blatant in their public disregard for propriety and godliness."

Nothing was said about the happenings of the previous night.

***

So far, it was all very 90s. The drunken father sneaking into the bedroom, the silence the morning after, the blame being cast on the child, even my father's little attack of Tourette's syndrome while he was violating my innocent person. Nothing, you say, has changed in five thousand years. But that is not quite true.

We had no support groups in the Bronze Age.

We had no runaway hotlines, no battered children's shelters, no psychiatrists, no Hard Copy. I had no way of knowing that my fate was not unique. My mother was dead, and there was no one else I might consider talking to; my sister was moody and self-involved, and seemed to have a boyfriend in every oasis, despite my father's efforts to keep her chained to the hearth.

My father's visits became more frequent.

I think I was about ten years old, although we measured time differently in those days, not being tied, as the city people were, to the cycles of moon, sun, and river. Our tribal god had rejected agriculture in favor of the hunter-gatherer lifestyle — that's why my great-uncle Cain had been exiled from the fold — but that's why our people had become so backward, wandering the desert instead of living in shiny cities, lacking a real notion of the passing of time. But I did grow taller, and my father grew crazier.

One night —

It was after one of my father's nocturnal visits. It was full moon night and I suppose I couldn't stand the pressure anymore, so I ran out into the night — a bitter cold night as many desert nights are — wearing only a shift of Egyptian linen. The stars put me in mind of the Queen of Gomorrah. It was bitterly cold, and I hid from the wind by snuggling against a line of tethered camels, comforted by their toasty, rancid body odor.

Presently, I saw that the patriarch's tent was aglow, and that shadowy people were moving around inside. I got curious. I crept along, lifted the tent-flap, and crawled among the sheepskins that were draped over everything. There were voices, and they were coming from deep within.

Flickering light, too. Around me, Abraham's wives and concubines huddled together for warmth. I moved toward the inner tent, conscious that I was doing something very wrong, very unwomanly; the Hebrews were perhaps the most chauvinistic culture of that period, and we girls were certainly not allowed to trespass into the holy of holies.

The patriarch was sitting on a woven reed mat, and my father was with him. In the background, surrounded by veils, were the emblems of our tribal thunder-god, which few had ever gazed upon and lived, which had been ours ever since the big flood.

I watched them, knowing that I'd probably get a severe whipping if I was caught — Dr. Spock had not yet informed the world's parents about how traumatizing it might be to beat your children — and I saw the patriarch in a foul mood, rubbing his beard and now and then glancing askance at the holy of holies, as though afraid it might emit a thunderbolt at any moment.

"I've been hearing voices again," said Abraham. "Voices from, you know, behind there." He pointed to the sacred veils.

"What are we supposed to cut off this time?" said Lot. "Our dicks?"

I narrowly avoided giggling. My father was returning to Abraham's recent vision in which our god told him that all the men would have to slice off their foreskins as a sign of servitude to him. Well, it could have been worse; some gods require the sacrifice of one's firstborn, and others expect female clitoridectomy; I hoped that idea had not occurred to the patriarch.

"No, no," said Abraham. "It's Sodom and Gomorrah. We have to teach them a lesson."

"So what is the Lord God planning to do?" my father asked. "Have us take over the salt mines?"

"Our Tribal Deity," said Abraham, "is going to blow those twin cities off the face of the earth as a punishment for their iniquity." He said it as casually as you or I might talk about snuffing a candle. That's what made him the patriarch, you know; he could make the grandest of concepts seem almost trivial; crossing Sinai was like crossing the street.

"Quite right," said my father. "Nothing but abomination. Should have taken care of it during the flood."

I hadn't realized that our patriarch's voices were now claiming responsibility for the great flood that almost wiped out Mesopotamia a few generations before. I wondered whether they'd be taking credit for creating the universe next.

Don't gape, Mr. Bigshot-Shrink. The world was a lot different then. Monotheism was still in the future. Every little society had its own god in those days, but no one had gotten around to claiming that other people's gods didn't even exist. That was a level of theological abstraction to which we hardworking nomads had yet to aspire.

"I want you to go to Sodom," Abraham told my father. "Scout the place out. I've told the Lord God that if you can ferret out ten worthy men in all of the twin cities, I'd like him to spare them the cataclysm."

"Good move," Lot said. "That way you don't lose face if — heaven forfend — no cataclysm actually takes place. Ten honest citizens won't be hard to find."

"True," said Abraham. "And while you're there, learn all you can about the salt business. You know, we're not going to be a bunch of desert-faring nobodies forever. One of these days, I see us taking over every city in the world — running the banks — the entertainment industry — taking charge, the way a Chosen People ought to take charge." I gasped. Another of his childishly simple, earth-shattering concepts. Talk about ambition! "Take your daughters," the patriarch continued. "Settle in. Keep an eye out for anything unusual. You'll be guestsof the King of Sodom, so you'll have diplomatic immunity. Try to keep kosher if you can. And whatever you do, don't go over to Gomorrah."

"Why not, patriarch?" said my father.

Abraham leaned over and whispered something in Lot's ear. My

father's eyes hardened; in the sooty light of the oil lamp he looked crazy, the way he looked sometimes when I sneaked a peek at him and saw him lumbering over me, sweating, in the night.

And once more, I thought of the Queen of Gomorrah, and wondered whether I would ever see her again.

***

Ur had been a dull city, all white and featureless. Sodom was beyond belief. Sodom had a night life — torchlight burning until the wee hours, taverns overflowing with wine. The salt mines had made the upper classes rich. People had slaves for everything. Even the public punishments were ostentatious — beheadings were accompanied with psaltery music and dancing girls, and whippings were performed by trained flagellants, wearing dark robes and golden goat masks. Nothing so simple or so interactive as a stoning.

Salt permeated the city. Their food was over-salted. The water held a hint of brine. Even the heaps of camel dung in the streets were encrusted with salt crystals. Salt caked the alley walls; you always saw a few dogs licking at the limestone.

Abraham had told us our host was to be the king, but at usual we were palmed off to one of his lower-echelon retainers; we were lodged in an apartment in the mansion of one of the royal salt accountants, who measured the salt into earthenware containers and employed a staff of six to tally the amounts on clay tablets. They went through a lot of tablets a day, and once I visited the archive, with itsstacks of cuneiform-covered documents. Being a girl, I could not of course read — those were chauvinistic times — but it was fascinating to stare at the little wedges, and wonder what they meant.

Gomorrah was dark as Sodom was colorful. Separated from its sister city by a narrow stream so briny from the nearby salt mines that no fish could live in it, Gomorrah was permanently in the shadow of a thundering mountain — the only active volcano in the region. The city's walls were black basalt; Sodom's were limestone. When any of the inhabitants of Gomorrah emerged, it was only at night. Sometimes they showed up at one of the nightly orgies which, as visiting diplomats, it was my father's tiresome duty to attend; but they never ate, and they never drank wine.

I suppose it was only inevitable that I should become obsessed with the idea of Gomorrah.

In the first place, I had been very strictly brought up. I knew nothing of fleshly things — strange to you, maybe, consider my father's now almost nightly invasion of my most private world — but think about it. We didn't have sex ed. in those days. I assumed, in my subservient way, that I'd been a very bad girl, and that I was simply getting what I deserved. It's not that surprising that I should become more and more drawn to that which was forbidden.

My sister Rachel, on the other hand, seemed to blossom in this place. The more my father came to me by night, the less depressed and moody she became; it was hard not to think there might be some causal connection between those two things. She took bellydancing lessons from one of the king's minor concubines (contrary to popular belief, buggery wasn't the only form of sex they practiced in that town) and soon became the life of the nightly orgies. My father never even bothered to scold her, though often, after she'd been particularly exhibitionistic, or ate too much barbecued pork, he would come home and beat me senseless with cedarwood cane he kept especially for that purpose.

I remember the cane well, because it had a curious knob in the shape of a dog's head, and it had come all the way from Troy. I also remember it because of some of the painful uses to which my father put it in those wee hours of the morning, sometimes not even bothering to anoint it with camel fat beforehand.

I don't want to dwell on it, but I think it's fair to say that I wasn't having a very good time in Sodom. If you check your Torah, the book of Genesis claims that "it" only happened once, that I got my father drunk, and that he never noticed a thing; well, that's what you get when the history books are written by male chauvinist pigs.

I started to wander the night.

It was safe to leave the apartments as soon as my father left my side; within minutes I would hear him snoring. My sister had taken to staying out all night, painting her face, and indulging in all the other Sodomite activities; my father no longer really gave a shit. Wandering alone in the streets, a young girl who had yet to even have her first period, I was self-conscious at first. But I found that if I kept to the shadows, if I darted quickly from alleyway to doorway, from pillar to gatepost, few ever noticed me.

Sodom was a tolerant city.

One night, I found the pit of discarded slaves....

It was by the eastern gate, the closest point in the city to Gomorrah. It was the stench that first attracted me. There was a temple dedicated to their hermaphrodite god by this gate, and a cloud of frankincense smoke, billowing out of the front portal, almost masked the odor of rotting corpses. The steps of the mini-ziggurat were lined with vultures. There was no one on the street, which was strange; in this town, no matter how late at night, you always ran into some drunken partygoer quirting his litterbearers, or a prostitute primping in a doorway.

Past the temple stood a low wall, and when I looked down I saw them: emaciated bodies heaped up, arms and legs and bony faces, staring eyes; in the bright moonlight the eyes glittered like polished onyxes.

Have you ever seen some of those holocaust photographs? This was just the same. Except that no one thought it particularly immoral. I gazed, but I did not condemn. We all had slaves. I was impressed at the quantity of the dead, the conspicuous consumption of the society. I was too young to feel much pity. But presently I heard the clatter of a cart, and I ducked behind a statue of Ishtar that overlooked the pit. An old man was pushing the cart, which contained a fresh load of corpses. He dumped them unceremoniously over the side of the wall, and left.

I heard a noise. Someone — or some creature, perhaps a jackal — was prowling through the piles of corpses. I heard the patter of its feet. Yes. Definitely an animal. It sprang from heap to heap, sniffing, searching for something in particular. I'm not afraid of jackals; they are cowardly creatures for the most part. He stopped now and then and howled. He listened. I froze. He ran up a body that was tilted up, arm hugging the lip of the wall, and now he was on the other side of the statue, a little upwind of me; I hoped the wind would not change.

Then it was that the eastern gate creaked open, and there came through the portal a palanquin completely draped in black. The litterbearers were all Nubians, and their loincloths and headbands were also black. I shrank back in my hiding place. The eyes of the Nubians were glazed, as though they had been drugged or in some magical trance.

They carried the litter to within spitting distance of where I was. I crawled between the statue and the wall, between the breasts of Ishtar. I tried not to breathe. The jackal was suddenly right next to me.

It snarled. I was trapped between the goddess's breasts. I could smell its hunger. It was salivating, shuddering. I didn't want to scream, but when it leapt up onto me and began tearing at my garments, I let out a startled whimper. Because there was something about the jackal that was a little like my father — the look in his eye, a faint whiff of desire — we did not know then about pheromones, Mr. Shrink, but we could certainly feel their effects. That animal was embracing me in a parody of what my father had done that night, itself an obscene parody of love.

When the jackal bit me on the breast, I did scream, and then I felt powerful arms pulling me out, felt the sharp stone graze my elbow, found myself suddenly face to face with the Queen of Gomorrah.

The jackal was whimpering. I saw a deep red scar on its

back, and the queen was handing her gold-handled whip to an attendant. "You should know better," she said to the jackal. "Roaming the slave-pits at night! Stupid, stupid, stupid."

In the moonlight, losing my terror, I saw that there was something human about the jackal. It was cowering from the queen. At length, it slunk away. She turned to me. "We meet again," she said, as though she had been expecting it all this time. "I see you have been bitten. Are you ready to come to Gomorrah?"

"My lady," I said,"the patriarch forbade us —"

She laughed. The sound was like the clatter of clay pots. I felt a certain comfort in that laugh. I dared to look her in the eye. I saw myself, twin images of a girl in those eyes, and I thought: How young I look, how vulnerable, how sad. And I knew she was thinking the same thing.

"You mustn't let men do all your thinking for you, Shoshana," she said. "Men see everything in black and white, and always in an adversarial relationship. Good and evil, man and woman, life and death. There are, you know, twilight areas where opposites intermingle, shadowlands you might call them. Sodom is such a land: in Sodom, the distinction between man and woman is blurred, and that's what your father calls abomination. But in our kingdom, it is the line between life and death that is crossed, you see."

"What do you mean?" I asked her."How can something be both dead and alive at the same time?"

She touched my hand. Cold, cold, cold; I had touched a dead man before, and I knew that cold. "My daughter," she said softly, and I thought she was about to weep.

"I cannot weep," she told me.

"Do you read minds?"

"No," she said, "but after the passage of a few centuries, one learns to guess what humans think; their emotions skitter across their faces; you can smell their thoughts, sometimes before they even think them."

"Humans?" I said. "You speak as though you are not one. Are you a goddess?" I knew that the gods took human shape sometimes. Our own god used to take long walks in Eden with Adam and Eve, our forefathers.

"I am more real," she said, "than any goddess."

She lifted me to my feet — in my confusion I had fallen on my knees before her, as though she were that very goddess she claimed not to be — and caressed my cheek, my hair; her hand moved slowly down to the wound in my breast, an ugly welt that showed through the tear in my sleeping-robe.

"Oh," she said, and her icy fingers tensed a little, "I see that the vile creature has already ... embraced you. That was not according to my plan ... but never mind. It's time you visited Gomorrah."

She enveloped me in her arms. I flinched. Her skin was bitterly cold. I buried my face in her bosom, heedless of the burning iciness that seeped into my pores, that seemed to invade my very veins. Even this cold comfort was better than my father's hot embrace. She kissed my brow. It was as though she were branding me with the imprint of her frozen world. I knew then that I loved her. That was what I had felt when I first looked on her face, long ago, in the city of Gilgamesh.

"Did you like that kiss?" she asked me. "Is this what you have longed for, secretly, in the middle of the night — to be sucked into a world deeper than death, colder than the grave, darker than shadow?"

"I don't know," I said, "but I know it's got to be better than the world I know." And she drew me by the hand and led me to her palanquin; a slave made a back for me to step up; I reclined against cushions made of human skin, stuffed with the feathers of exotic birds; and I lay in the darkness and let the queen kiss me, again and again, not even crying out when her kisses drew blood.

Thus it was that I share "d the palanquin of the Queen of Shadows, and came to the city of night, and learned the darkest secret in the world.

***

Things became a little better after that. My father remarried — rather, he purchased a plaything from the slave-market, and scaled new heights of perversion and sadism with her. I never found out her name, never attended the ceremony, which was a Sodomite one in any case and therefore not actually binding on us. I suppose her name is of little interest; nobody thought it important enough to record in the Torah.

They left out my name, too, and I'm supposedly the ancestor of an entire race.

Gomorrah —

By day, a tomb. The basalt mansions, some carved out of the side of the volcano itself, were desolate. Volcanic ash lay over draperies, furniture, statues, dimmed the once-bright murals. The citizens of Gomorrah lay sleeping; some in a communal catacomb, a network of tunnels that burrowed into the mountain; others in splendor, in sarcophagi of granite or marble or pure gold. The houses were like tombs, their contents piled up; treasure-hordes were guarded by skeletons in armor; statues of gods and heroes lay in disarray; there was no food or drink, except for the occasional depiction on a mural. A smell of brimstone lingered in the air, perhaps because they had burrowed deep into the side of the volcano, exposing clefts that spewed out fumes of sulphur now and then

By night, the court of the Queen of Gomorrah was lavish beyond all I had seen in Sodom. As the sun set behind the volcano, the courtiers would emerge from their hiding places. The megaron of the grand palace was cloaked with cobwebs and carpeted with dust; it was hard at first to get used to the darkness, but when I did, I saw that a different light suffused these creature's existence. The phosphorescence of their skin, the dust-motes scintillant in the starlight, the silvery radiance of the moon over burnished mirrors of bronze — the flecks of gold dust on their black cloaks — the crystalline intensity of their eyes — all these things illuminated a world that never needed lamp or torchlight.

On the third night, the queen led me by the hand to a garden in the heart of her palace. It was overgrown with blackened, twisted vines; here and there, a red rose bloomed; and in the center of the garden stood a mirror-still pool, bordered by four dragons sculpted from lapis and malachite. Incense spewed from their jaws, a bitter odor, mostly myrrh, I thought.

"Your father," said the queen, "has a god who speaks from behind a curtain, through the lips of a befuddled old man. Would you like to meet our god?"

"I've never met a god," I said.

She chuckled.

"Don't be afraid."

She led me to the edge of the pool and told me to look

into the water. The water was quite still. And now, the queen took a pebble from a little basin beside the pool, murmured words in a mystic tongue, and cast the stone into the water. "Now," she said, "repeat after me — Dracula, Dracula, Dracula."

"What does that mean?"

"It is a magic formula whose resonance opens up a gateway from the present into other times, other places."

She cast the stone into the pool. I repeat the words; they rolled richly off the tongue; they were words of power; I shivered, trying to blame it all on the cold, for Gomorrah was a cold city, even in summer.

The water shimmered in the moonlight….

Then, kneeling over the edge of the pool, I started to see things. I saw a man on horseback, darkhaired, with a drooping mustache and a helmet of some unfamiliar metal. He looked out at me. I heard him whisper in my head: Greetings, daughter from the distant past.

"Who are you?" I cried out. "What kind of god are you, that condescends to speak even to an unlettered girl?"

I am your people's future.

"My people?" I said. "You hold the destiny of the Hebrews in your hands? But I thought that our tribal thunder-god —"

He laughed. "There are a people even more chosen than your own," said the god. "Believe me. You are the ones who will influence all the events of the future. Nations shall rise and fall; empires, religions, and races shall came to power and be overthrown. But behind all these great events will be yourselves — the eternal ones — the ones who have embraced the world of darkness."

I turned to the queen in disbelief."I don't understand," I

said.

"What is he telling me — that I will live forever?"

"If you take good care of yourself," said the queen. "We are not gods precisely; we can't change the laws of nature; there are ways to kill us. But there is no reason you shouldn't survive for a thousand years."

"The way people used to," I said, "before the great flood."

She laughed again. "How superstitious you are," she said at last.

"Images in pools — isn't that some kind of heathen superstition?" I said. "Our patriarch says we shouldn't trust gods we can see and touch, but only the invisible one behind the curtain in the tabernacle."

The queen said, "Let me tell you something of our god, then. He is not so much a god as a visitor from the future. The word of power came to me in a vision long ago, when I was still mortal. In his time, he is some kind of great king, a voivode. He is feared. He impales his enemies by thousands and dines while watching their death-throes. A great mage captured his spirit in this pool, so that we can speak to him through the chasm of time; to him, in the time beyond, it seems as though he is dreaming. Because to him we are figures of history and legend, he knows more about us than we do ourselves; to us, he can serve as a kind of oracle. If you want, ask him a question about your future ... it will come to pass, I promise you."

There was really only one thing I wanted to know. But I was afraid to say it out loud. I have not divulged my shameful secret to anyone until tonight. Oh, I wanted the god to tell me whether my torment would ever end, but to do so I would have had to confess that this torment existed. So instead I asked about something I cared far less about. "Are there," I asked the god, "ten upright men in all of Sodom and Gomorrah? My father is on a mission—"

Dracula glared at me across the gulf of time. "our father, he said, is wasting his time.

I said, "You mean that he might as well pack up and go home, that he won't find what the patriarch has sent him to look for?"

No, daughter of Eve, he said, I merely mean that his search has become irrelevant. There are some things even the gods have no control over.

The queen took me by the hand once more. "Talk to me while I bathe," she said, "and I will tell you more."

We went into an inner chamber hewn out of the basalt, and there she commanded an attendant to draw her bath, which was a curious thing; for there were twelve young women chained to columns, and the attendant bled each one into an earthenware pitcher, and emptied its contents into the tub. The victims were drugged, perhaps; they stared dully ahead, not seeming to care that their lives were being siphoned away from them. She stripped, stepped into the frothing blood, and began languidly to scrape herself with a lump of pumice.

I sat beside the bath, handing her cloths and unguents as she requested them, waiting. One always had to wait with vampires; they have so much time on their hands; they do not move that fast, unless it is to attack, immobilize, and drain their prey's blood. I tried making light conversation. "Among our people," I said, "when a woman has her monthly bloodletting, she takes a ritual bath, a mikvah, to cleanse away every trace of blood ... but you are doing the opposite...." She only smiled.

"Don't chatter," she said. "Enjoy the profound silence of night."

I listened. The room was quiet, save for the groans of dying slaves. The walls were thick. At first I heard nothing more. Then I realized I was hearing more than I had ever heard before. Somehow the acuity of my hearing had increased. I could make out individual crickets. A nightingale halfway down the mountain. I thought I could hear the grass grow ... and yes ... if I really listened ... there, there, my father's drunken snores, and the quick, sharp breathing of his Sodomite woman.

Finally, she said, "The god is right. You see, Shoshana, our mages have been studying the mountain for some years now, and we are certain that it is on the verge of erupting — in a matter of days."

So it had nothing to do with divine retribution at all.

"But what will you do about it?" I said. "Will your people pack up all your belongings and found another city somewhere?" If, indeed, the inhabitants of Gomorrah knew that they were going to be buried under tons of lava, why didn't they seem remotely worried?

"Oh, some of us undoubtedly will leave," said the queen, "but for most it will be at best a minor inconvenience. The mountainside is honeycombed with tombs. We will sleep a little longer than usual, perhaps, but what is a century or two, or even a millennium, to those who must contemplate eternity?"

"What about the Sodomites?" I said.

"Why worry about them?" said the queen. "When your farm's burning down, are you going to waste your time rescuing the cattle? There'll be other prey."

I still couldn't believe this, couldn't grasp the long view that the vampires took of history. The queen smiled sadly. She touched my cheek, my forehead. She was no longer cold; the blood had warmed her body almost to burning, and I winced; but then, when a rivulet of blood dribbled down toward my lips and I tasted the smooth salt fluid, I felt something I'd never felt before. Orgasm only hints at its intensity. I shuddered. The warmth shot down my throat and seemed to rush directly into my arteries. I could hear my heart pumping, could hear the river of blood as it gushed through the capillaries of my brain.

"YHWH!" I cried out. I was shocked at my own perversity. To let the sacred name pass my lips ... yet there was no thunderbolt. "What's happening to me? Have I become a vampire?"

"You are not completely changed, my daughter. But a time will come when the daylight will cause you grief...."

"The blood! The blood!" She gripped my wrists now and drew me into the tub of blood with her. She caught me in the slippery embrace of gore. Blood seeped into every orifice of me. I was on fire. The room careened about; everywhere I saw the lifeless eyes of the chained slaves. I could not tell terror from ecstasy. With a slender finger she traced on my young breasts the outline of an apple. With her other hand she plunged down to my most secret places, touched what only my father had touched before; but he had not sought to kindle any flames in me. The queen's deft fingertips skirted my nether lips, snaked upward to caress a certain mound that made me tingle and finally quake and scream, and I profaned the holy name several more times, heedless that if one of my people heard me I might well be stoned to death; I no longer feared death; I knew that the woman who held me in her arms was death, that death was a new way to say love.

Before dawn, I went once more to the oracle of Dracula. I threw in a stone and repeated the magic formula, and once more I gazed into the visage of the impaler from a future time.

Daughter, he said, I dream of you again.

"Show me this future they're talking about," I said. "I suppose it's too late for me now, there's no going back, I don't know if I've chosen wisely, but —"

The water rippled softly. The moon was obscured by the mountain. Incense rose from the brazier. Through the wisps of smoke, in the undulating water, dimly lit by candlelight and starlight, I saw vague images. I saw the volcano burst, the city buried, the people screaming in the streets. I saw new cities, always new cities, bigger, shinier, dirtier,more and more crowded. I saw wars that spanned whole continents. Death was everywhere. Dracula's own victims cried out from their spikes. I saw my own people driven from their homeland time and time again — from Egypt, from Judaea, from Poland, from a thousand places with unpronounceable names; I saw them die by millions; I saw a weapon that killed more people in a single hour than the entire population of our known civilized world; and I knew at last the truth of the legend of Adam, my ancestor and the patriarch's; that man is a fallen creature, that our god is infinitely wrathful, destructive, and uncaring.

The only light in the world's future came from a place of ultimate darkness...

I saw the Queen of Gomorrah emerge from a thousand-year slumber, shatter her igneous prison, break out of the walls of obsidian. I saw her in the night, her skin luminescent in the starlight. I saw vampires everywhere — though I could not know what the scenes represented then, I now know what I saw — Auschwitz — Hiroshima — London in the Black Plague — Naples during the cholera season — vampires. Standing watch at the foot of a cross where a man was tied up and nailed alive; ruling in the courts of Egypt and England, Constantinople and Kazakhstan. I saw vampires dancing in the neon night of a thousand cities. I saw vampires in theaters and opera houses, vampires in darkened cinemas, vampires feasting on the numberless hordes of humans who populated an exploding world. I even saw myself. Yes. Sitting in an art deco office of the future, pouring my guts out to a roomfull of strangers. No, I didn't understand any of these visions. It was a kaleidoscope of alien landscapes.

Daughter of Lot, the dark god whispered in my mind, do you like what you see?

I couldn't answer. I was bursting with new emotions. All my life I had hungered for something without even knowing that I hungered. The taste of blood lingered on my lips. I felt fulfilled. I wasn't just some insignificant female anymore. I had a destiny.

***

Two messengers were at my father's house the a few days later. The Septuagint calls them angels, but angelos just means messenger in Greek; those Greeks do have a knack for fancifying the mundane.

They came from the patriarch, who was encamped in an

oasis nearby. It was a day of tumult and festivity, the annual ceremony of their god-king's sacred marriage to himself, which was also the city's fertility ritual, signalling the commencement of spring. Drums, conch-trumpets, harps and dulcimers could be heard coming from every direction. People jammed the narrow streets; palanquins rammed into one another; merchants jostled one another as they peddled shish kebabs and wine.

A parade was streaming past our apartment; we sat on a balcony, watching it go by. Abraham's messengers were young men, twins, and very attractive; my sister Rachel had been making eyes at one of them all through breakfast, and now my father's wife was winking suggestively at the other as she broke bread and poured out salt.

In honor of the hermaphrodite god-king, it was the custom for the men and women of Sodom to cross-dress. It was not unlike the mardi gras in New Orleans; drag queens everywhere, and music pouring from every tavern; the only difference was the constant death-gurgle of the sacrificial victims from altars all around town, for the sacred hermaphrodite god was propitiated by the flaying alive of dozens of young boys and girls, mostly culled from the children of the slaves who worked the salt mines. The flayed skins were hoisted up on poles and carried aloft by dancers; the smell of death mingled in the hazy air with the tang of salt and the odor of sweaty bodies.

Abraham's messengers weren't particularly disturbed at the bloodshed per se; you have to understand that this was before our tribal god banned human sacrifice.

The patriarch's wife, you may recall, bore a child at a very advanced age; it was naturally incumbent upon

Abraham to sacrifice his first legitimate son, but one of those revelations from heaven conveniently intervened — that's how it is when you have a direct hotline to the Lord God — and soon everyone was denying that the Hebrews ever practiced human sacrifice at all.

It was the scale of human sacrifice that appalled the two messengers — I mean, this was their first time in the big city — and the stench was making it hard for them to keep their breakfast down. They complained loudly about the abomination of it all, and my father chimed in now and then in hearty agreement.

At that point, a group of revellers stopped beneath our balcony and started hooting and whistling at the two messengers. The celebrants were drag queens to the nth degree. One wore a flounced skirt in the Minoan fashion, with fake breasts made from two large conch shells; another was dressed like an Egyptian, with a wig, blackened eyes, a chain of scarabs around his neck that rested athwart another pair of artificial boobs, these ones made from gourds; a third was actually in the costume of a Hebrew matron, which is to say that she was very plainly and concealingly attired.

It was the pseudo-yenta who cried out, "Who are those handsome young studs up there in the apartments of the Hebrew ambassador?"

"Send the fresh meat down," said the one in Egyptian garb.

"Yes," said the Minoan, "we want them for the sacred fertility orgy."

"Is it true you Hebrews are all circumcised?" said the yenta. "Show us yours and we'll show you ours, honey!"

Lot cried out, "Abomination! You would practice your

craven lusts even upon the angels of the lord?"

They hooted and jeered, and the messengers looked suitably embarrassed, and Lot got up and did what every good Hebrew does when confronted with abomination; he rent his robes and howled. I was glad he did not put on this exhibition too often; with the amount of abomination in this town, he would have had to spend all our barter goods on clothes.

At length, the procession moved on. At noon would come the solemn nuptials of the god-king. I wanted to go to the palace to watch, of course, but my place was at my father's table, waiting on the guests hand and foot; even now, I was oiling their feet as my father discussed the salt business and how our people might want to get a piece of the action.

"What about the patriarch's ten upright men?" said the first angel. "How's that going?"

"Oh, it'll be fine," said Lot. "I got a list from the king's treasurer of the most honest men in the city — they pay their taxes, are faithful to their wives, and don't indulge in any more abomination than absolutely necessary — so we can easily pick ten at random."

"Good," said the second messenger. It was the politically correct thing to do, to satisfy Abraham's mysterious voices while simultaneously managing to do business.

"Daughter," Lot said — I honestly think he could not remember my name at times — "Hurry up and finish drying the guests' feet; you're so slow — are you sick?"

No, father," I said. "It's just the sun. For some reason, it's really hurting my eyes. I think I'm burning up."

"Not even that hot," my father said. "You'd think she'd never been reared in the desert at all, she's become so spoiled by their soft city ways," he went on, but it was true that I was finding the sun almost unbearable, and I was glad that I was able to crouch under the shadow of the breakfast table. "I'll write a note to the patriarch," he said, "and tell him the ten good men are no problem; he can call off the apocalypse. The Sodomites will no doubt be very relieved," he added, winking.

I don't know why I even opened my mouth. Girls are supposed to be seen and not heard. But I had a acquired a new self-esteem during my visits to the Queen of Gomorrah. I piped up. "Father, the volcano is going to blow any minute. I don't think you'd better find any upright citizens in this town. You wouldn't want the Lord God to make a mistake, now, would you?"

"What?" my father screamed.

"I know," I insisted. "I've been to Gomorrah. I've spoken with the Dracula oracle, the voice from the future. You've never spoken with any god; you just listen to whatever Abraham says; every little whim he has is the word of YHWH."

My father gasped to hear the sacred name pass my lips, and the two messengers looked very sheepish. My father's wife, knowing nothing of Hebrew customs, just looked bewildered.

It was my sister who shrieked, "You stupid little girl. Don't you know you can be stoned for saying —"

"And who's going to stone me?" I shouted. I got up, hurled the basin of expensive oil at the wall, quickly backed into the shadow of the doorway, away from the sunlight. "It's not like there's a couple of hundred tribesmen here to pick up rocks. I mean, look around you.

These people are civilized. They don't go around stoning people just for saying YHWH."

My father slapped me resoundingly. I tasted blood. And that taste rekindled my memories of the night I spent in the Queen of Gomorrah's bloodbath; instead of cowering and backing down, I got right in my father's face. His breath, stinking of wine and garlic, brought back a flood of memories of traumatic nights, and I shrank back, but only for a moment. I looked him right in the eye and said, "YHWH, YHWH, YHWH, father, I don't see any thunderbolts descending from the sky; if that was true, you'd be burned to a crisp by now."

That was how my father found out that I'd been conscious all those times, that I knew what he was, knew him to the core. He exploded. He started to slap my face over and over, and finally he shoved me through the doorway into the apartment. "Go to your room," he said, "and you will receive neither food nor water until you are ready to apologize."

"Go fuck yourself," I said to my father.

He just gaped. I started to laugh. For the first time I felt that I had power, real power; that I was a real woman and not some defenseless child. I could just imagine what the two messengers were going to tell Abraham when they got home.

***

By sunset, my father was more drunk than he had ever been in his life. I could hear him shouting and throwing things, and cursing at the messengers. With my attenuated hearing I knew everything that was going on; heard the wine splosh out of the jug, heard my father's heavy breathing, my sister giggling, my father's wife pacing back and forth in confusion.

I lay on my pallet, brooding. At length, my father stormed into the bedchamber. He saw me in the half-dark, thought I was asleep.

"Bitch!" he shouted. "Whore! I'll teach you your place. You think that you're a woman now? You think you can defy me, little girl? You think that because I've neglected you of late, I can't come right back and give it to you all over again?"

He hulked over me. Seized me by the shoulders. Out of force of habit, I squeezed my eyes shut, waiting for the invasion of his touch. Sweat ran over my shoulders, slicked my narrow breasts. He shook me. His fingernails drove under my skin and I could feel blood welling up, and the smell of my own blood maddened me.

I bit him.

He raised his hand to slap me down.

At that moment, the volcano began to rumble.

There came an eerie red glow through the window-slats. I caught a whiff of burning sulphur. I opened my eyes. I didn't care anymore. My father looked defeated, spent, consumed with inner torments I had never seen before. He let go of me and crumpled down to the floor.

Then he left the room. I heard him shouting. "Rouse the messengers! Tell them to get word to Abraham that ten good men could not be found in Sodom! Get our camels — we're getting out of the city!"

He did not even bother to summon me. But I crept out of bed, and I too began gathering up a few pots and some fresh bread out of the oven, and a basin full of salt. My sister and I worked feverishly together with a new kind of solidarity. I knew she had heard everything in my room;

she had a newfound sympathy for me. "You too, Rachel," I said softly.

"Yes, Shoshana; me too."

And we embraced; it was the first tender moment we sisters had shared in many years.

In the streets, the drunken revelry was still going on. Only a few were surreptitiously marching in the direction of the westerly gate. The volcano, I suppose, had rumbled before, without much effect. But now, as I looked eastward toward Gomorrah, I could see that the mountaintop was coated in brilliant vermilion, and that smoke was funelling up toward the moon.

My sister and I and my father's wife sat in a cart; my father drove the camel; the messengers, riding a chariot, were disappearing into the distance. We reached the gate; the gate-slaves opened it; we entered the plain; we moved on without speaking.

We were only about a mile away when the explosions began.

"Don't look back!" said my father to us all. "The abominations are being wiped out! Great is the Lord God, the Lord of Hosts! Holy is he, the Lord of Sabaoth! Don't look back or you too will be consumed!"

We were traversing a ridge now. Below us were the salt mines.

Slaves were still working them by torchlight, and overseers still stood with whips. The ground was quaking. We hastened. Our camels grunted.

"I have to go back," said my father's wife. "You think I want to live in a stinking sheepherder's tent for the rest of my life?"

"You'll die!" my father said.

She leaped from the oxcart and began running down the slope, toward the salt mines. Behind her, Sodom was in flames. The sky was black with ash. The lava was hurtling down the mountain now. The twin cities glowed. Even from this far I could hear the screams.

If we didn't hurry, we too would be buried alive. My father urged us on, but I stood and watched her. I knew that I was not wholly human, and that even if I was buried in the ashes I would find a way to come back.

I saw the earth open up. I saw the mines collapse. Slaves blowing into the air, arms, legs, decapitated heads flying. I saw Lot's wife, standing there with her arms outstretched, gazing at Sodom, saw the hail of salt and brimstone descend upon her, whiten around her, turn her into a statue in mid-scream. I felt my sister grab me by the arm and drag me back to the cart. Heard the wheels clattering, felt the cart bumping over the stones; at length, when the plain evened out a little, the rhythm of the cart put me into a deep sleep, and I dreamed of the Queen of Gomorrah, and of nights of blood and shadow.

***

We lived in a cave. My sister and I were pregnant; I died in childbirth and they walled me up in that selfsame cave and returned to the tents of the patriarch; by then the story of Sodom and Gomorrah and grown to — dare I say it? — biblical proportions.

Why, then, am I here? Listen. I've ridden into battle alongside Vlad the Impaler, stalked the catacombs of Rome for lost Christians, gorged myself on the battlefields of Waterloo and Gettysburg. But always I was haunted by my father's face: not only the face of rage as he violated me on countless nights, but also the expression of helplessness and defeat on the night I finally overcame him. I was alone for a thousand years, and then I encountered the Queen of Gomorrah at a party in Antioch; she smiled, we talked of old times; but you know, we had drifted far apart in that thousand years. Since then I have known crowned heads and white trash, presidents and slaves, and I feasted on their blood. But buried deep within me … somewhere … there's an angry little girl.

For a hundred bucks an hour, I want someone to hold her, soothe her, wipe away her tears. For a hundred bucks an hour, I would like to learn yo weep again. I've lived with this so long I don't know what I'd do if I could be cured, but I think the time has come for me to try.

Can you help me, Mr. Big-shot Shrink? Can you hold Shoshana's hand? Can you read her a bedtime story?

Can you love her?

This story ended up in *Valentine,* the sequel to my 1984 novel *Vampire Junction.* Although the novel is set in the rock-and-roll and movie milieu of 1990s Southern California, there are a number of flashbacks to the earlier lives of Timmy Valentine, the twelve-year-old rock star protagonist who became a vampire during the destruction of Pompeii in an arcane sex magic ritual in which he was castrated by two shamans who were seeking immortality.

In *Chiaroscuro* the setting is Rome of the early seventeenth century. The characters of Caravaggio and Cardinal del Monte are based on history, and though there are numerous details of my own invention, the lifestyle of this cardinal's inner circle, with its orgiastic meetings, sexual deviancy, and corruption, is well attested. It is also a fact that Caravaggio's well known painting, *The Martyrdom of Saint Matthew,* contains almost an entire painting underneath with a radically different structure. X-ray photographs show a nude angel in the front, right-hand foreground.

Out of the historical mystery of why the angel was deleted comes my fictitious inference that the angel was, in fact, the eponymous hero of my novel *Valentine.*

Chiaroscuro

Rome, A.D. 1598-1600

Out of the first rustlings of the forest leaves come whispered words, images, odors, memories in stark chiaroscuro.

... gutted, the Colosseum rears up over the makeshift shelters of the homeless ... a full moon ... Corinthian columns matted with decaying leaves … the heat heavy in the moist air, a rank perfume of cloves and rotting oranges and crushed rose petals and human sweat …

To the boy the place has a strange familiarity, yet he cannot quite place the meld of fragrances. The night is alive. Boys with torches race down steep cobbled streets to light the way for a cardinal in a litter. The accents are familiar, but the tongue is somehow no longer Latin. How many centuries has it been since Pompeii? The boy does not know. This time he has emerged from the forest with very little memory at all. He has slept for a hundred years or more. The dirt of centuries crusts his eyes. He is still of the night, of the forest.

He runs behind the chair as it weaves through unlit alleys. The litterbearers do not notice him. They see a dark creature, perhaps a cat, sniffing at their heels; they do not know he smells their very blood as it races in their veins. The night is humid and the cardinal heavy; the smell of age and sweat is ill disguised by perfume and incense, and his blood is sluggish. Curious, the vampire creeps closer. He springs into the litter, blending swiftly into the ermine fringe of the cardinal's cloak. The blood oozes in this man's veins. It does not tempt. It is tainted with alcohol and unwholesome diseases. Wine dribbles from his lips.

The cardinal closes the drapes of the litter. Leaning back against cushions of velvet and damask, he reaches into his cassock and masturbates. Catlike still, the vampire scurries behind folds of drapery. There is candlelight. Grotesque shadows against the curtains. The cardinal sighs and drinks more wine.

"Ah," says the cardinal, "peccavi, peccavi, semper

peccavi."

Should he feed? the cat thinks. But the thirst is still dull in him.

The road is bumpy. The cardinal's silver goblet falls from his hand and grazes the cat. He remembers how silver once sapped his strength. Now it seems to have lost its power. A crucifix, studded with amethysts, dangles from a chain around the cardinal's neck. No magic emanates from it. A bible, silver-clasped, with a cruciform intaglio set into its spine, casts no spell either. Have the symbols of religion have lost their ability to harm me? he thinks. There is something different about the world. He cannot tell whether it is himself — whether the unremembered trauma that sent him to seek refuge in the forest has inured him to the powers of light and darkness — or whether it is the world that has changed during the time he has spent in the womb of the forest — whether faith has been sucked from it, like blood from the throat of a beautiful woman.

Or it is both: the magic draining from the world, the light seeping into the forest of the soul.

They come to a stop.

The cardinal adjusts his clothing. He wipes away the last drops of semen with a fold of the cassock. He crosses himself. He kisses the crucifix. He places his hat on his head and whisks aside the drapes. The cat leaps out onto marble.

A forest of feet: the sandaled feet of the litterbearers, the dirt ground in, rank; the feet of attendants, stockinged and gartered; the feet of the cardinal, his boots fringed with dead animals's fur. Cold. The marble stealing the warmth from his paws. Row upon row of candles in the distance;

an altar boy slouches past, swinging a censer. The legs are all stock still, standing to attention, except for two that shift neurotically from side to side. He darts between the feet. Whispers and murmurs everywhere. As his senses become attuned to the vastness of the chamber, he hears from somewhere far away, the voice of a lone chorister, singing the same phrase over and over to himself: *Miserere mei, miserere mei.* The shuffling of feet and the rustling of vestments and the mutterings and coughs all meld into one cacophonous echo. It is a cathedral, but one so vast his head spins when he looks up.

"His Eminence," says one voice, piercing the hubbub "Cardinal del Monte."

He sees the cardinal, bloated as the setting sun, making the sign of the cross through the incense mist. His eyes are smarting from the fragrance. He slips away, his paws sliding on the cold smooth marble. He follows the music.

Miserere mei....

He focuses his mind on that musical phrase. Music is the one thing he can still grasp. Furtively he moves toward its source. There is an oak door, but it is simple enough for him to wriggle past the threshold where countless feet have worn a hollow in the stone.

He is in a vestry. Cassocks and surplices hang on pegs. The room is drafty yet windowless. The smell of children's sweat pervades the air. The singing comes from a boy who is buttoning his cassock. The voice is a boy's yet not a boy's; the boy's face is smooth, yet the eyes betray some ancient pain. He is older than he looks, the vampire thinks. He too has had his manhood ripped away. In the service of music. We do have something in common, he thinks, though he is only mortal. How they strive to prolong the transient, these humans, though all must end in dust.

Perhaps I can show him my true shape, he thinks, and already he is resolving out of the incense and the dancing dust-motes, naked as when he emerged from the forest. The dirt of death still clings to him, but he shakes it loose. Boldly he takes a cassock and surplice from one of the pegs and begins to put it on.

"Oh," says the other boy. "I didn't know there was someone here."

"People say I'm quiet," says the vampire.

"You must be new around here. I haven't seen you before, but if we don't hurry we'll both be late and we'll get whipped." For the first time the vampire notices a streak of dried blood on the back of the chorister's cassock. "My name is Guglielmo; who are you?"

He thinks quickly. What names has he overheard in the streets? "Ercole," he says, "Ercole Serafini."

"Hercules! What a name for such a pretty boy." Guglielmo laughs. "I'll call you Ercolino. You must have come with Cardinal del Monte."

"How did you know?"

"His Eminence always goes for looks before talent. I'll bet he bought you for twenty scudi from some old peasant in Naples ... you've been freshly castrated too I should think ... I can still see the pain of it in your eyes."

"*Neapolis* ... yes, Naples." Is is true , Ercolino thinks, that I once lived in that part of Italy. He does not tell Guglielmo that it was fifteen hundred years ago, in a city long since buried beneath the brimstone of Vesuvio.

"Put on this ruff," Guglielmo says, tossing him one from a chest. It is heavily starched and presses to tight against his neck. "And hurry."

"Where are we going?"

"Vespers at the Capella Sistina ... haven't they told you *anything?* Then a private party at the cardinal's in honor of the visiting Prince of Venosa — there's a pervert for you! We're to appear *travestiti* there — I hope they can find women's clothes to fit you. Do you sit on the *decani* side or the *cantores?"*

"Don't know."

"Decani then. That way you can stand next to me, on the south side of the nave. And you can avoid being noticed by Ser Caravaggio."

"Ser —"

"Michelangelo da Caravaggio. A mad painter who's the cardinal's pet monkey at the moment. If he catches sight of you he'll want you to pose. Something pornographic I'm sure, though there'll be some religious excuse for the subject matter. If he wants to paint you, you take his money but tell him to keep his poxy hands away from your delicate flesh." Guglielmo crosses himself.

"I'll remember," says Ercolino softly.

Guglielmo leans down and wipes a patch of dirt from his cheek with his finger. He snatches his hand away. *"Maledetto!* Cold!" he says, blowing on his finger. "You've been down into the mausoleum, all that marble, those freezing sculptures of dead popes, they have sucked the life from you...."

Ercolino smiles sadly.

"Would you like to look in the mirror before we go?" Guglielmo says.

"No ... thank you ... I don't like mirrors."

"Come on then. There's over a mile of corridors to run

down before we reach the chapel.".

***

He stares upward from the decani choir stalls to the finger of God, the still center of the arc of the ceiling of the Capella Sistina, the moment of creation. Guglielmo whispers in his ear that eighty years ago a man named Buonarroti spent years painting that ceiling flat on his back. The boy continues to stare even though they are all kneeling, eyes downcast, murmuring the paternoster.

Our Father? he thinks. Surely not *my* father.

The boy gazes upward at the face of God. Is it only the painter's artifice, or has God changed so much during the time the vampire slept? Is that not a human God, who bears more than a passing family resemblance to Adam? Ercolino thinks: they are reflected in each other, God and man. This is a new thought for him. If even the highest, the most remote of supernatural beings, has become a little human, has the same thing happened to him? For the spirit that breathes life into the boy who calls himself Ercolino Serafini itself draws life from the collective terror in men's hearts.

I have seen God so many times, he thinks. I saw him in the eruption of Vesuvius, in the eyes of the statue of Capitoline Jove, in Bluebeard's madness and in countless icons and crucifixes, a creature conceived in pain. Other people's father, not mine. How is this God different? Could I have been bewitched by the dead hand of Buonarroti?

The choir rises. The boys cluster around an illuminated part-book which contains the notes for Prince Gesualdo's music. Ercolino is shorter than the others and squeezes in close to the parchment. A giant candle drips hot wax onto the page. He is unfamiliar with this method of notation, but it is not difficult for him to understand its principles. But as the music starts — it is the *Magnificat* – he gasps at its audacity. The melodic lines are twisted and fantastical. The harmonies are alien and abrupt. It is music that transforms itself before it can be grasped, and its eerie chords hang in the air, echoes clashing against echoes, like a series of unfinished sculptures....

Who can have written such music? It is not a perfect music. It is a music of anguish and uncertainty ... it is a *human* music. Again the vampire wonders whether it is he who has changed, or the world.

On their knees once more for a set of *responsoria,* he whispers to Guglielmo: "This Prince of Venosa, this Gesualdo — can you point him out to me?"

Guglielmo directs his gaze toward the altar, where there is a section reserved for the college of cardinals. Among the figures robed in crimson is a man dressed all in black. He seems sullen. He is fidgeting. Perhaps his own music has disturbed him. "They say he murdered his wife when he discovered her *in flagrante* with another man," Guglielmo says.

"Strangled her!" says another boy gleefully from the pew above.

"Nonsense — he ran her through with his sword — cut off the other man's balls, too," says Guglielmo. "And by the way, I'm sorry I said you had no talent. I'll never be a man, but I'm man enough to admit it when I'm wrong. You're well named, Serafini."

But Ercolino is not listening. His gaze has shifted to the man kneeling next to the mad composer. He is unkempt; he stares from side to side; his doublet does not match his cloak, and his left stocking is torn. He wonders who the man is, how he could be up there among the cardinals; he does not appear in the least bit embarrassed by his shabbiness.

"Don't look at *him!"* Guglielmo whispers urgently.

Too late. They have seen each other.

They rise for a reading from the *Book of Revelation.* It is a curious, stilted, ungrammatical Latin, he thinks, for he remembers well the severe cadence of that tongue as it was uttered by the pleasure-seekers at Baiae and the doomed denizens of Pompeii and the courtiers from the palace of the Emperor Titus.

"Look away!" Guglielmo says. "Nothing good will come of your attracting the notice of Ser Caravaggio!"

They look into each other's eyes. The boy knows what the man sees: a child, malleable, a sheet of virgin parchment — mortals have always seen him this way. He does not look away. The music begins again — it is the hymn *Ave Maris Stella.* Ercolino does not join in. He has smelled blood. Something has awakened the hunger, dormant so long. It is something about the man.

Suddenly he realizes why the man is so dishevelled. He has come from a brawl. His arm is crudely bandaged with strips of linen torn from a shirt. The blood is fresh and pungent. The odor slices through the incense and the scented wax. It is irresistable. The paean to the virgin swells; the voices of the choristers tremble with that hopeless passion only eunuchs can muster. But the cardinals are nodding off and the altarboys are half-drugged by the incense; it seems to Ercolino that only he and Caravaggio are truly alive at the moment. No time passes between desire and its fulfillment. Ercolino transforms himself into a fine mist and is wafted toward the painter amid clouds of incense. The man continues to stare at where Ercolino stood. But he is already at Ser Caravaggio's side, ripping at the bandages with his cat-claws, for all the painter can see is a dark furry creature lapping the lifeblood from his wounded arm. He closes his eyes. He smiles. He knows it's me, Ercolino thinks. He *knows!*

He feeds now. Blood spilled in violence tastes sweetest; sourest is the blood of the bedridden. This is an angry blood, a blood full of the spices of heightened emotions; it is the blood of an artist. The vampire exults. The warmth floods him. He drinks deep. He tears at the flesh, he thrusts his cat's tongue deep into riven muscle. Caravaggio murmurs. He utters a single sharp cry of pain or ecstacy and then snaps out of his rêverie. He has ejaculated. He moves his hand to cover the stain on his codpiece. The incense masks the smell of semen, but the vampire can smell it even through the intoxicating fragrance of fresh blood. The painter glances shiftily about him. The cardinals are snoring; Gesualdo is scribbling on a scrap of parchment.

Caravaggio laughs out loud. The cat mews and leaps off his arm, nestling between the brocade of his jacket and the dark oiled wood.

"Who are you?" says the painter. There is wonder in his eyes. Has the illusion slipped? Has Caravaggio seen his true form? He wrenches himself back into the catshape. He gazes up into the painter's eyes. He stares past those eyes into the eyes of God the Father.

I am a cat, he thinks. *I am a cat.* He does not think Caravaggio is convinced. How can that be? A few times, an innocent has been able to see through the illusion. A child who has not learned to separate the inner and the outer worlds — a village idiot perhaps — these are the only humans capable of seeing his true form. They, and the beasts of the forest in whose shapes he cloaks himself. He knows that the painter is not an innocent.

The cat retreats into the fog of incense. Panicking, he springs from the pew and swirls into the mist, resolving himself once more at the side of Guglielmo, picking up the *Ave Maris Stella* in mid-phrase, melding seamlessly into the arc of the music.

Without looking back he knows that the man is still staring at him.

I'm afraid, he thinks. I don't want to look back. When you drink someone's blood, there's a bond. It is the bond of hunter and prey, the love-death dance of the world. But with this man I don't know if I'm hunting or hunted. I'm afraid, he thinks.

But at last, with the borrowed life-force racing in his veins and lending him the illusion of warmth, he gives himself up to the music. The music soars. It is the music that allows him to pretend he has not lost his soul.

He sings.

***

The apartments of Cardinal del Monte: the announced entertainment is a masque penned by the celebrated poet Torquato Tasso. The boys are to appear only in the fourth act, as a chorus of odalisques, for the setting of the play is the seraglio of a Turkish pasha, and the plot, such as it is, concerns the efforts of Dionysus, a Greek mage, to rescue his beloved Francesca from concubinage and a fate worse than death. It slowly becomes clear that the performance is in fact a vicious parody of the poet's work, and that some wag has simply taken the noble Tasso's drama *Aminta* and cleverly turned it into a trivial tale by changing the names and bastardizing the rhymes. Double-entendres abound, as do references to Cardinal del Monte's none too secret fondness for the Turkish vice of sodomy.

Guglielmo and Ercolino have donned some androgynous tunics which bear little resemblance to the actual dress of Turkish harem girls. They have wreaths in their hair. They are there to mingle with the cardinal's guests. There are few women. There are many princes of the church, reclining on plump silken couches or sprawling across the floor like scarlet tents. There are dandies. There is a withered duchess whose face has been powdered to a marmoreal whiteness. The conversation is carried on in whispers and titters. Now and then one of the guests looks about him warily. They seem to live in terror of some scandal.

The walls are covered with artwork, but all of it is concealed with drapes. There are statues too, but they too are covered up. The apartment smells of the oranges stuffed with cloves that the rich carry on their persons whenever they must venture out into the streets, to sniff whenever the stench of putrefaction becomes too suffocating.

Cardinal del Monte sits on an overstuffed throne, a page boy on his lap. The boy is singing to the accompaniment of a theorbo. He cannot keep in tune because the masque musicians, sawing away at their viols from the next room, are in a different key. No one is watching the masque anyway, except for Prince Gesualdo, who squats on a stool with a bottle of wine in his hand.

"They'll be going on till dawn!" Guglielmo whispers in Ercolino's ear. "But with any luck, after we muddle through our little production number, we can slip away. I know a good shortcut to the choristers' dormitory."

"I can't stay until dawn," Ercolino says. He hopes he will not have to explain.

The cardinal is laughing. The throne's legs squeak against the marble as he shifts his bulk. *"Per bacco,"* he shouts, "the ancient Romans with their orgies were never as decadent as we!" The audience claps as though his utterance were a veritable pearl. But Ercolino thinks: If only they had seen what I have seen. After fifteen hundred years, the past seems more present than ever. "More wine!" the cardinal shrieks, "and after we have become very, very drunk, perhaps a peek at my secret paintings!"

Collective gasping in the audience. The secret paintings are what they have really all come to see. Ercolino sees Guglielmo chuckling to himself.

"Why, what is in those paintings?" Ercolino asks him.

"Street urchins masquerading as heroic figures of myth and scripture," says Guglielmo, "and all, of course, without a stitch of clothing. Oh, there are nymphs as well as shepherds; the cardinal knows his own tastes, but he has something for everybody."

Coyly Guglielmo adjusts the folds of his tunic so as to conceal as much as can be hidden with so skimpy a sheet of cloth. He straightens the wreath in his hair. He makes an attractive girl, Ercolino thinks, when he does not try to walk; his stride betrays him. Ercolino himself, though he has kohled his eyes and stuck a blood-red rose behind his ear, he feels no need to play the part of a woman. What is man or woman? he thinks. I am not even human.

Soon it will be dawn. The boy vampire has not yet slept since his emergence from the forest. He does not think the dawn will pain him as much as it used to. He is becoming inured to his own superstitions.

Cardinal del Monte has waddled off his throne. He has yanked the first curtain aside to reveal a startling Cupid, large as life . Attendants raise their candelabra. This is a brazen Cupid — one of the grubby children of the street, scrubbed clean and sporting a pair of ill-fitting wings. The child, still scrubbed, is right there — he is the one who has been sitting on the cardinal's lap. He giggles.

Another painting — the onlookers ooh and aah — depicts the blind prophet Teiresias as he gazes on the unholy coupling of serpents — the impiety, as the myth goes, causing him to sprout breasts and cursing him to live as a woman until the spell can be broken. Unable to control themselves at the sight, two of the cardinal's guests begin to couple themselves right there at the foot of the painting.

Cardinal del Monte trots off into the next chamber, where the depictions are still lewder. On a wall-sized canvas, an orgy is in progress; in one corner, a man in a flowing robe — an Israelite — views the scene with an expression of disgust; two *putti* hover around his shoulders, whispering into his ears. A muscular, winged youth stands beside him, brandishing a bejeweled sword.

"Ah," Guglielmo says, laughing, "the patriarch Lot and the Archangel Michael prophesying destruction to the Sodomites. The biblical subject justifies including the orgy."

"I see." He does not want to say that the orgy seems rather tame by comparison to what he witnessed during the heyday of the Empire. In fact, the proceedings at the cardinal's affair seem listless, the decadence selfconscious and contrived. He loses interest as del Monte moves on, whisking aside arrases lifting draperies. He is like an overgrown child, Ercolino thinks, this prince of the church.

He remembers a scene from the circus at Pompeii — a Christian being crunched in the jaws of a lioness. Others burned alive, crucified, raped to death by jackasses ... this is what they died for, he thinks. It is they who now rule in Rome ... and this is what they have become.

Inwardly he laughs. Perhaps the world is not so changed as he thought. Perhaps it is only me after all, he thinks. His mind floats ... he finds he has drifted unawares once more into the shape of the black cat.

It is good, he thinks. Good to forget being human, to partake once more of the forest.

The drunken laughter now comes from far overhead as he slinks across the costly Persian carpet stained with wine. In one room choirboys are giggling as they apply the feminine makeup of the odalisques. One room is empty save for a naked woman, pouting, in a copper bathtub. There is a corridor lined with busts and broken statues that seem to have been plundered from all the sacred places of the ancients. One room is hung with threadbare tapestries depicting the deeds of saints and sinners. A massive bronze Jupiter gazes down from a niche and he cannot help mewing a prayer in a half-forgotten language.

From behind a curtain he can hear a man singing softly to himself. *Miserere mei.* It is the same lilting strain he first heard from the lips of Guglielmo. He slithers past velvet into an inner room. Caravaggio is there. He is painting. A huge canvas dominates one end of the chamber, which is lit by row upon row of scented candles, like a church. The canvas is dark save for shafts of light that illumine the figures in the foreground. He sees St. Matthew, thrown onto the ground and about to be slain. His killer hunkers above him. A boy shrieks out in terror, while overhead, riding a whirlwind, angels watch, their faces impassive. Other figures are crudely blocked out.

Caravaggio works with profound concentration. He is clearly in terrible pain. He does not hear the mangled verse of Torquato Tasso or the jangle of the theorbo and the off-key choirboy. He is absorbed. He paints with deft flicks of the wrist, working one tiny area — the flesh-tones of a screaming child's face — over and over in infinitesimal gradations of color.

He still has not changed his clothes, and his blood is still dripping from his wound onto the marble. Blood runs onto his palette and streaks the pigments. He grimaces. Yet his wrist moves swiftly — it dances across the canvas to a music that the boy vampire can almost hear — the tortuous music of Carlo Gesualdo — the music of hell, the hell God made.

The hot blood wakes his hunger. Catlike he pounces. His paws slip along smooth marble till his tongue tastes blood again. Blood races through him like fire. Blood warms him into simulated life. He purrs.

As though in a dream the painter says: "Why do you stand over my shoulder? Have you come for me? Are you the angel of death?" Illusion is useless. The man has the power to see his true self. It is the same gift that has made him a painter, and the same gift that has made him mad.

"No, Ser Caravaggio, I am not the angel of death. I am Ercole Serafini, sir; I am a decani soprano of the papal choir." Only when he utters these words does he realize that this must be his new identity for a little while. The world has become more vast as well as more human. He must stay inside this microcosm until he has learned the new rules. "My friends call me Ercolino," he adds.

"Oh, beautiful and terrifying. Oh, but your eyes say so much more than do your lips. You are more than another one of del Monte's singing boys, bought from the slums, gelded by a cut-rate barber. I have seen you in dreams." He becomes animated. His eyes shine with passion and madness. "If I could only capture you on this canvas ... perhaps I'd be less afraid then." And he has not even looked at Ercolino yet! He has only seen him ... reflected in the oil of the painting, perhaps ... a reflection of one who can cast no reflection! Unless he is speaking to a creature of his imagination, an angel of his dementia.

"Why are you afraid?" Ercolino says.

He puts down his paintbrush for a moment. "Oh, it is the fever," he says. Beneath the tangle of beard, Ercolino can see that the skin is soaked with sweat and cracked and caked with pus. Caravaggio is ill. His blood is almost at boiling point. It is a sweet blood, made tart by the ineffective possets of the cardinal's resident quack.

"So much darkness," the boy says, looking at the painting. "And the light, painfully bright."

"But life itself is *chiaroscuro,*" says the painter, "a perpetual darkness leavened only by the lightning of love, inspiration, agony."

"You're not at the revels with all the other guests, Ser

Caravaggio? I've been told you're a lover of pleasure, a sensual man."

"Oh, no. They keep me here, the trained monkey, the caged artist. What would I do at the party? Oh, but they love my crude ways. I am so entertaining. Tell me, boy, when you sing, don't you feel like a whore?"

"I don't know."

"Well, just look at you!" He turns to the boy vampire. His blood stains the boy's lips. How strange I must look, the boy thinks, in my preposterous costume, a sexless creature radiating the sexuality of a borrowed gender. "Ah," Caravaggio says, "but you *are* the death-angel I've been dreaming of. You must come to my studio in the morning; I'll pay you half a scudo a week for your pains, until the picture is done. And meals, of course; His Eminence has supplied me with an excellent cook until such time as the *Martyrdom* is done."

"I can only come at night," says Ercolino, "and I won't need food."

"No, of course not," says the painter. "But can man live on blood alone?" He does not smile, but his eyes hint of mirth and irony.

"I can."

"But soon my wound will heal."

"You will have other wounds."

"Yes."

He hears the strains of the ode of the odalisques from the cardinal's private theater. "I must go," he says. He backs away, unwilling to look away from the unfinished painting. Its beauty is yet unborn; it is a cadaver with no heart, no blood, like a hungry vampire on a dark street corner.

"Give me the rose," says the painter. "A pledge." Unasked, he plucks it from the boy's hair. A thorn jabs his finger. Blood spurts; he seems to relish the pinprick. If the boy does not go soon he will have to feed again. The hunger is always there.

The boy escapes, transforms, darts through the mass of satiated flesh toward the candlelit theater to take his place with the choir of unmanned youths. The song of the odalisques is silly and though he has never rehearsed it it is simple enough for him to join in in the monotonous refrain:

Amor, amor, amor,
Vittorioso amor.

***

A single swath of brightness sweeps across darkness. Ercolino stands half in and half out of the light. False wings sprout from his shoulders. He cannot see the painter's face. Only the rapid motion of the brush, shadow dancing against the far wall, the plaster peeling, a cockroach circling a wine bottle.

But now and then he hears Ser Caravaggio's voice, whispering to himself: *my love, my death.* He wonders what the painter means. The man will not let him see the canvas. The boy stands in the light and the shadow. He does not feel the cold because he is himself the source of the cold. It is high summer and a hot wind blows from Ostia and the stench hangs heavy over the sewer outside the window. But the room is cool. The boy holds a pose of marmoreal stillness; the feathers shiver, but he does not; he does not even breathe; a rancid sweetness hangs in the air; a dew has formed on his pearl-smooth skin; his eyes are innocent of feeling.

The shadow of the paintbrush moves feverishly back and forth along the wall. *My love, my death* – what do those things mean?

"Do you know why you cannot see me in mirrors?" says Ercole Serafini.

"No, tell me," says the painter from behind the canvas.

"Because I am myself a mirror. Of myself I am nothing. When you look at me, you see only yourself, your shadow-half, the part you do not wish to see."

"Philosophy," says Ser Caravaggio, "don't speak to me of philosophy. I get enough of that from those fucking cardinals. Philosophy is the handmaiden of sodomy." He flings his paintbrush across the floor. He downs a quarter of the flagon in a single gulp, cockroach and all.

The boy has not even breathed.

***

"Why do you call me the angel of death?" he asks the painter. "I am no angel, and I am not death."

"Don't speak to me! I'm making the lightning dart across your eyes. I'm making your glance arc over the dying saint toward the portrait of myself I have put in, peeking timorously from an alcove. No, don't say a word. Don't move. Don't even breathe. Be. *Be.*"

***

He has come to the painter's apartments every night. Every night he has drawn a little blood, just enough to take the edge off his hunger; every night he has stood in the corner, half in, half out of the shadow, wearing nothing but the harness to which are attached two flightless wings. Sometimes he sings. Before dawn he returns to the dormitory where the choristers sleep, three or four to a bed; he lies, sleepless, next to the snoring Guglielmo, waiting for the bell that will summon them to breakfast and to matins; he is shunted from service to service, down dark hallways lined with ancient sculptures pilfered from the temples of pagan Greece and Rome; he never encounters the sun, though Rome in the summer is so sultry that the very stone of the walls sweats. Now and then a shaft of sunlight streams in through a chink in the ceiling, or into an atrium, or through an open window; the sunlight does not burn him any more. He has ceased to believe in good and evil; light does not kill him, night does not nurture him. He has seen too much of the darkness in men's hearts to be affected by their folly, their superstition.

In the hour before the dawn he settles on the cold marble like dew; he resolves into his familiar shape, tiptoes toward the bed. The smell of eunuchs sleeping is different from the smell that rises from the beds of whole men. The air is innocent of the pheromones of arousal or the scent of drying semen. There is a sweetness to their slumber; their sleep is the limbo of the unbaptised. Ercolino stands for a moment in a pool of twilight, not yet quite substantial. It is at that moment that Guglielmo pounces on him. When the eunuch's hands touch the icy flesh they quickly let go.

"Ercolino, Ercolino!" says the chorister. "I've been spying on you at night. Cardinal del Monte pays me. He wants to know all about you."

"You shouldn't. Sometimes it's hard to follow me."

"I've seen you go to the painter's house, the one I warned you against. I've climbed up the wall and stood on tiptoe on the shingles and seen you drink the man's blood … what does it mean? I never see you eat or drink. Ercolino, you're not human, are you?"

"Caravaggio calls me his angel of death. But that is his

own imagining. I am what people make me."

"I've heard about creatures like you. You are immortal. You were here before our Lord walked the earth. When you take enough blood from a man, he becomes immortal too."

"Half-truths," says Ercole Serafini, thinking of the painter grinding his very blood into the canvas, wringing his soul into the pigment.

"I want to be immortal too, Ercolino. Make me immortal."

"You don't know what you're asking."

"But I think I do. I think you are a vampire. I think I have seen you sucking the blood from the painter's fingers as he closes his eyes in ecstacy. There is something Satanic about you. Such beauty can only come from evil, put here to tempt men. Am I wrong?"

"You don't really believe that, Guglielmo." Though the room is dark, the boy can see with the clarity of one born from darkness. To him it is as though the chamber were awash with a soft sourceless light. Guglielmo only thinks that the shadow masks his emotions. The light that comes from the shunning of light shines so fiercely that it betrays every flicker of doubt in the chorister's face. Ercolino knows that his friend has seen something; he knows he does not understand what he has seen, and that for him all is confusion and terror and the yearning half-remembered from the time before he was unmanned. Ercolino says, "I can't give it back to you."

"I don't want that back," says Guglielmo, but the boy knows he lies. "I just want to be like you. And if I can't, then I will hurt you."

"I cannot be hurt," says the boy vampire. But that has

not been true for over a century.

***

The death-angel rears up from the shaft of radiance, his arm upraised, one finger pointing up to the sky. He is impassioned; there is a lasciviousness about his smile; the paintbrush has imbued his boyish musculature with a silky, sensuous sheen, as though it were kissed by moonlight. A line leftward from the crook of the painting touches the upraised weapon that will strike the doomed evangelist. A woman pleads, her arms reaching out toward the angels' knees; and old men look on, lugubrious and morose. To the far left, surfacing in abrupt chiaroscuro, is the face of a somber woman, her hand against her chin. Her emotions are unfathomable. Perhaps she is awed at the mystery of martyrdom; perhaps she is a little aroused at the sight of blood; perhaps, perhaps … it is the angel she sees. Perhaps it is he who stirs, within her, longings dark and profane. For the street-urchin curl of his lip, the insolent forwardness of his demeanor, the tantalizing *vade mecum* of his gaze, surely these do not spring from the divine in him, but from the earthly; perhaps the woman is perplexed that the eunuch of heaven is imbued with such sensuality.

The boy vampire hears the pause in the nervous rhythm of brushstrokes. Caravaggio has put down his brush and steps back to admire his handiwork. The room is full of dancing, flickering light; there are candles and oil lamps everywhere. Ercolino steps away from the wings, which have been attached to a free-standing metal frame against which he has been leaning, holding the same languorous gesture for about an hour.

A heavy arras has been drawn over the chamber's bay

windows, blocking the moonlight. The air in the room is stifling. The dust that dances in the dense and sodden air is peppered with powdered pigments. It is oppressive, but Caravaggio is oblivious to everything except the painting and the boy vampire.

"It is close to completion," the painter says, and drains the third wine bottle of the evening. The wine is sour and its vinegary odor pervasive. "Come, Ercolino, look at how I've immortalized you."

"But I already am immortal."

"My love, my death," Ser Caravaggio says. He always says this. Over and over he says it. "Yes, you are immortal, you beautiful child; you are immortality made flesh. Oh, it is a sin for you to be so beautiful; how can I dare to imprison such beauty in a cage of canvas, pigment, linseed oil?"

The boy laughs. "I am not imprisoned," he says.

He stands there, his expression a perfect vacuousness. He knows what the painter sees: a creature maddeningly erotic yet strangely inviolable. He sees the painter's gaze move downward from his unblinking eyes down to his unsmiling lips, the undefined musculature, the inhuman pallor of his skin, the flat and hairless pubis, the white scars of castration, the penis that cannot stiffen. Caravaggio's eyes are glazed from drunkenness and sleepless nights. The blood will be sour tonight from the alcohol, and sweet from the burning up of body fat; Ercolino smells the blood, and knows its composition intimately, as a wine-taster knows his vinyards and his vintages.

"Oh, Ercolino, I long to possess your body and yet … why do I find myself unable even to try? … Cardinal del

Monte sends over the pick of the choirboys all the time; he hired me, you know, because I … understand his tastes … I've had every homeless urchin in the street for the price of an evening meal … you, you, you … who come here willingly … not in fear of the Cardinal's wrath, not driven by greed or hunger … you I dare not have. Why do I fear you so much, my angel of death?"

"I have told you, Ser Caravaggio, I'm not an angel and I'm not death."

The painter's blood is racing. Yes, he can hear its music, joyous, like the rustling of mighty wings. The hunger wakened in him is akin to passion. I must feed, he thinks. I have stood here, motionless, playing at being his dark angel, creature of his fantasies. I have told him time and again that I am not what he wants me to be. It is always this way. Always I fulfil the dream-wishes of men, sometimes even their death-wishes; I can never be perceived as anything else. Perhaps I do not even have an independent existence apart from these mortal passions, the self-destructive yearnings, that men project on to me.

Oh, that music! It is the blood, responding to the hunger; that rhapsodic and chromatic surge of life's essence, driven by the rhythm of heart; oh, I am hunger, thinks the boy vampire, hunger is all I am. Oh, I must feed, I must feed.

Caravaggio says, "I am ready. Take me, dark angel of my passion. Is that not why you've come to me … to carry me to hell in some ecstatic transport of forbidden lust? You have already drunk my blood … now drink my soul!"

"I don't want your soul. I only want the blood itself."

"I demand that you take my soul!" the painter screams. He turns to void his bladder into a chamberpot. "My soul!" he cries again.

And he flings himself upon the boy, whose flesh is colder than marble. The boy reflects: To him, life and art are one; both are chiaroscuro, fragments of brilliance set against vast canvases of shadow. They are at cross purposes, and yet each feeds on the other.

Ser Caravaggio tears away at his own clothing, hugs the cool flesh with an ardor that cannot be quenched; he strokes and caresses, trying to waken a response that cannot come; he is on his knees before his dark angel, who is no spirit at all but the very opposite of the spiritual, carrion imbued with the illusion of life, carrion that thirsts so much for the life force that it drinks and drinks again and yet is never sated; oh, oh, I am carrion, Ercolino thinks, and bends down to sink his canines into the painter's shoulder, making him cry out with pain that is also lust. Ser Caravaggio sweats and moans but there is that about me which prevents him from becoming hard. What does it matter? Why should it concern me, the illusion that this poor mortal has fashioned for himself? Is he not prey? Is he not just a warm teat from which to suck the life-force? Oh, but the boy vampire is troubled where he was never troubled before. The encounter with Bluebeard has changed him utterly. Not long ago, he remembers, in England, I watched Kit Marlowe bleed to death in a Deptford tavern, and I did not even feel the hunger, not in the same way as before … the hunger was tinged with bitterness.

But here comes blood. Blood. Oh, oh, the blood … oh, it is warm, warm, warm … oh, it is a drug that feeds its own addition. Oh, yes, the bitterness that he has begun to feel is there too, but perhaps he is more used to it now. He tongues that gushing warmth. It tingles. It shoots into him and leaves him wanting more ... I could kill him, he thinks to himself. I could suck all of it out and still not be fulfilled. But I would kill his genius.

Caravaggio weeps. "I love you," he whispers.

What kind of love can this be? the vampire thinks. It is a pavane in which each partner dances alone. He sinks his teeth deeper into the painter's neck. His canines rend flesh now. The blood comes spurting. I must not take too much ... I must conserve ... gently ... gently ... the painter's body shudders with a terror that is like ecstacy.

They hear a tearing sound. It is the arras. It is ripped down, and two figures stand framed in the open window, one bulky and big-jowled, the other a slim and cowering.

"Shame, shame, shame, shame," says the voice of Cardinal del Monte.

"I told you, Your Eminence," says the voice of Guglielmo, "that the two of them were up to some vile perversion."

The boy looks up. His lips are blotched with crimson.

"Satanic blood-rituals," says the cardinal. "I tend to turn a blind eye at the vices of the flesh — ah, for is not flesh weak? — but heresy is another matter, isn't it, Guglielmo?" Guglielmo nods. "He has been a good spy, and well deserving of the extra scudi I have lavished on him." And the cardinal tosses him a purse, which the chorister pockets, never taking his eyes off Ercolino.

Who slowly licks from his lips the last traces of blood.

The cardinal and Guglielmo step forward. Del Monte, robed in crimson, each finger ringed with a different jewel, is shaking with hypocritical indignation; the eunuch Guglielmo looks at Ercole Serafini with trepidation and desire. Caravaggio sobs.

"You have drunk each other's blood, in savage mockery of the holy sacrament of the eucharist," the cardinal continues. "I witnessed it, and so did this boy. You're at my mercy."

Defiantly, Ercolino says, "He did not drink my blood, Your Eminence; I was the only one who drank. And not to mock the scriptures, but to fulfil a terrible need which is the curse of all my kind."

"And what *kind* might that be, boy?" says the cardinal.

Guglielmo crosses himself and looks away at last. "He promised me immortality if I would follow his dark ways … if I would sell my soul," he says. "He is a demon." The lie does not come easily; it is wrenched from him; Ercolino feels a certain compassion for him in his confusion.

"He is an angel," Caravaggio says. "He has come to foreshadow my death."

"Vanity, vanity, all is vanity," says the cardinal. He comes forward. His blood smells of cloves and garlic.

The cardinal glares at the painting. Caravaggio steps back. Somehow he seems lost.

Ercolino sees himself. Am I really this beautiful? he asks himself. He has never seen himself since his transformation, of course, since his world contains no mirrors. He cannot even see himself reflected in Caravaggio's eyes. The cardinal pulls a little hand-mirror from his capacious vestments and holds it up to Ercolino's face. He sees nothing, of course. He throws the mirror on the ground and the glass shatters. Then, turning to the table, covered with candles and with mixed pigments, he seizes the largest of the brushes, dips it in carmine, and proceeds to desecrate the figure of angel of death.

Caravaggio watches, stony-faced. An artist is little more than a liveried servant. He does not look away as the cardinal covers the angel's features with smears of red, as he daubs the crimson over the slender body. He takes particular pleasure in bloodying its genitalia. He laughs. He is as drunk as Caravaggio. He is as drunk with power as he is with wine. He laughs and laughs until Ercolino is afraid he will collapse in a stupor. But before he can do that, Guglielmo comes, supports him as he staggers back to the window; there is a basket and a pulley there. It must have been constructed just so the cardinal could spy on Caravaggio and play his little joke on him.

Just before he disappears, Cardinal del Monte says to Ercolino: "Go back to the gutter, *ragazzo;* we don't want any devil children in the house of God."

Gugliemo does not look into his eyes; Ercolino knows that he fears his silent reproach. If he were only to look, he thinks, he will see that I do not reproach him. They all grasp at me; when they can hold on to me, when they find me insubstantial as the air, they become angry; they turn their anger on me; even the cardinal.

The night air, muggy and oppressive, blows into the chamber. The candleflames waver and flare up.

"It is just as well," says Ercole Serafini to the painter. "I am not what you think me. Paint me out of the picture. Forget me. Let me step back into the *oscuro,* out of the beam of light."

Caravaggio seems stone sober now. He seems to be looking at the boy vampire in a completely different light. "You're right," he says. "You are no angel. You're just another one of those children of the streets, kinkier than the others, perhaps; you tricked me. I tricked myself. Go back to the gutter, boy."

"Addio, mio signore," says the boy vampire softly. Then he funnels into shadow and drifts down into the street below.

***

For many years he has haunted the back alleys of the eternal city. The city is rich in prey. It has been easy for him to hide in the squalor, in the shadows; like Caravaggio's chiaroscuro, it is a city where the bright places shine with the brilliance of the sun, and the dark places are utterly dark; where the marble still gleams on the walls of the Michaelangelo's Basilica of St. Peter, where prostitutes ply their trade in the shadow of the grime-crusted walls of the Colosseum, where the marble gleams no more.

He has had many names in the intervening years. Ercolino, Andrea, Sebastian, Gualtier, Orlando. He has lured countless travelers to their death, offering to show them the ruins of the Forum Romanum or Nero's Golden House, giving them instead surcease of feeling. He has been careful to kill cleanly and permanently. He needs no companions in the twilight world that he inhabits. He contemplates eternity alone.

One evening, strolling through the marketplace, he overhears the name Caravaggio. Pausing to listen to the chatter of apprentice artists, he realizes that the *Martyrdom of Saint Matthew* has finally been completed; that tomorrow it will be unveiled at the Chiesa di San Luigi die Francesi. It is not far from the market. He is seized by a need to see what has become of the painting, which he last saw blotched by the cardinal's wrath.

His form blurs, shimmers, condenses into the familiar

black cat. He races through the alley. His senses are made keen by the nature of the animal; the smell of blood is heightened. In a doorway a wounded soldier is bleeding. Inside a seedy apartment, a girl is menstruating. A child trips, skins his knee against the cobblestones. All these give off the sensual scent of blood. There is time for that later. Tonight he must see what has happened to the angel of death.

He leaps; he springs; his feet pad softly on the stones; soon he is at the Palazzo Madama, across the street from the massive portals of the church. How well he remembers that place; it housed the studio where he drank the painter's blood. Soon he has made himself into a mist and is funneling through the keyhole into the house of God. Incense and candlelight. Stillness. And there is the painting, still draped, still unseen, in a side chapel dedicated by the Contarelli family.

He has become a cat again. He sidles up to the altar, insinuates himself through the wooden railings. The shadow of the great crucifix dances in the flames of a hundred novena candles. The pain is but a pinprick as he slips in and out of the crucifix's penumbra; he has become more and more inured to it, understanding now that even the devices of the divine are stained with corruption. He leaps onto the altar. There is as yet no altarpiece. The *Martyrdom* hangs on a lateral wall. He leaps again, he scurries down the nave, he crouches at the foot of Caravaggio's painting.

He is close to the drapery; he could perhaps whisk it away with a flick of his paws, or return to human shape and simply pull down the eleven-foot-square velvet covering. But before he can make up his mind, he hears footsteps on the stone floor, echoing; he slides into a fold of the drapery; torchlight fills the chamber. It is Cardinal del Monte. He has put on weight; he leans on the shoulder of a young man … Guglielmo.

He is glad Caravaggio is not with them.

Guglielmo has changed. Because he is a eunuch, he does not seem to have aged that much; but there is a deadness in his eyes, like that of one whose mind has been dulled by opiates. The vampire watches.

"Pull down the veil, Guglielmo! I want to see." The cardinal manages to stuff himself into a front pew. Guglielmo opens the railing and pulls aside the velvet.

At first the vampire sees nothing but a jumble. Light and darkness jigsaw across the eleven-foot-square canvas. Out of the kaleidoscope emerge faces, arms with taut musculature, wings, a plumed hat; all flicker in the candlelight; all seem in constant motion.

This is the *Martyrdom of Saint Matthew.* The angel of death no longer stands in the foreground, lit up in all his grim beauty. The painting is full of darkness. Where the angel once stood, a boy is recoiling from the scene of the saint's assassination. Here and there in the front stand naked penitents, readying themselves for baptism. There is an angel on a cloud above; the angel's face is hidden; he hands the dying saint the palm of martyrdom; all that can be seen of the angel is the crook of the arm, the taut curve of a buttock jutting from the obscure æther around the cloud; a boyish leg with its foot pointing skyward, perhaps to the face of god.

Where the woman was sitting, on the far left, there are now other figures. In the middle distance, peering from the gloom, is the face of Caravaggio himself, an observer, within yet perpetually outside the world he has created.

It is beautiful, the boy vampire thinks.

Cardinal del Monte is speaking to Guglielmo, who squats obsequiously at his feet. "That devil-child is gone from the picture now," he says. "Pity."

"Why, Your Eminence?" Guglielmo says.

"It was a pretty thing, and I like to come to churches in the middle of the night and gaze at these ... divine manifestations of beauty and ... enjoy their profane aspects. If you know what I mean."

Still in his feline shape, the vampire slithers from darkness to darkness along the cold stone floor of the *chiesa*. He sits in the cardinal's shadow. The cardinal has loosened his cassock and allowed his penis to rear up from the folds of red fabric. Mechanically, his eyes devoid of feeling, Guglielmo begins to fellate him. The cardinal gazes at the painting and sighs. "That devil-child — such a pretty thing, with such a fine voice; a pity. A pity. He could no doubt have been trained to perform your function, Guglielmo, and he might have put a little more ardor into it than you."

Guglielmo does not answer. The black cat peers into his eyes. He remembers it all now: how the young eunuch begged him to give him immortality, not understanding its dreadful consequences; how, thwarted in his plea, he told the cardinal stories of blood-rites and devil-worship; how they had parted, with the cardinal angrily defacing the canvas, with Guglielmo unable to look his old friend in the eye ... How low he has sunk now! the vampire thinks. He is an empty thing. His betrayal of me haunts him; it has made him into the cardinal's whore.

It is not so the much the casual sacrilege of it that appalls him — is he not himself, after all, a sacrilegious thing to these people, a very concretization of the dæmonic? — but the vacuousness he sees in Guglielmo. It is as though he were already dead.

An uncontrollable anger rips through him. He cannot stop himself. He is changing from black cat to ferocious panther. He springs at the cardinal's throat. He claws his cheeks. He befouls the incense-laden air with his spoor. His hind paws strike Guglielmo in the chest and dislodge him, sending him reeling back against the neat rows of novena candles. Confused, Guglielmo tries to stem the blaze by throwing his cloak over the flames. They are plunged into darkness. The cardinal rises to his feet. His penis dangles flaccidly from his vestments as, making the sign of the cross, he cries out, *"Retro me, Satanas!* I adjure thee and conjure thee, spirit of darkness, to depart from this holy place!"

The vampire laughs bitterly. Through the larynx of the panther, the laugh becomes a roar. The cardinal slinks away toward the vestry. Should he pursue? Should he snuff out this bloated monster? The boy vampire feels only revulsion. The anger was a momentary thing; as it leaves him, he abandons the shape of rage and resolves into the form of the young boy once again.

"Guglielmo," he says softly.

"You came back!" the eunuch whispers. He turns to face him. He has retrieved his cloak from where the molten wax continues to burn a little. Once more there is candlelight, more subdued than before, throwing the chiaroscuro of the painting into even greater relief. "How I longed for you to come back," Guglielmo says. "I've hurt you, and it was only because of envy. I don't want to be immortal any more. I only want to die."

"I can bring that about," says the boy who was once known as Ercolino, chorister in the Sistine Chapel. "If it's what you really want."

For a fleeting moment the deadness leaves Guglielmo's eyes. He is remembering something; what, the boy vampire cannot fathom.

"Yes," he says at last, "I do want it."

He comes forward. He has become pitifully thin. He does not even possess a ghost of his old arrogance, his love of mischief and intrigue. Cardinal del Monte too is a vampire, the boy thinks. They are all vampires, these humans; they feed off one another in ways I cannot even conceive of. If I take his life, what will I give him? Freedom? Is there a hell beyond this hell? The boy vampire cannot know. To endure the torments of hell, it is necessary to have a soul; by his very nature, he is soulless.

Guglielmo loosens his ruff collar and tosses it against the railings. The boy vampire approaches him.

"I'm sorry," he tells him.

Guglielmo is weeping as the fangs, with a pitiless tenderness, pierce through his skin and into his jugular vein. The blood is sour; truly it is laced with opiates and other drugs to numb the awareness of life's bitterness. The boy drinks deep. Blood is blood. His body begins to tingle with the memory of having once lived. The color drains from Guglielmo's face. He grows limp and cold. The boy vampire lays him down upon the altar, beneath the glowering visage of a marble effigy of St. Matthew.

Then he hears a voice from the shadows. "So it was not for me you came, angel of death," says Michelangelo Caravaggio. He steps out from behind a stone pillar.

"Let me finish my work," he says softly. "I don't want him to awaken to eternal loneliness."

Gently, lovingly almost, he rips open the dead eunuch's chest and pulls out his still fibrillating heart. He licks a few last droplets from it as it grows still, and then he places it on the altarcloth, watching the red veins radiate outward from it. He breaks Guglielmo's neck for good measure. He does not want his friend to have to face what he has faced.

Then, wiping the blood from his lips, he turns to Caravaggio. "Thank you for removing me from the painting," he said. "I never belonged there."

"Ah, but I didn't remove you," says the painter. "Look." He points. "You are still there. I only concealed your face. In art, what is not seen is the most beautiful of all."

And the boy looks up, following the curve of the painter's hand, and he sees at last what he should have seen all along; the angel with his face concealed in shadow, leaning down from the sky to bestow on the saint the symbols of his martyrdom.

"There," Caravaggio says, "concealed in the shadow of the crook of your own arm, unreflected in the surface of the cloud, the perfection of your features only hinted at; there you are."

The candlelight flickers. The shadows dance. The shapes of dark and light seem to revolve, to flit across one another. There is life in the picture. Perhaps, in a moment, the angel will look up.

"No," says the boy vampire. "Until we see his face, he has no face. You only think he has my face because once, lost in the labyrinth of your own imagination, you saw me and thought me someone else."

It is true. The angel's face belongs to everyman now. Each man is free to picture it as a reflection of his own yearnings, his secret self. In that sense, it *is* my portrait, thinks the boy. In obeying the cardinal's forbiddance, he has painted me more truly than he himself can know.

"I must go now," he tells Caravaggio.

"Wait! Will you not — for old times' sake — a few quick drops of my blood?"

But the painter speaks to the empty air. Only the art remains.

In the distance, the painter can hear a soft voice, inhumanly sweet and pure, soaring above the music of night: *Miserere mei, miserere mei.*

Only the art....

***

Next is an original story about Timmy Valentine that did not appear in the trilogy. In fact it was written for an anthology of stories related to *The Crow.* Timmy also makes a cameo in some of my other novels; one day someone will write up a concordance.

I am fascinated by the world of jade artifacts and I own a collection of Chinese burial jades, some of them Neolithic. This, and the unusual way the jade trade is run at the Burmese border, is what inspired this story.

Red as Jade

1

Vampires can be your friends. No one fucks with a vampire. Even when, on the outside, he looks like a harmless little kid. I suppose that was my rationale for taking Timmy Valentine to the Golden Triangle with me. The underground jade market can be a dangerous place to hang out, and I look like an easy target — I'm a slip of a Chinese American woman, and at thirty I don't look a day over fifteen.

No one believed I would actually want to take over my father's business when he got sick. Most of our relatives believed that the Jade Emporium in San Francisco was just a laundering operation for my father's heroin smuggling, but actually it was the other way round — the drug trafficking was just a way for him to finance his consuming passion. That was how we were alike, me and Dad. Jade was my father's life … and mine.

It's hard to explain that to someone who doesn't share that passion. "Like explaining music to the deaf, I guess," Timmy told me, as we rode two bicycle rickshaws side by side down a banana-tree-lined dirt road.

"Or the undead to the living?" I said. The rickshaws squeaked, the hot air swimming with strange odors: dung, tropical flowers, exotic, decaying fruits. Sometimes I couldn't tell if Timmy Valentine believed his own hype, or if he was just really, really protective of his platinum-sales persona.

"Don't, Pauline," said Timmy. "I'm sensitive about vampire jokes." We rode in silence.

I don't talk much. When I was little, I didn't speak at all; then I stuttered a lot; with some people I still do. But although I hadn't known Timmy Valentine long, I trusted him; since our trip started, I hadn't stammered once.

It's true I had never seen him eat. It's true that this vampire thing got on my nerves sometimes. We'd become friends at one of my father's big mafia-cum-movie-biz dos. Both loners, I guess. Not that I saw him much, him being a busy celebrity, me constantly trying to make sense of my father's scribbled figures on old legal pads.

The market is not really underground; it's a ways past the last stilted house in the village of Dao Yok, in a mountainous country that's neither Thailand, Laos, or Myanmar; you start your journey at a five-star Hilton in Thailand, still well within shouting range of civilization, but within an hour you're in no-man's land. It was dark when you started, and now it's misty morning in a landscape dense with teak trees and wild orchids.

Now and then there's sniping. You have to realize that this territory is being fought over by various entities — the

Burmese military government, the rebels of the Shan Free State, a hill tribe or two — but a petty war is not enough to halt commerce. I think the jade trade finances all the warring parties one way or another — taxes, levies, protection money, whatever you want to call it.

I make this journey every three years for my Dad; this time I had a secret mission as well.

When the path starts to wind up a hill called Doi Sawan, you see a few thatched kiosks where children or old men watch over piles of boulders, but these are the ones that have already been picked over.

"Picked over?" Timmy asked me. "But they look —"

"Just the same as the others?"

That, of course, is part of the mystique of the stone. Jade boulders come with a skin around them, a dull, dirt-colored skin. No way of knowing what's inside — a deep, oily green, a delicate lavender, the prized white — or just plain old dirt-colored to the core. And you have to bid on it before you cut it open.

I told the rickshaw peddlers to stop a moment. Just as well, with a recalcitrant elephant hogging the road ahead. I showed Timmy one of the boulders, palm-sized, asked him what he'd bid on it.

He smiled a little — yes, that million-dollar smile, so enigmatic, so — what had the *Times* said about that smile? — "joyous yet melancholy, innocent yet pregnant with the promise of a undeliverable sexuality" — "Okay, I'll play," he said. "Five bucks."

I fished the money out of my pocket. Handed it to the giggling, gap-toothed vendor. Then, extracting a file from my jeans, I sawed away at a little corner of it to expose the jade's true color.

"Red," he said, and laughed. "Natural for me, I suppose."

"Not a bad color. Probably not a translucent jade, but rich, a little sinful even. Okay," I said, "now watch me."

I took a deep breath. Reached into the basket. They weren't all boulders — some were no more than pebbles — they tinkled as they slid, making the crystal-cold music jade always makes. I have a sense of jade, inherited from Dad, I suppose. Some stones seem to sing a little. Soon my fingers were tingling. A pebble slithering away from me. They were alive to me, those stones. Pushed my arm in deeper. *Touched it!* A shock wave through my body. Yanked it out.

"Five bucks?" I said, and threw the old crone the equivalent in Thai money. She wasn't so happy this time. Maybe she only worked the bottom of the hill, but she must still have had a bit of the jade-sense.

"So tell me," said the boy who claimed to be a vampire, "what's the difference between the two pebbles?"

"I couldn't tell you," I said. "From the outside, they're equally dull. But this one sets me tingling. I don't know how they could have missed it." I took the file and exposed a corner of it. Just as I thought: creamy white, translucent ... if only I could be sure it was that way all the way through ... but I was pretty sure. "You really don't feel anything at all?" I asked him.

"Well," said Timmy Valentine, and he looked at me with those strange, clear eyes, "I do feel something. But not this jade-sense of yours. When your fingertips grazed that stone inside that basket, the air around us was flooded with the scent of longing. A pheromone, I guess. Charged with eroticism. People think I can't feel love, but I do know what love smells like."

Timmy Valentine is a scary guy. I mean, this was broad daylight, and you knew that the boy was probably just a victim of his own handlers, but you could see how he had become the Prince of Neo-Gothic. He looks like he's around twelve, but I think it's some kid of hormone deficiency thing, probably, and that also explains his voice, which just doesn't sound human.

"Don't be scared, Pauline," he said, "I don't bite."

"Give me a break, Timmy," I said. "This is probably the one place in the world where you won't be mobbed by screaming teenage girls … you can be yourself."

"I am," he said. And stared into his brown boulder with the crimson streak, fascinated … as though it were a living, bleeding thing.

***

We came to the market at last. Canvas stalls everywhere, and old men playing the bidding game in tight, silent circles. "Watch me," I told Timmy. A monkey scampered across our path. The first pavilion was the most crowded. The boulder, of good size, had an edge exposed, brilliant green, kryptonite-colored — very attractive. There were about a dozen bidders, bearded old men, a few Europeans; the auctioneer was a bushy-bearded, plump man in a paramilitary uniform … Uncle Chang.

"Go away, girl," he said. "You know tradition. No women."

I said, "I am my father, not myself." I showed him the white jade *bi,* three thousand years old, that hung on a gold chain around my neck. The old men muttered and glowered. I placed my hand on the boulder. The other bidders did the same. Jade has always been auctioned this way, in silence, in a secret language written with the fingertips.

Uncle Chang threw a silken cloth over the boulder and the circle of hands, the signal that the bidding was now to begin. Immediately I felt the restless drumming and scratching, the time-honored technique of bidding, the fingers dancing while the faces stayed impassive. Beneath the cloth, my hand felt snared in a nest of snakes. I looked from bidder to bidder. But I felt no tingle. Usually there's a different vibe for every color; I trace my finger along the surface, I feel the traceries, the bumps, the bubbles of lucidity; I feel the stone's soul. But no. Nothing at all. Only the pinprick sizzle of neon green where the skin had been breached. So I did not bid.

There was one other man who did not bid. I had never seen him here before. He wore a double-breasted duster — a weird affectation for this climate — and a slouch hat. He did not seem Chinese, but there wasn't much of him visible — he was draped in shapeless black, and I didn't see his eyes because he wore a pair of silver-rimmed mirror shades.

Was he gazing at me? He seemed to be. No one else paid attention. The bids were climbing sky-high. I felt the frantic wriggling, the cursive outlines of Chinese characters that spelled out names, the tap-tap-tapping of units, tens, hundreds, thousands … greenbacks, cash, the only valid currency in this borderland … and then, at last, no movement at all.

The silk was whisked away.

A fat little man was unrolling a wad of Benjamin Franklins from his chest, and smiling smugly to himself.

"Is it over?" said Timmy Valentine, who had been sitting in a corner, watching a rerun of *The Waltons* on a battered black-and-white television. A chained gibbon shrieked from its roost in the awning.

"Yes," I said. "Nothing to see here. Let's move on."

But I did not move.

Because I felt the tall man's presence. He hadn't moved either, though the bidders had all left the circle, and the auctioneer was getting ready to heft another boulder onto the stand.

At length, the tall man gestured dismissively at the successful bidder, who was sipping a quick *café filtre* by the side of the pavilion.

"He will be disappointed," he said — he had a soft voice, high-pitched; you imagine eunuchs talking this way — and looked away at last.

"I-I-I know," I said. For the first time in a week, I was having trouble talking. Fuck! Not now, not in front of these people!

"I know who you are," said the man, "and I know why you're here. Be careful."

He took off his mirror shades and looked me straight in the face.

And his eyes were mirrors too.

I think I would have screamed if I hadn't felt Timmy's hand on my shoulder. The tall man loped away, uphill a little further, toward the cavern of antiquities — his real destination, and mine.

"What was all that about?" said Timmy.

"H-he's after the Empress of Jade," I said.

Everyone heard me say that; the chatter went dead — the kind of silence that tells you that the gunman has entered the saloon. Uncle Chang looked at me askance. "No be so blatant!" he whispered.

"Where is she?" I asked him.

"Up the —" He looked shiftily about. "Hundred tell you where she hidden."

I uncoiled the C-note from my sleeve and dangled it before his nose. He snatched it away. "Cheap theatrics!" he scoffed. "You think this is some cheap kung fu movie?"

"M-maybe," I said. "Well, not cheap."

Uncle Chang then proceeded to whisper in my ear the words that would take me to the thing my father most longed to possess. This buying of jade boulders, seeking out the finest, sending them to the best carvers to make precious objects for the homes of the nouveau riche of Chinatown, this was only part of the Jade Emporium's business. More important to my father was the room in the attic, the room of his secret treasures … the room that would one day be mine.

I was so excited that I wanted to rush to the viewing location right away, but I knew I had to pace myself. I would give the tall man an apparent advantage. He would spend all day thinking he had already won the prize, and I would swoop in the next day and snatch it from him.

"Who is he, anyway?" I asked Uncle Chang, and stuffed another hundred dollars in his hand.

"Nobody know," he said. "First time here. Some people call him the White Giraffe, because he very tall, and he albino. He very good jade-sense. Some people here think your father send him, come to senses this year, marry you off properly to rich American doctor."

"My father would never send someone in my place," I said, unsure of myself suddenly. I had to keep my cool.

Couldn't let it get to me — wouldn't they just love that! They'd nod their heads and murmur sagely about how a girl should never have slipped into their private little club.

So I spent the rest of the day buying up stones, and come evening we took two more bicycle rickshaws (downhill this time, so the extra weight did not entirely kill the peddlers) and trundled back down toward the village where we would get back to the Mercedes and chauffeur waiting patiently by the grove where the drivable dirt road came to an end, backtrack to the back street and finally to an incongruous fifteen-kilometer stretch of superhighway that would bring us back to the Hilton and the twenty-dollar hamburger deluxe and civilization.

Timmy didn't have dinner, not even a glass of wine. "I'll eat later," he told me. At midnight, when I woke up screaming, he wasn't there.

***

The nightmare sent me right back to childhood. It was the same one, though I hadn't had it for twenty years. I know the day it happened because it was the night before my mom died in a car crash.

It's a dark room. Here and there a shaft of cold light on a stone face. I know that I am trapped. I'm wearing a flimsy nightgown. Or maybe it's a shroud. The air is dense, putrescent.

I try to touch my face and arms and all I feel is something hard, chitinous. I try to scream but my lips are mandibles, and only a dry chittering issues forth. I crawl among the dead things. I have too many arms and legs. A burning drool oozes from my jaws. Who am I?

The dust hangs heavy. I'm here to fight someone. Who? What?

I skitter among the dead things.

There is a hall. An empty coffin. On the coffin, a crow perches. A dragon, coiled, asleep, around the tomb. And suddenly I know that it's my tomb, my bed, my place of rest, and if I can only reach it I won't be afraid any more … I edge closer to the sarcophagus … smooth and cold … white limestone.

If I can only slither across those glassy scales….

But as I graze one jeweled claw the dragon wakes. His eyes snap open with a metallic rasp, like the gates of a cemetery. And he exhales a searing, frosty fire, and in that fire's chill blue shimmering I see the faces around me, faces of sacrificial victims, women, men, children, eunuchs, dogs, horses, hecatombs of corpses overrun with rats and maggots, and the dragon lunges over the dead toward me, and all I can do is cry out, "Let me in, let me in —" and in the mirrors that are the dragon's eyes I see myself, not a human but a monstrous bug-thing —

The crow flaps its wings and shrieks, and then I scream —

In the Hilton at the edge of the country with no name, I remembered the first time I woke up from that dream.

Weeping, in my father's arms.

And I can't talk. The words don't come, "Tomb! Da-da-da-da-da — insect!" How old was I? Nine, ten? I know it was before puberty.

"Hush," said my father, "hush, my daughter; it's time for you to see the attic."

He put a terry cloth robe on me, and led me from my room, past the master bedroom where my mother lay snoring, my baby brother in her arms, past the lace and marble bathroom and the linen closet, to the door I had never seen him open. He took the big key that hung from the dragon-shaped hook — which made me shudder, because it brought back the dream a little — and the door creaked open, and — never letting go of my tiny hand — he pulled me upwards toward the landing where the moon shone through the round window, a circle inside a circle.

At length we reached the little treasure room. The room was legendary in our house, yet no one save my father had ever been known to set foot in it. "La, la, l-l-l-light?" I said.

"The first time," he said, "sometimes things are best viewed in the moonlight, my daughter." He spoke to me in Cantonese, which he never did in front of company, or even in front of my mother, who was Italian. "You will come here often enough by day."

For now the treasures were only glimpses — a mottled horse rearing up — an urn carved with flowers — a white dragon — the greasy luminescence of fine jade. That was when I felt the tingle for the first time. The air was electric. I knew the colors without seeing them, because I said at once, without stuttering at all, "Daddy, I thought jade was supposed to be green."

"That famous green," said my father, "come from Burma, and they only started mining it in quantity two centuries ago … you must learn to appreciate other jades too … celestial white … imperial yellow … blood-red." He sat me down on his knee and made me close my eyes and tell him the color of whatever he placed in my hand, and sometimes I felt laughter shake his whole potbellied frame, and sometimes I felt a tension rack him. At at last he gave me an object I knew was white — even through my closed fingers it irradiated my body. "Tonight," he said, "you dreamed of the cicada. That's a very important dream. In the Han Dynasty, two thousand years ago, the jade cicada was a symbol of the soul's victory over death … now open your eyes … and your fist."

I did. It was a stylized artifact, angular, ungainly. "In those days," my father told me, "they buried you with a jade cicada on your tongue. It ensured your immortality."

I looked at the cold white thing, me a whiny little girl in an attic room in San Francisco, the cicada reaching to me from my past, and from my dream.

"You want to try it?"

"Try?"

"Open wide."

He popped the jade cicada between my lips. I felt like gagging for a moment. Hadn't this thing been in some dead person's mouth before? With all those worms. A stone bug. I thought I was going to choke. I spit it out. My father caught it. I was shaking. My father wiped the cicada and put it in a jar with half a dozen others.

"There now," he said at last, "in your dream, you were trapped in the cicada. Now you've turned the tables on that mean old insect."

He made me laugh in the end, and I didn't have the dream again for years; but lately, lately it had been coming back, and this time I wasn't a child anymore, and I couldn't sit on someone's lap; so instead I lay in my bed in a suite in a five-star hotel and watched CNN for a while, until I heard a tapping at my window, and I saw Timmy, curled up on the sill, leaning against the air conditioner.

***

"Don't worry," he said. "I've eaten."

He climbed in and I closed the window behind him.

"You really go overboard with this method acting," I said. "I haven't seen you gag on garlic, or get burned by the sun, I mean you're petty damn selective when it comes to the trappings of vampirism ..."

"Myths, Pauline," he said, wiping the blood from his lips.

Then I looked out at the parking lot. There was a large gray mass lying between two Mercedeses.

"Don't worry," said Timmy. "He was old. He asked me to release him."

"Timmy, there's a dead *elephant* in the parking lot."

"He'll be gone by morning. His mahout already knows about it; it's been in his dreams all week; before dawn, he'll be here soon, with younger elephants to help bear their comrade away. There's a tiger loose, they say." He shrugged. "But you've been dreaming too."

It's weird. It didn't seem to matter that my companion was some kind of schizoid maniac and that I was stranded at the very edge of civilization. Somehow, I knew that Timmy would understand. His life had been stranger than mine could ever be. I knew he'd listen. I knew he wouldn't think I was crazy. I told him everything — the cicada and the dragon — I told him my secret reason for coming here this year — I told him how afraid I was, how the tall albino with the mirror shades made me almost want to turn tail and flee back to America.

And Timmy held my hand in his — his was as cold as a jade that has been in the grave for a thousand years — and said, "I'll tell you something about myself, then, Pauline Huang, and here it is: you have this uncanny jade-sense — touch the stone's skin, feel it's true color — some may think it's magic, but to you it's as natural as breathing —

and I have a soul-sense. When I touch the skin of a mortal, I feel that mortal's true colors — I see his soul. It's not magic for me, either. It's probably something to do with pheromones, or the subtleties of body language, or — well, you see what I'm getting at."

"What are you telling me?"

"The tall man with the mirror shades. He looked at you. Something happened. I know. My hand brushed against you at that moment and I saw inside your skin."

I was getting the creeps. Timmy has this way of totally sucking you into his vision of the world. When he speaks to you, no matter how absurd it all is, you know, at the time, that it's god's plain truth. Softly I said, trying to make light of it all, "And who did you see? Eleanor Roosevelt?"

"No, Pauline. I didn't see anyone at all."

"What?"

"You were gone, Pauline. Just for a moment. Until he turned away and walked uphill. You were empty. You were a shell. Your soul was somewhere far away."

2

All right. So what *was* my secret mission? It was an order from my father to bring back something — someone, I suppose you might say — from the cavern of antiquities in Doi Yok. The Empress of Jade.

My father is a shady man. Because of him, junkies share needles in back alleys, and kids die of AIDS. I can't help that. I love him. He has always been the best of fathers, and I am pretty dutiful and obedient, for an American — that Confucian culture runs deep in my blood. I love him, but I have a hard time telling him; it's then that the stammering comes worst of all, as though I had a big rock wedged in my throat.

My father is a bad man, but he's not without compassion. He inherited this business. He couldn't help it either. It was in *his* blood, you see.

My father has been ill for several years now, and my cousin takes care of the dirty business while I run the Jade Emporium. He won't go into a hospital, because he thinks that he'll never come back out; so he lies upstairs, in the attic, among his treasures, on a high-tech super-bed with IVs, a nurse on duty 24/7, even a machine that goes *ping*. A week before this trip, he made sure the nurse was out of earshot, and he told me to open a velvet box, one he hadn't shown me before.

"Time to understand the cicada and the dragon," he said at last. "Time to face down your nightmare."

"But, Dad," I said, "I haven't had that nightmare in a long time."

"Open the box," he said.

Inside were little rectangles of jade. Not the fine jadeite from Burma, but the ancient nephrite, muddy green streaked with a dried-blood brown. They were like *mah jong* tiles ... or like the scales of a dragon, perhaps. Each corner had a hole, and in some of the holes were scraps of gold thread.

"What are they?" said my father.

"Western Han Dynasty," I said, "they're pieces from a jade burial suit."

My father nodded … wheezed a little … indicated the Demerol dispenser with his head. I gave him a little shot of the painkiller, even though the doctor had told him to go easy on it. "Good girl," he said.

"When a high-ranking person was buried," I said, knowing how he liked to hear me repeat, word-for-word, the lessons he'd taught me, "nine orifices were plugged up with jade — the cicada for the tongue, jade pigs clenched in each fist — and then the entire body was encased in a jade suit. The body and soul, the life-essence, bottled within. Immortality ensured."

For a moment I thought he was going to ask me to have one made for *him.* He could have afforded it, but I didn't think he really believed those millennial superstitions … did he?

"No, nothing like that," he said, reading my mind, as usual. "But what if … somewhere out there … in the undisturbed burial chambers of ancient China … there was an Empress, preserved by the magic of the jade, the cicada still unborn upon her tongue, her body sewn into its shroud of magical stone … waiting through the centuries for —"

"There *is* such an Empress, isn't there?" I said. "And you want her."

"Chang sent me a letter," he said. "I think I'm in love." He pulled a wrinkled color xerox from under his pillow. "Look … look."

And there she was. Resting on a slab of concrete. No dragon coiled at her feet, no crow standing watch over her sarcophagus. In the background, a dirt road, a truck, a gang of peasants with shovels posing with crooked smiles. The whole scene bathed in a faceless sunlight.

"Can you bring her to me?" my father said. "Since your mother died I've been lonely. . . ."

"Dad," I said, "that's morbid. Sure, a jade suit would be the crown of your collection. But with a dead woman inside —"

"With jade," he said, "there really is no death. Anyhow, I get a special feeling from this jade, even from this poor reproduction of a photograph. It was found near the ancestral village in China. It calls to us."

"If you say so, Dad." My jade-sense didn't work over distance; my father always claimed that his did, though unreliably.

"And when something calls this strongly," he added, "there is also danger."

"Danger? Either I'll bid on it, and I'll get it and bring it back … or someone else will. You'll set a limit … I know you will … you'll be sensible."

"You are to bring it back at any cost," said my father, with such intensity that I reached for the Demerol button, thinking he'd have another spasm. "But no, the danger is not that we'll wipe out all our bank accounts. You will see."

"Then —"

"The danger," my father said, "is in your dreams."

***

So there we were. The crates of raw stones all ready for shipping, and now there was only one order of business left. The cavern of antiquities was the most labyrinthine sector of the underground jade market. It was not just a single cavern, but a whole labyrinth.

By the front, shafts of daylight streamed in from holes in the cavern vault. Here were dealers with new objects, or objects pretending to great age. Wagonwheel-sized *bi* incised with scenes of hunting and how-to guides to sexual positions. Goddesses with sweeping robes. Amulets by the thousands, carved into good-luck calligraphies or laughing Buddhas. The vendors mostly children or middle-aged women, some in their hilltribe costumes, bowed by the weight of their silver ornaments.

Further in, little chambers, hollows in the rock like side chapels in a cathedral, and now the *objets d'art* were more reliably authentic, though nothing much older than Ming. Here were rows of dragons, horses, goats, and turtles, and those ornamental urns with florid reliefs, and glowering lions and fu dogs, and yes, crows, too, perched on carves branches with cunningly wrought leaves. The salesmen were middleaged, and men, mostly; no native dress here but Armani suits, or, more casually, Versace jeans; here, improbably, were credit card machines linked via cellular modems to the world of commerce beyond the no man's land. Prices were in the five, perhaps even six figures here. But I had little patience for these trinkets; we had ones just as lovely back at the Emporium, made in our own workshop in darkest Palo Alto.

The directions Uncle Chang had given me were convoluted. At least once, Timmy and I found ourselves doubling back, or walking in circles. I suppose we were being tested, or something.

Presently we seemed to be descending deeper into the hillside. Not many vendors now, and we were regressing in time, to objects of Sung, Han, Zhou, Shang, or even Neolithic vintage. And the salesmen were older and more ferocious.

"This is it," I said at last. "This corner, and we should be

—"

We entered through a narrow gap in the rock. A misty space, echoey, and too dark to see the size of it; here and there, a naked light bulb swung. The stench of bat dung in our nostrils. I started to move forward —

The tall albino blocked our way.

"I'm sorry," he said, "I was here first."

"We get to look," I said. "The auction's not until tomorrow."

"I've made a preemptive bid."

I looked into his mirror shades and saw myself reflected … or was it me? Were those the compound eyes of a great cicada, the jointed limbs? Of course not. Letting him get to me, I thought. Can't do that.

I looked past him. Past the swinging light bulbs … to the wooden board that leaned against the far wall. She was there all right. I could feel each one of the scales, dark green jade spattered with the color of dried blood … she was near … my jade-sense doesn't work over distances … I couldn't see her yet, but my blood was singing in my ears….

"Oh, Pauline," said the tall man, "I've seen her. She is perfect. Not a scale missing, not a strand of gold frayed … she is beautiful. And inside that suit she's there, all of her, untouched by time."

"Well, let me be the judge of that," I said, but I knew he was right.

"Let's not fight over her," said the tall man. "This is history, this is the interface of truth and legend."

"Ya, ya, y-you're not going to turn this bidding war into some mythic battle," I said, though the man was clearly suffering from an Indiana Jones complex.

"Hardly," he said. He reached into his duster and pulled out a business card. "Just doing my job." He tossed it to me.

The card read:

David S. Coleman, Ph.D.,
Department of Acquisitions,
The San Francisco Museum of Ancient Civilization

"You're from a museum?"

"What did you think — that I'm some vengeful demon out of time, come to hound the old lady beyond the grave?"

"You do come across that way," I said.

"Well look, little lady," said Coleman, "this treasure's meant to be seen by millions, not locked up in some drug dealer's attic. So go home and let's not have a bidding war. I've got a resource you can never outbid — the tax dollars of John Q. Public."

This wasn't the battle I'd been expecting. There stood this man, as outlandish-looking as a comic-book villain, surely some ancient nemesis of my father's who had nurtured a grudge since some childhood spat and now was prepared for some mythic catharsis ... but no. He was making himself look like the forces of feel-good liberalism, and me like the villain. That threw me off guard.

It was Timmy who stepped in. "Pauline," he said, "there's something wrong here."

"Get out!" Coleman screamed. "You were never part of this equation!"

Well, I had come twelve thousand miles and then some, and suffered nightmares and wormed through this labyrinth, and I wasn't going to leave without at least touching the Jade Empress. I could see her clearer now, getting more used to the dark, and my jade-sense was jangling in my veins, in my brain, making me feel almost superhuman. I started forward, tried to shove Coleman out of my way even though he was a foot taller than me, but instead he whacked me with the back of his hand, casually, across the chest, and sent me sprawling hard against jagged stone.

How could a man be that strong? Confused, I tried to sit up. The stalactites wheeled overhead. It was then that I saw Timmy Valentine transform —

Transform? He shimmered against the phosphorescence of the limestone. Arms flapped into dark wings. Lips tightened to a beak. *I'm dreaming!* I thought, and kept hearing my father's voice: *The danger is your dreams in your dreams your dreams —*

Timmy cried out … and his cry was the harsh caw of the raven … and his eyes were amber yellow, and feral, and fire-bright … the naked bulbs swayed, and through the crisscross beams he flew, arrowing at the tall man's heart —

Coleman leaped up … suddenly he was on a ledge, ten feet overhead, like a demon in a kung fu movie. Timmy spiraled higher, shrieking. What was going on? Hadn't I seen crows in my dream, stone crows guarding the sarcophagus?

"Oh. no," said the tall man, "no, you don't. You're not the one I'm destined to fight, you're not even supposed to be here —" He pulled a revolver from his duster and squeezed the trigger, point black, as the crow prepared to swoop down on his shaded eyes.

I screamed.

There was no gunshot. It was a water pistol. A stream of liquid hit the bird and vaporized it. A flurry of feathers.

"Never know," said Coleman, tossing the weapon in his pocket, "when holy water's gonna prove handy." He turned his back on me and strode to where the Jade Empress lay. I looked down at my hands and saw they were the chitinous limbs of a monstrous insect —

And suddenly I was somewhere else: in a bed at the Hilton, being tended to by Timmy. Chicken soup and cold compresses. And Timmy sitting by the bed, normal as can be, in neatly pressed Versus casuals, just your ordinary underaged neo-Gothic superstar on his day off.

"You — a crow — what did it mean? —"

"When I transform," said Timmy, "I become the thing most feared. Obviously our friend believes that a crow will be his ending. But I was only an illusion … not his real death. I'm not the real enemy … am I now?" He turned to me as if I would have the answers.

"How should I know?" I said, and moaned.

"Pauline," he said softly, "are you ready to tell me who you *really* are?"

3

"Only," I said, "if you tell me who *you* are."

"Oddly enough," he said, "I've never lied to you."

"Well, I haven't lied to you either."

"But you *have* lied to yourself. Or rather, you've chosen not to see … certain things."

"There's another person inside Pauline Huang. A

person who cries out to be avenged. A person from an ancient time. A person you fear to let out, because you're afraid you'll lose your own self."

"The holy water? What was all that about?"

"I shouldn't have let it faze me. It took me by surprise, I admit. Usually my defenses are up a lot more. Anyway, it wasn't your everyday holy water from the local church ... it was blessed by a true believer ... it was pretty potent. I don't understand how he managed to carry on his person — although the water wasn't touching him directly."

"Why wouldn't he have been able to?"

"Oh, you don't get it?" said Timmy Valentine. "He's a vampire too."

***

Night. Still groggy, my head still throbbing, I went with Timmy from the Hilton, into the empty town. He had insisted that I make arrangements to ship all the jade I had already bought, though normally I would never do so until just before flying home.

"Where are we going?" I wanted to know, but he didn't answer me. "We can't call a hotel limo at this hour," I said. "We can't even rouse a bicycle rickshaw. How can we go anywhere at all?"

The streets of the border town were quite, quite vacant. To call it a town was flattery; the Hilton and its support system *were* the town. One bar was open a few blocks down. Peasant music — some people call it "Country 'n' Eastern" played from within — a whining, melancholy music. A couple of prostitutes sat outside, and an old man with a hookah puffed opium into the jasmine-scented air. In the window, a tall silhouette moved. *Coleman*.

"Ignore him," Timmy said.

We pressed on.

"He thinks you're beaten," said Timmy, "but he doesn't know that you still have a powerful connection to the past … your jade-sense."

We walked … rather, we ran, toward the hilly country. As we ran it seemed that our feet left the ground sometimes. It seemed that I was enveloped within mighty, dark wings, which held me close and were somehow comforting.

The night air was warm and moist. It rushed over me. My hair streamed. The embrace of the vampire held me tight. I had not felt this safe since childhood, wrapped in my father's sheltering arms. I looked down. We were racing toward the jade mountain. My jade-sense was more alive than ever. The whole hillside was thrumming with it. We swerved up toward the silvery moon. We swooped. I had felt this before. I knew it. I recognized it. I had flown before. Without help. Alone.

We reached the market. Deserted now. Guards with AK-47s — soldiers of the insurgent Shan army, perhaps — stood watch, but there was a fiercer protector than they — the spirit of the mountain itself, sitting in a shrine in a niche in the naked rock, a battered wooden image covered in gold leaf and garlands of decaying jasmine. The baskets of boulders were locked away in chests. Some of them had a child or a dog sleeping next to them.

There was the entrance to the cavern of antiquities. Unnoticed, cloaked in Timmy's private darkness, we entered. There were more guards, but we flitted from shadow to shadow. Aluminum shutters covered the private stalls, and the corridors were illuminated only by an occasional cigarette.

We followed the path we had followed before … quicker now, since there were no distractions … I don't know when we ceased to fly and took on human shape … I think we were flitting from form to form … the jade-sense seized me totally … color and texture whirled around me … *she* called out to me … *Pauline … Pauline …* only it sounded like some ancient Chinese name … *Pui Yi … Pui Yi …* the Empress of Jade was speaking to me, and knew my name, because, because —

"Don't shy away from it!" Timmy cried.

We stood in the innermost cavern now, with the swinging light bulbs and the bats, and there was the Empress, splayed out on a wooden platform, ready for shipping, and I reached out to touch the texture of the jade with my mind, felt every speck of cinnabar and scar of calcification, felt the deep green and the flecks of blood-red, knew there was real blood, too —

"Do you remember now?" Timmy demanded. "Do you feel, do you see? It wasn't any accident that you ran into me at that charity fundraiser … that you invited me to come on this trip just as I was feeling the need for a week of anonymity … there is someone else inside your skin … and that someone else and I have been together before, long ago, a thousand years, two thousand years ago…."

Then it came to me all at once.

I remembered who I was, and why I had come. It was as clear to me as if it had only just happened … and in a sense, that was true, for the time spent waiting in my carapace of jade had been a time outside time, a moment that was not a moment.

4

… brightness … I know it is bright outside because there is a chink in the wall of my litter. I am being carried through the streets of a city. I hardly dare peek through the curtains, but I know the litterbearers are husky and move in a rapid, even rhythm. Beside me sits the woman who has raised me, the woman I call Auntie Chiu.

She is dour today. She rarely smiles, and today she has not smiled at all. I am weighed down by layers of silk and ornaments of jade, bracelets carved with dragons, a ten-piece pectoral ornament that tickles as the litterbearers jog, their leader calling the beat of their running in a monotonous guttural melody. It is a hot day, and I am thirsty, but my aunt doesn't let me drink, because she doesn't want me to ruin my painted lips.

"If the Emperor chooses me —" I begin.

"He will not choose you," says Auntie Chiu, but I know that it is what she hopes for above all things. But to say so would be an ill omen.

I don't think of being chosen. Instead, I daydream about rejection, about returning to my cousin Wei, my true love, who has sworn to become a monk if I am chosen.

***

… brightness … it hurts my eyes to step down from the litter, because I have been traveling in it for days, stopping only after dark to sleep in secret places, for it would be calamitous if malicious eyes were to see me. But now, all at once, I face the light … not only the dazzling brightness of an inner garden, but also the luminescence of the high court of the Son of Heaven. I do not have time to take in the sculpted hedges, the chrysanthemum bushes, the terracotta statues of gods and goddesses. On a raised dais sits a tall, impassive presence with pale skin and white robes, so hung with white jade ornaments that I can hear him tinkling as he waves a languid arm to command that music begin, a raucous jangle of gong, fiddle, and fife. Surely, I think, the Emperor. Hastily I begin to make the motions of the prostration, but my aunt, embarrassed, stops me just in time.

"You fool!" she whispers. "Do you think the Son of Heaven would condescend to show you his Sacred Countenance?"

She indicates a screen behind the tall man's seat, a screen of bronze, jade, and ivory. Though no one sees behind, we all know that it thence that all power in this garden emanates. Before the screen is an empty throne whose arms are carved in a design of dragons.

I have no way of knowing that this is just a minor court ceremony, a little light entertainment to pass the Emperor's time in between more important duties, such as diplomacy or feeding the imperial crocodiles. I've been rigorously trained since I was six years old in case such a moment as this might one day occur. And now I see that there are other litters, too, and other young women stepping from them, and my heart sinks. All are beautiful. All, doubtless, have been trained.

Next to the throne sit a dozen court ladies, tittering, fanning themselves. One by one the tall man calls the girls to the foot of the throne. Most he dismisses in a moment or two. Many are already in tears. At last it is my turn. It is already late afternoon, and slaves are fetching torches. Humbly I inch my way toward the empty throne.

The tall man speaks. His voice is high and pure, and I realize that he is a eunuch. Of course he is … men would not be permitted in this inner garden … only the Son of Heaven himself. "Your name?" he inquires.

"Pui Yi, Excellency," I say, not daring to meet his gaze, trying to maintain the demure composure that Auntie had taught me. If he is a eunuch, he could be very important. The decision might even be entirely his, for why would the Son of Heaven concern himself which such mundane chores as choosing a bedmate for the night?

"They tell me that you sing," says the tall man.

"I've had a little training, Excellency. My master was quite distinguished in the title role of *The Daughter of the Raven.*"

"Impertinence!" he says. "Don't volunteer any information. *Yes* or *no* will suffice."

"Yes, Excellency."

This is already going badly. I can imagine the shame my auntie must be feeling. But then the eunuch claps his hands and says, "We shall see how this pupil of the late Son of Heaven's favorite opera star may perform."

The sun sets. There enters a boy with a *p'ip'a,* a graceful child with luminous white skin and large, hypnotic eyes. Surely he is a slave from one of the legendary empires far to the west. He kneels before the throne and begins to strum his lute. Fascinated, I find myself staring at him … silence has fallen. He has done what even the celestial radiance from behind the throne could not do: he has stilled the chatter of the court ladies.

The boy beckons for me to kneel down next to him. His

fingers stroke the strings of the *p'ip'a* in a way that reminds me of my many stern lessons in the sensual arts. "Don't be afraid," he says. "Follow my lead. We'll do the song together."

And so, raising his voice, he eases me into the song, which is a well known ballad about wine, and chrysanthemums, and being drunk on love. My voice is weak, but he supports me. He doesn't seem to breathe at all, but soars effortlessly through the song's convoluted melismas, and soon I'm soaring with him. It's as though I'm being borne on great wings to a eyrie high above the world. I don't think of the Son of Heaven at all ... only of my penniless cousin Wei, lost in his hopeless fantasy of wedding me. I know that the young boy sees this. He understands me. He too has lost something precious ... which he must mourn forever.

When the last notes die away, the tall pale man seems more displeased than ever. I think to myself ... good, at least there will be no more performances ... I will be assigned some cell in the women's quarters and be forgotten, like the thousand other gifts and tributary objects the Emperor receives each year ... catalogued and shut away to gather dust forever....

But no. "You will ready yourself," the tall man says. "Today, fortune smiles upon you, Pui Yi. May Heaven bless your womb."

The audience is over. I am led away. I have not even seen the face of the Son of Heaven, but without uttering a word he has already taken from me my past, my life, my soul.

***

"More!" cried Timmy Valentine. "Try to remember all of

it —"

I was shaking. My hands gripped the breasts of the Empress of Jade. Timmy *was* a vampire, and I had seen him before ... in another existence ... as the young musician who understood my loss ... was it a past life of mine, or was I somehow being possessed by this dead woman's spirit?

"Listen," said Timmy.

I did. There were stirrings in the cave of antiquities. I could not tell what time it was, but I knew the vendors would start to set up long before dawn.

I gazed into the thousand scales of jade, still glassy from their millennial interment, saw myself, saw the cicada's compound eyes, the flapping of the crow's wings....

***

Night. I am alone. The bridal chamber is hung with crimson silk and paper lanterns. The bed has been strewn with attar of roses, and I have been dressed, combed, rouged and painted by a dozen faceless maids. Now I lie in the bed, alone, in a sheer robe, awaiting my fate. It is a large bed, and the reeds are fresh and fragrant.

Time passes.

Presently comes the sound of a sobbing child. Who can it be? One of the imperial children? But they all have nursemaids. The sound does not go away. I keep thinking it is only the wind, but at times there are words.

My curiosity gets the better of me. I get up from the bed. My auntie has always warned me about my curiosity, but am I not a chosen consort of the Son of Heaven? I follow the source of the sound ... opening first one door, then another, growing bolder ... a woman in black banging a jade chime to attract the attention of the Goddess of Mercy

... eunuchs lighting joss-sticks ... nobody sees me, and nobody seems to hear the sound of the weeping child ... save I.

At last, sliding open a panel ornamented with a bas-relief of elephants, phoenixes and tigers, I see the weeping child. He is almost a man, really; he is a little past puberty, but he is dwarfed by the hugeness of the chamber, and by the thronelike chair of ebony inlaid with mother-of-pearl. Sitting at his feet is the young bard with the *p'ip'a,* the boy who sang with me earlier this evening. Incense wafts through the room, which is lit by moonlight from a window that overlooks a pond; the song of frogs and cicadas fills the night air.

The boy-musician sings another song now:

"Do not weep, my Lord,
for there will be many days ahead
when you will need those tears;
death, famine, war, destruction, pestilence are waiting.
Rejoice, my Lord, while time remains."

I recognize the song; it is from *The Daughter of the Raven,* and it is the song the raven's daughter sings to her father, knowing that she must sacrifice her life for his in a moving display of filial piety.

It is a strange choice for a song with which to cheer a weeping child, but in this chamber, where we are dwarfed by crimson columns and statues of beasts and bearded men, where a white jade *bi* hangs above the throne like an artificial sun, it does not seem out of place.

"This is the girl I was telling you about," says the boy singer.

"She seems very sweet, Musician," says the child.

"But she is sad too, Little Newt," says the musician.

"There's no reason to be sad here," says the child. "Here they have everything … picture-books, flowers, delicious candies. I'm the only one who is allowed to be sad."

"My life isn't my own," I say.

"Does that pain you?"

"I am told," I say, "that I have been selected for the highest honor a woman can attain. But sometimes I think of a man I left behind, who now must enter a monastery … have you ever left something behind? Is there someone who weeps for what you might have been?"

"There are so many things," says Little Newt. "If only I could tell someone —"

"You can tell me if you like."

"I'm afraid. I'm only a puppet. A pale, tall man is pulling all the strings." He comes down from his throne and he embraces me … he kisses me gently on the lips … there is a disturbing sensuality to his kisses, as though I were more to him than a woman intercepted by chance on her wedding-night….

And now we are both sobbing disconsolately, and it dawns on me that this is no ordinary child … even though the musician addressed him with no honorifics … even though he has spoken to me as a boy might speak to an elder sister … yes, a pale, tall man has been pulling all our strings. He is as helpless as I! He is only a boy, and he too is a prisoner in a gilded cage —

"Your Majesty!" I cry out at last, and hasten to perform the proper prostration. But before my head strikes the floor —

A wild-eyed man has thrust open the door and comes

running with a dagger in his hand.

"I can't bear it, Pui Yi!" he screams. "I can't let you be taken by another —"

"Cousin Wei!" I shout. He throws himself at the Emperor, but instantly the chamber fills with guards. Cousin Wei does not even finish his utterance. His head lies at the Emperor's feet, and blood gushes from his neck stump as his headless body flounders and collapses. We are drenched in blood, yet the entire scene of violence cannot have lasted more than a minute.

I am numb. I finish my prostration, hitting my head three times on the slippery floor. The guards are already wiping the marble clean and spiriting away the corpse … I barely have time to understand that this was a man who loved me, who died in a hopeless attempt to possess me.

When I look up from my kowtow, it is as though nothing has happened at all. Little Newt is still seated at the foot of his throne. But on the throne itself sits the real power … the tall, pale man with the empty eyes.

"General Zo," the Emperor says softly. It amazes me that a eunuch may be called *general,* but no one can question his power.

"You did well, Your Imperial Majesty," he says, and I can see that his formal obsequy conceals an absolute disdain. "The plot to overthrow you is utterly crushed."

"There was no plot," I cry. "There was a man. He loved me. It was stupid of him. He has been killed."

"Silence, woman!" says the general. "Your kind never ceases to astound me. How long did you and that cousin of yours plot? Which of His Majesty's ousted half-brothers financed your plan?"

I am trapped. I know he must have overheard my entire

conversation with the Emperor … heard me speak to him coarsely, as a girl to a younger brother … heard me confess of another love, another life … and all these things *are* treason … all are capital offenses.

Your Majesty, it remains only for you to sign this." He pulls a lengthy scroll from his capacious sleeve.

"What is it?"

"The execution order for this rebel," says General Zo. He pushes me down into a posture of submission with his foot.

"Help me, Little Newt," I gasp.

The Emperor clears his throat. In the moonlight, I can see fresh tears springing to his eyes. "Are you sure, General," he stutters, "that she is a rebel? Do you think she might be just … an innocent, lost amid things she cannot comprehend?"

The general laughs. It is the laughter of all mad villains, the laughter of pure evil. "Of course she's an innocent," he says. "How else could she have been duped into betraying you? Sign, Your Majesty."

He signs. He has no choice. We are all pawns. But, I think to myself, whose pawn is General Zo?

"I am sorry for you, Pui Yi," the general says, as he pockets the scroll and summons the guards to drag me hence. "You thought you would be an Empress, didn't you? And you will be an Empress, though your domain will consist only of jade."

Defiance is all I have left. I know there can be no countermanding of an Emperor's signature. The will of heaven is immutable. "May you live," I scream at the general, "until I find a way back from the grave to wreak vengeance."

"What kind of a curse is that?" the general laughs. "You have just condemned me to eternal life!"

As they lead me away, I hear the musician break once more into the lament of the raven's daughter, and I know that the Son of Heaven still weeps.

***

It is a terrible execution. It is not an execution at all. They do not kill me. They condemn me to everlasting torment.

To still the voice that sang so seductively, they slice away my tongue. They cut me in a thousand places, with such exquisite cunning that every nerve is exposed yet the blood still runs true and I cannot lose consciousness. Then, as I lie on a marble tablet in the executioner's chamber, unable to scream, they begin to prepare me for living burial.

Two jade pigs they cram into my fists, and plugs of jade they stuff into all the orifices of my body. Almond-shaped jades cover my eyes. At last comes the jade cicada, symbol of rebirth … now it replaces my tongue, a cold hard thing that grates against my teeth and pushes the back of my throat so that my gorge rises, only I am too weak, too drained to vomit. Now, with excruciating slowness, they begin to sew the jade platelets over my body, sealing in my soul. Each sliver of jade rubs the raw flesh and makes my nerves scream out anew. Each time the needle with the spun gold stitches one jade scale to the next, the sharp edge pinches my flesh. In my mouth, the jade cicada begins to suck the life from me, a larva wriggling in its stony casing. This anguish goes on day after day … it is a sacred process, and ritual must be followed precisely, for though I am a traitor I cannot be summarily killed like a common criminal … I am also a consort of heaven, whose life and death must reenact the cycles of earth and sky.

Once set in motion, the procedures of my execution are painstakingly prescribed. Entombment, too, is a lengthy process, with interminable rituals to go through. How much better to be dead! By the time I am to be buried, I am sure that the people at court have quite forgotten me. I suppose I have already gone mad by then; so much pain, and the life-preserving quality of the jade always keeping me at the fringe of consciousness, never finding oblivion. But in the end, someone does come to visit me.

I sense his presence through the searing pain. He has brought his *p'ip'a* with him. I am already in the burial chamber … he must have funneled in through some tiny crack or chink from the world outside … but when the music begins I am in a different place … the music soothes me a little, stops me from choking on the cicada crammed into my mouth, even sets my jade suit to chiming in sympathetic vibration.

"Your curse," says the young singer, whose name I have never learned, "will come to pass. I've made sure of it. The jade will not make you immortal … that is a myth … I, who am a myth made flesh, understand above all the emptiness of myths. But your anger is stronger than jade. It may be stronger than death. Vengeance is as old as mankind itself. I know. I've heard that vengeance comes in the form of a crow … perhaps that is why you have learned to sing the song of the Raven's Daughter so poignantly. I have a power, Pui Yi … for you must know by now that I am no boy, but a creature of an ancient time, one who preys upon mortals … and I have used my power on General Zo. He will die but not die. And there will come a day when you and I will stand together, and you will battle the dragon, and the treasure you both seek will be your soul."

The musician touches the jade that envelops my face. I know he does not weep — his kind cannot, though they can bring tears to the eyes of mortals — and he adds, "And Little Newt says he is sorry he could not say goodbye."

5

Only an instant had passed. I knew why I had come. "You made General Zo a vampire," I said to Timmy.

"Yes."

"David Coleman is General Zo."

"The secret of your resting-place was well hidden, Pauline. But with all those burial-grounds being dug up to make foundations for new shopping malls in China —"

"I see," I said.

I also understood why it had taken me so long to learn to speak, and why confronting Coleman brought back my childhood stammering....

More noise now. I took Timmy's hand, and together we merged into the nearest shadows. Uncle Chang had come into the chamber, and he had workmen with him, with tools and lumber.

"Box it all up, la," he shouted at the workmen. "San Francisco museum. Letter of credit. Finally, I retire!"

Bright lights now. Coleman was nowhere to be found. Perhaps he was more sensitive to daylight than Timmy ...

perhaps he was sleeping, gorged with the blood of some peasant prostitute, in a coffin in the basement of the Hilton.

I wanted to stop the workmen, cling to the jade suit that held my lost soul, but Timmy held me back. *There is another way,* he said. He spoke not in words but in a language of night, of the movement of ripples in the pools of shadow. He held me to him in a close and dark embrace. I understood him. I let myself meld into him. He flowed over me, and together, as a stream of shadow, we trickled toward the crate they were building around the Empress of Jade.

The coolies were pounding in the nails. We ran past them, noticed only as a momentary flicker, a sudden chill. Slid into the makeshift coffin through the micro-thin slits between the boards. In darkness now, taking up no space at all, for the Empress of Jade was the world.

"In the end," Timmy said to me, "it'll be like the last time. This is between you and the general. I'll only be able to watch."

"I know," I said.

I wrapped myself around the woman of jade. My ancient self, still trapped within, still frozen in her timeless agony, called out to me through her epidermis of chill green stone. It was time for soul and body to come together. I sank into myself and became one once again. And awoke to the echoing pain and rage.

In a corner of the packing crate, shrunk to the size of a rodent, Timmy too waited.

In time, I felt motion. This, then, was why Timmy had wanted me to ship everything home early. I was to go on a different journey. I made my mind very still. Now and then, I heard the lilting music of some ancient lullaby, and knew that Timmy was doing what he could to soothe my torment.

There was a journey by oxcart, I think, from the bumpiness of it and the constant lowing of cattle. Then a truck. At length, a much smoother ride … we must have reached the cross-country highways of Thailand.

Then many days of stillness. A warehouse, perhaps. Searing heat — my jade carapace sucked fire and moisture from the air, inflaming my rage and pain.

Then, finally, more motion. Eased onto another truck. Stop-and-go … jerky moves back and forth … clearly, we were now bouncing our way through in the legendary traffic jams of Bangkok.

And then, finally, the pounding of hammer and crowbar, and I found myself once more on display.

6

I dreamed....

In my dream, I dreamed....

I dreamed that I woke from the nightmare, that I fled into my parents' room ... my mother still alive then, her arms wrapped around my baby brother, never waking ... my father holding me....

(And Cousin Wei, too, holding me on the day they told me I was to be sent to court....)

My father is holding me. I am the cicada bursting from the earth. I am the crow of vengeance. I am a weeping child. In my dream I cry out to him, "Dad, dad, they tell me you're a bad man, because of you junkies die in the streets —"

My father lies on his sick bed. My hand is on the Demerol button. He groans. The IV tube sways in the wind from an open window. The walls are lined with artifacts. And suddenly there are tube everywhere, catheters, stethoscopes, wires, and they are jerking my dad into the air and they are not medical tubes at all but puppet strings, and my father is suspended above the bed and his arms and legs are wriggling and his lips open and close to the snap of a marionette string, and he cries, "Good and evil are just parts in a play ... we're just acting out ... for ever and ever...."

And I see that what is to come was writ millennia ago, and I'm destined to act it out, no matter that I've lived a hundred lifetimes in a hundred bodies.

"Why me?" I cry. It's a question others like me have

always screamed out, despairing, since the dawn of humankind.

My father's body dances. He is an empty shell of jade. He has lost his soul. And I can give it back to him … at the cost of my own … yes. Like the raven's daughter in that ancient Chinese opera.

Suddenly I see my mother's coffin flying back up from the earth and the cicada bursting from its chrysalis and above it all, wheeling, crystal-eyed, the blackwinged messenger of death —

One by one the scales of the dragon shatter like —

Shards of jade and —

***

Neon. I hadn't expected that. I'm lying on a marble plinth, I think. The neon is overhead, flashing in garish hues of pink and turquoise … the jade skin is welded to my flesh, it has become my skin, the almond-shaped jades over my eyes are lenses through which I see level after level, rainbow-diffracted, escalators, elevators, crystal, glass … Jesus Christ, I think to myself, I'm in a fucking *shopping mall.*

No people though. It's night but my senses are sharp because I perceive everything through my jade skin. The neon is flashing, and I make out words: ARMANI • VERSACE • TOWER RECORDS • CYBERCAFÉ. This is a shopping mall then. In Bangkok, a new shopping mall goes up almost every five minutes. Bangkok is the new mecca of consumer vulgarity. So this is where the Empress of Jade has ended up … as a centerpiece in a shopping mall! So much for Coleman's pretensions to being some kind of museum curator!

Timmy, where are you? I cry out. It's the language of

night, of course. And now I see him. On a landing atop a marble stairway, seated at a white grand piano, wearing his trademark Dracula cape, the one he does his concerts in.

There's nothing I can do, Timmy responds. *I am only a watcher. This is not my dream. I'm here to complete the picture, just as I was with you when these events were set in motion.*

He starts to play. Not a piece of music, but a kind of meditation on music, different motifs weaving in and out, sometimes a burst of singing, a half-formed melodic fragment. This is not a music designed to bring me peace. It is uneasy listening. The dissonances grate on my jade scales. It's a chaotic music … a music pregnant with the pain of rebirth.

As the music dies away, I know that David Coleman has entered the atrium where I lie behind glass, in a recreated model of my tomb. I see him now, but I'm not yet ready to reveal myself.

I can hear his footsteps echoing on marble. He wears a black Armani suit and a yellow "power" tie. He is carrying a briefcase. I hear ticking. A bomb. I do not move. I reach out with my heightened jade-sense, and I see him through a veil of green, his eyes still shielded by mirrors. What now? Has he gone from grand vizier to museum curator to pyrotechnician? I wait.

Timmy is coming down the escalator. His cape his fluttering behind him … it must be the air conditioning … and his hair is wild.

David Coleman holds out a crucifix.

"Not this time, General Zo," he says softly. They confront one another. Timmy touches the crucifix and it shatters. "I'm prepared this time, and you know that superstitions are losing their power."

"This is none of your affair," says Coleman.

"I know," says Timmy. "I'm just a thing in Pauline's dream, a watcher, an explicator. After all, we've reached the comic-book moment when the villain must reveal his dastardly plan ... and you need someone to reveal it to."

Coleman laughs. "It's all a big cosmic joke isn't it?" he says. "I don't even know why we go through the motions."

"We're vampires, you and I — we can afford to take the long view. But why are you about to blow up this spanking new mall, which has its grand opening tomorrow, complete with stunning jade exhibition on its way to the San Francisco collection?"

"You know as well I as do that the jade suit must be neutralized. I;I've searched for almost two millennia for Pui Yi's resting-place. After you made her curse come true, I've wandered the earth in torment."

"Believe me," says Timmy, "I understand. But blowing up the shopping mall?"

"Just a little side job — you know, the usual corrupt bureaucracy, crony deals with insurance companies, insider trading, stocks about to fall — all the banalities of villainy."

"All right then. I'll go back to providing the soundtrack, and leave the two of you to duke it out, good versus evil, the whole cosmic shebang."

Timmy turns, goes back up the escalator, sits back down at the keyboard, begins, improbably, a New Age rendition of *Melancholy Baby.*

David Coleman unlocks the glass portal. He stands inside the mockup of my tomb. He surveys the scene with a kind of pride. As, indeed, he ought to. The simulacrum is excellent. As he sees each object, I too, with my jade-sense, see what he sees, and it fuels my rage.

There are the terracotta statues of my entire family — poor Auntie Chiu never knew what hit her — all were quietly decapitated and their bodies thrown into the river, but the grave of a royal consort must contain the full complement of relatives and hangers-on, and so they are all there in miniature. There are valuable items, too, bronze vessels, an enormous jade *'tsong,* a basket of carved *bi,* a whole menagerie of jade beasts, both real and mythical.

Coleman sets to work. He opens the briefcase, sets the timer, carefully places it beneath the marble plinth so that I will be incinerated.

"Time to die, my little concubine," he says softly.

He looks down at me. Who does he see, Sleeping Beauty?

"I wanted you," he says. "Why should Little Newt be the one to fill you with his seed?

A song rings out from the landing above us:

"Do not weep, my Lord ...
death, famine, war, destruction, pestilence are waiting.
Rejoice, my Lord, while time remains."

He puts his arms around me, scaly, anguished woman encased in stone, and with exquisite tenderness he kisses my jade lips. I feel his tongue through the sliver of cold stone, feel it vibrate against the jade cicada, feel the final surge of fury that propels me back from the shadowland —

I am changing. My flayed flesh bonds to the jade. I stretch out my arms.

"Magnificent!" says General Zo. He loosens his tie. Is he afraid of nothing? I feel his hand shoving hard against my pubic region, ripping at the frayed flaps of skin, forcing my millennial blood to well up …

I sit up. Blood is oozing from between my scales of jade. Tears of blood are running from my blank green eyes. The general throws his jacket on the marble floor.

"If only you could sing to me," he muses. "But you can't anymore, can you?"

I want to scream but now, as in my childhood, I cannot. The cicada clamps my vocal cords tight.

He unbuckles his belt. What is he thinking of? Is he not a eunuch? How can a eunuch love any woman, let alone a corpse encased in stone?

But no. He is not about to rape me. He is changing. Growing. His teeth are lengthening. He shakes his head and his mirror shades fly across the tomb. His eyes are mirrors too, and in those mirrors I see —

No. I too am changing. Black feathers are erupting from the jade. Great wings are sprouting. The general spreads his arms and he too has wings, leathern, scaly wings, and his forehead flattens into a reptile's, and his nose elongates and breathes out brimstone —

He rips into my side with a claw. But the jade holds firm … the blood congeals and scabs over and binds the carapace harder.

The raven wheels above, flitting from level to level of the shopping mall, shrieking death. I fly at the dragon. I batter him with my beak. I curl into a ball as his flames roar over me. The glass that encases the exhibition melts.

The odor of burning sulphur is nauseating, but I cannot vomit. The jade cicada is a lump in my throat, choking off my voice, tethering me to the land of the dead ....

A full-scale dragon now, he rears up, claws on the balcony above, pulls himself to the next floor, smashes the glass panes of a fashion store, slams his tail into a Tower Records sign, which explodes in neon sparks. I run after him ... and suddenly I am aloft, a soaring chimaera of soul and stone ... I dart toward his eyes, I jab at them with my beak, a foul blue acid spurts from them and fountains over the marble floors, which fizz and hiss and dissolve ... I, the guileless girl with the voice of an angel, I have become the avenger, returning evil for evil ... rending the flesh from the cheekbones ... and still he flies, higher, higher, toward the garish cupola of this cathedral of commerce, a painted sky of electric constellations that spell out SONY PANASONIC JVC ... blinded, he smashes against that ceiling, and the signs short out and the constellations blink and sizzle ...

The dragon plummets, flailing. I dive after him. He smashes down on the dais where my body lay before. The statues of my ancestors shatter and dust flies up in the wind of the dragon's breath.

And finally, wounded, he speaks to me. My talons are deep in his flesh. Our blood gushes like lava, searing all it touches. "Pui Yi," he says, "why are you killing me? I *want* to die. What kind of revenge is it ... to end my torment ... to set me free?" I become angrier. I almost speak, but the cicada clogs my throat still.

I see my puppet father jerking up and down on his strings ... I see the boy emperor, helpless, manipulated ... I see myself. What kind of a choice is this? No choice at all.

To avenge myself is also to fulfill my enemy's desire. My strings have been pulled. A terrible despair wells up. I will burst.

"Do you think I'm a bad man?" I look into the dragon's eyes, and I don't see the enemy. I see my father. "You think I'm evil because I profit from the suffering of junkies and throwaway children?" A fuming tear rolls down his gnarly cheek, and I see that he too is carapaced in jade, he too is bound up inside an identity of stone. And the death-embrace we share is also a moment of tenderness. The coupling of lovers. The comforting hug of a father and child.

At last, the welter of emotion dislodges the cicada inside me. I feel it move, I feel it stir to life, feel the wriggling of protoplasm beneath its stone meniscus. It writhes behind my lips like an unwelcome penis. I feel its wings emerge. The insect legs gouge my cheeks and uvula. Slime oozes from the jade. At last, my lips are pried apart by the cicada's steely forelegs and my mouth rips open in a scream of unendurable anguish, and the cicada bursts forth, tearing my face wide open.

"Perhaps I came to destroy you," I say, "perhaps to release you. The cosmos is a grand eternal symphony, and good and evil are just the little dissonances and resolutions that propel the song to its end which is also its beginning. In the end it's not important which side we are on. Our destiny is to dance together, black and white, man and woman, good and evil, light and shadow, life and death. We have to believe in good and evil ... because ... if we start to veer from this world of absolute truths ... then what are we? We are nothing, and where once stood God, there is only emptiness. The dance of good and evil is the magic that holds together the illusion that is reality."

This is the awful truth that I have learned, the truth in the eyes of the dragon. I am free to forgive General Zo. I am free to love my father, even though he is not a good man. I see that a vampire, child of darkness, can be a harbinger of light. The scales of jade have fallen from my eyes.

I love myself. It is a bitter love, but true.

The cicada settles on the dragon's face and methodically begins to eat away at the flesh. I have a tongue again. My voice doesn't get swallowed up in my throat like a lump of lead. I can speak. I can sing.

The dragon is dissolving as the cicada devours it, sucking in blood and flesh and scales of jade. The cicada grows with every bite, molting, shedding its crystal carapaces, growing, growing until it has engulfed the dragon and seemingly the world....

And, as the young musician vampire plucks the plangent melody out on his *p'ip'a,* I sing the last words of the song of the raven's daughter:

Rejoice, my father, while you still have time;

Rejoice, rejoice.

Then the bomb goes off, and the shopping mall crumbles in a flash that barely goes noticed in Bangkok's noisy neon night.

7

I watched the explosion on CNN, in my father's sick room, in San Francisco, and so I knew that I had not dreamed everything. A brand new mall had collapsed before its opening, crushing the jade exhibit smuggled in from China. No mention of a bomb, though. Faulty structure ... complaints about the unregulated building boom ... heads were rolling, but nobody believed they were the right heads. David Coleman, respected archaeologist, Indiana Jones sort of reputation, reportedly killed. No one else.

There was a crow perched on the window sill.

"The Empress of Jade was crushed to smithereens, Dad," I said. "This was all I could bring back."

I put the cicada in his hand. Translucent white jade, carved in that stylized, almost postmodernist style that characterized the Western Han Dynasty. The flawlessness of it set off my jade-sense. A shudder ran through me. A cold thing, a thing of severe, uncompromising beauty.

"I've not been a good man," my father said.

"I know," I said, and I embraced him, frail and shriveled, a ghost before dying; I wept. "It doesn't matter," I said. "No regrets now, Daddy."

"This is beautiful," my father said, holding the jade cicada up to the dying light. The crow flapped its wings. It looked at me with the eyes of a young boy. "This is absolute," my father said. "When I die, put it in my mouth. Perhaps it will speak for me in the afterworld."

"Yes."

"Now, Pauline," he said, sighing deeply, "maybe you'll bring yourself to tell me that you love me."

I did not stammer. I did not stutter. For the first time in my life, the truth did not stick in my throat.

***

Timmy Valentine has a hit single out. The song in the music video is *Crucify Me Twice,* and it's got all the typical Neo-Gothic tropes — it's Nine Inch Nails for the *latte* crowd, with whipped cream and brown sugar on top — but there's a second song, too — a bonus track — a weird, whiny Chinese melody that's supposed to be two thousand years old. I don't see much of Timmy, but he has a habit of leaving private notes in the most public places.

The Enquirer pointed out that when you play that track backwards, it says, "Pauline, Pauline." Thus, I have been "romantically linked" to Timmy, although it's bullshit of course; vampires and humans just don't, you know.

I'll have to look him up soon. Apparently there's an underground jade market opening up in Yunnan, where a huge neolithic burial site's turned up where they were going to put in a new stadium. Maybe Timmy will feel the need to get away again.

Vampires, after all, can be your friends....

This is another story that can stand alone, but somehow managed to appear in the Timmy Valentine trilogy somewhere. It is about Christopher Marlowe, and, as always, some of it is true. But not the parts you think....

More Strange than True

memory: 1611

Ariel, chick, farewell....

Whitehall, artificial light, stage machines, the night made bright by a thousand candles, the aging actor weighed down with robes, and gold thread, and tinsel, and tassels, and amulets, and rings, and chains of silver, and an orb set with a polished onyx ... the boy, not weighed down at all, for only his waist-length hair, and the branches of a potted ficus, serve to conceal those parts which may not with propriety be shown to the ladies at court.

The flickering tallow weaves about his person such a luminous, sheer fabric ... one ought not call it baseless, that would be to filch the master's words ... he seems as much enrobed in light as the old man in damask, wool, ermine, leather, silk (but that silk must be returned to the merchant of Venice by dawn or there will be a forfeit of a halfgroat). Ariel steps out from behind the tree. The play has gone well and soon will come the epilogue.

Prospero has said goodbye to the world of magic. Prospero is Master Will himself tonight, and he has spoken the words with a peculiar poignancy:

Leave not a rack behind.

The boy who has been one of the children of the Blackfriars Theater when he was first noticed by Heminges, an actor in the King's Men, who has been inducted into Mr. Shakespeare's acting company, who has remained mysteriously young for three summers … age cannot wither her! the apprentices say of him when he struts about backstage in the leafy apparel of Titania or the dusky face paint of Cleopatra's Charmian … he knows it will soon be time for him to go too. Before they suspect the truth. And before they lay the deaths on him, for the past three years have been blighted with inconstruable tragedies: Lady Catherine Darling, a favorite lady-in-waiting of the queen and ardent lover of the stage, perishing from loss of blood despite the physician's unorthodox decision to use no leeches; Willie Hughes, another of the children ex Blackfriars, and the boy's chief rival, perhaps, in the affections of the court; some stablehands in the households of the Wriothesleys and Somersets.

All, were one to pursue the truth, linked only through having once been in a place, alone, with the pale boy of the dark tresses and the eyes that, like lodestones, impel the looker towards Polaris. Sometimes a drawing room, sometimes an alley; Lady Catherine was seated at a virginals, struggling with a Byrd that would not sing to her; the boy would sing, however, or Byrd, or Tallis, or Dowland, and her favorite air fast became her funeral march. It was a lovely funeral; the king came.

The king has come this evening too. But it is not the poet that he watches with those ratlike little eyes; it is the boy. The boy looks away.

Stage hands with giant fans stir up the wind. The boy reaches up to catch the golden harness, flies upward into the ether, his hair strategically draped about his hips; with his free hand he waves to the throng, all silks and brocades and brightly-colored doublets. Then, as he nears the balcony, he lets go, seems, to the audience, to defy the earth's pull, somersaults in the empty air and dissolves into the shadowy eaves … into air, into thin air.…

Applause for another miracle of illusion.

He is still up there, of course; but he has become one with the smoky evanescence of wax, with the tendrils of tobacco fumes (for the court is agog with the new-discovered vices of the western Indies), and from above them he can see them all, bepowdered, bewigged, bewildered; Prospero stands alone for the epilogue, thumping his staff on the boards like a master of the choristers, then like a slave craving his own masters' indulgence; and indulgence comes in the languid handclaps of the king, the squeals of delight of the ladies, the surly smile of Buckingham, the king's friend, catamite, some say.

And later, the poet kneels at the king's feet, and the rest of the company with them, and the king is pleased to grant the company five pounds in old silver, undebased, Elizabethan silver. The pound has been scruples lighter since 1604. And as a special token of favor, the king gives Shakespeare a choice of rings from his second-best bauble tray.

And then he asks, "But the boy, Master William, where is that excellent boy? We would see if his tresses be his own." The king's English is still intermixed with the accent of the north, though England and Scotland have been one for eight years.

Heminges looks nervously at the wings; the boy is suddenly there. He has shot down from the rafters in the shape of a bat, transformed too fast for any to notice; he too kneels, keeping his eyes downcast.

"Come closer; we would study that visage, for time soon spiles a youth's smooth features. Silver is too soon tarnished, and alabaster cracked."

And he looks down at a fold of the king's doublet, which, though it is cloth of gold, is frayed. He smells a rank desire inside that doublet. The king toys with the hair, twines it in a callused finger.

"Wilt not look us in the eye, bairn? Do we affright so much? Thinkst thou that we would smite those delicate cheeks, when, troth, 'tis thy puir monarch which lieth smitten? What do they call thee?"

"Ned, Your Grace."

"Why Ned, here's gold." He takes another ring from the tray — "Aye, there's a carbuncle of a manly size," and slips on the boy's finger. He gasps; for the boy's hands are colder than the metal. "He sucks the warmth from me," says the king.

"Then," says the Duke of Buckingham, "Your Grace must needs receive warmth in return."

The king's friends laugh. But the king looks dark, and says, "Take care, Buckingham. I have made buggery a hanging offense, for I will not have loose morals in my kingdom, now that our scriptures have been properly

Englished."

"And the commonfolk have finally found out what sins they have been committing," says Buckingham, "even without benefit of Latin and Greek." More laughter, some real, some merely polite.

"Hast thou sinned, Ned?" says the king. And that same gnarled finger is descending down the boy's neck now, glancing the left collarbone, tracing its way downward towards the nipple. The fingertip moves southward, stopping to count each rib. The more the finger lingers, the more the boy feels anger. But the blood does not come rushing to heat his cheeks; what blood there is in him is dead blood. "God's death, but thou'rt cold. I would see thee naked, yet —" tugging at the hair, "would I not distress thee," laughing, "for thou art bonny."

And the moving finger writes, scratching words on marmoreal skin, in a spidery scrawl, Ned Ned Ned Ned and Wilt thou to bed?

And the boy says, "But Your Grace — by your own decree —"

"There are no laws," says Buckingham, "for them which make laws; though we shall answer to God in due course."

"In due course," says King James Sixt and First. "Shall we compare carbuncles? I shall not have it said I gave thee too rich a jewel." And his hand has penetrated the thicket of hair and reached down to caress the place beneath. "What, no carbuncles at all?" he says. "Comely yet incapable. Thou sad wee thing." And the king laughs.

"I pray you, do not belittle me, Your Grace," says the boy.

"Belittle, quotha!" says the king. "Well, go thy way. But first thou shalt kiss my hand, that's little enough to ask."

The king stretches out his hand; forces it to the boy's lips. Ned looks at the king's face for the first time. Cannot these humans look at him without seeing some fantasy of lust? Do they not understand that what they want from him he cannot give, has never been able to give, has had that gift forever stolen from him in the fiery death that swallowed up Pompeii? For fifteen hundred years he has fed, and killed, and turned men's lusts against them, and deemed himself been completely evil, and content to be evil. But he has finally learnt that there is no evil; there is only that which is pitiable; he learnt it from a man most men would regard as the most evil man of all time, Gilles de Rais, Bluebeard, the child-killer.

That is why I pity the king, he thinks. Look at him. He desires; he does not love. I am a bauble to him. He cannot know that the bauble is death. And as he and the king gaze at each other he knows his shape is shifting, for men see in him not only what they most lust for but what they most fear. I must look away or I will betray myself. He tears his glance away, but as the king's hand pries apart his lips, instinct takes hold of him.

He bites.

The king guffaws at this. "Thou'rt unmanned in more ways than one," he cries, "thou strugglest like a vixen." And at that the court bursts into uproarious laughter and applause, as though the king has uttered the wittiest of euphuisms, and even Master William has a little smile, no a big smile (more lines than hath the new map with the augmentation of the Indies) and so, unwatched, the boy feeds, feeds, feeds, feeds on blood that is no bluer than any man's....

The king does not even see. He basks in the tumult of

sycophancy.

Tonight the boy will have to disappear. He has tarried too long among these people … it maddens him, for here, in the company of those who have brought about in the world a very renascence of poetry and song, he has found men who did not think him an abomination. Like Kit Marlowe. (Though there were those found Kit abomination enough.) Kit is dead now, and soon these will be dead too, and the rebirth of poesy will be re-death. The boy feeds. He will need strength. The blood of kings does have a kind of potency. Tonight he will flee.

Tonight: away from Whitehall, away from London … perhaps even across the sea … he will take passage to the New World … or to Cathay … or to the frozen uninhabitable north … the world's mortality weighs down his mind … it will all dissolve … into air, into thin air … all but himself, who is already air.

memory: 1593

"Oh Ned, I am slain," Kit cries to him in an upper room of the tavern in Deptford. "Look at me, I bleed from the guts, it is fatal."

And the boy who has called himself Ned Bryant comes to him from the shadows where he has been hiding, mouselike, since the brawl over the reckoning began.

He knows that the poet is right. The wound is the kind that kills by a slow inexorable hemorrhaging; nothing can reverse the course of death now. How could the man have been so careless? Did he not know how many enemies he had? Did he not know that half those who professed themselves his friends had sold his misdemeanours to the eyes and ears of justice?

A doctor with a tray of leeches is huffing up the stairs, preceded by the mistress of the place, one Eleanor Bull. "What a terrible thing," the innkeeper is saying, "he is the greatest poet of our times, for all that he's an atheist and a sodomite."

"Mayhap not the greatest, after all," the doctor says. "For I was even this afternoon at the theater, where I saw Romeo and Juliet."

"Oh, that old sack of bombast."

"I warrant not; 'tis a Romeo new penned by that Shakespeare …"

"Ah, the poet of Titus Andronicus. This Romeo, I take it, would be far more violent; the pig's blood gushing in torrents on the boards; mutilations, rapes, stabbings; faith, my son Peter did importune me to be taken to see Titus, but I would not have my children exposed to such modern extremities, for they are yet tender."

"This, sir, was not bloody at all; bawdy more like —"

Kit Marlowe groans. "Boy," says the doctor, "help me with my leeches, or thy master dies." The leeches wriggle in a glass jar, and the doctor pulls one out with a pair of sugar-tongs.

"Sir," says Ned, "he dies anyway."

"Begone," Marlowe whispers harshly. "If I must be bled, let the boy do it. Boy, suck the blood from my wound, as thou art wont to do."

The doctor and the innkeeper look at each other, wondering, perhaps, what strange perversities have passed between the man and the child; but then they shrug, go downstairs.

"The constabulary must know of it," Ned hears the

woman saying. "And I shall have to find a priest."

And then it is that the boy kneels by Kit's bedside. Blood is seeping from the poet's belly. The boy bends, laps up the blood with swift flicks of the tongue, as a frog plucks flies from the air. As he feeds, the playwright's features soften in a kind of ecstacy. The blood is potent, as it always is when a man lies on his deathbed, still young, unplagued by illness. "My Ganymede," says Kit, "my Hylas, my Patroclus."

"Those are all Grecian catamites, are they not? I have not been your catamite, only your extractor of gore."

"Greek, aye ... nay, rather Ganymede was Trojan. Oh, if you could have but been in my plays! You would have made a fine Zenocrate; as Helen of Troy you would have had no equal. But I know you cannot go abroad by day." Yet Ned knows Marlowe's verses well; he has many of them by heart. A few years past, following the scent of untainted blood through narrow streets wretched with rats and plague-ridden corpses, he saw the flicker of a candle in an upper room, and heard a voice mumbling to itself, heard the squish of a quill being sharpened, the scratch of pen on paper, and the voice was saying, pausing between each little phrase to set it down:

Sometime a lovely boy in Dian's shape
With hair that gilds the water as it glides,
Crownets of pearl about his naked arms,
And in his sportful hands an olive-tree,
To hide those parts which men delight to see,
Shall bathe him in a spring....

There was such music in that muttering and scratching, music that assuaged the horror of the death-strewn street, that the boy could not help but fly towards the sound; and presently found himself tapping at the sill, crying in a small piteous voice, that the window should be unlatched; and Master Marlowe lighting another candle the better to see what had flown into the upper room, saying, "Surely thou art no angel. It would be a hard thing for me to believe in thee, seeing I believe not in God."

"Hardly an angel," said the boy, "yet sooth, not human neither."

"An evil spirit then. That is more to my liking; for though I can no longer find it in me to acknowledge a higher good, evil is another matter altogether; why then welcome, evil spirit. What seekst thou here?"

"What were those words that danced about mine ears, and dragged me hither through the streets of death?"

"My words dance well — for thou hast caught their rhythm. Hast a knack for singing, I'll warrant. That was a play, boy! Hast never seen a play, sirrah?"

"Nay. I dare not stir forth by day."

"I knew it! An evil spirit indeed, why, thou hobgoblin, thou imp, thou puck! Not stir forth by day! We shall put on a play by night for thee, at court, with a thousand candles for the sun."

"Can you not merely speak the play to me, without actors, without a stage? It was words that drew me here, not spectacle."

"Oh, you are a flattering evil spirit."

But then, pulling a sheaf of paper from a chest … the ink was not dry on some of it … he did begin to read his Edward II to the boy. The boy listened without a sound. He did not even breathe; perhaps that unnerved the poet, but he did not seem so; he was caught up in the perfervid vigor of his lines, in the tragedy of love so hopeless that a king would lose his queen, his kingdom, and finally his life. The boy said not a word till almost the end, when the assassin Lightborn slew the king by thrusting a red-hot poker into his arse; and then he cried, "No more, I pray you."

"So! The evil spirit hath a delicate stomach, it seems."

"I have seen too much of such things."

"Thou goest to the gallows of a Sunday, dost thou, to watch the felons being hanged, drawn and quartered...."

"Nay. I mean that I have seen too many men, women, and children impaled through the fundament with stakes, spears, spikes, even red-hot pokers ... I once had a friend, you see, you loved impaling."

"But this is the sixteenth century! Such atrocities belong to some barbarous forgotten time."

"Indeed. But I have not forgotten. It was a hundred and thirty years ago...."

Thus it was that the boy, whom Kit christened Ned, began telling the poet stories of the dark past. He did not know if Kit Marlowe believed the tales; but many a dash of color in Kit's plays owed something to the boy's storytelling. And the boy returned to the upper room frequently, for the poet's blood was clean, and he never drank enough to harm his host; for how could he kill the source of so much music?

But now, Ned thinks, the man dies anyway.

This time he sucks the very life from him. And thinks, This one should come back from the dead; the world should not lose one such as him, though it call him an atheist and a sodomite. And so he does not desecrate the body, but leaves it lying as though asleep, bloodless and pale; and then, shrinking to a mouse again, he dives into a hole and flees through the labyrinth of tunnels that spirals through the house.

The sadness that wells up is still new to him; he has only been able to feel it for a century. It reeks of a human childhood he has not thought on for a thousand years or more. He feels this sadness now as he burrows through beam and plaster. It animates the blood and makes him a little less dead.

And in the night, his grief driving him to an overpowering hunger, he kills again and again; in another tavern, foaming at the mouth like a rabid mastiff, he bites a pregnant woman through the belly and gorges on her unborn child, spitting out the caul into a tankard of ale; snapping a drunken seaman's neck and quaffing from the upturned neck-stump as it were a wineskin; and then at last, overcome, he finds a resting place, which as it happens is in a sewer next to the river.

The next night he goes to Mistress Bull's boarding house once more. The body is still lying where it left, for there has been no inquest yet. The mistress and an agent of the queen's, one Walsingham, are deep in talk downstairs, next to the fire. The body lies untended, in the dark, but for one who sees with the eyes of night, the room is awash with cold dead light. A cross hangs above the bed; it pains the boy only a little; time has conquered his superstitions; but still, he does not like to look at it. Another, he sees now, has been placed above the poet's heart: a silver cross, encrusted with amethysts; a costly thing, surely.

"Kind Kit, you must awake now." The boy touches the corpse with a finger; yes, yes, he can sense the inhumanly slow pulse that is the heartbeat of the undead; but Marlowe does not open his eyes. "You must awake, and come with me; I cannot answer for you; they say you are an atheist; perhaps they will mutilate you; then I will have given you undeath for naught."

It must be that damned cross above his heart, he thinks, and he grasps it and flings it to the floor; it burns him only for a moment, and then the skin grows back over the cruciform brand. Then Marlowe's eyes open. And he says, very softly, "It seemed to me that the whole world weighed upon my breast. But that is gone now."

"Come," says Ned Bryant.

"Come? What am I now? What is this thou hast made me?"

"What you have written is immortal; why not then you yourself? Listen, Kit, thou and I are kin now … I do not take liberties with my betters, but now I shall thee and thou thee, for thou art no longer Master Kit, and great teacher, and by a score of years my senior. In this new life thou art many centuries my junior, and it is I who must teach. How to transform into creatures of the night. How to thin the body into mist — O soul, be changed to little water-drops — how to feast on the blood of the living. And most of all, how to feed on the blood of the living, as I have done since before Rome fell. Oh Kit," says Ned, "I have done this for the sake of thy poetry, and for myself, because of my terrible aloneness. I have been a child for fifteen hundred years, but my thoughts are not a child's thoughts. I could recite lost verses of Catullus to thee, and poems of Sappho that were burned with the library at Alexandria; I can repeat all of Dante, even the cantos he discarded. I can speak to thee of Pythagoras' metempsychosis, of Aristotle, of Copernicus, of Mohammed, of St. Augustine, for I have lived through fifteen centuries of philosophy."

"But what of love, my little Ganymede?"

"Oh, but there is that in the universe of night which surpasseth love; there is the contemplation of eternity; there is the coldness that breaks the mortal heart, but which for us does make the night burn brighter than the sun; these things are deeper than love, more powerful than death."

Kit Marlowe grips the boy's hands, pulls himself up from the sleep of the dead. He is not glad, the boy thinks. He is still afraid; mortality still clings to him. "What of the soul?" he says. "I am not a believer in souls. Death should be an ending. This likes me not, to die then have to wander once more in the world."

"Why trouble with the soul?" says Ned. "If thou didst have a soul, and hadst thou died an ordinary death, would not that soul be even cooking in the everlasting furnace?"

"Why this is hell," says Marlowe, "for it is not the vanitas I yearn for. Free me, Ned, free me, I implore thee."

How can I free him? Ned thinks. And how can he resist what I have to offer him? Is it not what all men most desire? Did not Faustus sell his soul to the devil for less than I have offered? Ned cannot understand at first that he is being refused. In fifteen hundred years, he has become secure in his seductive powers. No one can deny him. Is he not more lovely than any angel? So many have told him this, and come to him, and let him drink up their life. A savage anger rises in him. He seizes the silver cross, heedless that it chars his fists, and pounds it into Kit's chest, snapping bone and cartilage to penetrate his very heart; the poet does not cry out at all, but only, as he closes his eyes for the last time, whispers, "I thank thee, gentle Ned."

The boy casts the cross aside. He wounds in his palms are already healing. "I have been here long enough," he says. He must away. A long dark sleep of a hundred years will mitigate his sorrow. He has yearned for renascence and found himself stillborn. He almost weeps.

He leaps from the open window, and in mid-leap takes wing, and leathern-winged swoops down the fetid alley, toward the river, away from London.

memory: 1593

And, on leathery wings, swift as the wind, he swoops, swerves, sweeps along the narrow streets, thinking only that he must get out of London, bury the ugly memories and his identity, find another name, another time … he must enter the dark forest and renew himself so that he can emerge, healed, ready to feed once more….

Beyond the river … over the cathedral … past the palace … into the wood … swooping … down low. He drops to the ground and his wings disintegrate … he has become a rodent now, sniffing through the damp grass, each blade silvered by the moon.

He moves into a clearing. There are toadstools. There are human voices. He cannot help himself. He can hear the music of their blood, and his hunger rises a little. The hunger he can control; the grief will not go away. In human shape again, he rests in the shade of an ash-tree at the edge of the clearing. The ash does not sting him even though it has been said that, of the stake that must be driven through a vampire's heart, ash-wood is best, for it partakes of the most ancient of magics; it is an ash-tree after all which supports the world, so said the rune-readers of the north. He leans against the trunk and watches.

Three humans come into the clearing. Their faces are eerie in the chiaroscuro of moonlight and forest. They are laughing. One is a ravenhaired woman, dark, serious and soft-spoken, one a young man with a slight beard and an extravagant ruff, the other a younger man, a boy even, whose doublet is festooned with pearls. Ned has seen the young man somewhere before: now he recognizes him; it is the Earl of Southampton, Harry Wriothesly, who has occasionally visited Marlowe in his garret.

"Sooth, a fairy ring," says the young man. "Will, come see."

"Dare we enter it, Harry," says the woman, "with the moon so bright, and the hour of midnight fast approaching?"

"What, fear you hobgoblins, witches, pixies, pucks?" the young man says, and skips over a line of toadstools; he bows and beckons his two friends.

Ned sees that at the center of the clearing the toadstools form a circle. Solemnly, the three mortals enter the circle. They stand equidistant and link hands so that it seems that the magic circle circumscribes a triangle. And Ned moves closer, intrigued by the curious ritual of their interconnecting; for it seems to him that one loves the other who loves a third who loves the first yet none is loved by whom he loves the most; the boy has seen this from the way their glances dart, one to the other, the other to the third, and so on round and round in a roundelay that will not play its final chord, will not resolve. It is a game to them, yet the stakes are human hearts.

"I pray you, no more sonnets," says the fair-haired boy, "I am for plays: tears and laughter, revenge and retribution."

"Let us do a play now," the dark lady says, laughing. "A play for Will, and these toadstools shall be our groundlings."

"Groundlings! Toadstools should have more taste," says Will. "But truth to speak, 'tis an excellent open space for a play — look, yonder brake shall be your tiring house, this fairy circle the apron of our stage, and the moon hath all the light we need."

"All the world's a stage for you, Will," says the boy. And kisses him on the lips, daring him to go farther; and the lady covers her laughter with a coy clasped hand; and Ned sees in Will Shakespeare's eyes confusion and inner torment. "Why, what's the matter?" says Harry. "Inside this fairy ring, we are invisible; it is May; nothing is as it seems; nor night, nor day; nor love, nor death; nor man, nor woman."

"Harry, Harry, thou speakst in riddles."

"No riddles, Will, but visions!" He plucks a velvet sack from his sleeve, waves it past the others' noses, and cries, "Fresh nutmeg … this fruit of this, chewed thoroughly and long, induceth the condition called 'midsummer night's dream' — the mad enhancement of the senses — monsters, fairies, creatures of light and darkness dancing in the air — whorls, patterned patens of bright gold —"

The dark lady shrieks with laughter, takes the first bite. "'Tis bitter." And after a moment: "But now 'tis sweet." And laughs again. Her breasts are but slender; she too is young, Ned thinks.

"I am not one for drugged delusions," says the poet. "My brain is fevered enough." His two companions laugh. "But I would see you act, Harry."

"You see that often enough," says Wriothesly, "when I'm with my mother the Countess."

"But how would you act," says the dark lady, "and you were in a stage, and gowned and gartered as a queen?"

"I'll show you, if it like you. Lend me your dress. But you, lady of shadows, must play a man, for I would not have you naked in the wood."

"More nutmeg first!" she says.

And then the two skip over the fairy ring and into the shadows, leaving Will along in the moonlight. Closer, Ned thinks, I must come closer. Mist has begun to swirl up from the ground, and Ned attenuates himself and joins that mist, and floats above the poet's head, and smells his very breath, a cold clean breath quite unlike Kit Marlowe's, that was always clogged with cloves and wine. The poet is mumbling to himself....

"I know a bank where the wild thyme blows,
Where oxlips and the nodding violet grows
Quite overcanopied with luscious woodbine...."

Music again, thinks the boy, music surpassing even Marlowe's. How can I leave this place? he thinks. How can I retreat into the shadow?

And from the shadow come the dark lady and the boy. They are dressed in each other's clothes. The lady has become a dandy, beruffed, bepearled, and her hand resting on a jeweled pommel; the boy, corseted and enrobed in lace and satin, has become more girlish than ever. And the effects of the drug have made them even giddier. They laugh and point at one another and tell each other what they see: "A jackanapes!" "An ass-head!" and Will Shakespeare observes, inscribes their antics in the ledger of his mind, and says nothing at all.

They posture, they orate, they yell out random passages of bombast; and now and then, the poet smiles; and finally, exhausted, they fall into a heap in the middle of the fairy ring; and Will kneels down and looks from one to the other, and softly he says, "Thou master-mistress of my passion", but Ned, the funneling mist, cannot tell to whom he addresses those words, though he engulf the three of them within his vaporous arms.

And Harry says, "Tell us what play you are writing now."

And Shakespeare says, "I cannot tell thee much. It is in an elfin clearing such as this. A fairy king and his dark consort are battling to possess a boy, an ..." he thinks for a moment, "Indian boy."

"To possess him carnally?" says Harry. "Why, that rivals Master Marlowe." And he and the girl giggle softly.

A field mouse darts through the circle. Startled, the lady sits up; the nutmeg has made her easily affrighted. For a moment Ned loses control of his shape. But like quicksilver he pours himself back into the air.

"Behold — some personage — a beautiful boy — condensing out of the mist," says Will. "Tarry, thou wanton boy! Gods, but he was comely! If only he had played my Juliet, and not that snotty-nosed Alfred Walmsley, panting like a pregnant sow. Boy, come back!" And tries to pull young Ned back out of thin air.

"So, nutmeg after all!" says the lady.

"Nay," says Will, "I saw him. It was a thin, pale boy, seeming almost one with the mist and moonlight, not quite substantial."

"It was only a puck," says Harry.

Will sits awhile in thought. "If peradventure such creatures of the night could be conjured up on a stage," he says at last, "there would be magic indeed."

"How?" says the lady. "They cannot come abroad by day."

"Indeed," says Harry, "they do fear the dawn; the sun doth send them screaming back to Hell."

"But if," says Will, "the night become as day...."

"Yes!" says Wriothesly. "Thousands upon thousands of candles ... the great hall of one of our castles ... a dais set up, courtiers and royals in their most gilded vestments ... I have heard they plan such a spectacle at Blackfriars ... with the children of some chapel choir. A merry prospect indeed, unscrubbed young quiristers flouncing about in petticoats by candlelight."

"Yes ... in such a place, in such a time, a thing of darkness could recite my words ... and how such words would sing, an the tongue that sing them be not mortal, but itself of air excorporate; for poetry is air, though it err not; it is the air that the ear is heir to. Nay, 'ear' is too much; I must retool the conceit."

I cannot sleep yet, thinks the vampire who has called himself Ned Bryant. I must to this new theater that performs by night. I must bedazzle with my singing until they make me one of them. I must attract the notice of this poet until he gives me words to speak. I cannot depart this time till I be the thing of darkness he acknowledge his; I must become that immortal tongue.

In the pageant of blood that has played through his unlife for fifteen hundred years, there has been too much horror. He has apprehended so much evil that he has finally come to know there is no final evil. It is this that has mitigated his superstitions, so that he no longer recoils from the cross, or the sacred host, or the holy blood of Christ. I must have blood to sustain me in this half-existence, he thinks, but there are other things I need too; even a monster can know beauty, and yearns to utter honeyed words, and sing in languages other than the voice of night.

I shall to London....

***

This next piece, a novella, appeared in a remarkable collection, *Vampire Sextette,* created by my friend Marvin Kaye. It's presented as an absurdist parody of a courtroom drama, but has its roots in an actual case that is not *that* different from this story. Satire aside, it has a few disturbing truths in it.

S.P. Somtow

Vanilla Blood

Well, then. We might as well begin in the middle. Because the beginning has been done to death, hasn't it? The discovery of the bodies, the cross-country chase, even the allegations of police brutality ... you've seen it on CNN. Sixty Minutes. 20/20. Hard Copy. Graphic detail. You saw it all.

You saw her face. Pale as Ophelia in the bathtub of blood. The half-formed smile. The eyes, wide, emerald-green, the soggy blonde hair that wound about the corpse like a seaweed garnish; the skin, luminescent, of a piece with the porcelain she lay in; naked, of course, but they didn't show that on TV. If you were lucky, you caught the nudity when the camera lingered on the photos that first day on Court TV, marking the exhibits one by one, starting with the crime scene photographs.

You saw it; we can dispense with it.

You saw the perp on the cover of *Newsweek.* How young he looked! Anyone's kid, really — a nice Southern boy. Tried as an adult? You didn't really want to agree with the prosecutors — he seemed so goodlooking, so vulnerable, so — in need of a friendly social worker. Stared right through the camera and into your eyes … and into your heart.

Even the Pope sent a letter. As if that would have done much good here, right in the heart of Catholic-hating Klan country.

And then there was the lawyer. Pro bono, of course. A man who had been on every dream team in every high-profile trial in the last ten years. A talking head on Court TV. Once rendered Pat Buchanan speechless on *Crossfire.* He, too, had made the cover of *Newsweek.* But that was the "Superlawyers" cover story last year.

The prosecutor. An ice queen. Considered more robot than human … at least, until Flynt released the nude pics. You know this. You've spent whole watercooler breaks discussing her anatomy. Oh, yes, she was a natural redhead all right. Unless, of course, she had taken the trouble to dye … down there.

What a bitch! But an appealing one.

And the judge. He fumbled his way through the last big one, an eighteen month soap opera of celebrity murder, money, and sex. Now he had learned his lesson, and he was breathing fire, not taking any shit.

You are familiar with all these figures, I'm sure — there aren't many people in America who aren't. The *Saturday Night Live* parody alone said more than this brief memoir ever could.

So, instead, we'll start in the middle … just seconds after Judge Trepte kicked the cameras out of the courtroom.

We'll even go so far as to begin in the middle of a sentence.

***

— gone yet? Good, good.

— Sir? Get that thing out of my courtroom. Thank you. All the way out. When I kick out the cameras, sir, I kick out the cameras; I don't mean to have them lurking about in the anteroom. I mean, out, out, *out.*

— But, Your Honor, we've paid generously for the broadcast rights to — all right, Your Honor. Yes, sir. Goodbye, sir. Thank you, sir.

...

— and now, counselor, you will reveal to this court exactly why your next witness is arriving in so remarkable a fashion.

— He always travels this way, Your Honor.

— Objection! The defense is attempting to offer a *corpse* as a defense witness!

— You must admit, counselor, that the prosecution does have a point.

— He's not exactly *dead,* Your Honor. He just travels this way.

— In a *coffin.*

— Yes, Your Honor.

— Well, I'll be damned. Strike that. I think you will all agree that I made the right call in getting rid of the press. We can all relax now, and get to the bottom of this nonsense, without getting yet *another* lead story on the CBS Evening News. Miss Anderson, strike all that — all of it. This is not going to be a trial for the TV trial junkies. No. This is life and death ... some would add even undeath. Don't expect me to run this courtroom like Judge Itoh. More like Judge Dredd. Strike that too, Miss Anderson, strike, strike, strike, strike, strike. Now I'll stop pontificating and turn things over to you overpaid lawyers.

— The prosecution continues to object, Your Honor.

— Sustained.

— Your Honor, we cannot present this case without this witness's testimony.

— Then I will reconsider the objection when the witness deigns to get out of the coffin.

— He can't, yet. Your Honor. But I believe he will be able to in about five minutes....

— Five minutes you may have. The court will recess for five minutes ... no, let's say ten. Some of us still smoke.

***

— Well, counselor?

— I don't understand it, Your Honor, but the witness doesn't appear to have stirred.

— Does the defense counsel propose to attempt to resuscitate the witness? We do have paramedics on call, do we not? Or will smelling salts do the trick?

— Your Honor, this has gone on far enough. Defense's sense of the theatrical is a little ill-timed, don't you think? I mean, they defend a few big name actors, they think they're Perry Mason. Can I continue to state my objection?

— Your objection stands. Bring on your next witness, counselor.

— We confess, Your Honor, we're sort of at a loss. In view of the apparent immobility of our star witness, we'd like to ... ah ... may I look at my notes? ... Jeremy Kindred. Yes. He's on the list.

— Very well.

***

— State your name for the record.

— Jeremy William Kindred.

— How old are you, Jeremy?

— I'm … I don't know exactly. Fifteen, sixteen.

— Are you a vampire?

— Yes.

— Are you a member of the group variously known as the Brotherhood of Blood, the Cult, the Vampire Society?

— I was, sir.

— You were?

— I was for a while, sir, but it was just what you'd call peer pressure, and no sir, I didn't kill nobody, didn't drink nobody's blood.

— Just answer the question, young man.

— Uh, sure, Your Honor.

— Tell us about it … in your own words, if you'd like.

— Objection! This is all irrelevant. The witness wasn't even *at* the killing. He's just wasting the jury's time.

— I think it's important to my case, Your Honor, that we clearly illustrate the circumstances under which these kids could come to believe that these crimes were not only acceptable, but desirable.

— Listen. The cameras are off, counselors. There's no more need for posturing. The jury is going to zone out completely unless you entertain them with a good story. So, kid, let's have it.

— Uh …

— You may proceed, Jeremy.

— Well, sir, I really joined it for the sex. I mean, there was a rumor that the Brotherhood had these orgies in the old Hanson house.

— That's an abandoned house?

— Yes, sir, by the cemetery. I don't why it ain't been

tore down yet; it's kinda an eyesore. It's condemned, though. I always used to walk past it on my way to school. It's a big old place, creaky doors, peeling paint, scary statues of devils with leathery wings … and the big angel with the bronze sword … not shiny anymore, green mostly … not since the ringleaders of the Brotherhood was all put in jail. But that used to be the weirdest thing about that place. It was all crumbling and dirty except for that sword. That tall angel stood next to them wrought iron gates and it held its sword high in the air and the sword was all polished ... and you know, walking to school in winter, with the sun just rising, you could of swore that thing was on fire. The way it caught the sunlight. So the kids called it the Flaming Sword, like the preacher says about the Angel of Death. Anyways … there was this rumor that someone had wild parties there … you might call them raves, I guess … lotta E, lotta dope, lotta loose wenches if you know what I mean. So when Cat Sperling kept looking at me from the other end of the hall, she was a senior and all, with tits like balloons, you could say I was interested. Everyone knew that Cat had something to do with them parties. And everyone wanted that bitch, shit, even the girls wanted her. But there's something weird about her that you need to know. It wasn't no big Hollywood special effect kinda thing but … she carried the night around with her.…

— Could you explain that a little more clearly, Jeremy? Take your time.

— Well, sir, it didn't matter if the sun was out, or if all the lights was on inside that school room. She always had like a shadow on her. Her skin was real pale, and it glimmered … well, like the moon was shining … but just on her you understand, just on her. There was a silvery thing about her eyes, too … you know like when you're in the woods all alone at night and you catch the moonlight dancing amongst the leaves … you catch my drift, sir?

— You're saying she was attractive. She had a unique look. Some kind of makeup, perhaps.

— Yeah well, it was like on no infomercial about pearly essence face cream … a lotta girls use that shit … she was different. It was like she was the real thing, and the others were all just imitating her. Did I tell you about the black hair? It was long, all the way to her waist. And she wore black lipstick. It matched.

— A goth, then.

— More than that. Like I said. Not a wannabe. The real thing.

— Objection, Your Honor, I fail to see how this catalog of feminine charms has any relevance whatsoever to the defense's case!

— Stop posturing, counselor. I've sent away the cameras; and the jury looks awake for the first time since this sorry spectacle began. I'm going to allow it. You may proceed, Mr. Kindred.

— Just tell the story in your own words, Jeremy.

— Well, I still think he's fishing, Your Honor.

— I've already overruled your objection.

— Jeremy?

— Yessir. Cat Sperling, sir.

— Cat Sperling let you know, through some kind of sign language or eye contact, that she had something to discuss with you.

— Not exactly, sir.

— What did she let you know?

— She wanted to fuck me, sir.

— Watch your language, young man! Try to act in a manner consistent with the dignity and majesty of the law — what's left of it!

— I'm sorry, Your Honor; I don't know no other word for what she was trying to say.

— Very well, then. The court will take into account the deprived environment you clearly come from.

— I ain't no trailer trash, Your Honor!

— Quite so, young man, quite so. Why don't you finish telling your story to the court?

— Sure, Your Honor. Like I said, I got the Look from her. There ain't no mistaking the Look, sir. From all the way across the hall, and I knew she wanted me. Well, so there's a place you go to when you give someone the Look … at least that's how it works at Edward Kramer High. The place is up on a hill, you know, the hill just north of the cemetery. There's a road that winds up, and a hiking trail as well. At Kramer, we don't need to pass notes; it's a tradition; you get the Look, and if you give the Look back, then you go meet on the hill. If you hold up one finger, it means *tonight;* two fingers means we'll set a time later. Well, Cat held up one finger; everyone saw it, even if they didn't say nothing; Kramer ain't a kiss and tell kind of a school. — It's an ancient tradition, then.

— I'd say so, sir.

— One that your parents would know about. That even a few members of this jury may well have experienced, if they happened to have gone to your high school.

— Did Cat Sperling meet you on the hill that night?

— Yes, sir.

— Did she then proceed to initiate you into the

Brotherhood of Blood?

— Oh, no, sir. You can't get in just like that.

— Tell the court what happened, Jeremy.

— Well, that night, I went up to the hill. I borrowed my Mom's Malibu. I don't have a license, but you said I'd have immunity, right?

— This is a multiple murder case, Jeremy. I don't think the court is too worried about your license.

— Okay, okay. Well, she was waiting there all right. She was every bit as enticing as the rumors said. It was windy and her hair was flying every which way … and catching the moonlight. She leaned against a tree with a joint in one hand … I can say that, can't I? … and her eyes were wild. I couldn't believe my luck. I mean, to tell you the truth, I'd never done it before. Unless you count, one time, in summer camp —

— That's all right, Jeremy. I don't think the court needs an exegesis of your sexual experiences.

— Okay. So she says to me, Jeremy Kindred, I've had my eye on you. You're a good-looking kid. And I says, Yeah, they say that. I'm tall for my age, almost six feet already. And she says, You got that unplucked look. Like a glistening round apple in a tree … a fresh smell, apple-scented shampoo maybe, a little-kid smell in a big-kid body … and I know how much you want me, seen how you stare at me in across the hallway or last week when we had that big assembly with the Yankee AIDS speaker. Here, take a drag of this, it'll relax you, I know your heart's pounding, boy. Really pull on it, hard I mean hard. Come closer. You always wanted to touch them, didn't you? Here. Put your hand on them. Through the sweater for now, I ain't no whore … I know you like it, Jeremy

Kindred. So well, I felt them titties and they were fine. Firmer than I thought they'd be. Fairly straining against the wool they was. Got a rise out of me, lemme tell you. It was something to be alone on the hill with Cat Sperling. It sure turned my head. I didn't even think nothing of it when she asked for a drop of blood.

— So let me get this straight, Jeremy. This woman, this older woman —

— She won't but three years older than me, sir, if that! —

— Well, for the sake of argument, a slightly older and certainly much more sophisticated woman ... lures you to a well-known trysting spot ... gets you all hot and bothered ... and suddenly asks to drink your blood?

— She didn't say drink, sir. You're jumping the gun on the story. She just said, Jeremy, you cute-as-a-button boytoy, let me have a drop of blood. The drinking didn't rightly occur to me, not at that moment ... I don't know *what* was occurring to me, really, excepting I wanted to get inside her jeans something fierce. I knew she was a member of that Brotherhood thing, so blood had to figure in it somewhere ... like swearing blood-brotherhood with your best buddy in junior high or something. Well, she asked for a drop of blood, and by now we were in the back seat of the Malibu, I forgot to say that, didn't I? ... and I was reaching into her jeans ... it didn't feel down there like I thought it would ... more leathery ... and slick ... like a beat-up old wallet. And she was all, I have a needle here, and I just need a little bit, just a thimbleful would do the trick right fine. And she reached into a back pocket and pulled out a hypodermic. The needle glinted in the moonlight that reflected off the rear view mirror and you know what it made me mighty hard, more than I'd ever felt before in my life, cause I guess there was something dark about it, something forbidden ... and this was how she did it ... she yanked my pants down to my knees and kinda crouched down and pushed me up into her, and at the same time she jabbed that needle into my chest, like she was fixing to impale my heart. Well, I can't tell you how that made feel, I mean, I just about burst right then and there, after being inside of her only a minute ... and then I thought, well, I'm screwed for sure, because Cat Sperling ain't gonna want a green kid who can't last but a minute inside the famousest pussy in town.

— Your Honor, I simply have to object. I just don't see how this catalog of adolescent fumbling can possibly relate to the defense's case.

— If you'd bear with me for a second, Your Honor, I believe the witness is about to reach a crucial point of evidence in the defense's case ... the blood.

— All right, counselor. But if you don't reach some kind of relevance within the next two minutes —

— Jeremy, tell the court about what happened next.

— Well, sir, she didn't seem to pay no mind to the fact that I come inside her. She was only interested in the blood. When she saw that stream of red gushing into that syringe, she started thrashing and heaving and carrying on something fierce. She was all moaning, too ... and shrieking ... like a passel of cats in a back alley. I never seen anything like it, sir, and I've watched a lot of pornos. And then she's all shuddering to a climax right there in the back seat of my Malibu. And the blood's dribbling from her lips ... but it's not a scary thing ... it's warming her, lighting up her face ... her cheeks were pale before, but now they're all blushing just a bit. And then she says to me, I want you to join. Join what? I asks her, but I already know what she means. I said, I heard there's a lotta parties, and in them parties you all get down, if you know what I mean. Parties right in the cemetery's what I heard. She smiled. You're coming to the very next one, she says, and it's on Friday the Thirteenth … next weekend … but it'll probably last until Sunday morning … when some of us, the ones that aren't in too deep, who can still stand the vibes, why, we go to church. I'm thinking that it can't be *that* bad if they go to church afterwards. So I say, sure, I'll come. And she says, Be sure and bring your best friend Jody.

— Who did she mean by that?

— Jody Palmer, my best friend.

— The defendant?

— Yes sir, he sure is.

— I trust the prosecution is now satisfied as to the relevance of this witness?

— We continue to object, Your Honor. All this is fascinating in a prurient sort of way … I can see the reporter from CBS in the back there, desperately looking for an opening to demand the cameras back … but the fact remains that Jody Palmer killed several people, including his mother … and that he's being tried for murder.

— Your Honor, we must have some latitude here. The prosecution's perfectly aware that we're trying to establish that the defendant was under such crippling social and emotional pressure that he believed he no longer had a choice. You must allow the witness to —

— Your Honor! The coffin lid is shaking!

— Well, hold it down, bailiff!

— I can't! There's something inside … struggling to get

out!

— Jesus Christ, I forgot Daylight Savings Time! Sunset's an hour later!

— Cut the profanity, counselor.

— I'm sorry, Your Honor, but —

— I'm fining you a thousand dollars for contempt. Get your checkbook out this minute, counselor. Bailiff! Control that coffin!

— Blast! The lid's off!

— Well, put it back on.

— It's fighting back! Someone's inside — and he — she — it's trying to sit up!

— Well, restrain him, bailiff.

— It's a woman, Your Honor ... a young woman.

— Cat!

— The witness will refrain from speaking unless it is in response to a question from counsel, or from myself.

— Oh. Yes, Your Honor. Yes, sir. I didn't mean to —

— Counsel for the defense ... you've been referring to this witness in the masculine gender from the beginning. And now that your witness has deigned to emerge from her ... ah ... conveyance, she appears to be very, very feminine indeed. Exceptionally so, and flaunting it besides. Do you always instruct your witnesses to appear in court in flimsy negligees? Is this a courtroom or a Frederick's of Hollywood catalogue? For God's sake, madam, cover yourself! Bailiff ... a cloak for the witness. I won't have the jury distracted by her endowments. In fact, I won't have the jury distracted at all; counsel, I want an explanation.

— Your Honor, could we have a brief sidebar? This isn't the witness we had in mind for this portion of the testimony. There appears to have been a … misunderstanding.

— Oh, Jeremy … you sure are a sight! You look real small and scared and powerless up there in that witness box. But it's okay, baby. Cat's here now. Cat will hold your hand. It's gonna be all right. You didn't do nothing wrong … and it's not you that's on trial.

— But Cat … you're *dead!* I saw you die!

— Death ain't nothing, baby. Just another kind of doorway. And there's more than one way of going through that doorway … you can let them shove you through, and you can let them flush the key down the toilet bowl of eternity … or you can wrest that key out of their hand and take it with you … so they can't slam the door in your face … so you can live forever on the edge of life and death … I did it, baby, just like I said I would … I did it, baby. Oh, yes, I crossed over, and I crossed back. Just like the duke said. And you can do it too. Don't be afraid, Jeremy. Oh, and Mr. Counsel … the duke says he's sorry, but he can't be in court tonight. Something's come up. He sent me instead. I can give all the evidence you need.

— The duke, as you call him, Miss … Sperling, is it? … is under subpoena.

— Subpoenas don't work too good on dead people, Mr. Judge. If the duke wants to come to your court, he'll come; but your laws don't really apply to him. The undead have their own laws. There's nothing in the constitution about them.

— On the contrary, Ms. Sperling. Just because creatures you're calling the *undead* are not specifically mentioned in law doesn't make them outside the law at all. Anyone who is evidently capable of rational discourse and capable of appearing here and making remarks, relevant or otherwise, is a *prima facie* candidate for personhood and I can damn well hold them in contempt if I so choose!

— Your Honor, the witness is ... well ... she's sort of swirling, melting into some kind of mist … and now there's a black cat running around the courtroom … it doesn't seem very friendly, sir …in fact, it's got poor Mrs. Coates trying to climb up one of the pillars … it could be rabid, Your Honor.

— Shoot the critter! I won't have any more disruptions!

— Sir, the cat appears to have leapt out of the window.

— That's four stories, bailiff! Surely even a *cat* can't leap for stories and survive … now what? It's flying into the night? You see great leathern wings against the face of the full moon, bailiff? Is this *Batman* or is it a court of law? Put that camera away, Mr. Prinze, or I'm kicking CNN out completely. And I'm hereby instructing the jury to ignore all of this — the woman climbing out of the coffin, the soap-opera dialogue between Ms. Sperling and the witness, the bizarre metamorphosis from female to feline, *and* Mrs. Coates's screams. None of this ever happened, do you hear? *None of it!*

— Your Honor …

— What is it now, counselor? My patience is wearing pretty thin.

— In view of the fact that we have let the wrong … ah, cat out of the bag, and in view of the fact that the witness currently on the stand hasn't yet completed his testimony. …

— Quite, quite, counselor. I think there's been quite enough claptrap for one day. Court will reconvene tomorrow at nine o'clock sharp, corpses and all.

— The corpse ... and I will try to make sure we have the right one on hand tomorrow, Your Honor ... will not actually be able to *say* anything until sundown ... might an allowance be made? Please don't consider it contempt; consider it rather to be a medical condition that prevents the witness from testifying during daylight hours.

— All right. I'm going to give you a lot of leeway, counselor. But any cats, bats, or talking corpses are going to have to abide by my rules. Court will reconvene at three p.m, then — we will allow the current witness to finish his touching story — by which time sundown will have arrived and we will be able to continue with your key witness — assuming him, or her, to have completed his, or her beauty sleep at that time.

§

— So, Jeremy ... having had your blood sipped by the sexiest girl at Kramer High in what can only be described as a somewhat erotic experience ... did you then accept Ms. Sperling's invitation to an event which you believed would be some kind of wild, gothic, orgy?

— Yes, sir.

— And did you bring the defendant with you on that occasion?

— Uh, yes, sir.

— And did you and the defendant drink blood at that event?

— Yes, sir. Vanilla.

— Vanilla?

— When the new ones drink blood for the first time ... they mix it with vanilla syrup. Kinda kills the taste. Gets you used to it. It's like, uh, you wouldn't give your kid brother a straight shot of JD the first time, not without mixing it with a Coke or something. He'll get just as drunk, but it won't burn his throat as bad.

— What did you tell the defendant to get him to come to this event?

— Oh, that was easy. Jody's a big vampire fan. He watches vampire movies all the time, and he plays roleplaying games, live-action ones, too. Last year, we hitchhiked down to some sci-fi convention in Chattanooga, and he got into a live-action vampire thing that lasted the whole weekend, 24/7. He didn't even try to pick up no bitches or get fucked up, he was so caught up in the game. See, when it came to Cat Sperling's big event, orgy, whatever you wanted to call it, I was just looking to get laid, but Jody wanted something deeper. When I told him that she'd asked me to bring him, asked for him by name even, he got all glassy-eyed and weird, and he was all, "Finally. This is it. The call. The embrace of ultimate darkness." Which sounds like the script of a video game, but he said it all like it was for real. Jody has these deep eyes, that cornflower blue color, you know, that the bitches like so much; he could have had bitches, except he wouldn't play any of the games they wanted him to play. So when he starts talking about *ultimate darkness,* and he puts on this weird, toneless kind of voice, like he's, I don't know, *possessed* or something, it gets creepy. That's why the kid had no friends. He scared people. Even so, I wouldn't exactly call him guilty of murder.

— Objection! The witness is speculating wildly about the defendant's guilt … even without counsel calling for such speculation. He's not here to speak to these issues.

— Yes, yes. The jury will disregard that, of course; the

defendant's guilt is for the jury to decide, not this benighted young man. Please confine your testimony to the facts, Mr. Kindred … if any.

— All right, Jeremy. You do understand what the judge is saying, right? Just tell us what happened. No opinions, just facts.

— Yessir.

— You passed on Cat Sperling's invitation to the defendant.

— Yes.

— How did you convince the defendant to attend?

— I told him it was the wildest live action role playing game of all time.

— You didn't mention the … erotic element?

— Oh, yes, sir. I told him there would be an orgy.

— And how did he react to that?

— He said, you can have the sex, Jeremy, long as I can have the violence.

— So is it fair to say that the defendant had a tendency towards violence?

— He was just kidding, sir! I never knew Jody to harm a flea, except in some fantasy or game, and then, of course, he'd go crazy … ripping off heads or wrapping himself in entrails … you know, movie special effects kind of shit. But in real life, no sir, Jody was gentle. I've seen him walk sideways so he wouldn't step on a bug. Most guys kinda enjoy stepping on bugs … taking a life, you know, even if it's just a bug's life. Jody wasn't like that. Loner, though. At lunch, he'd always be by himself, because even though I'm his best friend, you didn't want to be seen hanging around with a loser; he understood that; we only hung together after school, or at the mall. But even sitting by himself, munching on them power bars which was all he ever had packed for his lunch, he had an audience … there was always bitches eying him from a distance, wanting him. I guess it was the eyes. That's why he was on the cover of *Time,* wasn't it? The eyes. I assumed that's why Cat wanted me to bring him. And I know he's been getting a lot of mail from bitches all around the country, since that magazine cover; he told me that one time when they let me visit him in jail. I thought he'd be more, you know, fucked up by jail, what with all them big dudes named Bubba, but he says ain't none of them touched him; they're all scared of him. It's been put out that he has powers, you know, going through keyholes, transforming into bats, and all that vampire movie shit; but what I wanna know is, if that's true, why hasn't he escaped from jail? Well okay, I guess I'm getting off the subject again. You wanna know about the party in the cemetery, the Friday the Thirteenth thing … and how my friend Jody come to be accused of wiping out his family and a passel of his friends.

— Yes, Jeremy. Take your time. I know some of this is painful. But the jury needs to get the whole picture.

— Where was I?

— Perhaps you could go back to the vanilla blood.

— Yeah. It was like a cocktail almost. They served it in tall cone-shaped glasses, flutes they called them; champagne comes the same way, I heard tell. When me and Jody got there, it was close to midnight. That's because Jody took some convincing, even though he loved vampires; these weren't his kind of people. Leastways, we assumed that it would be mostly the school Goth crowd, the Nine Inch Nails types, the Anne Rice readers; actually it was kinda surprising who *was* there. It wasn't even confined to kids from Kramer High. I mean, Miss Higginbotham, the social studies teacher, was there ... and she was bare-ass *nekkid,* and lying on top of a big old gravestone with her hippo-sized haunches in the air ... and moaning. And this ... well, this *black* dude was all on her shit, and he won't wearing nothing but a pair of black leather Pampers, and a nose ring the size of a golf ball, which must have tickled old Higginbotham's clit something fierce ... well, she was moaning every time his head bobbed up and down, and her titties were flapping around like a couple of beached flounders. Shit she was a sight, all moaning and wet in the moonlight like that. And there were other people scamming against grave markers; some guy was even trying to pork the stone angel that guards the cemetery gate. And there was this girl I'd never seen before, passing around the glasses, I mean flutes, filled with vanilla blood, and that was the only food they had at the whole party, if you can call it food. Well, just about everyone seemed occupied with someone else, and no one paid much mind to me and Jody, and the only one who said anything to us was the girl with the tray of blood; she stopped to ask us if we were new, and when we said yes, she told us drink up, it's real important for the new ones to drink up, can't really be part of the action until you've taken the first step; so we did.

— What sensation did you associate with drinking this, ah, "vanilla blood"?

— Hey, I don't rightly know if I should tell you what it was really like — this being a court of law and all.

— You're under oath, Jeremy. And also, you have immunity.

— So you can't use *nothing* I say against me? Nothing at all?

— Well — no.

— Objection! The witness only has use immunity.

— I'll sustain that, but I want to hear the witness's answer.

— Jeremy, the judge isn't going to do anything to you for what you say. He just wants to hear your answer.

— Well, sir, did you ever try E?

— Are you saying that the effects of this "vanilla blood" were somewhat akin to the drug E — Ecstasy — a drug popular among the "rave" segment of the student population?

— Well, if I answered that, I'd have to say that I'd *used* E before, and the judge just sustained that mean-looking bitch's objection. So I'll just say it gave me a boner the size of a baseball bat, and I wanted to screw the first thing I saw.

— Which was?

— Objection! Irrelevant.

— Actually, Your Honor, this answer speaks directly to the defendant's motivation.

— All right, I'll allow the question, but you'd better proceed very quickly to something important. Or the gentleman from CNN is liable to wet his pants.

— Jeremy, and what was the first thing you saw that you wanted to, as you so delicately put it, screw?

— Well, this is kinda embarrassing, sir. I mean, I wouldn't want you to think I'm gay or nothing, but I was so horny I wanted to do Jody ... well, okay, there was something about him, the eyes, or whatever, anyway, on Brother Thompson's Christian summer camp last year, we all learned about circle jerks from the brother himself, so it wasn't like …

— Order in the court!

— And I mean, people were going crazy in that graveyard. I swear, I saw Mr. Smith, the football coach, getting boned up the butt by Mr. Oliver, who's like a police sergeant down at —

— Order in the goddamn court!

— Your Honor, we're not hear to discuss the sexual antics of half the town. Could the witness confine himself to —

— Brother Thompson was even there, and he was handcuffed to a gravestone, and these motorcycle bitches were prodding him with cigarettes, and he was all moaning.

— That's enough, Mr. Kindred. Counselor, instruct your witness to get to the point.

— So, Jeremy, you, ah, made a pass at your best friend.

— Well, not exactly. It was more like this: I swallowed a couple of mouthfuls of that blood cocktail thing, and everything went all misty … well, okay, and I felt like my veins were on fire … like this burning sensation, this tingling, everywhere, especially, you know, down there … and the next thing I knew, I was on Jody's leg, like a dog or something, rubbing myself up and down on it. But he wasn't getting horny off that blood at all. It wasn't affecting him the same way. Even though there was couples, threesomes, getting down every which way, in the light of the moon, with a dark, pounding music pouring out of a ghettoblaster somewhere … like one of them imperial orgy scenes in *Caligula,* you know? … Jody wouldn't have none of it. He shook me off of him like you'd shake off, well, a dog. "Don't," he said. "You're like all them others. To me the blood feels different. I think maybe I ain't the same kind as you, maybe I don't belong with the likes of you. What you're all doing seems so empty to me. Blood sings a different music to me. When I look into the dark, I look right past all of you and all your sleazy thrills, your wannabe games, I see you all just flirting with the darkness … not willing to embrace it … to become a part of it … no, you're not like me after all, and it makes me sad because you've been a good friend to me, Jeremy, all these years when no one would talk to me because I'm like the school outcast, the mutant in the hallway … today I'm starting to learn who I really am."

— So the defendant had, as it were, an epiphanic moment from the drinking of human blood?

— I don't rightly know what that means, sir.

— Doesn't matter. That evening changed him, didn't it?

— Maybe so. What he said to me, though, was he found his true self.

— And his true self was what? A vampire?

— Won't that simple, sir. But anyways, I didn't have time to listen to him ranting on at that point, because, as I said, I was thinking with my dick. And soon my dick found something to play with. There was this mousy girl, no one anyone would look at twice in the daylight … her name was Constance Thorpe … and the only time I ever spent more than five seconds in her company was when me and her was paired off cutting up rats in biology lab one time. You know, she always used to make me nervous. She had nerd glasses, and she had a way of pulling out them rat intestines that made it look like she was enjoying it too much. And she dressed like a refugee from the 60s, parents must've been hippies or something and she forgot to rebel. Well I saw her leaning against a tombstone and she wasn't the same bitch at all, lemme tell you. She'd lost the glasses and she even had a spot of makeup on. But I didn't really give a shit, because of whatever it was in that blood; all I cared about was that she made a beeline for me and kinda nosedived toward my crotch. Before you knew it she'd unzipped me and she was all up on me like a noisy old vacuum cleaner. I mean, I wouldn't have been seen dead with her normally, but you should have seen her suck, I mean, that girl could suck. She was wild, too, licking up a storm on my balls and even thrusting down past them, I think she'd have stuck it up my butt if my pants had come all the way down, but the zipper was all tangled in her hair. Must've hurt, it yanking on that hair like that, sir, but she sucked with a will, like her life depended on it. So I sorta leaned back against the gravestone, closed my eyes, and slipped into like a kind of trance, just letting myself go with the flow of it … then I sort of came too with a shock because I could feel this pinprick, this sharp pain that wouldn't go away. I looked down and she had pulled out a syringe and she'd stuck me right in the shaft, and you know how much blood gets down there when you got a boner. I guess I kinda panicked, even though I knew that these people have a thing about blood, and I drew back, and well, I knocked the syringe out and I jizzed at the same time, and there was blood and cum everywhere … well, Constance was going crazy now, lapping up everything, sperm, blood, sweat, I could have pissed on her face and she'd've drunk it. Holy shit! I didn't like it. The high of the vanilla blood was coming down now. I was all dizzy. This wasn't how I thought it would feel. I felt all dirty inside. That's when I decided to go looking for Jody. I sorta pushed Constance out of the way. She was on all fours, the fucking nympho bitch, and already sniffing for a fresh piece of meat to chew on. I kept calling Jody's name, asked a couple people where he was, and they kept shrugging or being too involved with their own shit.

— And where did you in fact discover the defendant to be?

— Well, I'm getting to that, sir!

— Good. I see that the prosecution has become too, ah, involved in its prurient fascination with the material to object any further....

— There's no need for the defense to snipe, Your Honor, when it is clearly burying itself with every word this so called witness utters.

— Be that as it may … Mr. Kindred?

— Okay. Well, there's this big old structure bang in the middle of the cemetery, see, and it's the oldest monument there. I think it dates to long before the war.

— You mean the Civil War.

— Yes, sir.

— I think most of the jury are familiar with the monument you're referring to. It's the Forbin-St.Cloud Memorial, right? Built by a prominent French family, in the days when our little city was booming. Which times, since the banning of hemp cultivation, are long past. A bizarrely incongruous Gothic monstrosity, surrounded by a wrought iron fence with strange-looking gargoyles on top, rumored to have underground passageways, under whose sheltering eaves the homeless of this town often rest, as the local police force rarely bothers to kick them out, rarely even patrols this area because of the mysterious death of Police Sergeant McKinley, found garroted and disemboweled and spread-eagled over the —

— Why is the defense now regaling us with a history lesson, Your Honor? Objection!

—I'll stop, Your Honor. I just thought the local color would be helpful. The Forbin-St. Cloud monument has … *vibes.* I want the jury to understand that. Since all of them heard the ghost stories when they were kids, and few were brave enough to go there. I know the prosecution is anxious to get back to the dirty bits. So how about it, Mr. Kindred? Let's have 'em. The dirty bits.

— Like I said, sir, I thought I saw the back of Jody's head, and he was squeezing through the iron bars into the Fo-for- … well, we don't call it that, sir.

— What *do* you call it?

— We call it the Hellhouse.

— Why?

— Well, sir, on account of … it's big enough to be a house, what with all the underground passages it's supposed to have … and it's got this entranceway … well, a *fake* entranceway … that looks like the mouth of hell … a big old demon's jaw in stone with a stone door that can't be opened. Well … I didn't *think* it could be opened. But then … I saw Jody sort of standing there … at the stone mouth … you could see the sculpted flames of hell there … and he was just standing there. Just staring. Like he'd seen something … supernatural. Well, I kind of snuck up behind him. I guess I startled him because when he felt me breathing down his neck he screamed up a storm. I mean he had like a panic attack, and I hadn't *never* seen him lose his cool before. I got him calmed down. I kept saying, it ain't so bad, Jody, nothing bad's happened yet, maybe we just lost a bit of blood is all. Maybe we're a bit weak from that, you know, dizzy, seeing things. When you lose blood you see things. We learned that in school. But he was all, I saw what I saw. I said, What did you see? and he said, Nothing. Fucking nothing, and don't ask me again. I ain't crazy. I said, Nobody said you was. Just tell me what you seen there.

— And did the defendant respond?

— Yeah.

— What did he say?

— He more than said, sir. Well at first he just murmured, They went through the doorway, they just up and walked right on through there like it was air, I can feel them inside there, feel the heat of their souls inside the dead empty space … but pretty soon he was a-banging on that stone with his fists, like he should have been able to melt right through it. Well, what do you know? The wall started to give.

— He shattered a mausoleum wall with his fists?

— Not hardly, sir. I mean the wall and him seemed to kind of meld together, and he was sort of sinking into it.

— What did you do, Jeremy?

— I thought he was going to die. I mean, getting sucked into a jello kind of a wall, it was one of them *Poltergeist*-style special effects, like you see in movies. So I guess I grabbed on to him, and that's how I ended up getting pulled inside too. The stone felt mushy. Oily, you know. It made my flesh crawl. But the wall closed right up again as soon as we got through, and it was dark as shit in there, and won't no way to get back out. I almost shat my pants, I don't mind telling you, sir, it was that scary. The air was all moist and stale-smelling. I don't know how dead people are supposed to smell, but I could *feel* death there. Well, after a time, you could start to see a bit of light. Water was dripping. Where we were was a kind of corridor leading downward. And we heard voices. From down below. I was shaking, sir. And then Jody said the strangest thing. He said, Jer, we been buddies for a long time, but there's places you weren't meant to go … places I have to go alone. You weren't meant to pass through to this place, but you held on to me, and maybe that's good, because if anything ever happens to me, you can bear witness one day, you can speak the truth about me, shout it out, even if nobody ever believes you, or even understands what you say. I ain't long for this world, Jer, but I'm meant to go out like a comet, not like a lil old candle. You know that, don't you? I've always been different … like everyone's born facing the same way, their butts to the past, their faces to the future, but not me, I go sideways, past and future are a sidestream to me, a path I can never tread.

— Quite a speech for a teenager, don't you think?

— Objection! Calls for speculation.

— Ah, I see that the Madame Prosecutor has awakened. Sustained.

— That's all right, Your Honor, I was only being rhetorical. Mr. Kindred … Jeremy … I'll say it a different way. Did your friend, the defendant, often make long speeches like that?

— Not often. But more than any other kid I knew. If he got going, he could talk up a storm. Almost like a preacher, except it would be all about violence and death and dark things.

— Are you aware that the defendant hasn't said a word since he was taken into custody?

— I've heard that, sir.

— So he's definitely changed.

— Yes, sir. He ain't human no more.

— Literally?

— Well, sir, I was getting to that.

— Proceed.

— Well, like I said, there was voices. And the corridor leading downward. And the light, you see, the light came from down below. A flickering, red light, kind of like the flames of hell I guess. And even though Jody told me, No, you stay up here, this is for me alone … well, I guess I couldn't help following him down there. I was curious, sure. But it was also creepy as shit, and I didn't want to be alone.

— Did the defendant know you were following him?

— Sort of. But you see, he was like in his own world. He really didn't pay me no mind at all. I was like a puppy dog or something … no, a shadow more like, a nothing.

— To whom did the voices belong?

— Well okay, we kept going down deeper and deeper, because the corridor ended in steps and the steps led us deeper and deeper underground. Maybe we were going into the hillside, I don't know; I lost my sense of direction. Because now there were steps going up, and passageways leading sideways. It as like that story we learned in Mrs. Seymour's class one time, the one with the maze and the bullheaded man and the hero with his ball of yarn. The walls glowed. It was a cold light, millions of dots of light, you know, like you get in caves sometimes, phosphorescence I think it's called. I followed. After what seemed like a long time, it widened into a cave. I think it was part natural, this cave, but there was also a bunch of marble columns and statues of weeping angels and other cool gothic shit. The light came from flaming torches on the walls. Some parts of the walls had paintings, Egyptian stuff, guys with dog's heads, other parts had been painted over. It was all coated with soot, and when the torches flickered, it looked like them pictures was moving. And at the far end, there were niches in the wall, and in the niches were dead people. I mean some were long dead, like skeletons, but some were fresh ... and some of them I recognized. I mean, they went to my school. I mean, they weren't supposed to be dead at all. I mean, I would have heard of it if they'd died, I was in some of the same classes. Well, I wasn't that sure. Like I said, I was dizzy. And the sex thing hadn't totally worn off. I hid behind a big statue. An angel. The archangel Michael, I think, with a flaming sword. The sword was metal and sort of attached to his hand with a leather thong. And a bronze cross around his neck. His wings were wide enough that I could crouch down and peep through a little chink where his elbow lifted up against his robe. Apart from the sword and the cross he was all marble, and cold. And well, I wasn't dressed for the cold, so I was shivering as I huddled there, trying not to breathe too much.

— What did the defendant do at that point?

— He stood there, in a semicircle of light, facing all of them dead folks, and I saw there was three coffins laying there, fine old coffins made of carved wood with all gold on them. The coffins are just laying there, and the middle one, the grandest one of them all, is closed, but the other two have their lids on the ground next to them and they're empty, you see. And there's people here. They're hard to see at first, because they're all blended with the shadows, and it takes me a while to make them out. They ain't the same kind of people as the ones in the orgy up there in the cemetery grounds. They're, well, pale looking. What was that word for the way the walls was all glowing? Phosphorescent. Yeah. That was in their faces, too. When you looked at one of them a long time you could see the cold light clinging to their faces. They all wore black. I don't mean all Dracula capes and stuff. I mean, some of them had capes, but there were clothes from olden times, and clothes you could see down at the Goth coffee house over in the next town. There was leather and fishnet stockings. There was black lipstick. Sunken eyes. Some had sweeping robes, you know, the kind that rustle when you walk. And well, standing next to one of the empty coffins was Cat Sperling, and she was totally naked. And by the other coffin was … shit man, it's weird to think of it now, but it was Constance Thorpe, the little geek that done went down on me next to that gravestone up above. She was naked, too. She looked better than I thought she would. I couldn't believe it. The only two bitches I'd ever really messed around with, and they were standing around bare-ass naked in front of a bunch of ghouls in black. I gotta admit, it was making me, you know, all hot down there all over again. I watched my friend Jody. They didn't seem to notice him at first, them two girls, because they were busy staring into each other's eyes. I mean, I thought I was trapped inside of a lesbo porno. I mean, this was fucking wild. I never dreamed them two would have a thing for each other, I mean, the sexiest girl at Kramer High and some gap-toothed nerd with a thing for cutting up mice and frogs … secretly wanting to dyke it out? … I could see it in their eyes. Cat went without saying, but Constance looked different. A glow in her flesh. Gleaming. Maybe it was sweat. She had hard little nipples. They were inching toward each other. I was all, Holy shit, they're gonna get it on right here, in front of all these people … if they even *are* people. Cat's upper lip was quivering. The sweat was beading up on it. I could barely look at their pussies. I'd glimpsed pussy before, and in pornos you watch it all you want, but it's on a TV screen. This was different. I was afraid if I stared too long, I don't know, I was gonna have an accident.

— Your Honor, could the witness get to the point already?

— Sustained.

— I'm afraid he's right, Jeremy. The jury doesn't really need to know about your … accidents.

— Well, I didn't have no accident anyways, sir.

— Why?

— Just when I thought the two of them were going to really, you know, get down, the lid of the coffin in the middle started to creak open.

— A little like yesterday's little incident?

— Oh, no, sir. It was real slow, like. And then all the people there fell on the floor. I don't mean they tripped, I mean they fell to their knees, faces in the dust, even the two naked bitches. It was like, you know, I seen this movie about an ancient Chinese emperor, it was death to look him directly in the face. I could feel … fear in the room … and power. Real power. I was scared. I narrowly avoided one kind of accident, and now I was fixing to have another kind. Well, the lid was creaking open. Dust was flying.

The lid swung up and this old man was sitting up slowly. He was old, real old. Okay, he didn't *look* that old, but you could feel it in him. And he spoke. Slowly. Like he was having trouble remembering how to speak. Later they done told me that his kind don't have much use for talking amongst themselves; it's chiefly for the benefit of the ones that are still human. Oh, it won't English neither. But one of the guys in black got up off his knees and crept up closer, and he translated everything in a flat, echoey voice. The first thing he says is, The Duke asks what new creatures come before him today.

— Meaning the two girls?

— Yes, sir, I guess, because the sex goddess and the geek stand up, and they're all coyly looking at the floor and half-smiling, and their nipples are still hard. And they both say, Your Grace, we humbly beg for the honor of attending you. Well, his Grace mumbles something, and the translator says, How may you prove your worthiness? And they answer, We are yours entirely, body, soul, in life and death and undeath. We wish to become consorts of the darkness. We wish the everlasting night. We pine for the sunset. We abhor the light. We have listened in the wilderness and heard the music of the night.

— The sex goddess and the geek, as you call them, said all that? In those precise words?

— I reckon it was learned from a book or something, sir.

— So this appeared to be some kind of ritual?

— Yes, sir.

— Your Honor, I thought that this trial was about the defendant, not the erotic fantasies of some disturbed adolescent. I must continue to protest this undignified latitude in allowing endless filth to spew forth from the witness without any real connection to the defendant's guilt or innocence!

— Yes, yes, sustained, sustained, though I'm sure the lurid details will all be in your next book, counselor!

— I resent that, Your Honor!

— Be quiet and let the kid tell the rest of his story. If the defense would care to continue ... I'm as anxious to get to the relevance of this as anyone else here.

— Yes, Your Honor. Mr. Kindred ... Jeremy ... go on. Go easy on the sex. Unless it specifically concerns the defendant.

— All right, sir.

— Tell us about the defendant and his role in all this, then.

— Well, the translator guy, he says to the two girls, You know that before you can cross over, you must bid the flesh farewell ... and you must find a willing lamb ... a sacrifice. And Cat Sperling said, We have such a lamb, Your Grace. We've tracked him, we've lured him, we've cornered him, and we have him.

— And by "him", they meant the defendant?

— I guess so, sir, cause Jody done stepped forward.

— What was the defendant's demeanor?

— Huh?

— How did he look?

— Pale, sir, real pale. But determined, too. Whatever was about to happen, it looked like he'd thought it over and was gonna do it, no matter what. Grim, sir, real grim. It's amazing to me how young he looks at that moment. I know he's really older than me, but he comes off like a little kid. Scrawny. And so pale. Maybe that phosphorescence shit was rubbing off on him. He looked back only once. Looked me right in the eye. *Knew* I was there, knew I was watching. No one else saw, no one else knew. I thought about what he said to me earlier. *I ain't long for this world, Jer, but I'm meant to go out like a comet, not like a lil old candle.* Jody was fixing to die. I realized that. All of a sudden. Something had happened between him and Cat Sperling. Something that had pushed him over the edge. Like the preacher says on *Hour of Power,* into the abyss.

Well, the translator dude says to Jody, Do you come here of your own free will? And Jody's all, I do. Then the guy says, You will lose a lot of blood. Perhaps you will even die. But if you survive this ritual, you will be on the way to a different plane of existence. The one who brings you to us, the woman formerly called Cat, she was once such a lamb. To surrender yourself to the dark, to let the undead feast upon you, is to step blindfolded off the edge of the bottomless pit. You must trust. You must believe. Darkness will love you. Darkness will enfold you. Darkness will shield you. Do you accept such a destiny? If you do not, speak now, and in the morning you will wake up in your own bed, and remember nothing. But if you say aye, you will never again know where you will wake up in the morning: in your own bed, on a bed of thorns, in a coffin, in the wormy earth. Think carefully before you answer, Jody Palmer. It may be that you will never again see daylight. Some who have a special affinity for our kind … make the passage in a single night … and wake to eternal darkness. For most … well, for some there is the true death … but they would never had made the crossing anyway … it's a talent you're born with. And for some, a slow, agonizing sickness that may or may not lead to death and the crossing into undeath. We cannot tell. There is no science of vampirology. Do you understand what we are telling you?

And Jody was all, Yes.

...

— And?

— I'm sorry, sir. I was just trying to remember the details. After this it gets kinda all confused.

— Take your time, Jeremy.

— Yessir. Thank you, sir.

— You're telling us that these ... creatures ... made an offer to your friend, and he accepted it. An offer that, he believed, would bring about his death and transfiguration ... his metamorphosis into a creature beyond life.

— I reckon so, sir. I mean, there was nothing for him in the real world anyways. He was always kind of a throwaway kid.

— Did he give any impression of having been coerced into this choice?

— Maybe he didn't feel he *had* no choice.

— What did the defendant do next?

— He stepped forward. And the translator guy said, First comes the consummation of all carnal pleasure. Then comes the drawing of the blood. The first is your farewell to the flesh, you candidates for initiation into the Brotherhood of Blood; the second is your salutation of the spirit.

— So the defendant believed he was being initiated into some kind of vampiric existence?

— No, you got it all wrong. Them two girls was the initiates. Jody was the lamb, the offering, the sacrifice.

— He was willing to die for this?

— I reckon so.

— What happened next?

— It gets confusing, sir. Because the first part of the ritual, that was the "farewell to the flesh" thing, slowly shifted into the second part … the blood ritual. It started with the two girls undressing Jody, slowly, sexily … for example, Cat would undo one of his shirt buttons with her teeth, then Connie would do the next one down, while Cat was sort of sliding her tongue in and out between the buttons, teasing his chest. And they were all rubbing their titties up and down him. Now I knew that Jody really had never had no sex before, well, no more than third base anyways. But when they finally got the pants off him, he wasn't even hard. He just stood there, with a faraway look, fixing on some dark future he had always dreamed about. But the two girls were at him like there was no tomorrow. I guess, for them, in a way, there wasn't. They surrounded him. They were a blur of arms and legs and lips and tongues and gleaming pussies. I couldn't believe it, but mousy Constance was the wilder of the two bitches. She was squeezing Jody's scrawny ass, pumping against him, even thrusting her tongue in his butthole. But Cat was more playful. She skimmed her tongue along his arms, his fingers, and when she reached his balls and started flicking at them, he finally started to get aroused. I think he was holding himself in, trying to resist, thinking to himself that giving in sex was some kind of weakness, that he was there for the violence, not the sex … but no red-blooded guy could stay soft forever with them two working him over. And now they were taking turns, one holding him upright while the other slid up and down on him, spinning him around, making him dizzy, and he was moaning now, I couldn't make out all of it but it was all sick, private stuff, about his childhood, his parents, I don't know ... and then it started to turn toward violence ... first one girl then the other was raking at him with her nails, nails that seemed to get longer and sharper ... nails that seemed to curl up, tighten, into claws ... the girls were bucking and heaving as they pushed him down against the middle coffin, where the vampire master dude was still sitting, watching, his eyes slowly reddening ... or was that just the flickering of the torches? ... I don't know ... and the crowd in black was hemming in closer ... making it harder for me to see ... and I knew they weren't noticing me anymore, I even felt safe creeping out from behind the statue ... keeping low to the ground ... peering through the sea of legs and cloaks ... glimpses now ... the girls licking their lips ... their eyes slitting ... bending over him ... slicing at his chest, his abdomen with their animal claws ... and biting now ... I could see fangs. They all had fangs. All them black-clad people with them glowing white faces. Their fangs glistened in the dark like a thousand stars. And there were other sharp things. I saw spikes ... razor blades ... pocket knives ... hypodermics ... all ready to harvest my best friend's lifeblood. The girls were still all over him ... pleasure transforming into pain ... but the others were moving in now ... I could see a razor slice just beneath his nipple ... I could see a delicate mouth close in on his ankle ... and Jody was all convulsing now, I couldn't tell if it was from like an orgasm or whether they was *killing* the fuck out of him. Jesus I was scared. I wanted it to stop. Me against a hundred bloodsuckers, what was I thinking? But that was my best friend out there. But did you ever see a big that's been hit on the head in the slaughterhouse? That's how it looked. I mean, he was shaking like a fucking piledriver. I couldn't stand it. I mean, Jody, you know? Friends since the sixth grade. Campouts, swimming holes, dirty websites, all the shit young guys grow up together doing. Well, what I done was dumb.

— What did you do, Mr. Kindred?

— Well, I ripped the cross of the Archangel Michael's neck, and I pulled off the sword, and like a wild man I charged.

— You attacked a crowd of … sadistic vampire cultists?

— Cultists? Hell no, sir, these people was actual vampires. Cause when the shadow of the cross fell upon them, they started screaming. And scattering. And I was screaming too, a pretty damn impressive scream for a kid, a scream like a banshee, and swinging that big old heavy sword like it was nothing more'n a letter opener. Shit, I *scared* the fuckers. I think. There was this big flapping noise. Dust everywhere. Swirling. Mist. Everything was whirling and there was this roar, like a tornado or something. I don't think I actually hit anything with the sword. Everything was dissolving before I could smash bronze against flesh. I saw Jody on the ground there in front of the middle coffin. He was naked and I swear to God he was half drained already. There was so much blood, just sluicing from a hundred cuts on him, pouring out onto the rocky floor. I knelt down and tried to lift him up, but he was heavy, there won't no *give* to him at all, it was like he was already dead. I was still all crazed and I shook him, I was all, Wake up, Jody, this is your buddy telling you, come out of it, you ain't dead yet. And then the weirdest thing of all happened. You know all that swirling mist I was talking about? Well, it seemed to gather up the coffins and the cave walls and even the swordless St. Michael over there, and even the dirt beneath us, and it was all billowing about us and darkening, and the torches were blowing out one by one, and my friend was stirring a little, and I was all, Jody, don't die, don't die, don't die, when all at once the world seemed to melt around us … like a dissolve in a movie … and we were somewhere else. I smelled a fresh wind. Flowers. Old trees and rotting leaves. We were in the hills. The cemetery was way below us … and the moon was shining through the treetops. What happened? When I arrived at the cemetery there'd been cars every where, pickups, Mustangs, a Mercedes, a police car … now I couldn't see a one in that parking lot … and the graveyard was deserted. Jody was still lying across my lap … still bleeding to death … or was he? In the bright moonlight I saw … the wounds closing up … the scratches fading … the blood sort of evaporating, melding into the night mist … I didn't understand. I knew it won't no dream. I knew it had to be real … but … Jody was moaning now. I was all, Wake up, wake up … and, slowly, he did.

— I see. And I awoke and found me here, on the cold hill's side.

— Yeah. I guess so.

— You saved your friend's life.

— Maybe, but he sure didn't thank me for it.

— No?

— Shit, no, sir. When he come to, it was just about twilight, and I'd been watching him, and I'd covered him with my own jacket, and I was trying my ass off to make him come back into the world … and when he finally opened his eyes, well, he didn't look like he was fixing to thank me at all. He looked at me with slitted eyes, and I saw *hate.* Pure, naked hate. I sure was shocked. I said, Jody, it's me, your best friend, Jer. They were gonna *kill* you in there. I don't know what happened, but I got you out … somehow. And he whispers to me, gasping for breath between every word, like he's struggling to keep from slipping back into darkness, Jer, I wanted it. That was my chance. I'm nobody in this world. I was about to *be* something. Let go of me, Jeremy, and don't come near me again. And he shook off my jacket … stood up … just as the first rays of sunlight were breaking over the gravestones below yonder … he stood up, naked as the day he was born, stood up and walked away from me. He was so frail and thin he was almost like a little kid. But here's the weird thing … the scars was all healed. There won't a scratch on that boy. The sun painted him a golden sort of color, and he didn't hardly seem human. And he walked away. Away from the coming light … into the thickest part of the wood … like he was afraid of the sun.

— Did you speak to him after that?

— Not really. I think he tried to go back to one of their cemetery parties … they usually had them on the full moon … but I know he never was able to get back inside that monument. That stone carving of the jaws of hell … well, stone was all it was to him. He had lost the key. I took it from him. I was stupid, I guess. I really didn't understand him after all. He fell in with other kids. Started a new "secret society" of some kind. A wannabe vampire society. I heard about it mostly from —

— Your Honor, this is all hearsay now.

— Sustained.

— Your Honor, we have already heard evidence about young Jody Palmer's secret society ... from all sorts of expert witnesses as well as from the ex-members themselves. I'm not seeking to add anything to the record on that matter from this witness. In fact, I'm going to excuse him now. Perhaps my opponents would care to cross?

— Yes, we would. Just a couple of questions, Jeremy Kindred. You're still under oath.

— Yes, ma'am.

— Isn't it true that no one has related any of these outlandish incidents ... except you? I'm not referring merely to the supernatural events you claim to have seen inside one of the town's most famous landmarks ... but to these very imaginative orgies you describe as having occurred regularly at the cemetery. If these things were true, don't you think others would have reported them to the authorities?

— Hell no, ma'am. Half the authorities were *in* them orgies.

— So it's a kind of ... ah, conspiracy? Half the town involved in dark goings-on, and covering up the mess from the other half?

— You tell me, ma'am. After all, you were there, too.

— Well!

— Your Honor, the witness has just claimed that the state's prosecutor was present at those proceedings, in the light of which —

— Oh, nonsense, counselor. The boy's a raving lunatic.

— Your Honor, comments like that would tend to throw some doubt on your own impartiality —

— Shut up, counselor! I'm running a courtroom, not a

voodoo séance. If the prosecution would care to continue the cross —

— Ah … no further questions.

— The witness may stand down.

— I would like to remind the defense that this evening's extraordinary timing was designed to let us hear from whoever is supposed to be inside that coffin of yours, and that we are now ten minutes past sundown. And no one has been banging on the lid from the inside. Is that particular bit of nonsense over with?

— I don't think so, sir. At this time I would like to ask the bailiff to remove the coffin lid and invite the next witness to the stand.

— All right. Bailiff?

— There's nothing inside of here, sir, except a headless cat. And a large quantity of garlic.

— That, counsel, is in very poor taste.

— I don't know *how* that could have happened, Your Honor! Our resident vampirologist assured us that —

— Ew, Your Honor! It's stiff.

— Dispose of it, bailiff. So what is the meaning of this, counsel? Vampire hunters been calling, I suppose?

— I have no idea what's happened at all, Your Honor. We'll have the witness for you tomorrow, I promise.

— Don't make promises you can't keep, counselor; I'm told that the dead are notoriously inept at keeping their appointments.

— Your Honor is pleased to joke at my expense.

— My Honor has had enough for the day, and we'll reconvene tomorrow morning at … let's say ten o'clock.

§

— Dr. Shimada, you're a vampirologist.

— Just an avocation, actually. My day job is psychiatric resident at the juvenile division of the state hospital for the criminally insane. My study of vampires, real and imagined, grew out of the ramblings of a patient I have in my private practice; I can't elucidate further without breaching confidentiality, of course.

— And you've studied the defendant at some length.

— Oh, yes. Fascinating boy. Very disturbed.

— The defendant is not, however, in your professional opinion, a vampire.

— No.

— Nor any other supernatural creature.

— Well, I would take issue with the choice of "supernatural", sir, since, as I scientist, I would prefer a rational explanation for any phenomenon, however supernatural-*seeming*. But no, Mr. Palmer is by no means undead. He is quite, quite human. He's just like you and me.

— Except that he hasn't talked since … the events that have brought us all here for this trial.

— That is *almost* true. I was starting to make some progress with that. I think he needs a few more months before he'll actually … be able to say anything to shed light upon this case.

— You were making progress?

— He grunts now, sometimes. I even detected a whimper once. And one time, on my way out, in the doorway, I heard a distinct, if *sotto voce,* utterance of the phrase "Fuck off."

— I see. Will he ever talk?

— Everything he wants to say is caged up inside him. It only needs … a key. I've been considering the possibility of circumventing the lengthy period of therapy and just jumping to Pentothal.

— Sodium Pentothal? The old "truth serum," that cliché of 50s B-grade detective thrillers?

— The very same.

— How many sessions did you have with the defendant?

— I've seen him twice a week since the arrest.

— In your opinion, is the defendant insane?

— I think that would be obvious even to a layman.

— Was he insane at the time of the crime?

— Clearly he was unable to distinguish right from wrong at the time of the multiple murders.

— What is the nature of the defendant's mental illness?

— In Freudian terms, his superego, the inner voice we often think of as our "conscience", weak to start off with from inadequate childhood reinforcement, has disappeared entirely. It has been replaced by what he perceives as supernatural "beings", creatures who control him. He has experienced a transference of the normal youthful libido ... the sex urge ... in the direction of violence and bloodshed. The weakening of the superego causes him to be unable to control his beast within, his id. That, of course, is the basic reason for all crime, but in his case the weakening of the ego is clearly at a pathological level.

— I see, Dr. Shimada. I'd like to move that Dr. Shimada's entire report ... some 2,310 pages of it ... be admitted to the record as Exhibit, ah ...

— Defense Exhibit QQ.

— Yes. Defense Exhibit QQ.

— I hope you're not expecting our benighted jurors to

make head or tail of it, counselor. Even the last few minutes have been a little, ah, dry.

— Dr. Shimada's learned testimony merely adds to that of seven other psychiatrists, Your Honor, who have all agreed that the defendant is hopelessly, irretrievably insane.

— Quite so.

— Dr. Shimada, if you state again, in simple layman's terms, the defendant's state of mind before, during, and after the crimes were committed?

— In layman's terms, Jody Palmer was stark, staring bonkers, counselor.

— No further questions.

— Cross?

— Well, yes, I do have a couple of quick questions. Dr. Shimada, in this 2,000 page document which, I admit, I haven't read, although my researchers have combed through it pretty thoroughly … do you not basically say that the defendant had no conscience?

— I suppose you could put it that way.

— Well, well, well. No conscience. And for that, we're gonna let him off after he mutilated his parents, disemboweled his sister, devoured his two-year-old brother's liver, and led a gang of hooligans on a rampage that culminated in several more people becoming … unwilling blood donors … not to mention … necrophilia.

— Your Honor, the prosecution's grandstanding.

— Sustained. Just ask the questions.

— Right. Well, I really just have one more question. You say the defendant has retreated behind a wall of silence.

— Yes. It's called hysterical mutism. It's one of the ultimate defense mechanisms of the paranoid schizophrenic.

— So you compiled a 2,000 page report about this patient … without exchanging a single bit of dialogue with him?

— As I spoke to him, I monitored his vital signs, his brain waves, the surface electrical activity of his skin.

— But he didn't actually *tell* you any of this.

— Scientists can read a great deal from —

— He didn't actually *tell* you. Answer the question, please.

— Ah … no.

— No further questions.

§

— Natalie McConnell, you've been given immunity because you appear not to have participated in the actual killing. But you saw everything, and your insight into the defendant's state of mind is vital to the court's understanding of his motives.

— Yes, sir.

— Are you currently enrolled in Kramer High?

— No, sir. I dropped out. I had to go to work in my dad's doughnut store.

— So you never knew the defendant until a few months before the incident.

— Yes, sir. I met him at Cat Sperling's funeral.

— You know Cat Sperling, then.

— Oh, sure, sir. Everyone did. She was the town slut.

— How did you come to be aware of that?

— My daddy always said that if I behaved anything like her, he'd whup my butt till it was bloody.

— What kind of behavior constituted "behaving like Cat Sperling"?

— Um ... too much lipstick ... wearing leather ... standing a certain way ... talking in a sexy voice ...

— Your father ever carry out his threat?

— Shit yeah. He wore me out all the time. When he wasn't making me go down on him.

...

— Order in the court! Order! Order! Counselor, tell the witness to stay on the topic.

— Your Honor, the fact that the witness was one of the disenfranchised, the violated members of society ... is not entirely irrelevant to this defense ... although I did not intend to have the matter raised quite this abruptly.

— That's enough. The jury will ignore the witness's life story, and concentrate only on those facts she raises that bear on this case. Meanwhile, I'd like the bailiff to make a note of the girl's remarks and pass them on the the district attorney; we are state employees here, and there are mandatory reporting laws.

— Well, judge, if you're gonna turn in my dad, you might as well turn in the pastor of Hillside Baptist Church as well. And the Vice-Principal of Kramer High — he got me in the closet one day. Oh, and —

— Miss McConnell, enough of that. When your testimony is through, you are to report to Detective ... ah ... who's on duty out there? ... Detective Arnold. He'll take it from there. Meanwhile, if the court would care to turn its attention back to the case ... Counsel? Counsel?

— Oh. Yes, Your Honor. So, despite Cat Sperling's reputation, you went to her funeral?

— Yeah. Her dad had ordered ten dozen doughnuts, you see, for afterwards, and I stopped by to get directions to the house. And that's when I saw Jody ... the defendant. He was standing in the distance ... in the shade of an oak tree. He was all in black. Trenchcoat and all. He looked lonely. Not like he was really invited. He was staring at all the relatives, at the coffin, at everything. With a kind of longing in his eyes. The guy seemed so sad. I wanted to talk to him. So I did.

— What did you converse about?

— Well, at first, I was all, like, questions, how did she die and such. And he said, *Anemia.* Which wasn't what I heard, I'd heard it was from something to do with sex, AIDS or such. It didn't matter nohow, cause she was gone no matter how you looked at it. I got him to give me directions to the Sperling place, and then he got to staring at me in a way I never been stared at before. Like he could see right into my mind. And he said to me, Are you afraid of the dark? And I said, Yeah. And he said, Very afraid? And I said, Yeah. And he said, Why? And I said, Because things come to me in the night. And he said, I can take that fear away for ever. I can take you on a journey with me. Across the river of death. To the farthest shore. To the kingdom of ultimate darkness. I look into your eyes and I see you're like me, you don't got nothing to lose. I said, You sure are right about that. He said, I'm gathering a group of people to take with me on this journey. It's a quest, you see. Like searching for the Holy Grail. The cup of blood. I just know you want to come with me, Natalie. I can see it in your eyes. One time, I met these creatures from a place beyond our world. They called out to me. But I stayed behind. I had work left to do in the world. I wanted to go, but I thought of all the dispossessed of the world, all the young ones crying out for release, and I knew I had to bring a few with me in order to be worthy of my place among the dark ones.

— Did the defendant mention Jeremy Kindred at all? The fact that his friend physically prevented him from being sucked into the vampire world?

— No.

— So you had no idea there was any side to the story other than what you were being told.

— That's right, sir.

— Did you believe him?

— Not really, sir. I thought he'd lost it. But there was something real hypnotic about his voice and such. He was sexy, too. In a scary kind of way.

— Sexy and scary?

— He was pale and thin. His cheeks were all sunken and his eyes, too. He looked like he hadn't eaten in days and he'd stayed out of the sun … well, like he was dead, really. Dead but beautiful. I guess what was exciting about him was … there was a wrongness. About the way he moved. The way he smiled. Like they weren't *his* lips, *his* limbs. Do you know what I mean? Like something was animating his body and such. Possession or something. I touched his shoulder. Flinched from it. It was cold as ice. But then again I felt I wanted to warm him up all over. I wanted to give him what I'd denied all those other men who took what they wanted from me. He was different. I wanted to make love to him. And later, we went back to the doughnut van, and, in the back, I did make love to him. I think of it as that, though he didn't really do much. I did all the moving. I'd never used dad's van for that before, and it was sticky on account of all the bits of custard filling and the little patches of spilled powdered sugar and all. He sat back against a pile of delivery boxes and I didn't care that they were getting all crushed. I just ate him up, impaled myself on him, rode him up and down, wrapped my titties around his face, but all the while he was muttering about other things … about banging and banging on the gates of hell till his fists were raw and bloodied from the rough stone … I didn't know what he meant until that night, when I met him again at the Forbin-St.Cloud monument and saw him kneeling at the carved mouth of hell and beat his fists against the granite … but I didn't care you see because I'd found someone as lost as me, maybe even more lost, someone I could give to freely, someone I could love.

— So you became a member of his … secret society.

— If you could call it that. It was just him and three of us girls. He called us the Brides of Dracula. He drank our blood. He mixed it with vanilla syrup and ice in a blender. Said he needed the ice because the heat of the blood would send him straight to the other world, and he wasn't ready yet, he still had things to do in the human world. The other two girls were Ramona and Chastity. They're dead now. He found Ramona lurking outside a homeless shelter over there in the city. Chastity was a runaway. I know what we done was wrong, but Jody, well, he had a vision and such. When he talked, we felt we belonged to something big. He gave us a structure, too, our nightly hunts. He taught us to pounce on alley cats and bite their necks and slurp down the gushing blood. That was disgusting, but it was kinda thrilling too. And now and then as a really special treat he'd fuck us. But it was always with us doing all the work, and him staring off into space, thinking I guess about his great vision. Which he finally explained to us. The day before … you know.

— He told you … what? That you were going to go on a killing spree?

— Not exactly. I remember it perfectly because we were having another meeting in dad's van. We always used it for meetings now, because I could always get the van between deliveries, and now, behind the smell of apple-cinnamon and chocolate, there was also a permanent smell of sex. Because the three of us … the girls I mean, not Jody … we'd do stuff in there while we were waiting for him. Thing is, you know how it is when us girls hang out together all the time … our periods kind of fall into sync. And so all three of us were on the rag at the same time. And we were all laughing about it, how it had gotten closer and closer in the last two months and now, this time, third time lucky and such, bang, same day, same second practically. And we were all idly fingerbanging each other while we talked about our fucked-up lives. So finally he shows up. And he's all, I smell blood. God, I smell blood! It makes me feel all … oh, I want it, I want it. And since we're all already with our panties down, and all moist from playing with each other, he's all over us, pulling out our tampons, lapping at us like a cat cleaning its ass. God, it was hot! I never felt that way before. The way he flecked my clitoris, the way he tickled my lips, teasing out every last flake of coagulating blood …

— Your Honor, spare us this pornography! Objection, objection!

— Your Honor, this evidence speaks directly to the nature of the defendant's mental illness … his delusional obsession with the, ah, sanguinary aspects of the human body.

— Young lady, get it over with, and proceed to the

question at hand.

— Yes, Your Honor. Um … what were you going to ask me, sir?

— Well, Natalie. You've just explained that Jody became unusually animated as a result of the smell of blood.

— That's true, sir. As I say, usually he would just lay there while we rubbed up and down on him, but that day he was excited. He even came. I mean, he just *spurted.*

— I don't think we need to know all that, but did the defendant then say anything about his grand vision?

— Oh yes.

— What did he say?

— Well, as we all lay there in the back of the van, there was this good, warm feeling, you know, us against the world and such, a little tiny piece of heaven. But then Jody begins to talk about the dark path we have to trod. I had my foot in the door, he said, and I was pushing my way in, and they sent me back out into the world. They didn't think I was good enough. But I'm gonna show them. I'm the king of the vampires. No dead dude in a coffin is gonna be badder than me.

— Did this statement contradict previous statements of his to you and your group of followers?

— Yes, sir. He always told us he was sent up here from the other world, that he had given up the world beyond so he could find disciples and teach all of them the dark path before he went back. Now he sounded bitter and angry and we didn't know what to do.

— What did he say next?

— We're going to do something really big, he said. An orgasm of blood and pain. We're gonna kill, maim, disembowel, decapitate, swim in the lubricious life force that spews from the veins of the dying. The way he said it, you gotta believe, it sounded … poetic … beautiful … I could feel the blood rushing joyfully from my pussy to meet his eager tongue … I could think about nothing but all that blood, swirling over me, carrying me toward the final climax in waves of crimson passion, oh God, Jody made me feel that good, all of us, he made us want to kill and to die the way we wanted his arms around us, his cock inside us and such.

— And how do you feel about Jody now?

— I love him, sir.

— Do you think he hears you, hiding as he does behind his wall of self-imposed silence?

— I don't know. Yeah. Maybe not. Maybe he doesn't hear any of us no more, maybe he's listening to a different music, the rushing of the river of death.

— I want to spare the jury yet another description of the crimes themselves … the slashing, the torture … all the things you witness but did not participate in … because you … had a twinge of conscience.

— I chickened out. I shoulda done them things. Like all the other girls did.

— Then you would be in trouble, Natalie.

— I don't care! Do you understand? I love him. I want to go with him! Into the ultimate kingdom. Into the dark country. Jody, listen to me, you motherfucker … I didn't mean to betray you … I'm here because I want them to know the truth … what you mean to me …

— Your Honor, the witness isn't supposed to be talking to the defendant.

— Sustained. Kindly confine your comments to the questions asked of you, Miss —

— Your Honor! The coffin! It's busting open! The lid is sliding again!

— Got a stake handy, bailiff? You can use my gavel as a mallet, you superstitious nincompoop. You people are … screw it, let whoever it is come out. If the ladies and gentlemen of the jury would refrain from panicking — and just what the hell do you think you're doing in my courtroom, young lady, in the nude? Have you no sense of propriety at all? Bailiff, fetch the witness a damn cloak.

— Jody.

— Young lady, you're not on the stand yet. Go and sit down right this minute or I'll cite you for contempt.

— Be silent!

— How dare you!

— In this human world, you may be a judge of men, Mr. Trepte, but there are darker courtrooms, and there are punishments more dire than death. I stand before you, a naked woman, whose flesh is colder than the grave. Touch me if you dare.

— Madam, there is no higher authority present in this chamber than this jury and this judge. If you have anything to say, you will have to wait your turn.

— So what do you plan to do, asshole, cite me for contempt?

— Bailiff, cuff her!

— Your Honor, she's just ripped off the bailiff's head!

— Sobering isn't it, Mr. Kangaroo Court, to see your enforcing officer's torso twitching on the carpet. I'm sorry that I won't be paying the dry cleaning bill. Where I come from, we don't have money … or credit cards, for that matter.

— Uh — uh —

— Speechless, at last, Your Honor! Give me a minute while I take a sip from this poor man's gushing jugular. Excuse me while I wipe my lips clean with his matted hair. Where shall I throw it? You have a basket? Thanks. Now … where was I? Oh yes. The defendant. The silent one. You who heard voices in the night, who were labeled a paranoid schizophrenic by Doctor Shimada over there … you who have been true to your deep dark self, all this time, you who have kept the faith … I've come for you. I ain't Cat Sperling, the town slut, no more … I've worked on my accent some … you learn a lot when you hang with the undead … plenty of sixty-four dollar words in *their* vocabulary when they've been around a couple of centuries. Look at me, silent boy. I like that you kept silent after it was over. You betrayed no one. Oh! bullets! My, my. They go right through me. I feel nothing. No feeling, you know, when you cross over the river. No mortal feelings anyways. Look at me, silent boy. I'm still beautiful, ain't I? Beautiful as the day you saw me. My body is as firm as when you first touched it, but now it's cold as marble. It's a dead body, Jody, a corpse. But oh, a corpse that everyone in this room wants, man *and* woman, a corpse that exudes a sensuality that the living can't match, a corpse that breathes *eternity, eternity* … Oh, Jody, you don't know how long you were watched, how long you were groomed for that moment of sacrifice that your friend ruined for you. Oh, he meant well. But he's just an ignorant human being. And human beings are just cattle. They're here to serve us. Their lives are over in an instant. I watched over you … saw you grow up alienated … knew you were marked to become one of us. In this world a throwaway, one of the disenfranchised … in the world beyond … a prince. When you had your fantasies of death … when you dreamed of death and woke up with a stiffie in the night … one of us was watching … perhaps in the shape of a mist, coiling about the keyhole of your bedroom door … or a black rat, sniffing its way along the floorboards … smelling the crimson of your dreams. Oh, Jody, it was all meant for you … my seduction of your dumb, sentimental friend … the party at the cemetery … partly real, partly a fabric of hypnotizing illusions. Do you understand that? Oh, your doctor noted it all down as a dementia — delusions of grandeur — megalomania — paranoia — when it was all nothing but the truth. You heard the music of the night when others heard only wind, rain, the rustling of leaves, frightened children murmuring in their sleep. Oh, we were disappointed when you didn't die the slow death that night! You have always been special to the dark ones. All your life you've heard that whispered in your ear, you've wondered if you were going mad. Those whispers were all true. You have been anointed from birth, Jody. I wasn't kidding when I called you a prince. That's exactly what you are. The Duke couldn't welcome you into the kingdom himself. His coffin has been taken far away, for safekeeping. It's getting dangerous for us here, with all these movies and role-playing games. Lies, but flirting with the truth. He's sent me to fetch you, Jody. I told you we were all sad when you didn't come to us. Some of us wanted to fetch you by force. But the Duke said, in his wisdom, Leave him be. The darkness is strong in him. If he cannot find the true kingdom right away, he will strive to build his own kingdom … he will mirror our world in his own world … and he will make himself worthy … and when he is ready

… we will bring him in. That's what I'm here for. To finish what we started. Look at me now. Look at me, translucent as alabaster, pale as moonlight; come to me. That's right. You don't need that ugly orange prison suit anymore. Those cuffs are useless now. Come to me. I twist them off with a flick of my wrist. The undead have great strength. They draw their strength from the womb of mother earth herself. Oh, Jody, come, come. Unzip that uniform and stand before me naked. Touch me. Look at the horrified faces of the judge and jury. They are so unimportant now. Slide your finger against the bailiff's blood, congealing on my breasts. Lick them. Lick the blood from the areola. Slow now, slow. I kiss you now. My teeth meet soft flesh. I taste blood. Give me your blood. Warm my stone heart with your last life-force. Oh, Jody, Jody, you are beautiful. Give me all of you. I bite your chest … your abdomen … my fangs tease at the sensitive tip of your penis … blood engorges it … blood stiffens it … blood that will soon run gushing down my throat … oh, Jody, Jody, this is the end for you, the end and the beginning … drink me now … as I drink you … the cold of death is absolute … the warmth of life is but a shadow … and now … come … come into my coffin … I don't want to sleep alone anymore … come into the coffin … into the womb … into the tomb … oh, Jody, this is love … this is death.

§

The transcript ends here. At least, the decipherable portion of the transcript. What follows on the tape is chaos. Screaming. Here and there a single word: blood, shit, fuck, no, no, no.

There was also the fire. The courthouse razed to the

ground, the judge, the superlawyers, many others hospitalized for third-degree burns. There was also the complete disappearance of the defendant. Not a charred husk of him … not a bone … not a tooth.

There was also the silence. Not a word in the press. Not a picture in the paper. Not a clip in the news.

But you know all that. You follow the media.

Perhaps you even know about the transcript, which has been pronounced a hoax by almost every expert who has been given the privilege of examining it.

Does it matter? As a certain Roman procurator once said to a certain rabbi, in a courtroom not unlike this courtroom, two thousand years ago … *What is truth?*

It really doesn't matter to most of you. So stop reading now. Close the book. There's nothing to be gained from idle speculation about the nature of light and darkness … about the relationship between love and death … between desire and self-destruction. Get on with your lives. Go on. Do it.

Unless, of course, you can hear the music of the night....

Really my favorite of my vampire short stories, I saved this one for last. It appeared originally in an anthology called *Urban Legends,* edited by Josepha Sherman and Keith DiCandido.

The Ugliest Duckling

But you know, he wasn't ugly exactly; in some ways he was the most beautiful of all those changelings of the twilight who blend in with the shadows of dumpsters, who flit from alley to alley, who lurk in the doorway of an all-night grocery store till, with a reticent half-smile, they find their mark and move in for the kill.

I know them well; I have been a connoisseur since I first started coming to the all-night coffee shop, thirty or forty years ago; it was still there then, though not yet owned by Greeks. I moonlighted—the way it is with me, moonlighting is the only way I can work—as a photographer. Exactly. That kind of photographer.

And this part of town was the best place to find subjects for my peculiar branch of the art.

My studio was a bungalow, a guest house with a private entrance, up in the hills, ten minutes' drive from the alley with the back door of the coffee shop; that door was always locked in the '60s, but now the new owners always leave it open; it gives the homeless somewhere, inconspicuously, to go to the bathroom; Stavros the manager, son of a Thai prostitute and an Athenian bookmaker, feels that it's the compassionate thing to do.

These days, I am called Estelle de Vries; the French first name, the Dutch surname, I suppose that makes me Belgian. I appear to be in my mid-to-late forties, but in the right light I can appear ageless, and when you really look deep into my eyes, you can't help knowing my real age, give or take a millennium.

"Estelle," Stavros said to me, as he poured me coffee, knowing I would never drink, "you see him too, don't you?"

"Efkharistô," I said, putting one hand over my cup. "You know I never drink…coffee."

"I am sorry," he said, as he always says, "force of habit."

"Who did you mean?" I said.

"Over there," he said, and pointed with his lips.

Across the street, in the window of a doughnut shop owned by Cambodian refugees, is where they tend to gather. The light is more flattering there. There are more boys than girls, but you can hardly tell them apart. They are colored the same: dirtied by the grime of the streets, sickly in the radiance of the lime-neon store sign. That night, though, there was one who stood apart.

"His name is Luke," said Stavros, who always knows everyone's name. "I know, I know, he's beautiful."

Human beings are nothing if not shallow. How can they be otherwise? They barely live before they are consumed by darkness. Youth is a flash, adulthood an instantaneous decay. Attractiveness, for them, is telegraphed by a few simple signals: wealth, beauty, and a frenetic pheromonal hyperactivity which they call love. The boy had at least one of the three attributes; and even through the window of the coffee shop and the tang of pollution in the night air I could smell a faint taint of another. With two out of three, it should have been easy to acquire the third.

Cars cruised the boulevard. Now and then, one stopped. None stopped for Luke. Stavros and I talked of many things. We talked about how blue the sky is in Greece. I told him how I used to sit beneath the stars in Syntagma Square…ride the steep highway past Arakhova to the oracle at Delphi…stand on Parnassus and look down at the gray-green valley. I did not tell him that it was long before he was born; I did not tell him that it was not a car I drove to Mount Parnassus; that would have confused him too much. Now and then, Stavros would try to pour me coffee. I do eat there, sometimes; you have to keep up the pretense. Tonight I didn't eat, though the special, lamb souvlaki, rare and dripping with blood and brine and lemon juice, was one of the few dishes my delicate appetites could stand. I just wanted to watch.

"There goes Gloria," Stavros said. "She finally found a regular; he's an Indian john, I mean from India or Bangladesh or something; he pays her with one-ounce gold bars."

I had photographed her before. She wasn't that pretty, but with a chiaroscuro kind of lighting effect she achieved a certain voluptuousness.

I sold the photographs to Busty Bitches magazine for three hundred bucks. Only paid her fifty. You get what you pay for. I was glad she'd found a steady source of income.

I watched the others as they loitered, but in my peripheral vision there was always Luke. By four in the morning there was only Luke, steadfastly staring at the street, his blond hair haloed by the blinking neon, his eyes flecked with trepidation.

"In fifteen minutes," said Stavros, "he will come into the coffee shop and I will be forced to feed him."

"What do the owners say about that?"

"Oh no, scraps, leftovers, doggie-bag food really; he can get it here, he can find it in the dumpster in the morning; might as well get it while it's still 'luke'-warm, no?"

The doughnut sign fizzed; the bulb was going bad I supposed; one day there would be no alien glow for the street kids to stand in; I didn't think they'd fix it. Things do not get fixed on this street corner.

We talked about the way the water glistens in the Isthmus of Corinth. How dazzling-white the houses are on Mykonos. How the Aegean sparkles beneath extinct Thera. I did not tell him I can no longer see such things except in the cinema of the mind; I did not tell of my curious allergy to sunlight. I wonder how much he knows. Probably nothing; human beings are notoriously unperceptive; but Stavros is intelligent.

Then Luke is standing behind him. Stavros doesn't see him, can't possibly smell him—humans just aren't that sensitive—but somehow he happens to slip away at just that moment—a waitress calling for his attention, perhaps. Luke says: "You take pictures, don't you?"

"Yeah. My name's—"

"Estelle. I know. He told me."

"Are you hungry?"

He grinned. "Fucking hungry," he said. "Thanks." He

turned, winked at Stavros, who was now puttering around with the coffee machine; gave him a thumbs-up sign. It had been a conspiracy of sorts, I suppose. Luke sat down in the booth across from me.

He was thin. I don't think he'd changed his clothes in a month.

Through the holes in the sleeves of his beat-up Bulls jacket I saw scars: cigarette burns, needle marks; he put his hands on the table and I saw deep, white gouges in his wrists.

"Where are you from, Luke?" I said, expecting the usual: Oklahoma, Michigan, the Hollywood dream, the Greyhound, the disenchantment.

"I'm from Encino," Luke said.

"Oh. Then what about—"

"My parents? Fuck 'em."

"But you do have a—"

"Yeah. I'm not totally homeless. Don't make no difference."

"You don't talk like you're from Encino."

"Sometimes I do," he said. "When I forget I'm living on the street." His accent has shifted, almost imperceptibly, over the hill, toward the nouveau-riche valley of the valley girls.

He hadn't ordered anything, but a waitress brought Luke a plate of French fries and two slices of Boston cream pie. Luke ate both at the same time, stuffing them alternately into opposite sides of his mouth. The waitress didn't stay long, exchanged no pleasantries, hustled away as though Luke had the plague.

Which, of course, he did. I knew. Because I, unlike the others who share my world, have a sense of smell.

Everyone's blood smells different, and every disease has a different taint to it, a different bouquet.

"Don't worry about it," he said. "I'm used to it."

"Are you on anything for it?" I asked him. "AZT, maybe, or one of the new experimental drugs?"

He laughed. "Need insurance for that." He went on eating, and didn't volunteer any more until both plates were completely consumed. He was beautiful. Breathtaking, except that I don't breathe. The eyes were wide, clear, blue as that same Aegean sky I may no longer look on; his skin had a familiar pallor even though I could hear his heartbeat, hear the blood sing in his arteries, sense the Brownian motion of dust-motes in the air between us as he exhaled.

"I know you don't wanna fuck me," he said. "Nobody does no more. They all know somehow. Everyone talks to everyone else on the boulevard. But you could take my photograph. I'll let you take my picture for twenty, no, ten bucks, 'cause you bought me dinner."

"I think you're pricing yourself way too low."

"Maybe. But you're a nice lady. Who gives a shit anyways? I'll be dead soon. Ten will keep me going for another day. One day at a time." Sufficient unto the day is the evil thereof, as a wise young rabbi once told me; on the other hand, they crucified him.

"Okay, Luke. I'll take your picture and I'll give you ten bucks. I wouldn't be able to sell them anyway; you're too young."

"Older'n I look."

Me too, I thought. "But these days, we have to have proof of age on file; otherwise, we can get busted."

"Fuck 'em," he said softly. But when he said it, he

sounded curiously tender, vulnerable even; he was only playing at toughness, hiding a lifetime of pain.

We cruised around for a while in my '66 Impala. It impressed him that someone like me would have a cholo car. Actually it was bequeathed to me by an…acquaintance of mine. Not entirely voluntarily.

I was getting hungry now. It would be dawn in only a couple of hours. I had no intentions on young Luke. I am finicky about picking fruit before it ripens. A boy should have a chance at being a man, even if that chance was a flimsy as Luke's.

"Tell me about the dude who gave you the car," Luke said.

We turned up Highland, drove past Sunset and Hollywood, up toward the hills on the other side of which lay the life he had rejected.

"I don't know that much about him," I said. "We didn't know each other long."

"But you were, you know, intimate."

"Yeah."

The War of the Worlds church loomed above a Chevron station, just beneath the Hollywood Bowl. Intimate in a sense. Alfonso had tried to rape me in an alley. Thought I was just some white bitch walking around in the wrong 'hood, chased me down the alley in the Impala, thought he had me trapped between the front end and the graffiti; didn't know that I can't be squashed; I can make myself as insubstantial as a puff of smoke.

We were intimate for about five minutes, and I had a new car; no one really missed Alfonso; luckily, the sticker had eleven months to go. Alfonso may have been young, but he had certainly ripened enough to pluck; his existence was a dead end; I had no qualms.

"What's it like?" said Luke. I decided to eschew the freeway and go uphill toward Mulholland. The streets were narrow and twisty, the houses cramped and overpriced.

"What's what like?"

"Being intimate."

"You don't know? I thought you—"

"Nah," he said. "I look like a hustler but I don't have what it takes to kill my own kind."

"But you have—"

"Born with it," he told me. "Mom was an intravenous drug user."

"In Encino?"

"Yeah. Sucks, don't it?" Oh, I thought to myself, such innocence.

By the time we turned onto Mulholland Drive, my hunger had become noisome in its persistence. But I knew where we were going, and I knew that the boy was in no danger. Here in the hills, we were above the smog. You could even see the occasional star; but the stars were almost drowned out in the lights of the city; to my right, the valley sparkled like a Christmas tree carpet; to my left, more subdued, were smears of rainbow radiance that were Hollywood, West Hollywood, even, like a wispy distant galaxy,

Bel Air.

"Cool," the boy said. "But there's no stars."

"One or two," I said. Some joker had altered the speed signs from 30 to 80. "Yeah, there's one." We rounded a sharp bend.

"Actually, I think that's a satellite."

"And then there's you. Estelle means star, I think."

"You knew that?"

"Had a book once. What to name your baby. George means 'farmer.' David means 'beloved.' Never looked up my own name, though."

"Okay. We have to stop for a moment."

After another hairpin came a lookout popular with lovers. I pulled into the lot; as I suspected, there were other cars parked here. There were couples, lost in each other's arms, eyes, saliva; in a convertible, a man leaned back against black leather and a tousled head bobbed up and down; above us hung the moon, huge and purplish in the alien L.A. light. No one noticed us, a middle-aged woman and a boy; why would they? That would be almost the least perverse sexual combination in town.

"I've never been up here before," Luke said. "Saw it in a movie though. I think it was E.T."

I ignored him for a moment. Above the parking area there was an earthy rise; a fence discouraged tourists from seeing the real view; but I knew there would be someone on the other side.

Luke followed me at a distance; I could smell him. I stood awhile in the bushes, carefully listening for signs of trouble. There was always trouble on a Saturday night. The chill air sweated booze and indica fumes.

I saw trouble in a clump of oleander, a little way down slope; I was downwind and caught a whiff of the phero of fear; I blended into the cold hill's side, shifted with the breeze until I was right on them. It was a woman, bound and gagged with gaffer's tape—how very Hollywood—and all over; the moon made her blood all quicksilver black. Hunched over her was one of the many serial killers who ply their trade in this town; I had had my eye on him since the last full moon, when I'd found a victim of his, dying, in an auto graveyard in Sepulveda, and sniffed him scurrying away. It was too late to save the woman, and so, regretfully, I fed. But this time, I could hunt prize quarry, hunt the human hunter of humans.

The woman saw me. She was so close to death that she could penetrate the veil of shadow I had cloaked myself with. I smiled at her. I don't know what she saw; perhaps I was a good Samaritan, perhaps an avenging angel with a flaming sword. Enough of this. I turned to the serial killer, who had just removed a hacksaw from a battered tackle box. I attenuated myself, engulfed him, sucked out all the blood in one quick whoosh through every pore in his skin so that he wrinkled up, all at once, like a dried shiitake mushroom, then broke in a thousand pieces, brittle as brickle. It happened so fast. I don't know what the victim saw; I flicked the gag off her and coalesced back into my human shape, and, sated, climbed uphill to where Luke stood.

Presently, I heard the woman screaming, screaming, screaming; she had held in that scream so long, and now she could not stop.

"I saw that," Luke said. "Dude. You're a—"

I shushed him with a finger on his lips. He smarted; always and forever, my touch has the coldness of the grave about it. "There's no need to say the things we both know," I said. "Listen. Listen. You people never listen; you fill your lives with your own noise, drowning out the music that fills the space between spaces. Listen, Luke, listen."

The purr of a passing Porsche. The breeze. The screams of the woman gradually subsiding, subsiding…footsteps, tennis shoes on gravel on dirt, lovers breaking off their bracketed entanglement, curiosity getting the better of passion…I thought to myself: I know he hears these things, but can he also hear a different music?

Can he hear what songs the veiled stars sing beyond the city's mist and smog? I wonder. No. Surely not. He is mortal. Beautiful and mortal.

We got back in the car. Luke was not afraid. That was strange.

Perhaps not so strange; he believed himself doomed; he knew no possible redemption.

We drove a little further down Mulholland; and then I turned on Beverly Glen, took a sharp slide down Coy, heading for my bungalow. He didn't speak much. Even I became a little nervous.

Usually they can't stop talking. They can't help themselves. I'm so alien to them, so scary, so mythically familiar. We reached the house; I had a private entrance round the back; the main house belonged to some big-name screenwriter, who had put on so many additions, turrets, minarets, and balconies, that the whole resembled a kind of Arabian nightmare.

My own humble dwelling was dingy and unkempt. Gorged, I went to the coffin—it doubles as a coffee table—and sat on the lid for a moment, letting the blood slow to a sluggish crawl, resetting my metabolism. When I looked up, Luke had already taken off his clothes.

He stood, unselfconscious, in the swath of light from the open doorway of the bathroom, against a kitchenette counter stacked with pristine coffee cups.

"I guess I forgot to ask," he said. "The pictures. You want me naked, I guess."

"Oh, yeah. The pictures. I forgot. Ten bucks." I reached into my purse.

"Not right now," he said. "The money. I mean like, I'll take the money but, I mean, dude, I mean...not everything's about money. I mean, maybe I'd like to think you were just all taking my picture, just to, you know, take my picture. Like a mom would. Yeah I mean, I guess you will end up selling them to someone but, I would have done it anyway. 'Cause you're a nice lady."

Nobody loved him. Nobody cared. He stood there and sure, he had no clothes on, but he wore over his scarred body so sublime an aura of purity that he seemed innocent of all those human pecadilloes they call sin. I took pictures, dozens of pictures. I used the 1600 film so I wouldn't have to use the big lights; I posed him in the chiaroscuro of the light from the bathroom door and the dark of the kitchenette. He was a natural. He was one of those models who stares right out of the picture, out of the printed page, whose eyes seem to have something special to say to you alone; but one of the ways you do that is to have your eyes be wide, vacant, reflective, so that the viewer can fill the void with his own fixations, his own private delusions; perhaps that's all love really is, the art of polishing the mirrors in your eyes until you are the beloved's reflection reflected, back and forth, toward an infinite intensity.

Luke had that look. I speak of his eyes only because they drew the viewer's attention so intently that one barely saw the rest of him; the scars, the self-inflicted stigmata, the flat, firm pubis coyly figleafed by a slender hand that I had not the heart to move out of the way of my camera's uncompromising eye.

And this is what he said as he stood in the half-light.

"Can you really be intimate, Estelle? I know what you are now. Can you, like, love us? Or do you only hunt us down?"

I said, "There are some things I love. The night. The dark. The cold. The first sip of blood as it gushes up from a freshly severed artery. The cadent decrescendo of a heart as it pumps its last; oh, that's a kind of music. I wish that you could hear it."

"So," he said, "do I."

He kissed me; not in an erotic way, but as a child who seeks comfort in a comfortless world.

"Be careful what you wish for," I said.

"How fucking careful do I have to be?" he screamed. "I'm gonna die, ain't I? What difference does it make?"

I didn't answer him. I just put down my camera, went over to the refrigerator, fixed him a sandwich and a Coke, and waited for him to calm down.

It was an hour till dawn; my blood was beginning to run cold.

"Do you want me to go?" Luke said. "You have time to drop me off, before, you know, the sun…"

"Don't take those myths too seriously," I said. "But yeah, the sun; I don't like the sun too much."

"Or do you want me to stay?"

That was not my decision; it never could be. Not every ugly duckling is a swan. Most ugly ducklings are precisely that. To embrace eternity is a kind of destiny; it comes only to those who hear the music. I could not tell, really, if Luke could hear it.

I said to him, "Wait awhile. I'll have to retire soon. If you feel like staying, stay; otherwise you can always take the Impala."

"But how will I give it back?—I mean, I don't know if I can even find this place again."

"For me," I said, "there'll always be other cars, other rewards, other…intimate moments."

"Thanks," he said softly.

"Hey," I added, "you can probably sell it for a couple of thousand, make a deposit on a place, have a real roof over your head for a while; even, I don't know, get a job; there's a law that says they have to hire you, they can't discriminate. Who knows, you might be able to hang on till they find the cure. And I'll still be here if you need me."

"I'll think about it," he said angrily.

I opened up the coffin. It was crushed velvet inside, deep purple, with a pretty pillow of Chantilly lace; and a velvet pouch full of soil from a place so far away and so long ago I'd just as soon forget it. I went into the back and got into, as they say, something comfortable; a nightie, a shroud, whatever you want to call it. I lay myself down in the coffin; I didn't close the lid yet. I wanted my last image of the day to be the boy; they are beautiful, you know, these humans, beautiful mostly because they are so ephemeral, because they dare not cross the river to the cold dark shore; oh, he was beautiful. Even with the dirty air between us I could feel the warmth of his skin. I could hear the trickle of his blood. I could smell all his emotions: his terror, his dread, his hope.

"In a moment," I said, "I'm going to close the coffin lid. Be a good boy, Luke. In the kitchen, in the cookie jar, there's a little more money. If you need a hundred or so, help yourself; I trust you."

He seized me by the wrists. I didn't know a human could grip so hard. His pulse pounded against my dead flesh. "Take me with you," he said.

"You don't know what you're—"

"Yes," he said, "I do. You don't know what it's like to be this way. I'm sick without even looking sick, without acting sick; I ain't come down with nothing, nothing wrong with me on the outside, everyone says I'm beautiful and then, then they find out, and then I'm like, they can't look at me, can't touch me, can't even breathe the same air as me cause they think they're gonna die too. I'm nothing in this world, the world's like a fucking candy store window and I'm just standing out there in the cold with my nose pressed to the glass, I'm all craving all that sweetness and all that chocolate but I know I'm gonna die before I can taste it. Fucking Jesus, I want to be someone, something—like you. The world grows up, grows old, drops dead, and you just go on and on, dude, I want to be like you."

"But you don't even like killing your own kind—"

"They won't be my own kind anymore, Estelle."

"If only you knew," I said.

"I don't need to know," he said. "Right now I'm as good as dead. I feel too many things. I want to give up feeling. I want to be cold and hard. Dead is real. Dead has meaning. Dead is alive."

"But you're beautiful the way you are," I said. "Beautiful is brief.

Beautiful is fleeting. Beautiful is transience."

"I love you," he cried out. "You're my hope, my future, my star."

He threw myself on top of me, slammed the lid shut, and now there were two of us in that cramped space and he was hugging me, making love to me, trying to force my lips wide so that he could pierce his skin with my razor canines; oh, he wrapped his legs around me, thrust against me, his death wish stronger than any sex drive; he jabbed his wrists against my teeth and forced his blood down my throat, and inside the coffin's confinement the air was drenched in the perfume of his lust and fear; oh god, but he was beautiful. Even as my tongue swelled at the touch of the warm fluid, even as my sated innards gorged, even as the heat shot through my jaded veins, even dying, he was beautiful. I wrapped my arms around his perfect body, squeezing out his half-life and sending him to a new half-death; we were intimate, for the first and only time, for such intimacy is too searing ever to be repeated.

True love is as painful as it is transcendent; that's why mortals can't feel it; it would burn them up alive. But Luke had immortality in him, even though his disease bespoke mortality. That was why he would not be consumed by this love.

I knew then that he had heard the music; that he knew what song the stars sang.

So I embraced him, and I drank myself into the stupor of daylight; and at sunset I awoke, and found him still in my arms, dead yet not dead; the ugly duckling had, indeed, become a swan.

We went by the coffee shop one night, Luke and I, many days later.

Stavros tried to give us both coffee; and Luke would not touch his French fries or his pie. Stavros smiled a little. He did not step back in revulsion when Luke touched him, lightly, on the arm, to ask him some trifling question, the name of a new kid who had only just started working the block. The waitress, taking away his plates, looked him in the eye and was as civil to him as she ever is to anyone. I thought: Stavros knows more than he lets on, I suspect.

He set this up, somehow. I wonder if he's dropping a subtle hint. I wonder if he wants to be a swan, too. A country 'n' western love song crooned from the jukebox. How strange that humans are so obsessed with love when they can experience it only once before they die…or metamorphose into us. We spoke of the sky in Greece: how blue, how clear, how bright. Luke spoke of the dawn in Hollywood: purpled by pollution, tie-dyed by clouds of smog, spectacular; already there was a twinge of the eternal longing.

And Stavros tried to pour coffee, and I knew he was bursting with repressed envy. "You people," he said to me, "you people."

"We people," I said.

"So full of passion," said Stavros, "so full of life. One day you'll drift away from here, and I'll be an old man minding a decaying coffee shop in West Hollywood, staring through the glass at a new crop of street kids, waiting for death."

Luke looked up at him. Touched him gently on the back of his hand. Stavros didn't flinch, even though the cold must have startled him. "Don't worry, dude," Luke said softly. "I'll send you a picture."

And smiled, the subtle, sensual smile of the beautiful and the damned.

Thank you for reading this book and for sharing my dark visions. If you want to read more of what I've done, feel free to visit www.somtow.com, where you can even sign up for a newsletter.

If you read this on Amazon, feel free, if you are so inclined, to leave a review. You can do so by clicking right here: https://www.amazon.com/Lost-Valentines-Collected-Vampire-Stories-ebook/dp/B0BNZHXVFJ/

— S.P. Somtow

www.ingramcontent.com/pod-product-compliance
Lightning Source LLC
Chambersburg PA
CBHW020528310726
48979CB00014B/2254/J

* 9 7 8 1 9 4 0 9 9 9 7 6 0 *